THE TAILOR'S DAUGHTER

THE TAILOR'S DAUGHTER

Maggie Bennett

This first world edition published in Great Britain 2006 by
SEVERN HOUSE PUBLISHERS LTD of
9–15 High Street, Sutton, Surrey SM1 1DF.
This first world edition published in the USA 2006 by
SEVERN HOUSE PUBLISHERS INC of
595 Madison Avenue, New York, N.Y. 10022.

British Library Cataloguing in Publication Data

Bennett, Maggie
    The tailor's daughter
    1.   Female friendship - Fiction
    2.   London (England) - History - 18th century - Fiction
    3.   Love stories
    I.   Title
    823.9'2 [F]

    ISBN-10: 0-7278-6329-0 (cased)
                    0-7278-9163-4 (paper)

*My thanks as always to Judith Murdoch, my literary agent, and to
Maureen Delaney Hotham for her patient listening and wise advice.*

Typeset by Palimpsest Book Production Ltd.,
Polmont, Stirlingshire, Scotland.
Printed and bound in Great Britain by
MPG Books Ltd., Bodmin, Cornwall.

One

1771

On any other day Tabitha would have been delighted to run an errand for her father; she loved to see the inside of the fine houses in Bloomsbury Square, to get a glimpse of the sort of lives the nobility led. She'd have enjoyed a brisk walk on such a clear, windy February day, not yet spring but on the verge of it, with a promise of lighter, brighter days to come. On any other day she would have gazed up in admiration at the narrow, elegant facades and graceful porticoes; but today she drew her woollen cloak around her plump shoulders and lowered her face beneath its hood, so that nobody could see she had been crying. For if anybody asked her what was the matter she might burst into tears and she had promised her father that she would be brave.

As she hurried along the pavement, a carriage entered the square from Russell Street. Tabitha slowed her steps as it approached the west side of the square and drew up outside No 14, the home of the Dersinghams, the very same house where she was to call. She stood back a little as the coachman reined in the horses and climbed down from his seat to open the carriage door. Tabitha waited while an old lady, swathed in shawls, stepped down to the pavement, aided by a maid who was not young but well used to her mistress's needs. Another lady appeared at the front door, some five-and-twenty years younger than her visitor, and bearing a strong family resemblance. As they embraced Tabitha got a brief glimpse of a high-ceilinged hall and a curved staircase before the door was firmly closed behind them. She hesitated; surely this was not a good time to show Lady Dersingham her father's samples, and maybe she ought to call again tomorrow – but no! She must try, and if she was sent away, so be it. She hoisted her basket over her arm and made her way down the steep area

1

steps to the tradesmen's entrance, where she knocked on the plain wooden door; it was opened by a sharp-faced maidservant who eyed her suspiciously.

'You from Prewetts wiv the bits o' clorf?'

'Yes, I've got them here,' answered Tabitha. 'My father couldn't come today.'

''Er ladyship won't be best pleased,' remarked the girl, but she stood back to let Tabitha in. A black and white cat also squeezed in before the door was shut, nearly catching its tail.

In her well-appointed drawing room Lady Dersingham poured tea for her mother and fingered the squares of wool worsted in various thicknesses and colours.

'It's impossible to make a choice without Prewett to advise me,' she complained. 'I need to ask about the quantity I'll require for two morning gowns, and Sir Julian won't know which colour to choose for his breeches. They all look rather dull to me.'

'Dark is more practical for gentlemen, Stella,' said the old lady, picking up a sample with a bejewelled hand. 'He can't go wrong with black or brown.'

'But he likes light-coloured breeches, Mother, they're much more in fashion,' replied her ladyship. She beckoned to a maid standing discreetly near the door. 'Chapman, go and ask the girl to step up here – and make sure she takes her shoes off before treading on the carpet.'

Tabitha entered the room silently in stockinged feet. Lady Dersingham frowned at her.

'This is most unsatisfactory, girl. I need to see the tailor. Are you his daughter?'

'Yes, m'lady.' Tabitha gave a brief, bobbing curtsey as she had been taught.

'And why isn't Prewett himself here to assist me in making a choice?'

'Beggin' your pardon, m'lady, my father couldn't come today. He – we – my little brother was buried this mornin' at St George's.'

'Oh. Oh, dear. That's very sad for your family. How old was the child?'

'Nearin' a year an' a half, m'lady. He – he took sick a week ago, and – an' he got worse and then he died.' Tabitha's voice shook slightly, but she took a breath and spoke up clearly. Lady Dersingham turned to her mother with a shrug.

'So many young children die in London, Mother. There's a burial at least once a week, sometimes two or three. They have such large families, you see, far more than they can cope with.' She turned to Tabitha again. 'How many brothers and sisters have you got, girl?'

'Four, m'lady, no, three now. There's Michael, he's the eldest an' goes to school over in Hackney. Then there's me, then Jeremiah, he's nearly nine, an' then there was Jabez, he died last year of a fever, an' there's Thomas, he's three. An' poor little Andrew died on Monday.'

Now it was the old lady's turn to ask questions. 'So you're the only girl. You're no beauty, but you may improve in a year or two, and you look strong. How old are you – ten or eleven?'

'Ten, er, ma'am,' answered Tabitha, not sure how she should address her ladyship's mother.

'I hope you help your mother with the housework, and with looking after your little brothers.'

'I do my best, er, ma'am,' Tabitha replied. 'We have a maid to help in the house.'

'A maid?' asked the old lady in some surprise.

'Some of these tradesmen do very well, Mother,' said Lady Dersingham in a lowered tone that Tabitha could hear quite clearly. 'Bloomsbury Square is surrounded with them, living above their shops in sidestreets. And there's Barter Market, just to the south of the square, where butchers set up stalls and all sorts of pedlars and street sellers gather. It's convenient, of course, but Julian says that they'll lower the tone if they move in any closer.'

Her mother nodded, still curious about a tailor's family with a maidservant. 'And did I understand you to say that your eldest brother attends school, girl?'

'Yes, ma'am.'

'A charity school, I suppose?'

'No, ma'am, a grammar school. My father pays for him to learn to read an' write well, an' know his tables, an' a bit o' Latin an' Greek.'

'Why, what good will that be to a tailor's son? What will this boy do when he grows to manhood?'

3

'Go into the tailorin', after Father, him bein' the eldest son, ma'am.'

'Hmm. This tailor must think a lot of himself, for a tradesman.' The old lady glanced at her daughter who was turning over the samples. 'The boy will still have to serve his apprenticeship, I suppose, and what use will Latin and Greek be when he's cutting and stitching?'

Her ladyship did not reply, and Tabitha had no reply to give, though she felt her indignation rising up against this patronizing old woman, and the question went unanswered.

'I really cannot make a choice without Prewett to tell me what I need,' said Lady Dersingham, 'especially for Sir Julian's clothes. You had better leave these with me until your father can attend, which I hope will be tomorrow.'

'That's what my father thought, m'lady. I'm to leave the pieces here for you and Sir Julian to look over an' see what you like – an' then Father'll come tomorrow an' answer your questions – an' maybe take your orders.'

Tabitha stood still with her hands folded together as she spoke; her round brown eyes betrayed little of the sadness she felt inwardly for her dead brother and her grieving parents.

'Very well, then – tell Prewett to come early – but not too early, about ten o'clock – no, before then, before Sir Julian leaves for Westminster.'

'Very good, m'lady. May I go now?'

'Oh, yes, run along, run along. Would you care to take some more tea, Mother?'

Thus dismissed and out in the square again, Tabitha made her way to the corner where Bloomsbury Mews led off to some stables; she descended the ancient stone steps known as Frenchman's stairs, which brought her to Orchard Court, a paved area where Prewett's Quality Draperies dominated the milliner's and upholsterer's on either side. A shoemaker and a bookseller also shared the limited space of the court, with living quarters over their shop fronts. All knew each other's business in more ways than one, but there was no rivalry between their different services; all were respectable freeholders with premises rated at no less than £15 a year. No stink of butcher's shambles or fishmonger's slab polluted the air of Orchard Court, and street sellers were unwelcome. To Tabitha it was a miniature version of Bloomsbury Square, with Prewett's Quality Draperies as good as, or better than, any other dwelling in it.

The shop was closed today, and Tabitha went through the narrow alleyway between Prewett's and the milliner's to the shared yards where the washing lines were. She let herself in by the back door to the kitchen where Nan, the maid-of-all-work, sat by the hearth darning stockings; she had just put another piece of coal on the embers of the fire, using her hands instead of the tongs, and stared at Tabitha as if defying her to notice and tell Mrs Prewett. Nan's once white cap drooped limply round her face, and her apron was stained with gravy, but Tabitha said nothing. She was almost relieved when her brother Jeremiah broke the unnatural silence in the house by clattering down the wooden stairs.

'Oh, Tab, what a time ye've been! It's just like a Sunday here – no singin', no games, no playin' outside,' he grumbled, and she immediately put her finger to her lips.

'Hush, Jeremy, it *is* like a Sunday for us, 'cause our little brother Andrew's been laid to rest.'

'Then why've yer gone out visitin' the gentry for Papa?' he demanded. '*He* never works on a Sunday, an' he's sent Will an' Rob away for a holiday – oh, hello, Papa!' He stopped talking and put on a solemn expression as his father entered the kitchen.

'Did ye get to see Lady Dersingham, Tabitha?' asked the tailor. 'And did ye explain about the funeral?'

'Yes, Papa. She asks if you'll go tomorrow mornin', not too early nor too late, to help her an' Sir Julian to choose what they want. I left the samples there with her.'

'Good girl.' He patted her shoulder, and muttered half under his breath, 'I wish that ye were a son, to go to school in place o' Michael.'

This was a new idea. 'And can't I do so, Papa?' she asked in sudden eagerness, looking up into his face: he looked much older without his wig, his thinning hair almost grey.

'No, my girl, I wish ye could, but it'd be a waste o' time to teach ye. Ye'll have yer years taken up with bein' a wife an' a mother, like yer own poor mother.' He sighed, for Martha Prewett was inconsolable over the death of her precious baby, Andrew, and he imagined Tabitha's life taking on the same pattern of frequent child-bearing and grieving for the loss of

5

the ones who did not survive. If only he *could* have sent young Tabitha to school, she would have shaped a sight better than poor Michael, he thought. The lad was slow to learn and was not making much headway at the Reverend Wyatt's School for Sons of Clergy – to which were added such respectable tradesmen as could pay his fees.

Young Jeremiah looked up into his father's grave face. 'Will I be a tailor, too, Papa?'

'Good heavens, boy, ye're nearly nine years old, but yes, one day ye might learn to cut an' sew for the gentry.' And maybe ye'll take over my place in the shop instead o' your elder brother, he added to himself.

'What may we do if we can't play, indoors or outside, Papa?' persisted the boy.

'You must be quiet for yer mother's sake, my son.' Prewett saw the boy's face fall, and chided himself; he should put on a good face for the sake of his remaining children.

'Come, now, both o' ye, I'll show ye the globe, and ye can find England and all the lands held under the King. I'll put it on the table for ye, and ye must take care how ye turn it round.'

Tabitha exchanged a smile with her brother, for they liked learning from Papa who taught them lessons in geography and history, and listened to them read from the Holy Bible. So often he had not enough time, but today was different, and Tabitha sensed that a lesson with the globe would ease the sadness in her father's heart as well as her own. She and Jeremiah listened in fascination as he pointed to the British Isles and showed them the new colonies that lay across the wide Atlantic ocean in America; he told them that they were just as much subject to the King and his Parliament as Scotland, Wales and the troublesome province of Ireland.

For an hour John Prewett taught them, until his wife came downstairs to tell Nan to put the kettle on for tea and to attend to the chamber pots upstairs, not emptied since this morning. Little Thomas had woken up from his afternoon nap, and was demanding bread-and-milk, which disturbed Kitty the cat from her snooze on the rug.

'Now, don't ye go pullin' her tail, Thomas,' said his mother. 'Don't tease the poor creature, she's soon goin' to—'

She left the rest of the sentence unsaid, for Kitty was big with kittens, and Mrs Prewett felt for her, knowing that all but one of the new arrivals would have to be drowned, or the place would be overrun with them.

As with many another bereaved household, life had to go on as usual. The two apprentices, Will and Robin, returned from their day's holiday and Nan was severely chastised by Mrs Prewett for letting the meat burn dry in the oven, and for her sluttish appearance. Mr Prewett urged his wife to take the girl in hand and talk to her seriously but gently, to find out if there was anything troubling her.

'She's only seventeen, an' probably missin' her parents. Maybe she feels overworked,' he suggested.

'Overworked? What nonsense!' retorted Martha. 'Why, she don't do half as much as Tabitha, nor does she work half as well. Certainly I'll talk to the lazy wench, and tell her that if she don't improve by the end o' the month, she can go back to her parents in Seven Dials!'

Prewett dared say no more while his wife was in such a mood, and between Martha's sharp tongue and the girl's sulky silence, the atmosphere remained as charged as the air before a thunderstorm. Prewett hoped that it would soon blow over, but Saturday morning brought more bad news: their eldest son Michael returned from Wyatt's Grammar School with a letter from the Reverend Mr Wyatt saying that he could no longer remain there.

Prewett read in dismay that his son was unable to keep up with the rest of the boys, even though he had been put in a class with younger pupils. Mr Wyatt felt that he should not be pressed into an education so far beyond his natural abilities, for fear of endangering his health, and suggested to Prewett that the boy be put to some simple trade that would not demand more than he could give.

It was another bitter blow, following on from the loss of their youngest son. Prewett muttered to Tabitha that troubles never come singly.

'Your mother's very upset, an' thinks he's been harshly treated, so ye must be very careful what ye say,' he said heavily, for he did not blame the school for Michael's lack of progress; Martha had had a very difficult time bringing her firstborn into the world, and Prewett wondered if the child's head had been harmed, and if this was the reason for his slowness.

'All right, Papa, I'll do my best,' Tabitha answered, for she pitied both her mother and brother. Michael, the eldest of them, had lost weight and his eyes held a wary look that had not been there before he was sent to school at the age of twelve. He had always been a friendly, affectionate boy, happy to play with his younger brothers in the safe circle of his family; but his slowness to learn even simple arithmetic had now become too apparent for others to ignore, and being made to sit in a corner of the classroom wearing a pointed dunce's cap had not made him any cleverer. From being naturally happy and trusting, he had become fearful, and Tabitha had to listen silently to her mother's angry protests against the Reverend Mr Wyatt's treatment of her son.

Tabitha loved both her parents dearly, but sometimes she longed for a friend of her own age, a girl with whom she could share her innermost thoughts, her hopes and dreams; she thought of how they would laugh together, perhaps tease each other, even have an occasional quarrel, for it would give her such happiness to kiss and be friends again. But in this household of men, she kept these thoughts to herself.

'Good day to ye, Mistress Tabitha,' said Robin Drury politely when she passed him entering the cutting room.

'Good day, Master Robin,' she replied, thinking what a well-mannered lad he was, almost like a gentleman's son, and only a year or two older than Michael. He was at the start of his apprenticeship, and she much preferred him to Will Feather who, at eighteen, would soon be at the end of his. Will had a familiar way of talking to her, and she was never sure whether he was serious or just teasing. He gave her sidelong looks and winked at her as if he knew something about her that others didn't, or as if he could read her thoughts. She did not quite know why she found this objectionable, and there was nobody she could confide in, least of all her mother who she must not bother. Oh, for a friend to share such things! They would giggle together about Will Feather, she was sure – and then she wouldn't mind any more.

For the time being she had to comfort poor Michael, who blubbered openly when he was told about little Andrew's death, and seemed afraid to open his mouth to speak to anybody other than his mother and sister. Rob Drury tactfully looked away when Michael began to cry, but Prewett suspected that

Will Feather had been making fun of his son, perhaps reminding him of humiliations inflicted by other boys at school.

It wasn't the only misgiving the tailor had concerning Master Feather. When the two lads had returned from their holiday after the funeral, Will arrived late, and had the pale, muddy complexion and crumpled appearance that follows heavy drinking and dissipation. Prewett had questioned Rob about how they had spent their day of freedom.

'Er – well, we strolled down to Bankside to see the cock fightin', and there was a performin' bear,' said Rob hesitantly. 'And there was prize fightin' with a boxin' champion – he only looked a little feller, but he threw down a big chap double his size.'

'I'm surprised that ye didn't go into St George's church an' say a prayer for the innocent child who was buried on that day, which was the reason ye had a holiday,' said Prewett reproachfully, and Rob coloured.

'I would've done, Mr Prewett, only Will wanted to get down to Bankside straight away,' he replied, looking down at the seam he was tacking. 'I stayed with him till it started gettin' dark, and then I went to see my mother.'

'And were there other temptations on offer at the Bankside, Robin?' asked the tailor bluntly. 'It's not a good place for a young man to go. There are certain kinds of women who . . . Do you know what I'm speaking of?'

'Er – yes, Mr Prewett, I think I do, but I didn't take any notice of 'em,' muttered Rob, acutely embarrassed, though he looked up and met the tailor's eye.

'I believe ye, Robin, but I'm responsible for yer health an' virtue while you stay here under my roof, an' I don't want you fallin' under a bad influence,' the tailor said sternly. 'The world is full o' dangers for honest young fellows like yerself, and I'm sorry ye spent so much o' yer holiday with Master Feather.'

'I won't again, Mr Prewett, truly I won't.'

'I'm very glad to hear it, Robin. Master Feather will be leavin' us when he finishes at Easter, and I'll tell yer now, I shan't be askin' him to stay on as my assistant.'

Meanwhile another idea had come into Mr Prewett's head, and he knew he would have to be circumspect in breaking it to the family.

To his wife he said, 'Our eldest son'll never be a book lover, Martha, and we can only pray that Almighty God has some other plan for his life beyond our knowledge. I'll keep him in the shop beside me for a while, and find him simple tasks to do at his own pace.'

'I'm glad to hear it, John,' she answered. 'It'll be much better for him than pinin' at that horrid school.'

Mr Prewett let this pass, and added carefully, 'Jeremiah might benefit from schoolin', but I'll wait until he's ten before sendin' him away from home.'

'I'm thankful to hear that, too, John. Ye're quite right.'

He cleared his throat. 'And while I'm not keepin' a boy at school, I've made a decision to let Tabitha have the benefit of a year's schoolin'.'

'*Tabitha*?' Mrs Prewett thought she had misheard. 'But she already reads an' writes well enough, an' can add and subtract. What else does a woman need in the way o' book learnin'?'

'It isn't just books, Martha. The girls at Mrs Kelso's Academy learn the piano and how to do needlework, drawin' and paintin' – and they're also taught French. Silas Holmes, the bookseller, sent his daughter there for a year, an' ye know she came back so accomplished she married a banker's son.'

'*French*? What good will that do for a girl who'll get married and have children to look after?' Mrs Prewett demanded. 'Some use *French*'ll be to her when she's wedded an' bedded an' bearin' children to live or to die.' Her face fell, and her eyes filled with tears. 'Besides, she's a good girl, an' I need her help at home, an' even more when the next child comes. That creature Nan is no use at all.'

But John Prewett's mind was made up, and his wife's arguments served only to strengthen his resolve. He drew his daughter into the little office in the corner of the cutting room and said he had something of importance to say to her. When Tabitha understood what her father was saying, she could hardly believe it.

'Mrs Kelso's Academy, Papa? Is that in Hackney?'

'No, my girl, it's in Islington, a very healthful spot with nursery gardens to supply London's markets, and herds o' dairy cows to supply milk and butter. Mr Holmes's daughter went there for a year, an' it did her a great deal o' good. I've decided that ye should have the same privilege. How do ye feel about that?'

10

'Oh, Papa – oh, Papa, thank you, thank you!' she cried, overwhelmed with surprise and delight at the thought of a girls' school where no doubt she would make lots of friends. 'When shall I go?'

'I'll write to Mrs Kelso and ask if she can take you after Easter,' said her father, smiling at her excitement but realizing at the same time how much he would miss his only daughter.

From then on Tabitha went around in a dream. She would meet other girls like herself, talk with them, read together, help each other with their lessons – and share secrets. But as the special day approached, she began to realize that she would miss her parents and brothers very much, so was quite pleased to hear that she would be a weekly boarder, allowed home on Sundays.

Her father set to work making new gowns and a cloak for her, and her mother made sure that she was well supplied with white cotton petticoats and drawers. When she tried on her new outfits and stood in front of the full-length looking-glass in the cutting room, her father nodded in satisfaction; his girl would be the equal of any of the others at the academy.

Two

'Did you notice that long, curly black hair on Miss Dacre's chin while she was reading to us this morning?' asked Penelope. 'I couldn't keep my eyes off it!'

'Lord, I could hardly keep my eyes *open* while the poor old thing was droning on about the Wars of the Roses!' groaned Margaret with a melodramatic yawn. 'Does history have to be *quite* so tedious?'

'Geography's even duller, at least when Miss Dacre reads it,' responded Georgina. 'I'd have been bored to death if I hadn't got dancing to look forward to this afternoon.'

'O-ho! Do I detect a blush upon your maiden cheek, Georgina? Does your heart beat faster at the prospect of

Monsieur Joubert and his nimble feet?' Margaret threw a side-long glance at the other girls. 'Yes, look, she's gone as red as a beetroot!'

'I don't think it's his *feet* she has in mind!' added Penelope, and the three of them collapsed into a fit of giggles, lounging on the chaise longue in Mrs Kelso's parlour while they waited for dinner, served at twelve noon.

Tabitha sat silently in the window seat, looking out at the wet garden on a chilly April day, pretending not to hear them. She was the youngest of a dozen pupils aged from ten to sixteen; the one nearest to her in age was eleven-year-old Cynthia White who aped the manners and speech of her seniors, which Tabitha found impossible. Her one attempt to put on a sophisticated drawl had been a disaster, and had sent the girls into shrieks of laughter.

'What do *you* think of our Monsieur Joubert, Tabby-cat?' asked Margaret with a knowing smile at her companions.

The French dancing master, who came to the academy on Tuesdays and Fridays, seemed to Tabitha a pleasant enough man, although at thirty or forty years – there was some differ-ence of opinion about his age – he might have been as old as Methuselah to a girl of ten.

'I think he's a good teacher and I want to learn to dance,' she replied simply, for she was a complete beginner at what Mrs Kelso said was an essential requirement of a young lady. After three weeks at the academy she had not made any close friendships, and did not understand the whispers and giggles when Monsieur Joubert was mentioned. The girls' talk when out of classes was all about romance and intrigue, flirtations and exchanging of letters and love tokens; and when they weren't talking about romance they whispered about the changes in their own young bodies: the enlargement of their breasts – 'mine are bigger than yours, and Margaret's are enor-mous!' – and the growth of hair in hidden places. Then there was the all-important sign of womanhood, the monthly flow of blood which had half a dozen different names – the menses, the courses, the terms, the curse of Eve and the flowers. When *that* began it seemed that you were ready for something – whatever it was, lurking in the shadows ahead, waiting for you. Coming from a mostly male household, Tabitha had not even heard about the women's monthly flow, for her mother had never spoken of it. No wonder, thought Tabitha, it sounded quite messy and horrid.

The older girls continued to talk and laugh at their own jokes in a way that made the new girl feel excluded. When the dinner bell summoned them to the dining room she was last to rise, letting the others go first, and found herself seated beside Cynthia White, who was apparently far above Tabitha in social status. The daughter of a gentleman, Cynthia had been placed in Mrs Kelso's care as a permanent boarder, her mother being dead and her father in the diplomatic service and often abroad. When Cynthia heard that Tabitha's father was in trade, her initial interest cooled, and she might have withdrawn her overtures of friendship altogether if the two of them had not had to share a bed, as was Mrs Kelso's established routine for the younger girls. She was a stout, motherly woman who did much of the cooking herself, and fed the girls excellent fare; the bedlinen was regularly washed, and the girls' clothes kept clean and mended. Morning lessons were given by her sister, Miss Dacre; the girls would sit in a circle and listen while Miss Dacre read aloud to them from a book on the history of England and showed them the great continents of the world on a globe. Another lady tutor, Miss Brambell, came to teach reading, writing and mathematics; the latter involved applying numbers to household accounts. The girls were taught how to manage money wisely, and the cost of various necessary items a lady needed to order from the suppliers, be they butchers or bakers. (Or tailors, Tabitha heard Cynthia whisper to the girl next to her.) In the afternoons there were classes for drawing and sketching and playing the pianoforte with Miss Dacre, and cooking and needlework with Miss Brambell. After tea at four o'clock the girls were free to roam about the grounds, read in the little library or sit and chat with each other in the parlour until supper. Permanent boarders wrote to their parents on Sunday afternoons, but Tabitha was happily free to visit hers, and she could hardly wait until Saturday dinner was over and a hackney cab arrived around one o'clock to collect girls who were going home for the week's end. She quickly settled back into family life for twenty-four hours, and tried to answer the questions put to her by her parents and Jeremiah about life at Mrs Kelso's. What were the other girls like? Were the lessons very difficult?

Had she learned any French? – her answers were: chatter-boxes; no, not really; and yes, a little. Mrs Kelso taught them French, having been to Paris for a visit some years ago, but there was not much evidence of it being grasped by the older girls, for none of them spoke it in the dining room or the parlour, preferring to exchange gossip and read the *Lady's Magazine* or surreptitiously play at cards.

On her third Sunday at home Tabitha noticed the tension in the atmosphere, but nobody seemed to want to tell her what the matter was. Jeremiah was puzzled, and told Tabitha that Mama was very cross with Nan who was leaving tomorrow, and Papa had been cross with Will who had finished his apprenticeship and had already left. Nan looked wretched and her eyes were red from crying, though when Tabitha tentatively asked her what was the matter, she just shrugged and turned away, muttering, 'Me ma'll kill me.' Tabitha noted how clumsily she moved, and that she had grown fatter. She had always been a sullen girl, but Tabitha felt sorry for her, perhaps because of the haughty manners of the girls at school. She would not look down on poor Nan as they looked down on her.

'Why are you sendin' Nan back to her parents, Mama?' she ventured to ask as they were dressing for church on the Sunday morning.

'Because she's been a very bad girl and can't stay in a respectable household,' was the reply, in a tone that held a warning not to enquire further. Her father was also unapproachable on the subject, and rather cryptically remarked that she would find out such things soon enough. She was further mystified when she heard her father telling his wife that Will Feather was coming to see him the following morning.

'And if he accepts my offer o' twenty guineas to do his duty by her, I'll tell him he can stay on as an assistant, at least until she's brought to bed,' he said.

It occurred to Tabitha that her mother too was getting bigger, like Nan. Her memory stirred, and she remembered how, when little Andrew had been born, her mother's belly had got very big, and one day she had gone into the bedroom she shared with Papa, and Mrs Carter, a neighbour, had gone in with her and firmly closed the door. Papa went out very quickly, and came back with old Mrs Hitchcock, who carried a large leather bag. Tabitha was terrified by the agonized cries that came from the closed room, which got louder and louder until all of a sudden they had ceased and were replaced by another sound, a high-pitched repetitive cry – 'lah! lah! lah! lah!' – which signalled baby Andrew's arrival. Papa, down in the kitchen, had groaned, 'Thanks be to God!' and when Mrs Carter emerged from the bedroom carrying a pail with something in it, Tabitha had got a brief glimpse of bloodstained sheets and a soiled nightdress.

'Mind out o' the way, Tabitha, ye're not supposed to be here,' the woman had said sharply. Turning to Papa she had said, 'I'll take these home with me, Prewett, an' see to 'em. She'll be all right, an' the baby's yellin' its head off.'

As this memory of eighteen months ago returned to Tabitha, it now acquired greater significance. She remembered that when Mama had got up from her bed, she no longer had a big belly. But now Mama was getting big again, and so was Nan.

On the Sunday afternoon she took a big breath and asked her mother, 'Mama, is there goin' to be another child?'

Martha Prewett's reply was so sharp that Tabitha jumped. 'What've they been teachin' ye at that school?' she demanded harshly. When she was cross or upset, Martha relapsed into the manner of speech used in the laundry where she'd worked when young Johnny Prewett had seen her and wanted no other for his wife, whatever his parents said.

'Nothin', Mama, only lessons. Only – when Andrew was born ye were very big, an' – an' ye're gettin' big again, an' so is Nan—'

'Once and for all, girl, this ain't a matter for children, so be quiet and don't ask questions until ye're older. Ye'll find out soon enough, but ye're not ready yet.'

'Yes, Mama.' Tabitha answered meekly, wondering if she would be 'ready' when she started the mysterious monthly flow. She overheard her mother saying to her father, 'I think that girl's been pickin' up things she's no right to know yet. I never liked the idea o' her goin' to that place an' mixin' with them hoity-toity girls. Hussies!'

'She's a quick, clever child, Martha, an' I don't see how there'd be any harm in lettin' her know there's goin' to be a new brother or sister,' said Prewett mildly.

'I won't have her robbed of her innocence, John! It's bad

15

enough havin' that slut o' a girl sulkin' away in the kitchen. I'm packin' her off tomorrow, whatever ye say.'

'Ah, Martha, don't be too harsh. Wait until Feather's heard my offer, an' see whether he's goin' to behave like a gentleman or not. If he refuses, I'll send him packin', an' the girl can have the money to take home to her parents.'

Tabitha's mind was a whirl of new but imperfect information when she returned to Islington that Sunday evening. She suddenly thought of Will Feather and his knowing winks and smiles, and pondered the connection between him and Nan.

That night after lights out, in the close proximity of a shared bed, she made an attempt to ask Cynthia a vital question.

'Cynthia, d'ye know how – when a baby's born – where does it actually come from? How does it get to its mother?'

Cynthia gave a yelp of laughter. 'La! I never did hear the like! Did you hear what the tailor's daughter just asked me, girls?'

'No, what?' The four other occupants of the room were eager to be told.

'She doesn't know how newborn babies get to their mother!'

Amidst the general derisive laughter, poor Tabitha in sudden panic changed her mind and begged to be spared from further knowledge. 'Don't tell me, please don't tell me, I don't want to hear about it – don't want to talk of it!' she pleaded, putting her hands over her ears. 'Don't tell me, *please*!'

But they did not spare her: they vied with each other in forcing on her the full details of what her mother said she was not ready to know.

When all had fallen asleep except Tabitha, she lay staring at the curtained window through which the moon's rays coldly gleamed. She felt as if she had embarked on a new road in life, a dark, mysterious road from which she shrank, but along which she had to travel, like it or not. Some facts about life were rather frightening, and Tabitha felt very much alone with her new knowledge. She uttered a silent prayer in her head, and followed it with the Lord's Prayer, then feeling a little better, she turned her back on the softly snoring Cynthia, and fell asleep.

During the days that followed, Tabitha made a resolution to learn as much as she could from her teachers, and not to be upset by her fellow pupils if they made fun of her and called her Tabby-cat; much as she longed for friendship, she was not prepared to flatter or grovel for it. Her father was spending good money to give her this year of schooling, and she did not intend that he should repent of his generosity: on the contrary, she would make him proud of her. Yes! She'd make them *all* proud – her father, mother and brothers.

April passed into May, and Islington was a picture, with fruit-blossom out in the orchards, and cows standing in lush green meadows jewelled with buttercups and daisies. Tabitha had never imagined that the country could be so beautiful, and her spirits rose in the warm spring sunshine.

The girls were allowed to walk into the village in groups of two or three, but Tabitha was quite content to walk on her own within sight of a group, with either Miss Dacre or Miss Brambell keeping a watchful eye on them. Islington stood on rising ground, and from the hilltop there was a splendid view over the city, as far as the Thames, with masts of every kind of vessel pointing up. The other girls liked to parade in the High Street and Colebrooke Row where fine houses had been built for the gentry but Tabitha preferred to admire the fields and colourful nursery gardens which supplied much of London's fruit, flowers and vegetables.

Praise from the lady tutors did nothing to increase Tabitha's standing among her fellow pupils, but when Monsieur Joubert singled her out, it was a different matter. He actually asked them all to stand still and watch Mademoiselle Prewett demonstrate a figure with him. Standing opposite each other, they advanced and retired, advanced again and locked arms, swung round and repeated the movement, this time with a dos-à-dos: he bowed, she curtsied, and taking her arm he led her back to her seat.

'*Merci, chère mademoiselle* – you are as light as a fezzer, and 'ave a natural grace,' he said, while the girls looked on open-mouthed. 'Ze rest of you weel do well to eemitate 'er.'

Reactions ranged from reluctant admiration to frank envy of the girl they called Tabby-cat: to be shown up like that by the ten-year-old daughter of a tradesman! For Monsieur Joubert it had been a relief to dance with a young, unaffected girl who actually followed what he said without ogling him with smiles and sidelong glances; and for Tabitha it was a modest triumph. Her one regret was that she had nobody with whom she could share it; her mother would not have been pleased to think of her dancing with this Frenchman, and Jeremiah was – well, he was a *boy*, and wouldn't appreciate it.

Her Sunday visits home marked the passing weeks of the summer term. She heard that her father had been totally disillusioned with Will Feather when he had accepted the twenty guineas and promised to marry Nan, but had then absconded with the money and disappeared, leaving the girl waiting at the church gate of St George's. She had gone tearfully home to her parents, and Prewett had given her mother ten guineas, being unable to afford another twenty, and Martha had scolded him and called him a fool. She was getting bigger and slower, and little Thomas had to be tied to a table-leg to prevent him from running outside and falling over on the cobblestones of Orchard Court – or running into the other shops and causing mischief.

There was interesting news however. No 9 Bloomsbury Square was being refurbished for the arrival of a new owner; it had been previously occupied by an old lady and her invalid daughter who had now died, and the mother had gone to live with other relatives. There were all sorts of rumours going round; the newcomers were foreigners, but friends with the royal family, it was said, though there were hints of them having had to flee their country, like the Huguenots; another tale was that they had been involved in a scandal at the French court, and various suggestions were put forward as to what that scandal might be.

'Whoever they are, they'll need clothes made up for 'em, I don't doubt,' said John Prewett, smiling at Tabitha who was home for the weekend.

'How are ye gettin' on at school, girl?' he asked her quietly when they were walking to church with Jeremiah. Mrs Prewett had stayed at home, saying that she could not keep up with their long strides, and needed to rest. The new maidservant, Prudence Briggs, was a pleasant, lively girl who had been brought up by an aunt in the country, and was capable of roasting a shoulder of mutton and preparing vegetables, while also keeping an eye on Thomas.

Prewett looked affectionately at his sturdy daughter whose features resembled her mother, but there was a determination, a strength in her face that reminded him of his own mother who had brought up nine children without losing one, but who had died of a haemorrhage after her last confinement. He wanted a better life for his daughter.

'Are ye happy at school, my girl?' he repeated when they were out of earshot of Jeremiah. 'Have ye made any friends there among the other pupils? Ye never seem to mention any o' them by name.'

'I get on well enough with them, Papa,' she replied lightly.

'But no-one in particular? What about the girl who shares your bed?'

'Cynthia White? We don't have much to say to each other. I tell her that she snores, and she says I do, too. *And* she takes up most o' the room in bed! I like being back in my own room on Saturday nights.' Tabitha smiled up at her father who continued to question her.

'Does this – er – Miss White go home on Sundays, too?'

'No, she's a permanent boarder. Her mother's dead, and her father's often away abroad.'

'So the poor girl's motherless, with no home to go to?'

'Yes, Papa.'

'Well, then, how'd ye like to ask her to come home with ye one week's end, an' let her meet yer family?'

Tabitha's heart sank, and she did not know how to reply. He asked her again.

'I said ye must invite this poor girl to come home an' spend a Sunday with us, and share our table. I've spoken to yer mother about this, and she agrees, if ye would like it.'

Tabitha felt her cheeks reddening. She would not hurt her father's feelings for the world. 'It's very kind o' ye, Papa – and Mama, too, to – to give me leave to ask a friend to come home with me, but I don't think it would be, er – con-conve-nient,' she answered awkwardly.

'Why so?' he asked, smiling.

Tabitha thought what a joke it would be at the academy, if the tailor's daughter, nicknamed Tabby-cat, invited a fellow pupil to come home and meet her family: how it would be talked about and laughed over – how she would be humili-ated! But dear Papa must never know this.

'Please, Papa, don't ask me to invite her – the truth is that I don't *want* to ask her into my home – yer home, I mean.' She dared not raise her eyes to his in case he should read her thoughts. 'I'm really sorry, Papa, but I just don't *like* Cynthia, and I don't want her – or any o' the girls stayin' with us. I'm pleased to get away from them all at the week's end.'

'Well, I'm sorry to hear that, Tabitha. I thought 'twould be a pleasure for ye and a change o' scene for her, to have a short stay with us. But never mind, never mind,' he added, seeing her discomfiture. 'It's enough for yer mother an' me to see ye once a week.' He patted her shoulder. 'But if ye should change yer mind, our door's still open to any guest o' yours.'

'Thank you, Papa.' Tabitha felt shamed by her father's well-meant kindness and her own deviousness in wanting to spare him pain. Though if she had heard her parents' conversation in bed the night after she had returned to Islington, she would have appreciated her father's goodness of heart even more.

'Ha! Ye don't surprise *me*, John! I told ye it was a silly idea. *Any* o' those little madams'd take one look around our home, turn up their noses an' carry tales back to that school, laughin' their heads off at a humble tailor's shop! No wonder Tabitha turned it down – the poor girl would've been shamed.'

'Oh, surely not, Martha. We mustn't always think the worst o' people—'

'Much good it did ye for thinkin' the best o' that scoundrel Feather! Givin' him all that money needed for yer wife an' children, all for the sake o' that slut of a girl – how he must've laughed at ye behind yer back – just as these young madams laugh at Tabitha, I shouldn't wonder!'

She continued to scold, and John Prewett suffered in silence. At one point he opened his mouth to remonstrate with her, but closed it again. To utter a word would only prolong her diatribe, and besides, he had to admit, if only to himself, that there might be some truth in what she said. And if she was right, it meant that his much-loved Tabitha was the butt of her fellow pupils' jokes for being merely a tradesman's daughter. It would explain why she so seldom mentioned any of the girls by name – and had actually confessed to disliking the unfortunate girl who was her bedfellow. What should he do? Offer to remove her from Mrs Kelso's Academy? Or leave her there to do her best and shame the young madams?

He sighed, turned over, and bid his wife goodnight.

*   *   *

20

In June Mrs Kelso wanted her girls to make the most of the sunshine, and classes were held outdoors when practical. This made it even harder for the pupils to concentrate their attention on Miss Dacre's drone and Miss Brambell's neat solutions to financial exercises on the blackboard, carried out and placed on its easel in the shade. In the afternoon the girls brought their sketch pads and needlework outside, though pianoforte practice and Monsieur Joubert's classes had to remain indoors.

Tabitha threw herself with dogged determination into all her studies, and gave herself extra tuition from the books in the little library, formerly the study of the late Reverend Kelso. She practised the arithmetic taught by Miss Brambell, and learned the multiplication tables by heart. It made her think of her father doing his accounts, adding up the purchases of materials – needles, buttons, frogging and sewing thread – and calculating the hours spent making the finished garment and pressing it with a clean, damp cloth and heavy irons heated by an open fire at just the right stage of glowing coals with no flames or smoke. She also remembered going shopping with her mother at the Barter Market, and learning to balance prices against Mrs Prewett's purse. In such practical matters she was better informed than the daughters of clergymen, attorneys and army officers, so being in trade did have its advantages, and Tabitha learned to close her ears to ill-natured remarks, finding silence to be the best response. When Miss Dacre and Miss Brambell enthused over her essays, and pinned them up on the wall to be read and admired, Tabitha sat quietly with her eyes discreetly lowered, so that nobody could accuse her of pride or call her a crowing hen. The Tabby-cat had learned how to appear equally indifferent to praise or mockery, and this was to prove useful to her later in life.

Cynthia White and the other girls who were permanent boarders also looked forward to the freedom that the weekend brought. They took full advantage of the summer weather to dress up in their prettiest gowns and straw hats, and dawdle among the other strollers along the High Street and Colebrooke Row, where the nursery gardens created a splendid background for their youthful charms. On Sunday mornings they had to attend St Mary's Church with Mrs Kelso and Miss

Dacre, but in the afternoons they liked nothing better than to head for Islington Spa where the fashionable ladies and gentlemen gathered to 'take the waters' for their health, and parade along the lime walks and gardens that adjoined the marvellous well.

'What sport was to be had, if only we could have lost Miss Dacre!' sighed Margaret who had caught the eye of a red-coated officer. Cynthia had been ordered to stay close to Miss Dacre and keep her engaged in conversation for at least twenty minutes, and as a reward Margaret and Penelope had bought her a glass of lemonade from one of the booths that were set up around the well, while they had boldly ventured to drink ale.

Tabitha heard this tale when she returned on Sunday evening; in bed she was forced to listen to Cynthia's description of the handsome young officer who had surely fallen in love with Margaret and would certainly have led her to one of the arbours and sat her on his knee if Miss Dacre had not noted her absence and started calling out her name. 'Oh, it was simply *too* embarrassing!' Cynthia told them, amid much stifled giggling.

Tabitha silently resigned herself to being kept awake for hours, and when she finally managed to doze off, it seemed as if she was immediately disturbed again by a low moaning close beside her.

'Oooh! Aaah! Aaah!' The sudden scream woke Tabitha to full consciousness, and she found it was her bedfellow making the noise. Cynthia was groaning loudly, writhing and clutching her belly.

'Cynthia! Whatever's the matter?' cried Tabitha, sitting up in the dark. The other occupants of the room were murmuring, disturbed by the noise. Then poor Cynthia made a retching sound and vomited copiously all over the bed. Tabitha sprang out of the way, and stumbled to the door, where she called out, 'Mrs Kelso, please come! Cynthia's ill!'

Mrs Kelso and Miss Dacre came with haste, shawls thrown over their nightgowns, and both carrying candles.

'It's Cynthia, Mrs Kelso, she has a bellyache and is vomiting,' Tabitha explained. By the light of the two candles Cynthia's face was seen to be deathly white, and her eyes dark and staring. 'It's my belly – I'm going to die!' she groaned, and as Mrs Kelso drew back the sheet, Cynthia's bowel discharged a quantity of semi-liquid matter in the bed. The stench of it filled the room, and for one terrifying moment Tabitha thought the girl was dead.

'Merciful God, it's the putrid fever – she's got the flux!' cried Miss Dacre in horror, but Mrs Kelso kept her head.

'If it is indeed the flux, we must stop it spreading through the school,' she said, and quickly took charge of the situation. Between them the ladies carried Cynthia out of the room, to be cared for by Miss Dacre and put in a room by herself. Mrs Kelso called a maidservant to help her strip the bed, and Tabitha passed the rest of the night on a sofa in Mrs Kelso's room, her head on a cushion covered by a quilt. In the morning Mrs Kelso checked every pupil for signs of the malady, and laid a hand on each forehead to test for fever. One or two of the girls said they felt unwell, and one had a griping pain in her belly, but this was due to the commencement of her menses. A doctor was summoned, and after seeing Cynthia, he suspected typhus fever, possibly the dreaded cholera, always more prevalent in the summer months, and caused by drinking tainted water. He was assured that Cynthia had eaten the same food and drunk the same water as the rest of the girls, though Margaret and Penelope remembered the glass of lemonade they had bought for Cynthia when they had both taken ale – but they decided not to mention it.

Letters were written and messages sent to all parents to warn them of the outbreak, and over the next two days many journeys were made by worried mothers and fathers who came to take their daughters home. Only three remained: Cynthia, whose father was abroad, and two other girls whose parents were out of the country. The summer term was precipitately ended a month early, and Tabitha secretly – and rather guiltily – rejoiced at her release.

As it turned out, Cynthia took forty-eight hours to recover from the inflammation of the bowel due to drinking tainted water, and nobody else caught the infection. The good Mrs Kelso may have wished that she had waited a day or two before notifying all of the parents, but she gave thanks to God that it had been no worse.

At Orchard Court life was going on as usual. The tailor spent most of each day working in the cutting room, and there were plenty of orders, so he was glad of the assistance of Rob

Drury, a willing worker with a real interest in the craft of tailoring. One of Prewett's problems was finding some simple tasks for Michael to do; the boy could sweep the floor and gather up the snippets of cloth, but could not follow the finer points of tailoring: the measuring, both of the customer and the cloth, the calculations of how much cloth would be needed, to include the seams and linings, to say nothing of the special features that ladies and gentlemen often wanted. In the end Prewett decided to improve Michael's skill at reading and writing by getting him to copy pages out of the order book, so as to have duplicates of every transaction; but many pages of expensive paper were wasted due to Michael's omissions and inaccuracies, and a fair number were too blotted with ink and finger prints to give to a customer. Prewett said nothing of these problems to Martha, who was feeling the heat as she proceeded slowly from kitchen to parlour; she used the stairs as little as possible. Prudence was a quick but thorough worker, and was also blessed with a sunny nature. Prewett was thankful for her cheerfulness, a virtue not much in evidence in his home at the present time.

It was Mrs Markham, the milliner next door, who first brought news that the new owner of No 9 Bloomsbury Square had arrived and moved in; and Jeremiah, on his way back from the Barter Market, reported seeing a carriage outside the house, and a coachman taking two horses round to the mews at the back. A very fine lady, accompanied by a pretty, fair-haired girl, had been seen entering at the front door, and even Martha Prewett in her weariness and discomfort was stirred to take some interest in the new arrivals.

The tailor sent Rob round to the tradesmen's entrance of No 9 with a polite handwritten notice advertising Prewett's Quality Draperies, which the apprentice was to give to the servant who opened the door. He warned Rob that he must not be seen outside the house, and if the front door was open or any of the family was around, he was to postpone his errand. Everybody was curious to find out about the newcomers, but nobody wanted to be caught spying or vulgarly canvassing for business.

A messenger boy had then arrived with a short letter from Mrs Kelso, informing Mr Prewett that a fever had broken out at the academy, and that his daughter should be removed forthwith. The academy would open again in September, she wrote, and he would be reimbursed for the time lost. All other considerations were at once forgotten in Prewett's fear for his daughter.

'Oh, my God, not Tabitha!' wailed Mrs Prewett when her husband told her that he was going to bring their daughter home. 'What wrong have I done, that I should lose three o' my children?' Her words found an echo in her husband's own heart, though he did his best to hide it. And, to her parents' joy, Tabitha was not lost; she was restored to them in perfect health, and overjoyed to be home. On that very same day a note arrived from No 9 Bloomsbury Square, asking the tailor to call on Monseigneur le Comte de St Aubyn and Madame la Comtesse, to give them more details about the service he offered.

'Praise be to Almighty God, Martha, who has shown mercy to us an' spared our daughter!' he said with tears of joy. '*An'* sent us a new customer, into the bargain.'

The tailor lost no time in attending the St Aubyns, taking with him a basket of swatches of cloth in a variety of weaves and colours, together with haberdashery samples – the buttons, braids and lace edgings he kept in stock. Mrs Prewett and Tabitha were left with Rob in charge of the shop, speculating on Prewett's reception and what orders he might receive. Mrs Prewett set out a tea pot and cups on a tray, ready for his return, but after an hour had passed she made the brew and poured it out for Tabitha, Jeremiah and herself, and told Prudence to call Master Drury from the cutting room to come and join them.

'Now, Jeremy, make room for Master Robin,' she said, and the apprentice lad gave the boy a wink as he sat down at the kitchen table where Prudence was chopping vegetables for a stew. Tabitha handed round the cups and exchanged a smile with Rob. He had become almost like one of the family since the departure of Will Feather and poor Nan. Rob lived with his mother in a little tenement building crowded into a narrow street near to Spitalfields Market, and appeared to have no other relatives, though at some time he had learned how to read and write and good manners, which were friendly and engaging, without the over-familiarity of Feather. Tabitha felt at ease with him, his chief recommendation being his kindness and patience towards Michael.

'Papa, Papa!' cried little Thomas, running to meet his father as Prewett entered the kitchen, all smiles. He was eagerly questioned by his wife and daughter who wanted to know what the St Aubyns were like, and how had he got on with them, though by his cheery air they could tell that it had been a profitable visit. Martha boiled the kettle again to make fresh tea as he talked.

'They're French, an' very gracious,' he said. 'It wasn't easy to understand them at first, but I showed them my samples an' the sketches o' the various styles, an' used my hands to demonstrate how I would make them up. The – er – Count spoke a little English, but she had only a very few words, an' when they gabbled to each other nineteen to the dozen, they might've been plottin' a revolution for all I could tell!'

'Are they really on friendly terms with the King and Queen?' asked his wife.

'I couldn't be sure, but I've heard tell the Count has corresponded with His Majesty. He's quite a bit older than her, an' he's over here because of some scientific work he's done – he attends the meetin's of the Royal Society, an' must be reckonin' to stay for a while, because he says he wants to dress like an English gentleman – a coat, waistcoat and breeches. "All in the English style, Mr Prewett!" he said to me. And his lady wanted a riding jacket.'

'We'll be kept busy, then, sir,' said Rob.

'Yes, lad, we'll have our work cut out,' said the tailor, laughing at his little pun. 'And that's not all of it. There's a daughter, a pretty little thing, about the same age and size o' Tabitha, who's to have a riding jacket like her mother's – that'll be quite a challenge, 'cause I don't do much work for children. When this little lady looked at the buttons, I remembered I'd got some brass ones with a horse's head engraved on 'em, and would you believe it, I hadn't taken them with me, so I said I'd go over again with 'em, an' in any case I'll have to collect the sketches I left, so they said to call again tomorrow.'

'Oh, mayn't I go with ye, Papa?' asked Tabitha, her eyes pleading, for she longed to see the inside of No 9, and the French aristocrats who had received her father so graciously.

'Any other time I'd've said no, my girl, but this time ye're lucky,' he said smiling. 'I happened to mention that I had a daughter about the same age as theirs, an' how she'd learned to speak a little French at school – and the lady said I might bring her over with the horse buttons.'

'Oh, Papa, did she say so?' cried Tabitha, clapping her hands together.

'Yes, I think she wants to compare the two girls,' said Prewett, nodding towards Tabitha and then at his wife. 'So ye may come with me, girl, an' meet yer French counterpart. We'll call tomorrow at noon. Make sure ye're neat an' tidy, with clean hands an' face.'

'Oh, I will, I will, Papa! I'd like it above all things, to see a real Count and Countess!'

'Don't raise yer hopes too high, girl,' he warned. 'These sort o' people could easily forget about us, an' go out somewhere leavin' a servant to take the buttons an' give back the sketches with their orders.'

But as it turned out Tabitha got all she wished for, and more.

For the second time John Prewett presented himself at the tradesmen's entrance to No 9, this time accompanied by his daughter in her best gown and pelisse, with a straw hat tied under her chin with a white ribbon. A maidservant led the way upstairs to the elegant reception room where a footman ushered them into the presence of Madame la Comtesse and her daughter. Tabitha suddenly felt very shy, and bobbed a curtsey when her father bowed, keeping her eyes lowered.

'*Monseigneur le Comte n'est pas à la maison aujourd'hui,*' the lady said with a smile. ''E go to veesit wiz gentlemen. You bring ze buttons wiz a 'orse's 'ead?'

'Yes, Madam,' answered Prewett, and stepped forward to open the leather satchel in which he carried the haberdashery. 'Here they are, for yer daughter to see.'

'*Pour la jeune fille,*' added Tabitha softly, and the lady looked at her with interest. She spoke to her daughter in French, and added, '*Voici ma petite fille, Mademoiselle de St Aubyn.*'

The girl stepped forward but did not look at the buttons. She looked straight at Tabitha who raised her head and gave an involuntary gasp at the vision before her. Mademoiselle was a little taller and thinner than herself, and had the most

27

beautiful violet-blue eyes that Tabitha had ever seen, framed by long lashes. Her complexion was fair, with a delicate blush that made Tabitha think of a damask rose. Her flaxen hair hung in silky waves on her shoulders, and her rosy mouth was smiling.

'G-good day, Meess. I do not know how you call—' she began uncertainly.

Tabitha spontaneously bent her knees in a deep curtsey. '*B-bonjour, Mademoiselle. Je suis*— Oh, no,' she corrected herself, '*Je m'appelle Tabitha, si vous plâit.*'

'Tab-ee-ta. Tabita,' repeated the girl. '*C'est un très joli nom. Moi, je m'appelle Mariette, et je veux* – I want – to be a friend. *Je me sens très seule ici. Leve-toi*, get up from the knees,' she added, holding out her hand. '*Donne-moi la main!*'

Tabitha straightened herself up, and clasped the proffered hand. '*Oui, merci, ma chère Mademoiselle,*' she said, oblivious to anyone or anything else in the room. '*Moi aussi, je veux être votre amie. Pour toujours.*'

'*Pour toujours, ma chère Tabita.*'

This halting exchange was the beginning of a friendship that would continue and deepen over many years, though nobody could have foreseen it then. For the present both the St Aubyn and the Prewett parents were astonished at the change in their daughters during the bright summer days that followed that first meeting. From being lonely and homesick for the countryside and the friends she had left behind in Compiègne, Mariette became interested in her new surroundings, and not only the comings and goings in Bloomsbury Square; she was soon shown the way to the mews behind the narrow fronted houses, and the Frenchman's stairs that led down to Orchard Court and its respectable shopkeepers. John Prewett was horrified when Tabitha first brought her friend into the cutting room, and left his work at once to escort the young Mademoiselle back to her parents at No 9. Instead of being rebuked, Madame la Comtesse thanked him for the friendship between her daughter and his, and the great benefit to Mariette; she cordially invited Tabitha into the St Aubyns' home where the girl sat at table with the family and shared their fare.

When Monseigneur le Comte asked his wife if she thought it wise to encourage this friendship, she waved him aside with a smile.

'Ne t'inquiète pas, mon cher. Elles sont comme deux papillons, heureuses et innocentes!'

He gave her an indulgent smile; he thought the tailor's daughter, with her plump cheeks and round brown eyes, could hardly match his own Mariette in beauty or charm, but if his wife thought them two pretty little butterflies, who was he to disagree? After all, they were only children.

And marvellous as it seemed to the tailor's family, a day came when Mademoiselle de St Aubyn happily sat at their own table. The friendship was a blessing to Tabitha, as could be seen by her new vivacity in place of the wariness she had learned at Mrs Kelso's Academy. Her father began to realize that she had not been happy there; her determination to study hard and learn all she could had resulted in ridicule from the haughty girls who looked down upon the tailor's daughter; the fact that she had stoically persevered and said nothing of her loneliness to her family made him yet more proud of her, though he now had to make a decision whether or not to send her back to school in September. She had been doing so well at her lessons, and her teachers had praised her progress; and yet if she was miserable there . . .

Prewett sighed, for he could not talk it over with his wife, she had never approved of sending Tabitha away to school.

Tabitha tried not to think about September: she only wished that these carefree July and August days might never end. She and Mariette became inseparable, never tired of talking to each other about their most secret hopes and dreams; they believed that no sisters could be closer in spirit than they. The difference in nationality, social status and upbringing meant nothing at all to them, and as for the language, both their families were astonished at the speed at which they learned to converse in both English and French, and were never short of something new and absorbing to tell each other. Tabitha learned that Mariette was the only daughter of the Comte de St Aubyn by his second marriage; he had three grown sons and a daughter by his first wife, all married and living in France.

There was just one difference between them that they could not understand, and which gave both the St Aubyns and the Prewetts a certain unease; this difference was their religion. Both girls had been brought up as Christians, and firmly believed in God the Father who had sent His Son Jesus Christ to die on Calvary's Cross to save them from their sins. They were used to saying their prayers morning and evening, and attending church regularly. The Prewetts attended St George's Church, conveniently near at hand, where many of their noble patrons sat in the best pews; Tabitha expected to see Mariette there on Sundays, but found that the St Aubyns disappeared down towards Lincoln's Inn Fields, to some place of worship that Tabitha had never heard of.

'The chapel of the *what*, Mariette? Is that a church, then?'

'No, *ma chère* Tabita, it is an Embassy, and we worship in the chapel there.'

'What's special about this chapel, that you go so far, dear Mariette?'

'It is a Roman Catholic chapel, and we are Catholics,' her friend replied a little awkwardly, because she knew that her parents would have preferred her dearest friend to be a Catholic also; neither girl knew much, if anything, about the difference between the Church of England and the Church of Rome, or the situation of Catholics in a Protestant country; they only knew that they worshipped the same Father, Son and Holy Ghost, though the Roman liturgy was spoken entirely in Latin instead of English. The fact that the St Aubyns quietly made their way to the Sardinian Embassy, a fair walk away from Bloomsbury Square, was an unimportant detail to two adoring little butterflies who knew nothing of bigotry.

Three

Three weeks into August the warm weather continued, but the evenings started drawing in, and Tabitha noticed a change in the light; the mellow slanting rays that bathed the roofs and spires of London in a series of golden afternoons also presaged the approach of autumn. All too soon she would have to return to school, which meant parting from Mariette.

She could hardly bear to think of it, yet it was drawing inexorably closer, and would soon have to be faced.

For Martha Prewett the weather was still uncomfortably hot, and every ungainly step she took made her short of breath; she still liked to preside over her family's dinners and suppers, and refused to invite Prudence to join them at the table, which Tabitha thought was unfair to such a willing worker. When Mrs Prewett winced and clutched at her side, gritting her teeth and muttering about backache, Tabitha dared not comment, for she was not supposed to know about the new life her mother carried; if Martha had known how her daughter had been forced to hear what she wasn't supposed to know, Tabitha could only imagine the outcry it would cause. Her spirits sank at the thought of facing those other girls again, for she had not a single friend among them. Meanwhile it was her duty to prepare her real friend for the parting.

'Dear Mariette, ye know I'll soon have to go back to Mrs Kelso's school, and then we can only meet at the week's end,' she said sadly, and saw the French girl's beautiful eyes fill with tears at the prospect.

'I shall be so lonely without you, *ma chère Tabita*.'

'We can write to each other, dear Mariette.'

'That is not the same as to see you every day. I shall cry for you every night.'

Tabitha put an arm around her friend's little waist. 'Before we have to say goodbye, let's spend a day together, just ourselves and nobody else,' she said daringly, for she was not allowed to walk far from Bloomsbury Square without a parent or at least Prudence, and lately her father had been too busy, her mother too tired and Prudence too constantly occupied. 'We could walk down to that very long Oxford Street, they say it's full o' shops of all kinds – and more goin' up all the time – or we could go to High Holborn, that's not so far, 'cause I want to buy a keepsake for ye before I go.'

'Keepsake? Is that like a souvenir?'

'Yes, a little present that ye can keep an' think o' me – like a pretty bracelet or pair o' gloves. Ye can look in the shop windows and tell me what ye'd like, dear friend.' Tabitha had a crown piece that her father had given her one Sunday when she had been home from school; now seemed the right time to spend it.

'I will beg Maman to let me go with you, dear Tabita.'

And indeed Madame la Comtesse gave her daughter permission to walk out for just one hour with Miss Tabitha, whom she knew to be a careful and trustworthy girl. They fixed on the following Monday morning, the beginning of Tabitha's last week at home.

'I'll meet ye at the top o' Frenchman's stairs, Mariette, at ten o'clock Monday mornin'.'

'I will be there and waiting for you, Tabita,' replied her friend solemnly.

Fate, however, decreed otherwise.

At breakfast on that memorable Monday, Mrs Prewett looked flushed and anxious; she drank a cup of weak tea, but ate nothing. For the next hour she was restless and short of breath, and walked from the kitchen to the parlour and back again, unable to settle anywhere, though Tabitha noticed that every so often she leaned over the back of a chair and gasped for a minute or two, then straightened herself up and breathed normally.

'Are ye not well, Mama? Would ye like to rest in bed for a while?' Tabitha asked, thinking that Mariette would soon be waiting for her – but how could she leave her mother if something was about to happen? Tabitha knew in her heart that the child her mother carried inside her must be almost ready to be born, and the thought filled her with fear. What should she do?

Prudence had been washing the breakfast cups, but she suddenly took down her cloak from the peg behind the door, and told Tabitha that she was going out to fetch Mrs Hitchcock.

'Has Mama asked you to go for her, Prudence?'

'No, Miss Tabitha, but I reckon she'll soon be needin' her. Just ye stay here like a good girl, an' wait till I get back.' And off ran the maid, clearly alarmed at her mistress's condition.

Mariette will be waiting for me by now, thought Tabitha, and called to Jeremiah.

'Jerry, will ye go to the top o' Frenchman's stairs, an' tell Mariette that I can't meet her today, 'cause me mother's ill?'

'Why, is Ma ill? What's the matter with 'er?' asked the lad, catching her worried look.

'Just do as I tell ye, Jerry – run an' tell Mariette I can't come, an' say I'm very sorry – go on, do as ye're told, an' be quick about it!'

No sooner had the boy left the house than Mrs Prewett gave a loud cry, and to Tabitha's horror, a gush of water suddenly splashed on to the floor, wetting her mother's stockings and shoes, and forming a puddle beneath her. And there was no chamber pot downstairs.

'I should've gone upstairs afore now, and – and now it's too late,' gasped Martha. 'God help me – *help* me!'

'Papa!' Tabitha screamed. 'Come and help Mama, she's ill!'

Nobody answered, for John Prewett had seen Prudence leaving, and when told her errand, he sent her back and said he would go for Mrs Hitchcock himself. Martha Prewett gave another groan of pain and tried to hold on to the table, but sank helplessly down on the kitchen floor. Tabitha rushed to her side and supported her head. Nobody was taking notice of Thomas, who began to howl loudly, adding to the confusion.

'Mrs Hitchcock's comin', Mama, don't worry,' Tabitha whispered, praying that the handywoman would get there in time – but the first person in at the door was Prudence who gasped and whispered, 'Oh, my God!' at the sight that met her eyes – though she made a big effort to overcome her fear, and did not fail her mistress.

''Tis comin' on sharp, an' 'twill soon be born,' Prudence muttered. 'Ye shouldn't be here, Miss Tabitha, but ye'll have to help now. Let's get this rug underneath her, steady now—'

A voice full of reproach called to Tabitha from the open door. 'Tabita! Why do you tell me to go home?' It was Mariette de St Aubyn, standing and staring at them, taking in the scene. '*O, mon Dieu!* I shall pray to La Vierge for her – and for you, *ma chère.*'

Prudence also uttered a silent prayer as she knelt down facing her mistress, putting out a hand to lift the soaking skirt and petticoat. 'Let me just see if – Oh, 'tis the child's head, by my life! Take hold o' her hand, Tabitha – and Mariette, ye take her other hand. All right, Mrs Prewett, we're here with ye, don't be frightened – oh, where in God's name is the midwife? Oh, here it comes, the child's head!'

'*Je vous salue Marie, pleine de grace, le Seigneur est avec vous, vous êtes bénie entre tous les femmes,*' recited Mariette, doing as she was told, kneeling down beside Tabitha, and taking Martha Prewett's left hand.

John Prewett, hearing the shouts from the kitchen on his

return, strode through the cutting room and into the kitchen just in time to witness the birth of his seventh child who immediately set up a loud, repetitive cry. 'Lah, lah, lah, lah, lah!' The baby went on and on, competing with Thomas's aggrieved yells at being ignored.

'*Et Jesus, le fruit de vos entrailles, est beni,*' said Mariette. '*O, merci, Sainte Vierge!*'

''Tis a boy,' panted Prudence, nearly as flushed and breathless as her mistress, who was raising her head, trying to see the child, but meeting only the circle of faces around her.

'Another son, Martha,' Prewett groaned in relief. 'But why didn't ye *say* somethin'? Why didn't ye go upstairs to bed?'

'I wasn't sure – it was too quick – it's not due for another three weeks,' muttered his wife in utter bewilderment. 'A boy, did ye say? To take the place o' the lost one – another Andrew.' Then she seemed to become aware of the situation. 'Merciful heaven, what're *you* doin' here, Tabitha? – and Mam'selle? Who on earth let *them* in here?'

'We were already here, Mama, an' everything happened so quickly,' explained Tabitha. 'We were the only help that Prudence had—'

'Thank God ye're here, Mrs Hitchcock!' exclaimed Prudence as the midwife came bustling in at that moment. She immediately took over from the maidservant, and praised her presence of mind, though she quickly dismissed the husband and the girls from the kitchen, and gave Thomas into his sister's care. After cutting and tying the cord, and seeing the afterbirth expelled, she called upon Mr Prewett to carry his wife upstairs to her bed, while she washed the baby and bound him round with a long linen band of swaddling.

Prudence cheerfully cleared up the debris of the delivery and did the washing; she still found time to prepare and serve a mutton and vegetable stew with barley bread for the family's midday dinner. She stood by the table to serve them all – Prewett and Rob, Tabitha and Mariette, Jeremiah and Thomas. She was about to take her own portion away to eat alone, but Prewett bid her sit down with them. Tabitha took her mother's dinner upstairs on a tray, but found her and the new baby sleeping.

Once Mr Prewett had got over the shock and relief of his wife's delivery, notwithstanding its suddenness, he became extremely embarrassed over Mariette's involvement in it, and told her that he would go and apologize to her parents; but it seemed that she and his daughter had already discussed the matter, and decided that Mariette's parents need not be told the details, only that Madame Prewett had given birth to a son.

'I was happy to be there with *ma chère amie, Tabita*, Monsieur,' Mariette told the tailor with a confiding smile. 'I pray to La Vierge, and she take care of us all.'

Prewett could only bow and thank her gratefully for her services, though he knew he would live in constant expectation of a summons from No 9 Bloomsbury Square if the truth ever slipped out, which would be worse than voluntarily owning up in the first place.

The two friends had more to say to each other after dinner when they were out in the yard, tossing a ball for Thomas.

'Tell me, dear Mariette, did ye know how babies were born, before this happened?' asked Tabitha curiously. 'Ye didn't seem surprised.'

Mariette smiled. 'Non, *ma chérie*, I am not old enough to know such matters.'

'But then how *did* ye know—'

'When I see Madame on the floor and crying, La Vierge told me in my heart that an infant is coming – and that you have need of me, my Tabita. And I was not afraid.'

'Dearest Mariette, how good you are, and how wise!' cried Tabitha, throwing her arms around her friend. 'But who is La Vierge?'

'Why, the Mother of Christ, the Blessed Marie, Notre Dame!' replied Mariette in some surprise. 'Do you not call upon her for help in trouble? She is the Mother of us all – just as we are as sisters, my Tabita!' She laughed at her friend's uncertain look, and Tabitha laughed too, both aware that this adventure had drawn them even closer.

So Madame la Comtesse was told of the arrival of a new baby boy in the tailor's household, and assured that both mother and child were well. She sent her felicitations and a basket of fresh fruit as a gift for the family, blissfully unaware of the part that the two pretty butterflies had played in the drama.

When a couple of days later John Prewett received a note asking him to attend the Comte and Comtesse immediately, his heart gave a lurch. They must know! Somehow or other

35

they had got at the truth from questioning Mariette, and now he was about to lose his good name, possibly his livelihood, if the details of the birth on the kitchen floor in front of the innocent French girl had come to light. Trembling, and wanting only to get it over with and know the worst, he presented himself at the tradesmen's entrance, and was shown up into the presence of the aristocratic couple. He was breathing quickly and his heart was pounding as he entered the drawing room and bowed low.

'Ah, Prewett, we 'ave a favour to ask you,' said Monseigneur le Comte, and when the tailor raised his eyes, he saw that they were both smiling. He managed a half-smile, and waited.

'Our daughter Mariette 'as changed much since she made friends with your Tabitha,' said the Comte, and Madame nodded in happy agreement. 'We understand that Tabitha 'as to return to school next week, and Mariette is desolate.'

'Ah – er, yes, m-monsieur, Tabitha is – er—' Prewett hesitated as words deserted him.

'Mariette has had a governess up until now, as we did not want to send her away to school,' the Comte went on. 'But we feel that the time has come to let her meet with other girls and learn the same accomplishments as we see in your own daughter. And as Mariette does not want to part from her very special friend, we are agreed in sending her to the same academy for girls in Islington. Will Tabitha be willing to take Mariette under her wing, *c'est à dire*, and help her to – er – settle into such new surroundings?'

As soon as Prewett had regained his breath and composure, he gave the couple a courteous reply. Depend upon it, he assured them, Tabitha would be delighted to introduce Mademoiselle de St Aubyn to her friends – and he recommended the care taken by Mrs Kelso to ensure the health and well-being of all her pupils.

From tearful repining to wild rejoicing, both girls astonished their parents yet again by their enthusiasm, for they were hardly able to believe their luck. Mariette expressed an earnest desire to turn herself into an accomplished young English lady, and Tabitha could hardly wait to show off her special friend, Mademoiselle de St Aubyn, to the society-conscious young ladies at the academy. Mrs Kelso herself was flattered to be thus patronized by the French aristocracy, especially after the scare that had curtailed the summer term, and she undertook to attend personally upon the newcomer.

For Tabitha the new arrangement had many consequences. There was no need now for her father to hire a hackney cab, for the St Aubyn carriage was at the disposal of both girls and their luggage. Even Martha Prewett, still opposed to her daughter going away to be educated, had to admit that her status at the academy would be greatly improved, and her father's uncertainty turned to a deep satisfaction: there'd be no more hoity-toity condescension from those older girls who envied his Tabitha's success at her lessons.

'Let's take that walk to the new shops in Oxford Street, Mariette, before we go to Islington on Saturday,' Tabitha begged, for she still had not bought a keepsake for her friend. Even though they were not now to be parted, she wanted to celebrate with a love token for Mariette.

'I will walk wherever you please, my Tabita! Anywhere you shall go, I shall go also,' said the French girl, a sweet picture in her white gown with a muslin scarf around her shoulders.

'Take Thomas with ye, an' get him out from under the maid's feet!' ordered Mrs Prewett, as she suckled her new baby son. 'She can't get on with her work, with him pesterin' all the time.'

'Oh, Mama, can't Jeremy look after him?'

'No, he's not careful enough. *You* take care o' him, you and Mam'selle – do summat useful afore ye go skippin' off to that school again!'

So they set out from Orchard Court with Thomas between them. He held a hand of each and chortled as they bounced him up and down.

'Me go that way! Me want to see long-legs!' he yelled, tugging them in the direction of St Giles-in-the-Fields, where street vendors gathered and a troupe of entertainers wandered among the bystanders on tall stilts, to much wonder and applause.

'Let's go an' see them, just to keep him quiet,' said Tabitha, and saw Mariette's blue eyes widen at the antics of the stilt walkers, who took great strides like giants, and turned round in circles, as if it was the most natural thing in the world.

There were also jugglers throwing plates up in the air and catching them; women sold lavender from baskets over their arms, and a one-eyed man carried half a dozen small cages within which captive wild birds twittered helplessly.

'Oh, look there, those two men are dancing!' cried Mariette, though the two pugilists were in fact fighting with bare knuckles, circling round each other, alert for an opportunity to land a punch, and at the same time avoid the opponent's flailing fists. The crowd around them roared encouragement to one or the other, and Thomas wanted to go nearer, but the girls pulled him away and found themselves at a spot where seven roads met and a clock stood at the centre, telling the time in seven directions. Houses that had once been new had become ramshackle, and dirty-faced, bare-footed children played among the refuse that littered the unpaved thoroughfare. Tabitha became aware of shifty-eyed men and women looking at them suspiciously, and remembered her father's talk of pickpockets and cutpurses who preyed on pedestrians. It was time to get out of this area, she decided, but no sooner had she muttered this to Mariette than they were surrounded by a circle of beggars, mainly children, demanding halfpennies and farthings. Tabitha was not going to show them her purse, and told Mariette to hold Thomas's hand tightly as they turned back towards St Giles's. Suddenly she was accosted by a young woman carrying a baby.

'Miss Tabifa! Can't yer spare a penny for a poor babe wiv no milk, an' a muvver wiv nuffin' to eat? Give us a penny, Miss Tabifa!'

Who on earth could know her name? Heavens, it was Nan, their former maidservant, abandoned by Will Feather and now burdened with a baby. On hearing her cry, the number of beggars doubled, all calling her by name.

'Miss Tabifa! Miss Tabifa, give us a penny for bread, Miss Tabifa!' they shouted, and the ragged figure of Nan clutching her puny baby came and stood directly in front of the trio.

'Yer ain't forgot poor Nan, 'ave yer, Miss Tabifa?' she whined.

'Er – no, Nan – I'll give ye a penny,' she said, aware of her companion's shocked expression. 'You hold on to Thomas, Mariette, so I can reach for my purse – no, keep off, all o' yer, stand back!' she cried as hands stretched towards her, and everybody seemed to be shouting, 'Miss Tabifa, Miss Tabifa!' Her purse with the crown piece in it was hung around her neck on a leather strap, and the purse was tucked into a pocket. She had no sooner closed her fingers on it and taken it out, when a long arm shot forward and grabbed it from her. She caught a brief glimpse of a swarthy man's face grinning as he pulled on the strap, jerking her forward. Mariette shrieked, Thomas howled, and the strap was pulled off over her head by her assailant who disappeared forthwith into the crowd. Gone was the purse, the strap and the crown coin.

'Lor', Miss Tabita, yer gorn an' lorst it!' wailed Nan, clutching her baby.

'I'm sorry, Nan, I never thought—' Tabitha was close to tears, for now she would not be able to buy a keepsake for Mariette. 'I'm so sorry, poor Nan. I'll tell my mother, an' maybe she can sort out some clothes for yer baby. Is it a boy or a girl?'

'She's a girl, an' I nearly died givin' 'er life, Miss Tabita, an' I wish I 'ad. Me ma turned me out, an' now I 'as to beg. Me baby needs milk, an' I ain't got none for 'er, Miss Tabita.'

Tabitha stared at the still, white face of the baby wrapped in a stained shawl, and a dreadful, helpless pity seized her. 'I'll speak to my mother, Nan, I promise I will. Come, Mariette, we'd better go back home.'

They walked along in silence, with Thomas bouncing between them. 'I'm so sorry, dear Mariette. That poor girl used to be our maidservant, but my mother sent her away because she was going to have a baby – that baby.'

'Yes, poor girl, it is bad for her to live in this place,' replied Mariette. 'Do not worry about the keepsake, dear Tabita. I think this is another matter I must not tell to Maman and Papa.' Tabitha felt even more ashamed. She would have felt worse still if she could have known that Nan was in slavery to the thief who used her and her baby as a bait to move the hearts of strangers, giving him the opportunity to shoot out his hand and grab their purses. Nan would receive only a pittance of his takings.

'*What?*' cried John Prewett when she told him what had happened to her purse and its contents. 'Ye took Mademoiselle an' young Thomas down to Seven Dials? Good heavens, girl,

I thought ye had better sense. Say nothin' to yer mother, for God's sake, an' let's hope yer friend says nothin' to hers!'

To reinforce the lesson, Prewett did not reimburse his daughter, and no money or clothing was sent to poor Nan. The incident lingered long in Tabitha's memory, and was her first intimation of a dark pit of human misery, a seething underworld lying not far beneath the surface of life in Bloomsbury Square and the respectable tradespeople in Orchard Court. Tabitha knew she must shield her dearest friend from it whenever she could.

At the academy Tabitha's life was transformed. Arriving in the St Aubyns' carriage driven by a coachman and accompanied by a footman who stood up behind and took care of their luggage, the tailor's daughter could afford to be gracious towards Cynthia White, and make no apology to the older girls for her superior skill with words and figures. Her beloved Mariette now became her bedfellow and constant companion in class, dining room, library and wherever the girls gathered. Mrs Kelso smilingly dismissed Mariette from the French lessons, saying that she had no need of them, and gave her Mr Horace Walpole's novel, *The Castle of Otranto*, to read and help her with her English. It turned out to be full of murders and imprisonments, knives dripping with blood and a ghost thrown in for good measure. Mariette was both impressed and terrified by it, and kept the others awake at night by re-telling the story after dark. This proved to be a deliciously effective way of frightening the other girls, while reducing its terror content for Mariette herself. It also led to a demand for gothic horror stories, and when Mrs Kelso tried to recommend the essays of Dr Johnson and Mr Addison, and the sermons of Mr John Wesley and George Whitefield, she was disappointed at the response. Regarding the French lessons from which Mademoiselle de St Aubyn had been tactfully excluded, Tabitha had by now mastered enough French to note that Mrs Kelso's grammar and pronunciation left much to be desired, but it never occurred to her to betray the kind-hearted principal.

Similarly, after one dancing lesson with Monsieur Joubert, Mariette told Tabitha that the gentleman was no more French than the Prewetts' cat.

'And I can see on his face that he knows I know it, dear Tabitha,' she said in a low voice that none of the others could hear. 'And I think to myself, he is so polite to us, and a good teacher of the dance – so we shall not tell of his secret, shall we, Tabita?'

And their kindness was rewarded by poor, masquerading Mr Jenkins's grateful smiles; as Monsieur Joubert, he continued to captivate his pupils for another decade, and earn twice as much as he would as an English dancing master.

In these happy circumstances four summers and winters passed, in which the girls bloomed into early womanhood; for, as Tabitha pointed out, Shakespeare's Juliet had been no more than fourteen. John Prewett had intended his daughter to have one year's schooling only, but she was so enjoying her new popularity with teachers and fellow pupils, that when the St Aubyn parents begged him to let her stay on for their daughter's sake – and actually offered to pay her fees, which Prewett declined – he was willing enough to agree. It meant that she was there when the school was honoured by a visit from Monseigneur le Comte de St Aubyn and his wife after he had received a medal from the Royal Society in recognition of his contribution to the broad field of natural philosophy, encompassing the science of astronomy, the nature of matter and the mysterious force of gravity. He had proclaimed Sir Isaac Newton to be a greater mathematician than his own countryman Descartes, and his daughter and her friends at Mrs Kelso's Academy basked in the reflected glory of this distinguished émigré.

Tabitha commenced her menses three months earlier than Mariette, and was not much inconvenienced, but the French girl suffered cramps and irregularities that made her nervous about being caught without the necessary rolled cotton squares and bandages. Mrs Kelso pronounced her to be a delicate girl, which gained her privileges like having rest periods when the others were taking exercise.

At Prewett's Quality Draperies life was satisfactorily uneventful, and to the relief of John and Martha, their second Andrew proved to be their last child. Jeremiah became a pupil at the Reverend Mr Wyatt's School for Sons of Clergy and did well there. It was hoped that he would follow his father's craft, and eventually take over the business, which would include taking responsibility for his elder brother. Michael was well liked in Orchard Court, and did not wander far from it, for fear of encountering louts who made loud fun of his lack of wit. He was adored by seven-year-old Thomas and sturdy little Andrew who rode pickaback on his shoulders at every opportunity, especially on Saturdays when they went up the Frenchman's stairs to look out for the St Aubyn carriage that brought Tabitha and Mariette home each weekend. Prudence was now twenty-one, a great favourite of all except Martha Prewett, who dimly resented her without quite knowing why: she could not fault the girl's cheerful efficiency, compared with her own discontent. While she was also sometimes irritated by her daughter's close friendship with Mademoiselle Mariette, at least it was preferable to an intimacy with the maidservant, which would have annoyed her far more.

It was Prudence who quietly informed Tabitha of Nan's death from gin-drinking following her baby's death after admission to the Foundling Hospital.

'That place was meant to be a refuge for poor bastard babes whose mothers couldn't look after 'em, Miss Tabitha, but the trouble is that it's so overcrowded – they don't get mother's milk, ye see, an' so many of 'em die. I wonder what poor Captain Coram thinks of it now. He had it built, ye know, 'cause he was upset by all the abandoned babies he saw.'

Tabitha heard this in dismay, and turned away, blushing with shame. Poor Nan, who had sat at their own hearth, who had scrubbed and mopped their floors and emptied their chamber pots, and had then been abandoned by them, just as Will Feather had betrayed and deserted her; her own mother had turned her out, leaving her to fall into a brutal, destitute life. And Tabitha had promised to send her clothes for the baby. So much for her empty pity . . .

Robin Drury glimpsed her stricken face, and longed to be able to ask what was the matter, so that he might comfort her, but of course he couldn't. He had finished his apprenticeship, and was a pleasing young man of eighteen who admired Miss Tabitha from a respectful distance, doffing his cap to her and the young lady from France. Mr Prewett had advised him to gain experience with another tailor before looking for a permanent position with prospects, but there was another and more exciting possibility open to young men at this time. There had been rumblings of resentment from the American colonies who objected to paying taxes to the British government, and there were even calls for independence from some rebellious spirits. The King was totally opposed to this, and Parliament was split between those who supported the King, and the more far-sighted ministers who saw American independence as inevitable. Britain was blundering towards a wasteful, futile war, and the Army would need new recruits. His mother was utterly opposed to Rob enlisting, but there was adventure and maybe glory to be gained for a strong young man with no family ties; he was thinking it over.

None of these weighty matters occupied the minds of the girls leaving Mrs Kelso's Academy that summer. Tabitha and Mariette had heard about something called a regatta, a race between decorated boats on the Thames that was to take place in June. It had caught the imagination of London society, and everybody who was anybody would be flocking to Ranelagh Gardens, a splendid park adjoining Chelsea village, and full of attractions; it extended down to the very edge of the river. The twelve boats were to take off for London Bridge where they would turn round and come back again, cheered by spectators on either bank and ending at Westminster Bridge, where the first to arrive would be declared the winner.

'Oh, what better way to celebrate the end of our schooldays!' exclaimed Tabitha. 'Will your parents attend, Mariette?'

'I hope so. And yours, *ma chérie*?'

Tabitha shrugged. 'I don't know. My mother probably won't, so I hope Prudence'll have charge o' Thomas and Andrew, or else I will. Father might like to come – and Rob Drury.' She gave a little smile as she said the apprentice's name, which was not lost on Mariette.

And indeed young Drury was determined to persuade his erstwhile master to let him take charge of the two girls and find them places on one of the spectator boats that crowded the river to get near to the regatta.

As it turned out, Monseigneur and Madame de St Aubyn came to join the thronging spectators in Ranelagh Gardens, and so did Mr and Mrs Prewett, with Prudence and the two small boys. Jeremiah was there with friends from his school, and Michael stayed at Orchard Court to take tea with the milliner Mrs Markham and her sister. Rob Drury had managed to get his way as escort to the girls on a boat following the race called the *Lucky Lady*, decked out in ribbons, flags and twirling paper wind-wheels.

And there were three girls, not two. They had agreed to ask Cynthia White to join them. She had received a bitter blow when, on reaching the age of fifteen, Mrs Kelso had gently informed her that her father now wished her to be placed with a gentleman's family as a lady's maid or possibly a nursery maid. The awful truth was that her father was no political diplomat; she was the natural daughter of a prosperous brewer who had been willing to do his duty by her, but could not openly acknowledge her, as he had a wife and family. Most of her fellow pupils had been equally amazed and amused at discovering her humble origins, and the consequent blow to Cynthia's self-esteem. Tabitha had felt for her, and included her in the outing to the regatta. So there they all were on a cloudy afternoon in June, with a stiff breeze blowing up-river. A makeshift jetty had been constructed, and the passengers in their finery stepped on to the boats, of which there were twelve, lining up and waiting for the pistol shot that would signal the beginning of the race . . . and off they went, to deafening cheers.

John Prewett narrowed his eyes to pick out his daughter standing beside the beautiful but delicate Mariette and poor Miss White whose history he had been told. Tabitha's kindness to her, when she might have crowed over past slights, had given him great satisfaction. He also saw young Drury standing a little apart from the girls but with his eyes on Tabitha. Prewett knew how the land lay there, and indeed, there would be no objection to a tailor's daughter marrying another of that craft, especially a good, reliable worker like Drury; but Prewett had no wish for her to be tied down too soon; some girls were married at fourteen, but Tabitha had plenty of time to look further afield.

The boats were now out of sight, and heavy clouds had gathered; raindrops began to fall, and a collective groan went up from the spectators. Soon there was a steady downpour, parasols had to do the work of umbrellas, and the crowds tried to find shelter in the gardens, many of them making for the Rotunda, a huge circular structure with an orchestra in the middle, and tiers of boxes all around. Into these gathered a widely mixed collection of courtiers, citizens, mechanics and shopkeepers, all jostled together, to Martha Prewett's great annoyance.

'I told ye this'd be a waste o' time, an' tire us out!' she grumbled. 'Where've them boys gone? I hope that girl's keepin' her eyes on 'em. The sooner we all get out o' here, the better!'

But having seen the boats off on their race, Prewett wanted to be assured of their safe return. He would have been alarmed if he had seen their arrival at London Bridge where they had come up against the barges that ferried passengers to and fro between the banks. The bargees resented what they saw as an inconvenience, and deliberately rammed the pleasure boats, to loud consternation. Oars were tangled, and the boats swayed madly, their decorations limply dripping. The *Lucky Lady* got her share of noisy opposition, and the girls clung together, afraid that she would capsize. By the time the competing vessels reappeared, making for Westminster Bridge, the tide had ebbed, and the boats were separated from the jetty by about three yards of mud; no landings could be made, and there was no choice for the passengers but to wade to the bank in pouring rain, amidst much protesting and complaining. The ladies' summer clothes were soaked and their carefully dressed hair hung in rat's tails. Some of the younger ones like Jeremiah and his friends found it fine sport, and Rob Drury saw an unexpected and delightful opportunity to be of service.

'I'll have to carry yer across the mud, Miss Tabitha, an' then come back for the other two,' he told her gravely.

'Oh, Rob, you must take Mademoiselle de St Aubyn first, for I fear she will be chilled,' replied Tabitha, torn between amusement and anxiety. 'And Miss White is our guest, so she must be next. I'll be able to wade across if I take off my shoes and stockings.'

'Certainly not, Miss Tabitha!' he said firmly. 'I'll take all three o' yer, one at a time, startin' with Miss – er – St Aubyn. I'm ready to take her now.'

But the beautiful French girl, her silk gown clinging to the curves of her slender body, had already been seized by a bold youth in military uniform, and lifted up into his arms.

'Oh, mon Dieu!' she cried in alarm, though she put her arms around her rescuer's neck. 'You will drop me, Monsieur, and we both shall fall in the mud!'

45

He laughed and stepped out of the boat with his lovely burden, and waded ashore. The mud was smelly and full of half-rotted detritus left behind on the tide. He almost slipped at one point, and Mariette screamed, but clasping her tightly he righted himself and reached the dry ground. Tabitha, suddenly noticing her friend's passage, also screamed when she saw the youth nearly fall, and she was desperate to get to her friend's side.

'Mariette, wait for me! Take me over next, Rob, and then come back for Cynthia! *Quickly!*'

Once deposited on the ground, Mariette turned to thank her protector, but found herself still encircled by his strong arms, for now he was ready to claim his reward.

'Excuse me, er, Monsieur—' she began, but he was smiling down at her.

'Can you not put your arms around me again, little sweetheart?' And he lowered his head until his lips were almost touching hers.

'Let go o' her! Take yer filthy hands off! Don't ye dare insult Mademoiselle de St Aubyn!' Tabitha shouted, having just been deposited on the bank by Rob, and quite forgetting the ladylike way of speaking she had learned in her four years at school. 'Don't ye mind him, Mademoiselle, yer parents are waitin' to take ye home – come with me now, this way.'

'Don't be too angry with him, Tabitha, he saved me from the mud,' gasped Mariette as her arm was seized by her friend who hurried her along to where both the St Aubyns and the Prewetts were waiting by the Rotunda. Rob had gone back for Cynthia, and Jeremiah had just turned up with his two friends, all three so covered in mud as to be practically unrecognizable. Mrs Prewett was furious, but Monseigneur and Madame were so thankful to have their daughter safely returned to them that they had smiles for everybody, and hired sedan chairs to take them home straightaway, to get Mariette out of her wet clothes. The Prewetts and Miss White, accompanied by Rob, made their way back to Bloomsbury on foot.

'I have to thank you, Master Rob, for carrying Cynthia and myself over the muddy water,' Tabitha muttered, as they reached Oxford Street and continued along its straight length towards St Giles's Fields.

'It was my pleasure, Miss Tabitha,' he answered, remembering the brief happiness of bearing her weight in his arms.

With a smile he added, 'Yer friend was carried just as safely by that soldier, but I noticed how ye dismissed him! Why was that?'

'Oh, Rob, did you not see who he was? That scoundrel Will Feather! He tried to be familiar with Mademoiselle de St Aubyn, and would've insulted her further if I hadn't sent him off with a flea in his ear!' replied Tabitha sharply. 'Ugh, the very thought o' him touching my lovely Mariette makes me feel sick!'

'Are ye sure t'was he, Miss Tabitha? I heard that he'd joined the militia.'

'Then I hope they send him over to America,' she said with a shudder to think of that brute, as heartless as he was lecherous, so much as looking at her precious Mariette. 'Please excuse me, Master Rob, I must ask Miss White how she does.'

Riding home with her mother in the sedan chair, Mariette wondered if the handsome young man would have kissed her if Tabitha had not come along – and how it would have felt and whether she'd have liked it if he had. She recalled seeing his eyes upon her when she'd been clinging to Tabitha and Cynthia on the swaying boat, and remembered the feel of his arms around her. For the first time Mariette de St Aubyn thought seriously about love – the romantic kind, that led to marriage and having children – and decided she was thankful that Tabitha had come to her rescue.

Four

1779

J. PREWETT & SON,
LADIES' & GENTLEMEN'S TAILORS.

The newly painted sign, black letters on white, gleamed in the thin October sunshine, and John Prewett regarded it with pride. He nodded to his neighbour, the milliner Mrs Markham who had come outside to admire it.

'O' course, we do a lot more for gentlemen than for ladies, but we have to show that we do both,' he said. 'And I've left off the word *quality* – no need for it, our name's enough these days. To speak truth, it should be J. Prewett, Son and *Daughter*, because Tabitha does the home visits to ladies, and takes their measurements. Jeremy's a good boy, but ye need a female for lady clients, and Tabitha's got just the right manners.'

'Yes, I can see that she's a great help to you.' The milliner smiled, adding with a sidelong look, 'and what about that civil young Mr Drury? I notice that he still calls on you quite often.'

'Ah, Robin, yes.' Prewett's features relaxed into a look of affection. 'Comes to church with us every Sunday mornin'. He'll make a name for himself one day, that lad. He's in charge o' half a dozen men and women at Davidman's – they've got a workroom over in Whitechapel, an' they turn out any amount o' reasonable clothes, much cheaper than ours. Customers look for the size they want, an' maybe try on a few – it's not the same perfect fit, but Rob thinks it's goin' to be the tailorin' o' the future, with so many more o' the middlin' sort lookin' to dress decently. An' with these new spinnin' jennys and flyin' shuttles turnin' out more woollen and cotton materials than ever before.' He gave a little shrug. 'Rob's probably right, but I don't know what my old father would have said!'

'I'm sure there'll always be a demand for top quality tailor-made clothing, Mr Prewett,' said Mrs Markham. 'These machines may be able to turn out woven material in quantity, but when it comes to making up the actual garments, it will always have to be done by hand. There's no machine that can put in those tiny little stitches!'

He nodded. 'Yes, I agree. And Tabitha studies the latest fashion plates in ladies' magazines, an' makes sketches o' them to show to my regular customers.'

'Like the St Aubyns,' said Mrs Markham, for Madame and Mademoiselle were her customers also.

'That's right, and then I can make a copy so exact that nobody can tell the difference.' John Prewett allowed himself a moment of self-congratulation, for his high reputation had been built up entirely on personal recommendations.

'And do you think that Master Drury will come back to you?' asked the milliner curiously, for all of Orchard Court knew of the young man's pursuit of the tailor's only daughter.

'That's in the Lord's hands, an' not for me to say, Mrs Markham. There's a place for him at Prewett's any time he likes, but the business'll pass to Jeremiah or one o' my other sons, though they be but youngsters now,' he added, referring to Thomas and Andrew, healthy, high-spirited boys who would try their hands at tailoring after leaving school. Poor Michael would always remain a likeable but simple boy, good for carrying written messages, sweeping the cutting-room floor and able to heave heavy bales of cloth for his father or parcels of books for Silas Holmes – jobs that required brute strength but no great reasoning ability.

Prudence appeared at the shop door. 'Mrs Prewett says ye're to come for yer tea now, sir – and Mrs Markham too, if she wants.'

'*And* Miss Prewett, too, I hope!' said Tabitha, coming into the Court at that moment, breathless from hurrying down the Frenchman's stairs. She undid the ties of her cloak, and beamed at them both.

'Good afternoon, Mrs Markham. Lovely weather for this time o' year, but the leaves are falling fast, and they're slippery when they're wet. I nearly fell over in Bloomsbury Square!' She turned to her father. 'I've been to Lady Dersingham's, Papa, and she sent me on to Mrs Legge and the Comptons in Russell Street. You'll be getting orders from there, for sure.'

'There's a message for ye, Tabitha, from Mademoiselle,' said her father, smiling at the bright-eyed girl. 'She wants ye to call an' see her as soon as ye can.'

She was at once alert. 'Oh, does she? Have I got time to go over there before – no, better have tea first, or mother'll let me know of her disapproval.' She caught her father's eye for a brief moment, and gave a wry smile. Martha Prewett at fifty had become a scold, and wore a habitually pained expression; her family had learned not to tell her things that would disturb domestic harmony. Her chief complaint recently was Tabitha's refusal to accept Master Drury's offer of marriage. He had asked for and received her parents' blessing, and Tabitha was clearly fond of him; she walked at his side when he came over to attend Divine Service with the family on Sunday mornings, and they sat together in the Prewett pew at St George's, flanked by Thomas and Andrew on his side and Michael and Jeremiah on hers, next to Mrs Prewett and her husband at the end, ready to do duty as collector of alms. But Tabitha never stepped out with young Drury unchaperoned, for they were not betrothed in marriage. She had asked for another year before committing herself, and promised him an answer when she reached nineteen. Perhaps by then her beloved Mariette de St Aubyn would also be promised in marriage, for she was not short of suitors. John Prewett was willing to accept this situation, but Martha was infuriated by it, and it divided the husband and wife, as such disagreements will when they continue for weeks that stretch into months.

'She's only got to give Rob her word, an' then he'll know where he stands,' she said over and over again. 'If she's got any sense, she'll take his offer now, an' marry in a year's time if that's what she wants anyway. 'Tisn't as if she's a ravin' beauty, far from it – her face is as round as a bun, with two black currants for eyes. *She* won't catch the eye o' some rich landowner!'

This was a reference to the succession of offers for the hand of Mademoiselle de St Aubyn, another topic of speculation in Bloomsbury Square and Orchard Court, where the continuing close friendship between the two girls over eight years had surprised everybody. John Prewett looked fondly at his daughter, now in the full bloom of youthful womanhood. He thought he understood what young Rob saw: a dark-eyed, sunbrowned, bustling girl with a pleasingly rounded figure, neatly but not showily dressed, with her straight, dark-brown hair drawn back under a little linen cap. He was in no hurry to part with her, not even to the excellent Robin Drury, and not just because of her indispensability to J. Prewett & Son.

'Oh, Tabitha, *ma chérie*, what do you think? I'm invited to stay with Lady Farrinder at Heathfield House in Chiswick!' said Mariette dramatically, kissing her friend. 'For two whole weeks,' she added in answer to the question she saw hovering on Tabitha's lips.

'Well, that's not an eternity, my love, and Chiswick isn't the back o' beyond, is it? Who's Lady Farrinder, an acquaintance o' Monseigneur and Madame?'

'Well, yes, in a way. She met them at a Royal Society dinner, and she and her daughter Hester have since been to dine here. She's a widow with married sons and this young daughter. She has connections in Ireland, a cousin married to a – what do you say? A baron? He's called Sir Somebody Townclear who lives at Townclear Hall in somewhere called County Kerry.'

Tabitha was mystified. 'So what's the reason for inviting you to stay with this Lady Farrinder? A widow living with a daughter, and connections in Ireland – what is she to you? Are you asking for my approval?' She smiled as she spoke, but Mariette was deadly serious.

'Don't tease me when I need your support as never before, my Tabitha! Of course there is a reason! This Sir Somebody Townclear and his lady have a son called Conor and a daughter called – er – something like Mary, I think – and these two are coming to stay with their aunt and uncle in Chiswick.'

'Ah, now I hear you more clearly, my Mariette. And the name that stands out from all the rest is Conor – Conor Townclear. Is he a Mister or a Sir? How old is he?'

Tabitha was smiling, but a note of anxiety had crept into her voice, and her dark eyebrows were raised as she put these questions to her friend.

'He is called Mr Townclear because he is a younger son, and his age is – oh, somewhere in the twenties, I don't know. But there is something more important than his title or his age – or even his character, *ma chérie* – the family are Roman Catholics.'

'Oh, I see,' replied Tabitha, for now she felt that she really did see. 'And your father and mother, do they agree that you go to Chiswick and meet this young Catholic man and his sister who's called something like Mary?'

'I have already told you they do. Don't be frivolous with me, Tabitha.' Mariette's deep-blue eyes were not smiling, and the implications of this meeting were suddenly obvious to Tabitha, with all the possible consequences – the *desired* consequences of the visit. She flung her arms around her friend and hugged her close.

'Nobody can make you fall in love for the convenience o' your families, my Mariette,' she whispered. 'You mustn't be led into making a decision. You must take your time.'

'As you are doing with Mr Drury, and it is the joke of Orchard Court,' returned Mariette with a sharpness that made

Tabitha draw back and look into her friend's face. 'If only you had consented to become my personal maid when we left school! If only you had come to be my constant companion as I wished, and Maman wished! Then you would come with me on this visit, and give me your opinion and we would talk all through the night, and you'd help me to make up my mind, dearest Tabitha.'

'Oh, Mariette, I'm sorry. Forgive me,' replied Tabitha, silently recalling the uproar of four years ago when the St Aubyns' invitation to Tabitha had first been mentioned.

'Yer father didn't send ye to that school for four years, just to end up as a servant in the house o' French papists!' her mother had stormed, and Tabitha's father had taken her aside and told her that he would rather she stayed at home and exercised her new skills as his lady assistant, dealing with his lady clients. Of course he was thinking of her eventual marriage to good Master Drury. So, after being strongly tempted to take up the St Aubyns' offer, she had let herself be advised by her father. Sooner or later she knew that Mariette would be married to somebody or other of her parents' choosing, and then . . .

Perhaps that time had now come, and Mariette was destined to be the bride of this Mr – what was his name? Mr Conor Townclear of Townclear Hall, County Kerry. And perhaps that was where her dearest friend would go to live. Forever, for good or ill.

Tabitha clung to Mariette again in sudden panic, afraid of losing her.

It was decided that Madame should accompany her daughter to Heathfield House, and stay there for three or four days, after which Madame would return to Bloomsbury, leaving Mariette under the chaperonage of Lady Farrinder. This arrangement, Mariette confided to Tabitha, would provide a means of escape if the visit did not go well, and Mr Townclear failed to come up to expectations: in that case both mother and daughter would leave together, without loss of face or dignity.

'Of course, Maman and Papa and Lady Farrinder all hope that Mr Townclear and I will like each other, or they would not go to such trouble, dearest Tabitha. Oh, how I wish that you were coming with me.' She sighed for the hundredth time, and Tabitha could only advise caution.

And so, on a dull, chilly, misty day in early November,

Mariette and her mother left Bloomsbury Square in the St Aubyn carriage. A short distance behind them a groom followed in a horse-drawn cart carrying Mariette's two trunks, full of clothes, and her hat-boxes.

Tabitha waved goodbye and watched as the two conveyances vanished into the mist, the sound of the horses' hooves clip-clopping on the paving; she stood watching until it could no longer be heard.

It was not an auspicious start to a meeting with the partner of a lifetime.

'Tabitha, my girl, I've got another visit for ye to make – well, for both of us, really, at the home of a clergyman, no less!' John Prewett smiled as he spoke. 'It's a Reverend Mr Sands who lives in Clerkenwell, and whether 'tis he or his lady or their daughter who requires a tailor, I don't know, but we'll make our way over there tomorrow with our samples an' fashion plates, an' see if we can come back with some orders.'

Tabitha was glad of the diversion, and she and her father set out the next day in a hackney cab. They were soon out of the town and rising gently uphill; the open fields and gardens reminded her of Islington, even in the grey of winter, and passing by Clerkenwell Green they came to Red Lion Street and a respectable house which Prewett identified as the Reverend Sands' residence by the description he had been given, although they could see no church nearby. He paid the cab driver, and they made for the tradesmen's entrance, but before they reached the house, the front door opened and a gentleman appeared, beckoning them to enter.

'Mr Prewett? Come this way, my dear chap – and the young lady. Mr and Mrs Sands are expecting you, I believe?'

This cordial welcome was encouraging, as was the pleasant drawing room into which they were shown. Mr Sands, dressed in clerical black with the white collar and bands of his office, said that he needed a new jacket in tweed, and his lady and their daughter likewise, to protect them against the cold winter weather. Tabitha got out her measuring tape and notebook, and asked if there was another room where she could retire with the ladies; they led her up a flight of stairs to a landing from which other rooms opened. Mrs Sands opened the door of her bedroom, where a maid was dusting.

'Come in here, Miss Prewett,' she said. 'I must ask you to leave us, Cynthia, we have to be measured.'

Tabitha quite forgot her manners and stared at the girl with the duster in her hand: she was none other than Cynthia White, from Mrs Kelso's school. Tabitha had not heard from her for nearly four years.

'Cynthia!' she cried, before she could stop herself. 'Oh, to think we have met again.'

Cynthia glanced at Mrs Sands and said nothing, and immediately Tabitha wished she had not spoken, for fear of embarrassing her former school friend. Mrs Sands came to the rescue.

'Ah, do you two girls know each other?' she asked pleasantly. 'I'm sure there will be an opportunity for you to talk when Miss Prewett has finished her business.'

The measuring proceeded, and Mrs and Miss Sands pored over the sketches and chose the style of long jacket they fancied, with a good deal of comparing and arguing in favour of this or that. Did they want hoods, and if so, did they want them fur-trimmed? Taught by her father, Tabitha waited for them to suggest a fur, to give her some idea of what they were prepared to pay; ermine was expensive and fox was economical: the word cheap was never used in the presence of customers.

When the choices had been made, and Tabitha had entered the details in her notebook, the ladies went downstairs to the drawing room, and Tabitha eagerly went to speak with Cynthia who was waiting on the landing, having been given permission to see her friend.

'Well, fancy meeting you again, Cynthia, and in the home of a clergyman. How are you these days?' Lowering her voice, she went on, 'Is it a good place? Are they good to you? Can you talk to them?'

'Yes, it was surely the Lord that brought me here, Tabitha,' replied Cynthia with an odd little smile. 'I've been fortunate to find a place in the home of true believers.'

'Oh, I'm so glad for you,' said Tabitha heartily, remembering this girl's humble background and the humiliation she had suffered. 'Which church is Mr Sands? I mean, is this his parish?'

'He hasn't got a living at present, he's given it up to serve Lord George Gordon who has a seat in the House of Lords, and works very hard to preserve the true Protestant faith in England.' Cynthia's eyes shone. 'It's a great privilege for me to work in such a house as this.'

'What exactly do you mean by preserving the Protestant faith?' asked Tabitha. 'This is a Protestant country, isn't it?'

'Ah, yes, it's supposed to be, but heresies and false doctrines creep in whenever the church drops her guard, and we have to keep vigilant,' Cynthia answered with conviction. 'Lord Gordon has revived the Protestant Association, in which we should all enroll as members.'

Tabitha smiled at her solemnity, remembering her frivolous attitude to social life, fashions and romantic intrigues when a schoolgirl at the academy. 'Oh, Cynthia, you *have* grown prim and proper! What particular heresies have you in mind?'

'Need you ask? The Scarlet Woman of Revelations, chapter 17, the pagan church of Rome, with all her idolatry, superstitious practices, *popery*! You may shake your head, Tabitha, but beware! Only last year Parliament brought in this so-called Catholic Relief Act, which enables heretics and idolaters to hold office, take a university degree and betray our nation to France and Spain, put a Jacobite king on the throne again—'

'Oh, stop, stop!' cried Tabitha, half-laughing at what she thought nonsense. 'I've never even heard o' this Catholic Relief Act – and I thought a Scarlet Woman was a – well, you know – a whore. Oh, Cynthia, I ask you, how can you possibly believe all this?'

'Don't be complacent, Tabitha, but be on your guard. Be vigilant, be strong in the face of the enemy!'

'Do you realize, Cynthia, that you're calling our Mariette de St Aubyn an *enemy*?'

Cynthia came up close to her, and taking her by the right hand, looked straight into her eyes, and said in a deep, fervent voice, 'Hear what I say. Tabitha. Have nothing more to do with that family, or it will be the worse for you and yours.'

Tabitha drew back, chilled by the depth of feeling in the words. 'Thank you, Cynthia, but Mademoiselle de St Aubyn will always be my dearest friend. And now I think it's time for me to be leaving. Good day to you.' She gave a stiff little bow, and went down the stairs, to find her father in the entrance hall with Mr Sands and the gentleman who had let them in, a Mr Pole. He was saying something to the tailor, gesticulating with his hands to make a point. Prewett looked relieved when she appeared.

'Right, then, my girl, we've got others to see this mornin', an' mustn't dally. Good mornin' to ye, sir – and you, sir. Come along, Tabitha.'

Once they were seated in the hackney cab, Prewett said firmly, 'They're fanatics, Tabitha, an' wanted me to join their Protestant Association. Ye're not goin' there again.'

'Oh, Papa, I feel so sorry for Cynthia. She has no mother to turn to, no father to advise her, so she's been easily taken in by these people.'

'Yes, poor girl. Well, I've taken the orders for their jackets, so I'll have to call again for a fittin', and then deliver the goods,' he replied. 'And that'll be the last I have to do with 'em.'

'All right, Papa.' She gave him an affectionate smile, but John Prewett was worried, and did not tell her of his suspicion that the Sands, whoever they really were, had only asked them to call in order to sound them out, and ascertain their acquaintance with the St Aubyns – those French papists, as his own wife had called them.

Five days after the St Aubyn carriage had left on the six-mile journey to Chiswick, Madame la Comtesse returned alone, and sent a maidservant over to the Prewetts with a note from Mariette. Tabitha tore it open and read it eagerly.

> *Ma chère*, Tabitha,
>   O, how I miss you and wish you here to share the pleasures of a beautiful house with many comforts, and also to share my thoughts, dear friend. Lady Farrinder is very charming and goes out, or should I say comes out, with her daughter Hester and nephew Conor and niece Moira and me to walk in the park, and in the evening we sit by a good fire and play backgammon. Maman is waiting, so I must finish and send you my love, *chère amie*. I long to see you soon. From your own Mariette de St Aubyn.

It was a sweet, affectionate note that told her very little; apart from giving Conor Townclear's sister's true name, Moira, it said nothing factual about the brother or sister.

Eleven days passed following Madame's return, and then the St Aubyn carriage was seen to leave the square on a chilly, misty morning with only the coachman and groom, which caused some surprise: had it gone to fetch Mademoiselle home, and if so, why had not Madame or at least a reliable female servant gone to accompany her on the homeward journey?

All was explained when the carriage reappeared in the square that afternoon, and three people stepped down from it to be welcomed by Monseigneur and Madame at the door of No 9. Tabitha, working in the cutting room, did not see their arrival, and it was Jeremiah who reported to her that Mariette had returned with two others, a lady and a gentleman.

A note was delivered to Miss Prewett, which merely said, 'Dearest Tabitha, I'm home again with Moira and Conor Townclear, and will see you tomorrow. Love from your own Mariette.'

Tabitha read this with a dash of disappointment; Mariette had not only a prospective husband at hand, but a sister-in-law as well, gentlefolk who shared her faith and could walk boldly up to the front door of the house in Bloomsbury Square; perhaps she would soon have no further need for a humble tailor's daughter to be her confidante. Tabitha stoically made up her mind that if this were to happen, she would strive to behave with dignity, whatever hurt she felt.

'Tabitha! Oh, Tabitha, *ma chère amie*, at last, at last!' cried the beautiful French girl, enfolding Tabitha in her arms, and kissing her on each cheek in turn. 'I am so sorry because I could not see you last night, but I had to show my guests to their rooms and then take them all over the house. Also introduce them to Papa. And then it was so soon dark, and Maman said I must wait until tomorrow – that's today – and here I am! How are you, my own love? Are you well? And is it well with your parents and brothers? When can you come over and meet my guests? This afternoon? They are staying until the end of the month, so we shall have much pleasure together!'

This was reassurance indeed, and Mariette's sincerity instantly lightened her friend's heart and brightened her eyes. She went straight to her father to ask if she might be released from the cutting room that afternoon, and he agreed, though he had his doubts about the wisdom of this hob-nobbing with the gentry, mixing with them on an apparently equal footing; he feared that once Mademoiselle de St Aubyn was married, she and her kind would leave the tailor's daughter behind in Orchard Court, where the attractions of an honest young craftsman would be her best consolation. He kept his own counsel, however, believing that experience would teach her better than any amount of advice or admonition.

It was almost one o'clock when Tabitha presented herself at No 9 Bloomsbury Square. Should she pull the bell-rope or go down to the tradesmen's entrance? While she hesitated, the door was flung open, and there stood Mariette with her arms outstretched. She looked exquisitely lovely in a pale-blue gown, her flaxen hair drawn back with a blue ribbon, leaving short curls framing her face.

'Come in, come in, my Tabitha, to meet Moira and Conor! We are going shopping in High Holborn, and you are coming with us!'

Tabitha returned her embrace, then drew a deep breath before facing the visitors. A smiling girl of about their own age was introduced as Moira: she had a creamy complexion, brown eyes and dark-brown hair, accentuated by a green, fur-trimmed pelisse.

'Mariette has told us so much about ye, Tabitha, that I'm half afraid o' meetin' ye,' she said in the prettiest, softest accent that Tabitha had ever heard, having never met any Irish before. She returned the girl's handshake warmly.

'Thank you, that's – er – very good o' you, er – Moira.'

'And this gentleman,' said Mariette, leading him forward, 'is Mr Conor Townclear.'

Letting go of Moira's hand, Tabitha found herself looking into the dark eyes of a young man who was clearly Moira's brother. His complexion was clear and healthy like a man who spent much time out of doors, and his thick, black, wiry hair curled at the nape of his neck. He was looking straight at her and holding out his hand, apparently waiting for her to speak first. She realized that she was staring, and lowered her eyes, blushing at her bad manners, then raised her face again and put on a polite smile. He offered her a warm, strong handshake, and simply uttered her name, 'Tabitha.' He smiled and said again, 'Tabitha?' as if he was considering the sound of the word. She had never heard her name spoken in such a lilting way. He almost dropped the *h* from it, as Mariette had done at first, but not quite: the *h* was still there, but very softly pronounced.

'I never did hear of a name like that for a girl,' he said, 'but I'll say your parents chose right!'

And just as she had done on that first meeting with Mariette, Tabitha bent her knees in a deep curtsey to this man, simply because it seemed the right and natural thing to do.

'Come on, everybody, get your cloaks and bonnets on, and let's go forth!' ordered Mariette, her blue eyes dancing with happiness at seeing her dearest friend and probable future husband so obviously approving of each other. 'We're going to see the shops.'

Tabitha felt a moment's alarm, as she had brought no money with her, but it seemed that this was no shopping expedition, but literally to *see* the stylish shops now opening in both the West End – Mayfair, Piccadilly and Bond Street – and the City – Oxford Street, High Holborn and Cheapside, to which they now headed. High-grade retailing of all kinds was on show: jewellers and goldsmiths, clock and watchmakers, glovers and milliners, tobacconists, perfumeries and scores more.

'Look here, did you ever see the like of it?' cried Mariette, leading them to William Hamley's toy shop in High Holborn, which he had named Noah's Ark. Displayed behind the window was a painted wooden Ark against a backdrop of rainclouds and a storm-tossed sea, with Noah and his wife and their three sons and daughters-in-law, all beautifully carved and painted, watching the pairs of animals obediently going in through the Ark's door.

'Will ye look at those naughty monkeys already inside, and wavin' from the windows!' said Moira, laughing. 'Oh, may we go inside and look at the doll's houses? All that tiny furniture, isn't it just amazin'!'

Mariette agreed that she and Moira would go into the shop, but Conor declined.

'You stay outside with him, Tabitha, we won't be long,' said Mariette, as the two girls disappeared into the Aladdin's cave of the toy shop.

'Ye must excuse my sister, Miss Prewett,' he said pleasantly. 'We don't have anythin' like this in the length and breadth o' Kerry. London has taken our breath away quite!'

'Mariette says that Heathfield House is very grand,' she answered shyly. 'Is it anything like your home in Kerry – Townclear Hall, isn't it?'

'Oh, I'd say Heathfield has the most comforts,' he smiled. 'One thing in common with Townclear Hall is the little chapel where Catholics can come to join the family in worship. Lady Farrinder even has a resident priest, a very old man with a long beard who walks with a stick but performs all his priestly duties, in return for his bed and board.'

Tabitha could think of no answer to this, but his mention of the Roman Catholic faith reminded her of the threatening words she had heard at the Sands' house in Clerkenwell; she would not tell Mariette about that, or even mention that she had met their one-time friend Cynthia again.

When the two girls emerged from the toy shop, Mr Townclear continued to walk at Tabitha's side, taking her right arm in his because the pavement was slippery and uneven. He asked her about her own family, and she told him about her four surviving brothers, and the sadness of two deaths.

'Ah, yes, Miss Prewett, 'tis sad indeed to lose a child,' he said quietly. 'Among the poor Irish peasantry the number o' deaths among young children is very high. With our own tenants it isn't so bad, because my father takes care o' them and treats them as his own people – which is somethin' different from most o' the Anglo-Irish landlords, half o' them livin' in England anyway, but still collectin' their rents.'

'Oh, but that's terribly wrong, Mr Townclear!' she exclaimed, realizing that she knew nothing about Ireland and its grievances. 'Er – your father's a-a – baron, isn't he?'

'A baronet, Miss Prewett, so he gets called Sir Bernard Townclear, and my eldest brother who's also called Bernard, will inherit the title. I'll stay plain Mr Townclear, which doesn't worry me at all! The fact is, you see, we follow the same faith as our tenants, so they come to worship at our chapel, and they trust us. Not like the majority o' the Anglo-Irish who belong to the Church of Ireland, that's Protestant, ye see, and peasants have to pay tithes to a church they don't belong to. As if they didn't have a hard enough time scrapin' a livin' from the land, feedin' their children on potatoes and butter-milk. I'm tellin' ye, Miss Prewett, there's a lot o' bitterness against the English – but listen to me, ye don't want to hear all about that.'

'Oh don't worry, say no more, Mr Townclear. What you've said has given me a lot to ponder on. The truth is that Mariette and I never even think about the difference in our faiths, and I didn't realize that it was such a – a problem in Ireland.'

He stopped walking and stared at her. 'Miss Prewett! D'ye mean to tell me that ye're a Protestant?'

'Yes, Mr Townclear, all my family belong to the Church of England.'

'Heavens above, and there was myself thinkin' ye must belong to the Church o' Rome, bein' such a close friend to Mariette.' He paused, and looked at her questioningly, as if afraid he had offended her. 'Miss Prewett, I didn't intend to – forgive me.'

'Oh, say no more about it, Mr Townclear! Mariette and I have never had a minute's unease over our churches,' she told him, anxious to put his mind at rest. 'We both worship the same God – Father, Son and Holy Ghost – and the very fact that she's never told you I'm Protestant must show you how little we care about it. Truly, we never think of it.'

'I see,' he replied thoughtfully. 'Well, I must apologize for any remarks I've made that might be upsetting to ye, Miss Prewett.'

'I haven't heard any, Mr Townclear. Please let's say no more, or we'll upset Mariette.'

'Ah, Mariette, yes,' he said softly, his eyes on the beautiful girl walking in front of them with his sister. He smiled. 'As ye may know, Miss Prewett, I've come to look for a good Catholic girl, one who will support me in my endeavours, just as my mother does for my father, and my brother Bernard's wife does for him.'

Tabitha felt rather uneasy, and said bluntly, 'But I was under the impression that you'd already found this good Catholic girl, Mr Townclear.'

'Yes, I've been led to understand that Mademoiselle de St Aubyn and her parents are in agreement, but—' He hesitated, and then seemed to make up his mind to say something. 'Miss Prewett, ye're her closest friend, ye must allow me to speak openly. A good Catholic girl she most certainly is, but do I deserve such a sweet, beautiful young woman?'

'That, surely, is for her to decide, Mr Townclear,' answered Tabitha with a little smile. 'I'm not in a position to give any opinion on a matter that's no business o' mine.'

'But what do ye think o' me, Miss Prewett, based on the little ye know?'

'Too little to be able to answer you, Mr Townclear. She's my dearest, closest friend, and all I want for her is a husband who'll make her happy. If he doesn't, well, he'll be no friend o' mine.'

'What nonsense are you two saying to each other? I demand to be told!' cried Mariette, turning round and facing them, all smiles. 'Look, we've arrived at this marvellous old-style jewellers – he sells many antique brooches and rings—'

Rings? Townclear was at once attentive. 'My dear Mariette, d'ye wish me to buy—?'

'No, no, Conor, what I want is a ring for Tabitha, a keep-sake. Come into the shop with me, chère Tabitha, and tell me what you like.'

All four of them crowded into the lamp-lit room, and Mariette asked to see some silver rings. A sharp-eyed old jeweller set a tray on the counter in front of her, and watched as she asked a blushing Tabitha to choose one she liked.

'But I never wear rings, Mariette—'

'And I say you *will* wear one, *chérie*, just for me. Look, do you like this one, all these knots and plaits woven together in the metal? Try it on your finger.' She took hold of her friend's right hand and pushed the ring on to her third finger, easing it over the knuckle. It was certainly a pretty ring, and the Celtic whorls and twists in the pattern suggested lover's knots; it also suggested the work of a highly skilled silver-smith, reflected in the price.

'I can't possibly accept this, Mariette—'

'Thank you, I shall take it and pay now,' Mademoiselle told the jeweller, opening her purse and nodding her satisfaction as he wrote out the receipt. 'There you are, my Tabitha, wear it always for me—' She kissed her friend's flushed cheek.

'But I should get one for you,' protested Tabitha, knowing that she had no money with her.

'No, you must not. I can remember our friendship without the aid of a trinket. Come on, let's go and find a coffee house.'

'But Mariette, let me get ye a ring that *you* like,' interposed

Conor Townclear, holding up his hand to the jeweller, signalling that he was to leave the tray on the counter. 'Come and choose one similar to Miss Prewett's – what about this one?'

'Oh, no, no, there will be time enough for me to think about rings, Conor. And now I insist that we find a coffee shop and indulge ourselves in luxury – hot chocolate and Chelsea buns! And you may pay for us all, Conor, seeing that you are so ready to part with your money.'

Coffee and chocolate houses abounded in every street, and they settled on one near to Covent Garden, which seemed to be full of pearl-buttoned, powdered and bewigged wits with all the latest news and voices loud enough to relay it to the whole of the room. Heads turned to look at the trio of girls being steered to a table by Townclear who ordered chocolate and the buns recommended by Mariette; the atmosphere was thick with tobacco smoke, but at least it was warm after the chill dusk outside. Tabitha soon realized that they were attracting the attention of a noisy group of gentlemen at a nearby table.

'By my eyes, that young shaver's in luck! Such an abundance of beauty!' said one of them.

'But is he man enough to pleasure them all?' answered another with a leer. 'I could offer him some assistance if need be.'

'O, most obligin' o' ye, sir, very kind to be sure!'

A roar of laughter greeted this, and Tabitha blushed crimson, thinking that Conor must have heard. Mariette and Moira were chattering happily, oblivious to any other sound, and she glanced at Conor, to find that his dark eyes were regarding her intently, so she quickly looked away again, afraid that he might suspect her blushes were for him. She concentrated her attention on drinking the delicious chocolate and eating the bun. Neither he nor she uttered a word, but left the talking to Mariette and Moira.

When they came out it was quite dark. Tabitha knew that her parents would be wondering where she was, and Mariette must have been thinking along the same lines, for she gave Conor her arm and steered them all towards Drury Lane and back to High Holborn and Bloomsbury. Oil-burning street lamps had been lit in the wider thoroughfares, and the illuminated shop-fronts gave an impression of an unreal, magical town. Tabitha took Moira's arm as they followed the pair in front, and thought again how strange it was for Mariette to buy *her* a ring, rather than to have one bought by Conor Townclear for her own finger: she wondered what on earth he must think about it, and whether he minded.

In Bloomsbury Square there were no lights other than those in the windows of the houses, seeming to beckon them home to the comforts of blazing fires and toasted muffins; when they reached No 9, Tabitha wondered if Mr Townclear would be asked to escort her back to Orchard Court, and if so, what her reaction should be – but as they drew close to the door, she saw something that drove every other thought from her mind: a sight to make them all gasp in incredulous horror. Tabitha began to tremble uncontrollably.

'O, mon Dieu!' cried Mariette, instinctively turning to Tabitha who feared that she was going to be sick. The Townclears simply stared at the huge red letters daubed across the woodwork in – was it *blood*? No, it was not blood but wet paint, glistening obscenely, dripping down in trickles from the crude letters:

NO POPERY!

Five

W ho on earth could have committed this act of vandalism? Whoever he was, he had been quick, choosing a moment after dusk when nobody else had been around in the fashionable square, daubing the foul message on the St Aubyns' door and vanishing again into the dark.

Mariette and the Townclears had been shocked, but Tabitha had been more truly sickened than the others because, not being a Roman Catholic, she immediately felt that her family came under suspicion. *She* had been in the company of Mariette and the Townclears, but any other member of the Prewett household could have crept out with a pot of paint and a brush, and as quickly disappeared. Her father? Of course not, he was no religious bigot, and the St Aubyns were valued customers. Jeremiah? Never! Like the two younger boys he looked on Mariette as a family friend, and liked her. Martha Prewett, even when in a jealous mood, would never dream of taking such a risk, and Prudence had not a malicious thought in her head, neither had poor Michael.

She thought of Cynthia White. Could it have been some paid lackey of the Protestant Association? This seemed the most likely answer, and it distressed Tabitha, for if she had not met Cynthia at the Sands' house, she would not have drawn the girl's attention to the St Aubyns' religion. She had not told Mariette of that meeting, but now she wondered if she should do so. Certainly she had to consult her father, for the news of the incident would be all over the square and Orchard Court within hours.

She lit a candle and asked him to come with her into the cutting room, where he listened gravely, putting his hand to his head in a gesture of dismay.

'I wish we'd never set foot inside that wretched house, Tabitha! What exactly did Miss – er – White say to ye?'

'She warned me to have nothing more to do with the St Aubyns, or it would be the worse for me,' replied Tabitha miserably.

'Ye should've told me that at the time, girl.'

'But what could you have done, Papa?'

'I could've gone to the Comte and told him what we'd heard at Clerkenwell.'

'It wouldn't've prevented this from happening, Papa.'

'Maybe not – but I'll have to tell him now, an' let him know what we know. It could be due to us that the scoundrels came an' did this thing. Ye'd better come with me, girl. No need to say anythin' to yer mother, it'll only worry her.'

By which he meant that he would never hear the last of it from Martha who would blame him for getting involved with religious controversy.

Monseigneur le Comte listened attentively to the tailor who described his meeting with the Reverend Mr Sands and Mr Pole, and the way they had tried to press him to join the

65

Protestant Association, and how he had refused. Tabitha was then asked to tell them what Cynthia had said to her, at which the Comte had frowned.

'So – you say this Miss White was a pupil at Mrs Kelso's Academy when you were there with Mariette?'

'Yes, Monseigneur. She was a – an orphan, and came with Mariette and me the year we left school to see the regatta on the Thames – that time when we got so wet in the rain and had to be carried ashore.'

'Ah, yes, that comes back to memory. Madame and I had to take Mariette home quickly to get her dry and warm. But you remained friends with this – er – girl?'

'No, Monseigneur, we didn't meet again, not then. She said she was going to be a lady's maid in some gentleman's house. That was four years ago, and then when Papa and I went to see the Sands family to measure them for new jackets, Cynthia was there. She must've told the men that you were – that the St Aubyns were – oh, Monseigneur, I am so sorry about this!' Tabitha could not contain her wretchedness. 'If only Papa had not gone there!'

'I shan't go there again,' her father broke in. 'They can go without their jackets, an' I'll go without the payment for 'em. Like my girl here, I'm deeply sorry if we've been the cause o' harm to ye, sir.'

'Thank you for telling me this,' said the Comte gravely. 'We have lived here for eight years, and this is the first time we have – er – encountered anti-Catholic action. To be frank with you, I am inclined to think that the Catholic Relief Act of 1778 has done us more harm than good. It has drawn attention to the Roman Catholic community, and stirred up the – er – opposition.' The Comte did not want to mention the word Protestant in front of the Prewetts, but Prewett himself had no such reticence.

'This so-called Protestant Association is made up o' fanatics, and I don't want anythin' to do with 'em, sir,' he said grimly, and the Comte smiled and nodded.

'May I ask that you say nothing of this to Mariette, my dear Tabitha? Her mother and I do all we can to protect her from unpleasantness. And I know that she is waiting to see you, so do not keep her in suspense! Now, may I tempt you to a glass of claret, Mr Prewett?'

66

Mariette embraced her friend with tears and reassurances that nobody suspected the Prewetts. The cleaning of the front door would be a difficult and lengthy process, and it would require revarnishing. The whole incident had left a cloud over the square, causing old prejudices to be taken out and aired.

Mr Townclear and his sister stayed with the St Aubyns until the end of November, attending Mass on Sundays in the chapel at the Sardinian Embassy with their hosts, and also went on some expeditions to see the sights, including the Tower of London and Mrs Salmon's amazing waxworks exhibition in Fleet Street. They also went to the play, and Moira was entranced by the alluring actress Mrs Robinson as Perdita in a performance of Shakespeare's *A Winter's Tale* at the Theatre Royal in Drury Lane. Although Tabitha was invited to join them, she declined, advised by her father that theatres were hotbeds of immorality. More importantly Prewett had felt that with the prospect of a husband for Mariette, it would be best to let Tabitha's friendship with her decline. They were no longer children, he reasoned, and if there should be further unpleasantness by anti-Catholic extremists, he wanted his daughter out of it, free from any taint of suspicion.

Mariette however begged Tabitha to accept an invitation to dinner with the St Aubyns on the last evening of the Townclears' visit, and Tabitha told her father that she could not refuse without discourtesy. It was not an entirely easy evening, however. The Townclears faced a long journey, and Conor in particular was reluctant to leave London. He and his sister were due to leave Chiswick in two days' time for Bristol, travelling by stage coach and spending a night at Reading. From Bristol they would sail to Cork Harbour, and travel by an uncertain post-chaise along the Cork to Killarney road, where they would be met at a place called Poulgorm Bridge and proceed by a long, winding track to Townclear Hall near Tahilla, a remote spot on the Iveragh Peninsular.

'Ah, you mean your father's carriage will come to meet you at this bridge?' said Madame.

'Oh, no, Madame, 'twill be a donkey-cart,' answered Conor with a rueful smile. 'That track's much too narrow and stony for the carriage horses, and I wouldn't call it a comfortable ride. We will need three days, perhaps four in all, to get back to Townclear Hall from here.'

He acknowledged his hostess's sympathetic remarks about the discomforts he and Moira were about to face in winter conditions, but added that the trip had been a grand experience for them. 'London will see me again in the spring for sure, when I'll be stayin' for longer – much longer,' he added significantly.

Glances were exchanged between the Comte and Comtesse, for this was a reference to Mr Townclear's decision to settle in London for the forseeable future. His elder brother would inherit Townclear Hall and the title of baronet, and Conor said he wanted to make a life for himself in the great metropolis. As a Catholic there would be a limit to the opportunities open to him, but the Comte was more than willing to use his influence to find his prospective son-in-law a position in the City, perhaps in the accounts of the proliferating administration of the Pool of London, or possibly at the Admiralty. The St Aubyns knew that in April this excellent young man would arrive to claim his lovely bride who had promised him an answer when she reached her nineteenth birthday on the fourteenth of that month, just as Tabitha had told Rob Drury that she would give him an answer on her nineteenth birthday in June – not that Mr Drury's name was mentioned at the candle-lit dinner party, for Tabitha's romance was known only to the two friends. In both cases the young suitors were quietly confident of a favourable outcome, a sweet and shy assent from softly smiling lips, confirmed by blushes and loving looks. No wonder that glasses were raised and a toast proposed, 'To spring time!'

Inevitably there was some reference to the progress of the war in America, and the St Aubyns found themselves in broad agreement with the Townclears, that it was an ill-judged war on the part of the British government, and that ultimate victory over the rebel colonies seemed increasingly unlikely. France had officially recognized the newly declared 'United States', and with the recent British defeat at Charlestown, Conor remarked with some satisfaction that the King's supporters in Parliament were tottering from one crisis to another.

'And we Irish can't be expected to shed too many tears over that, surely.' He grinned, and was answered by an amused nod from the Comte.

'What are your thoughts on this American war, Tabitha?'

asked Mariette, partly to remind the gentlemen that they were talking in front of an English girl who might have views of her own.

'I really don't know very much about it,' Tabitha apologized, for in fact her only concern was that Rob Drury might decide to join the army; she hoped Will Feather was already engaged in active warfare in America, the further away the better.

When dinner was over and the gentlemen were taking port wine and cigars, Madame de St Aubyn confided in Tabitha how happy she and her husband were that Mariette would not be leaving them to go and live in Ireland.

'It is an ideal arrangement, Mademoiselle Tabitha,' she said. 'We shall not be so far away from our darling, especially when she – if a time comes to send for her mother.'

And I will not be so far away from her, either, thought Tabitha, when she needs *me*.

It was nearly ten o'clock, and Tabitha thought it time for her to leave; she had spent half the evening wondering whether Conor Townclear would be requested to escort her home to Orchard Court; she anticipated this short farewell walk with a mixture of nervousness and a strange excitement, betrayed by the rapid beating of her heart.

'Well, perhaps it is time to say good night,' said Madame la Comtesse, and Tabitha held her breath as the lady's eyes caught those of Mr Townclear. 'I wonder if perhaps, Conor, you would oblige us by taking our guest Miss Prewett home? It is not far, a mere five minutes' walk at most, but as it is dark—'

'With pleasure, Madame,' he answered at once, standing up and bowing to Tabitha who smiled her thanks and relief that neither he nor any of the others could know how her heart raced at the thought of his arm in hers, his deep voice speaking to her in that soft accent – words that would no doubt refer to the weather, the pleasant evening they had spent, and how long it would be before he was reunited with his lovely Mariette. She only hoped that she would have the breath to answer in a sensible and matter-of-fact way; for by now Tabitha was conscious of Conor Townclear's effect upon her, and it was very different from the sisterly affection she felt for dear Rob.

'Thank you, Mr Townclear, I'll go and fetch my cloak,' she said, glancing at Madame in acknowledgement of her request.

''Tis my pleasure entirely,' he repeated. 'I'll get my great-coat, and then I'll be with ye.'

At that moment there was a ring at the door, and a maid came quickly up the stairs to announce that Mr Prewett had come to take his daughter home.

'Oh, just in time!' exclaimed the Comtesse. 'How very considerate of Monsieur Prewett. Let Conor know that he has no need of his greatcoat.'

Tabitha's heart plummeted to a normal rate, and she expressed her relief that Mr Townclear need not be inconvenienced. As she took leave of her hosts and Mariette, Townclear came and stood beside her.

'So, I'm to be denied the pleasure o' taking ye home, Miss Prewett,' he said, smiling. 'The winter will seem long indeed, away from Mariette and yeself – but I'll be lookin' ahead to April.' And saying this he took her outstretched hand and raised it to his lips.

Hurrying down to meet her father, Tabitha thanked him for coming to fetch her. 'I'm sorry you've had the trouble, Papa,' she told him, linking her arm with his.

'It's no trouble, my girl. I guessed that somebody, a servant or maybe even Mr Townclear, might be asked to see ye home, an' I reckoned that was my duty, not anybody else's.'

'It's still good o' you, Papa,' breathed Tabitha, bewildered by the mix of emotions she felt.

With the departure of the Townclears, Tabitha expected that she and Mariette would revert to the comforting and uncomplicated friendship they had enjoyed for the past eight years, the one between two little butterflies, accepted by their families and giving a lustre to the everyday events of their lives, however humdrum, because all of it was shared with each other. Yet by the time Christmas arrived, she knew that there could be no going back to a time of what now seemed like innocence: a time before their awakening to the realities of life, future marriages and the changes it would bring; nor could they ignore a new and unpleasant aspect of religion. Their separate places of worship had never troubled the girls before, yet after the ugly daubing of the St Aubyns' door, their faith could never be quite the same: there would be a wariness, a suspicion contained in the very word *religion*.

Tabitha would have liked to confide in her mother, but Martha Prewett was going through a mysterious phase in a woman's life that their neighbour Mrs Carter said was called the *change*. It caused sudden outbursts of temper and a tearful reproachfulness towards her husband and children for imagined slights and unkindness. John Prewett bore it patiently, only to have his silence denounced as sulking. Thomas and Andrew roused her jealousy by turning to Prudence rather than herself to settle their arguments and to tell of their daily happenings. She accused Tabitha of contrariness in the matter of Robin Drury, and became increasingly resentful of her daughter's friendship with the St Aubyns, though John Prewett rebuked her firmly when she referred to them as French papists, and said he would allow no bigotry in his house. Martha hardly spoke to Prudence, and John apologized to the good-humoured young woman, begging for her forbearance.

'She's not herself, Prudence, an' worries over things that never used to bother her. I'm grateful for yer good-will, an' so is Tabitha an' the boys.'

'That's all right, Mr Prewett, don't ye fret yeself,' the girl replied as she bustled between the oven and the table, serving them mutton stew, bread and cheese and small beer in her capable way, her neat white cap tied firmly over her hair. Accidentally hearing this exchange, Tabitha's new awareness caused her to imagine an unspoken undercurrent in the words, as if Prewett had said, 'Thank ye, Prudence, I don't know how I'd bear it without ye' – and as if the maid had replied, 'Never fret, John Prewett, I'll never leave ye.'

Nothing was quite as it had been, and when she and Mariette exchanged kisses and Christmas gifts, she hugged her friend close, as if those two imponderables, time and change were conspiring to separate them.

'Is something the matter, *chère* Tabitha? Are you not happy?'

'Dearest Mariette, don't mind me. If only we could go to church together on Christmas morning!'

'Ah, that is something we cannot change, and must not care about. I always pray for you to the crucified Christ and his Mother, La Vierge,' said the French girl simply.

'And so do I for you, my Mariette – but – but when Mr

Townclear comes again he'll take you to be married by a Roman priest in a Catholic chapel – and will you still pray for me then?'

'*Mais naturellement*, why should I not?' asked Mariette in surprise, and Tabitha could not explain the strange unease which continued to trouble her like a pain aching on and on, never quite leaving her in peace.

When the New Year of 1780 came in Thomas, now nearly twelve, was enrolled at the Reverend Wyatt's School for Sons of Clergy, leaving Andrew with only Michael to entertain him, for Jeremiah had taken to brushing his hair and his shoes with equal vigour, and studying his reflection in the full-length cutting-room mirror. 'Quite the little dandy,' Silas Holmes had remarked, to Prewett's annoyance. The cause of this sudden interest in his appearance was not far to seek: a Mr and Mrs Sargent who were customers in Hart Street had a rosy-cheeked maidservant, Betty Topham, and young Jeremiah found endless excuses to call at their home with inquiries about their orders. He confessed sheepishly to losing the notebook in which he had scribbled Mr Sargent's measurements, so needed to take them again; in fact John Prewett had already copied them into his order book, a large, leatherbound register in which all transactions were recorded under customers' names, dates, addresses and requirements.

'What's all this fuss about the Sargents, Jeremy?' asked Prewett. 'I'm half-way through makin' up their orders, an' they'll be due for a fittin' on Tuesday.'

'Is that right, Pa? You'll be wanting me to come and assist you, then,' said Jeremiah, who had learned to speak more or less like a gentleman's son at the Reverend Wyatt's school.

'No need. I can fit Mr Sargent easily enough, an' Tabitha can see to Mrs. Ye can stay here in charge o' the shop.'

Jeremy's face fell, and Tabitha felt a flicker of sympathy for him, though she gave no sign that she knew about Betty Topham and her brother's youthful stirrings of the tender passion that had begun at the same time as the changes in his growing body. Boys had no breasts to start getting bigger, and no messy monthly menses, though having been brought up with younger brothers, Tabitha knew about their male appendages, and because of the knowledge enforced upon her by the older girls at the academy, she knew in theory how

72

they were put to use in the marriage bed – or out of it, as in the case of Will Feather and poor Nan, the thought of which still filled her with anger and contempt. It seemed that Jeremiah did no more than stand around blushing and stammering while Betty Topham simpered at the Sargents' kitchen door, but Tabitha dearly loved her brother and had no wish for him to be made to look foolish; so she smiled kindly at him after their father's rebuff, and did not discourage his hesitant confidences.

'Tabitha, you know how Rob Drury comes over on Sundays and walks to church with us – does that mean that he likes you? I've seen the way he looks at you, and Mother and Papa don't seem to mind. Is it because he's going to marry you when you're older? – if you don't mind me asking,' he added politely, which made Tabitha smile to herself. This time last year he would have teased her about Rob Drury, but now he too had fallen victim to the universal malady, and had become moonstruck.

'Ah, Jeremy, that's a hard question,' she answered carefully. 'There's no harm in walking and talking together, but there's a lot o' things to be considered, like how old you are, and how much money you've got, and whether your parents – well, they have to approve o' the match, you see.'

'What exactly is a *match*, Tabitha? Is it like getting married?'

'Yes, or when you promise each other that you'll get married one day when you're older, or when it's more convenient, and when you've saved up enough money.'

'D'you need a lot of money to get married, Tabitha?'

'Yes, o' course you do, to buy a house to live in.'

'I can't see that I'll ever have that much.'

'Father will help you, Jeremy, just as he'll help me when I give my promise to marry Rob – but you'll have to wait a few more years before you're ready to marry. It's different for boys, and a great undertaking, you see, getting married, and it means that you – you'd become a husband to a wife, like Mother and Papa. And *that* means that you'd have children.'

Jeremy blushed scarlet. 'Oh, Tabitha, I wouldn't want to have *children*. Not yet – not for years to come.'

She smiled and shook her head. 'That's what I thought, you're much too young. So it'd be better not to get too close to – er – any girl you're fond of. Talking's no harm, but keep your distance.'

'Uh-uh,' he grunted. 'I see. Thanks, Tabitha, it's very good o' you, and I'm obliged. But as to – er – Betty and me, I mean – would you say there was any harm in a – a kiss, once in a while?'

Tabitha shook her head. 'I'd leave that to her if I were you, Jeremy. A young man should never do anything a girl doesn't want.'

And with that Jeremiah Prewett had to be content, though their conversation echoed around his sister's head, for she knew herself to be in even greater need of advice. She would be nineteen in June, and Rob was waiting patiently for her answer. Her parents also expected her to make young Drury happy, and though her father was inwardly reluctant to part with his beloved only daughter, he had his eye on a comfortable little house for them, off the Whitechapel Road, conveniently near to the Davidman workshops, and not too far from Bloomsbury, so she would be able to visit her parents at least once a week. He wanted his daughter's happiness above all things, and young men such as Rob were not to be found every day, honest and hardworking, one who could be relied on to keep his marriage vows.

As winter came to an end, June still seemed a long way off, but April was drawing near, bringing with it Mariette de St Aubyn's nineteenth birthday – and Conor Townclear to claim her. Tabitha noticed a restlessness in her friend, an anticipation tinged with apprehension, such as all brides must feel as their wedding day approaches. Lady Farrinder had offered the use of her private chapel for the wedding, but the St Aubyns decided on the Sardinian Embassy chapel in Duke Street where they had worshipped for the nine years they had lived in London. A pleasant three-storeyed house had been found for the young couple in Gerrard Street, and Madame la Comtesse had purchased the kind of strong, well-designed furniture suitable to withstand the wear and tear of little new arrivals with all their demands and necessities.

Mr Conor Townclear was due to arrive at the beginning of April, and the wedding was fixed for May 6th, a Saturday.

'Sir Bernard and Lady Townclear are coming for the wedding, with Conor's elder brother and his wife, and Miss

Moira,' explained Mariette. 'They will stay here with Maman and Papa, but until we are married Maman thinks that Conor should not stay under the same roof as I, as it is not proper. He is to stay with Lord and Lady Mansfield who have a house on the east side of Bloomsbury Square. She has been a very kind neighbour.'

'Are they Roman Catholics?' asked Tabitha.

'Oh, no, he is a judge, very grand! And he has shown sympathy to the Catholic Relief Act, and says there should be religious toleration on all sides. Oh, Tabitha, Conor will soon be here – you will not leave me, will you, *ma chérie*?' They were sitting on the couch in Mariette's boudoir, and she suddenly flung her arms around her friend. 'Promise me that you will always be my dearest, closest friend – *please!*' she begged, and Tabitha felt her trembling.

'Of course I will, Mariette, you'll always be my friend,' she soothed, though a little alarmed by this display of nervousness. 'But you know, you'll be even closer to your husband when you are a – a wife. And in the course of time you'll be a mother, too.'

She felt Mariette stiffen, and asked gently, 'Hasn't your mother told you about the marriage bed?'

'Oh, yes, I know what I must do, and I trust that Conor will be patient with me, but that is all to do with the body, *n'est-ce pas*? The love I have for you is of a different kind,' said Mariette with innocent candour. 'I cannot bear to think of losing what we have—' Her violet-blue eyes filled with tears as she went on quickly, 'Oh, Tabitha, let me ask you again what I asked four years ago and you refused – come to live with me! Other people will call you my lady's maid, but I will call you my dear friend and companion. Will you not consider it for my sake?'

With Mariette's smooth arms around Tabitha's plump shoulders, the tailor's daughter closed her eyes. The idea had not come entirely as a surprise, for both girls had in the past referred to the possibility that one day they would live under the same roof again, as at Mrs Kelso's Academy. And now here was Mariette suggesting it – no, urgently requesting Tabitha's closeness during the early days of her married life. In another ten weeks Rob Drury would be presenting himself as her own affianced lover, her husband and protector, and what sort of girl would choose instead to be a lady's maid, a paid servant in the house of a married friend, however dear? What could she say? What could she do? What would her parents say? What of the St Aubyns? And most important of all – what of Conor Townclear? Would he welcome a lady's maid forever at his wife's side, sharing her every thought, sleeping in an adjacent room? Tabitha foresaw a great many objections if she gave in to her friend. And one overwhelming temptation to do so.

Mariette was still sitting beside her; she felt the light weight of the lovely fair head on her shoulder, the comforting arms around her neck, the warmth of their close friendship. In giving an answer, Tabitha tried to look honestly into the recesses of her own heart. At length she spoke. 'Mariette, if your parents agree and if Mr Townclear does not object, I will be your lady's maid for the next two months—'

'*O, merci, Sainte Vierge! Merci beaucoups!*'

'For the next two months,' repeated Tabitha, for Mariette was kissing her joyfully, bouncing up and down on the couch, sending cushions flying in all directions. 'Listen, Mariette, I said *for the next two months*, for I must marry Rob Drury in June. He expects me to be his wife, and my parents wish it.'

'And do *you* wish it, *ma chérie*?'

'Life has to go on, Mariette, we all have to grow up and grow older,' replied Tabitha with a kind of desperation in the face of life's uncertainties, for she was as reluctant as her friend to accept change to the life they had known.

'You do not answer my question. Do you wish to marry Rob Drury?'

'Yes, Mariette, I do. And thank you for making me realize it,' said Tabitha with a note of briskness, and getting up from the couch she added, 'We are both very fortunate to have found good men who want to marry us, and we should be grateful.'

'Oh, but I *am* grateful, my Tabitha! And especially now that you will come to be my very special maid. Can you start tomorrow, so that you will be already here when Conor comes?'

'I'm sick an' tired o' this everlastin' givin' in to these people!' stormed Martha Prewett, and on this occasion John tended to agree, though he kept his own counsel and made the best of it.

'It's only for eight or nine weeks, Martha, an' they've been friends for nine years. The family have been good to us, after all.'

'Good to us, fiddlesticks! They've *used* us, that's what they've done. That French girl's only got to crook her little finger, an' Tabitha dances to her tune! Wouldn't surprise me if they talk her out o' marryin' Rob, just so's she can stay there at that girl's beck an' call!'

'Now that's just silly, Martha. It'll be good for our girl to have the experience.'

'Experience o' what, may I ask? 'Tain't proper to be hangin' around a newly wedded pair, an' her not even married herself. If that Mam'zelle comes round here, I'll tell her just what I think o' the arrangement!'

Prewett rolled his eyes and took himself off to the cutting room where Jeremiah was employed in stitching twenty-five buttonholes on a gentleman's long jacket, while the dreamy smile on his lips showed that his mind was far away, reliving Betty Topham's last kiss. Prewett sighed heavily. He was to be robbed of his daughter's company for the next two months, and then give her up to young Drury for good. It was difficult for a father not to feel a little bit sorry for himself sometimes, he reflected.

Lady Mansfield had indeed been a good neighbour to the St Aubyns, and welcomed them into her treasure-filled house on the opposite side of Bloomsbury Square. Lord Chief Justice Mansfield's law library was full of priceless books gathered over the course of his long career as a judge, and being known for his advocacy of religious toleration, he and his wife were more than happy to give hospitality to the likeable young Irishman, prior to his wedding. Conor, for his part, was deeply interested in the library and also Lord Mansfield's gallery of fine pictures and the rarest collection of manuscripts ever owned by one person, or so it was said. And as it happened, Conor found himself with plenty of time each day to enjoy them. Mariette was unable to receive him without the presence of her mother or her dear friend, Tabitha Prewett – and Tabitha had been suddenly called upon to cope with sickness in the family. Both Prudence and eight-year-old Andrew had been struck down with a fever and had to take to their beds with stomach pains, nausea and a distressing looseness of the bowels. It reminded Tabitha of the symptoms displayed by Cynthia White at Mrs Kelso's school, when tainted water had been the cause. Martha feared that the whole household would be affected, and told Tabitha to take over the nursing of Prudence and to keep away from Andrew who was to be cared for entirely by herself. The fear of plague was ever-present in London, and John Prewett closed the shop while the dread shadow of sickness hung over the house. Remembering his mother's dictum in times of any outbreak of infection, he ordered that all water drawn from the Orchard Court pump was to be boiled before drinking or being used in cooking. This was Tabitha's duty, as well as washing soiled bedlinen and attending to the noxious-smelling chamber pots. Martha did the necessary cooking, and fed the family on vegetable soup and barley bread with cheese. She made gruel for the invalids, and gave them a little wine and water, though Prudence's cheerful presence in the kitchen was sadly missed. Madame la Comtesse sent two bottles of red wine and a pound of honey on the comb, and Rob, who was not allowed to enter the house for fear of infection, brought them a side of cured bacon, much to Prewett's gratitude.

At the end of four days the invalids were over the worst of the fever, though they were much weakened by it, and Prudence had never looked so pale. Tabitha had no doubt as to where her own duty lay, and it was ten days before she could safely leave them, to take up her role as lady's maid to Mademoiselle de St Aubyn.

'I was in agony in case you would fall victim to the fever, *ma chérie*,' said Mariette, and Conor Townclear nodded.

'That's right, she was half out o' her mind with worryin' about ye, Tabitha,' he said a little wearily. 'I tried my best to take her mind off the fear o' ye dyin' o' the fever, but I failed entirely. It made me see how much she depends on ye, an' that surely must mean that I do, too!'

His dark gaze rested on her as he spoke, giving weight to the words; he was most certainly not joking, and Tabitha was left in no doubt that the St Aubyns – and Townclear? – thought her essential to Mariette's well-being. It was a timely reminder that sickness or accident can strike at any time, and turn the best-laid plans upside-down.

And not only the chance misfortunes of sickness or accident. On the first day of May the Mansfields woke up to find that their front door had been smeared with dog excrement and daubed with white paint which spelled out the message:

IRISH PAPISTS GO HOME – OR DIE!

It was the sheer, vicious hatred shown in this second act of aggression that was truly frightening, and Conor said he could no longer accept hospitality from the Lord Chief Justice because of the risk involved to his hosts; he moved out that same day and found himself a lodging in a roadside inn on the outskirts of the city, used as a staging post. He did not tell anybody where it was, not even the St Aubyns, and it meant that he saw much less of his future wife.

''Twill not be for long, Monseigneur,' he said philosophically to the Comte. 'It wants but five days to our weddin', and yer family will see more than enough o' me after that!'

So Mariette and her lady's maid were thrown upon each other's company, with time to ponder on the threat of religious bigotry that was poisoning the air of London. There were murmurings at gatherings – as diverse as private dinner parties and gentlemen's clubs, men who met in respectable taverns, and drunken brawlers and name-callers who haunted the lower kind. Speeches were made in Parliament, and Lord George Gordon got up in the House of Lords to warn his fellow peers of the dangerous influence of Rome, and the greater danger of ignoring it.

At No 9 Bloomsbury Square Tabitha endeavoured to raise her friend's spirits in preparation for the wedding, while John Prewett longed for the day when he would receive his daughter back into the safety of her family, to prepare for her own wedding at St George's church.

He did not know that her heart was being torn in two: for how could she leave her dearest friend at such a time?

Her dearest friends . . .

Six

'*Elle est comme un ange,*' whispered Madame de St Aubyn, tears springing to her eyes at the sight of her daughter dressed all in white: from her simple silk gown and length of Chantilly lace over her head, held in place by a coronet of white May blossom, to her dainty slippers of white kid. 'Surely he will fall on his knees at her feet!'

Tabitha, the only bridal attendant, wearing a similar gown in blue, was putting the finishing touches to Mariette's hair which fell in pale golden waves on her shoulders. She placed a small bunch of white carnations in the bride's hands, and smiled in agreement with Madame, though the thought crossed her mind that Conor would be embracing a wife tonight, not an angel; in less than an hour's time he would take her hand and they would exchange solemn promises before a priest and a small circle of close relatives in the chapel of the Sardinian Embassy.

Mariette went to her wedding in the St Aubyn carriage with her parents and bridesmaid. Conor travelled in a hired carriage with his parents and brother Bernard who was also his groomsman. His sister Moira and sister-in-law Roisin accompanied Lady Farrinder and her daughter in the Farrinder carriage. The day was fine and clear, and a small group of bystanders and barefoot children, seeing their stately progress, gathered round to stare round-eyed at the bride as she emerged into the sunshine.

Inside the chapel Tabitha was over-awed by the ornate carved and painted statues, the candles and the smell of incense; it was far more elaborate than St George's, though the ceremony was completely unintelligible to her, being all in Latin murmured by a priest in richly embroidered vestments, and there were no hymns. She saw Conor's dark eyes open wide when he saw his bride coming towards him, and he took her hand with something like awe, as if seeing her for the first time; it seemed to Tabitha that everybody present gave a gasp at the sight of her virginal beauty. In twenty minutes the vows had been made and the wedding ring placed on Mariette's finger. The priest proclaimed them to be husband and wife, and prayers were said for their marriage, that they would be blessed with children and courageously bring them up in the true Catholic faith of their fathers.

It was over. The party left the chapel to return to their carriages, only this time the bride and groom sat side by side, and her lace veil was drawn back to show the lovely face of Mrs Conor Townclear. Tabitha sat behind the couple as the bride's attendant, smiling as was expected of her on this day of days.

Back at No 9 Bloomsbury Square a lavish wedding breakfast was prepared, and a large party of guests awaited them, friends and neighbours of the St Aubyns, Lord and Lady Mansfield and members of the Royal Society with their wives. Mr and Mrs Prewett were seated in a corner, Martha looking disapprovingly around her. Although it was not usual to invite one's tailor or any of one's tradespeople to a wedding, the Comte and Comtesse had decided that it was only courteous to invite the parents of the bridesmaid, but no other members of their family.

Congratulations, handshakes and kisses were exchanged, and Mr Townclear was told by the men that he was a very lucky fellow, at which he smiled and agreed. The young ladies clearly felt the same way about the bridegroom, but shared their admiration with each other rather than with the bride who looked so ethereal and had very little to say; besides, there was that round-faced bridesmaid fussing round her like a mother cat with a delicate kitten.

''Twould get on my nerves if I'd just caught such a handsome, charming beau!' laughed one of them. 'Mark my words, he'll chase *her* out of the bridal chamber tonight!'

At one point Tabitha left the bride to go and speak to her parents who looked rather awkward, sitting alone.

'We don't know anybody else here, an' might as well've stayed at home!' grumbled Martha.

'Now, then, Martha, ye'd've had plenty to say if they hadn't asked us,' John pointed out, and Tabitha suggested that they should go to the table and take a glass of wine. The Comte and Comtesse approached the couple and spoke glowingly of their daughter, and how much her friendship had meant to theirs, which mollified Mrs Prewett somewhat, except that there were none of her own friends or neighbours present to hear Tabitha praised.

By three o'clock in the afternoon the party was beginning to break up, and the bride and groom went off to change into the outfits Prewett had made for their wedding trip. They were to be the guests of Lady Farrinder at Heathfield House for a week in the quiet of the countryside and parkland around Chiswick. After that they would move into their new home in Gerrard Street, where their married life would truly begin, and Conor would start his new and important occupation as a personal assistant to a Mr Shenstone, a fellow of the Royal Society who had inherited a library and needed help with sorting it into categories and making an inventory of the volumes it contained. The Comte de St Aubyn had suggested his son-in-law's services, in the hope that the appointment would lead on to better things. Conor had a good head for figures and might have been recommended as a government clerk in the Exchequer at Westminster, had it not been for his religion, but thanks to the Comte's discreet introduction to Mr Shenstone, that gentleman had been delighted to find a book-loving secretary. In every way, the outlook for the young couple appeared bright and promising, and Tabitha happily complimented her friend on how well the ceremony and reception had passed off, while remembering that the main business of the day was still to come: the wedding night and the bridal bed. Lady Farrinder had given them the master bedroom and the dressing rooms on either side of it.

'Take care of her, Tabitha! I trust you to watch over her!' had been Madame la Comtesse's emotional plea as the bridal pair said their farewells and got into the Farrinder carriage with Lady Farrinder, Tabitha and young Hester. Tabitha had promised that she would – but how could she? Tonight Mariette would lie down with her lawfully wedded husband and submit to him as a dutiful wife, yielding up her virginity and becoming part of his own flesh, as God Himself had ordained. Catholic or Protestant, that particular activity was the same. Tabitha's treacherous memory sent her back to that night at the academy when the older girls, prompted by Cynthia White, had forced her to listen to the physical facts in graphic detail, and she had covered her ears: was her sweet Mariette truly prepared for what was to happen before this day was over?

Tabitha longed for the reassurance that the next morning would bring.

Arriving at Heathfield House, Lady Farrinder ordered tea and tactfully invited Tabitha to come with her and Hester to see the embroidered quilt that the mother and daughter had been engaged upon, while the newlyweds spent some time together, walking in the grounds or seated on the south-facing terrace, out of sight of the rest of the household.

Tabitha duly admired the fine stitching of the quilt and the watercolour sketches of the house and garden that fifteen-year-old Hester had done. They met with the bride and groom again at dinner, and by nine o'clock their hostess, covering a yawn, remarked that they must all be tired after such a long and exciting day, and begged to be excused, saying that she and Hester would retire. The rest of them willingly followed her example, and a maidservant was ordered to carry two pitchers of hot water up to the master bedroom, where Tabitha was to sleep in the bride's dressing room, to be on hand if Mrs Townclear needed anything in the night.

The lamps were turned down, and the candles put out. Tabitha knelt beside her bed and said a prayer for Conor and Mariette. There was a distant sound of voices somewhere in the house, and a clattering in the kitchen. A dog barked, and then there was silence. She settled herself down in the bed and let her mind rove back over the day, and all that had happened in the course of it – and over the last nine years, in which Mariette had been part of her life. They had grown up together, gone to school together where they'd shared a bed, and watched each other's transition from childhood to girlhood: and now her dearest friend was a married woman, a young matron, bound to love, honour and obey her husband, Mr Townclear.

Conor Townclear. Tabitha now let her thoughts dwell upon the man, lying only a few yards away in an adjoining room, alongside Mariette. Was *he* happy tonight? Was he kissing his bride, touching her, whispering words of love? Tabitha found that she was holding her breath, straining to listen in the darkness for a sound, any sound from the master bedroom. But there was complete silence, and at last, wearied by her own confusing thoughts, she fell into a fitful sleep from which she awoke suddenly, hearing a cry. She sat up in the strange bed, her heart pounding, listening intently: but there was only silence, as deep as the night itself. Had it been her own voice that had awakened her? She came to the conclusion that it must have been a silent cry from her own imagination, a sound heard in a dream. She lay down again, willing herself to go back to sleep – and straightaway dreamed that Conor Townclear had come to her, pulling back the bed covers and getting in beside her.

'Tabitha,' he said in that beautiful voice, only just sounding the *h*, softly, caressingly. She put her arms up and held his head, feeling the crisply curling hair at the nape of his neck. Her nightgown was white as a cloud, and he began to pull it up, up, up and over her head.

'Tabitha,' he said again, naked beside her, stretching himself over her, kissing her, stroking his hand down over her body and between her legs: his forefinger was on her very entrance, a fiery touch that sent a flame through her whole body, so that she sighed for joy, for sheer pleasure . . . and now he was speaking to her. 'Tabitha, help me.'

'Yes, oh yes, Conor, I will, I will,' she said in her dream, and woke up.

'Conor!' she cried, sitting up again. 'Conor, where are you?'

But only silence answered her, for it had been but a dream, and could not be recalled. When she fell asleep again, she did not wake until morning. The sun was up, and the servants were busy in the kitchen. Somebody knocked on the outer door. 'It's eight o'clock, Miss Prewett, and your hot water's here,' said a maidservant, moving on to knock on the next door. 'It's eight o'clock, sir – and madam. Your hot water's here.'

'Thank you,' came Conor's voice.

'Do you want tea, sir?'

'No, we'll go to Mass first.'

'Very good sir.'

Tabitha remembered that it was Sunday, and Lady Farrinder attended Mass in her private chapel at nine. And then came a tap on the inner door connecting their rooms, and before she could answer, Mariette bounded into the room, leaping on to the bed and leaning over to kiss her.

'Good morning, Tabitha, *ma chérie!* Have you slept well?'

'Oh, Mariette my love, yes, thank you,' sighed Tabitha, banishing the imaginations of the night. 'And did you sleep well, too? And – Conor?'

'Oh, yes, we were both tired to death. Yesterday seems just like a dream, does it not?'

'Yes, my love – just like a dream. But Mariette, are you – was it – did he—?'

'He was most kind and obliging, Tabitha. As I told you, we both fell fast asleep in each other's arms.' Her blue eyes danced. 'You don't expect me to tell you any more, do you?'

'I don't expect you to tell me anything, Mariette – only that you're happy.'

'Then rest assured and stop worrying, *chère* Tabitha,' said Mariette, and kissed her again.

At nine o'clock they all filed into the chapel, led by Lady Farrinder and Hester, followed by the newlyweds and some local Catholic families who regularly worshipped in this chapel; then came the servants, and finally Tabitha who entered timidly and sat at the back while a very old priest intoned the Latin liturgy of the Mass. When the Host and Chalice had been raised, Lady Farrinder led the congregation forward to partake of the Sacrament, though Tabitha kept her seat; she recognized the order of the service which was like Holy Communion at St George's, except that there it was held only once a month, after the usual Morning or Evening Prayer. Try though she would, she could not keep her thoughts on the proceedings, but kept looking towards Mariette who seemed much the same as yesterday; Tabitha could hardly raise her eyes to look at Conor, though once he caught her eye and smiled. Everything must be all right, then, and she had no need to worry: perhaps her mother had been right when she said that when Mariette had a husband she would no longer need a tailor's daughter for a friend. And in June Tabitha too would be nineteen, and a bride herself – Mrs Robin Drury.

She quietly got up and went out, so that nobody could see her foolish tears.

*   *   *

In the afternoon Conor and Mariette went out walking together, and Hester asked Tabitha if she would like to play back-gammon. No games of any kind were played on Sunday by her family, but she did not like to refuse, so the backgammon board was brought out, and the little leather bag of dice. She found Hester a pleasant girl, very interested to hear about Mrs Kelso's Academy, and over tea and almond biscuits Lady Farrinder asked her point-blank whether she thought Hester would benefit from attending such a place, being a Catholic girl. Would she have to attend daily prayers based on the Protestant prayer book? Would provision be made for her to attend a private Mass on Sundays? Tabitha could only answer that Mariette had been a Catholic girl, but as a weekly boarder she had been able to attend Mass with her parents on Sundays. It had never been an issue at that time, and Lady Farrinder's concern was a reminder of the growing swell of anti-Catholic rhetoric being stirred up by Lord Gordon and his followers: the sort of fanatics who daubed hate-filled messages on doors.

The newlyweds returned from their walk, and Mariette greeted Tabitha with her usual open affection. 'You should have come with us, *ma chérie*, we have been looking at the peacocks and wondering where they make their nests!'

Conor looked at his wife's friend, and she thought she saw something in his expression that was not quite as happy and contented as a newly married man should be; she turned away from his eyes and continued talking to their hostess.

The days passed in spring sunshine, the beauty of May all around them in trees, flowers, hedgerows and birdsong. On the Thursday morning Hester claimed Mariette's attention, wanting to talk to her about school and her longing to meet and mix with other girls. They had gone off together after breakfast, and it was then that Tabitha looked up and found Conor lingering at her elbow.

'Tabitha, could ye ever spare me half an hour?' he asked, giving her his arm. 'Let's walk out o' the garden and up to that gate at the end o' the lane. Mariette loves the view from there.'

She obediently took his arm and walked at his side, listening to his talk of country sights and sounds, knowing all the time that he had something else on his mind. She answered him in short, polite observations, and waited.

Once they were out of the grounds of Heathfield House, he took a breath. 'Has Mariette said anythin' to ye, Tabitha, about how she feels to be a wife?'

'No, not in so many words,' she replied slowly. 'But there's no doubt that she's very happy. Anybody can see that.'

He breathed out a sort of sigh, and shook his head slightly. 'She may seem to be happy, Tabitha, but the fact is, y'see, she has not become my wife. Not yet.'

Tabitha's heart gave a little lurch, but she said nothing.

'D'you know what I'm sayin' to ye, Tabitha? D'you understand me? Ye're a girl who knows more o' the world than she does.'

She gave the slightest of nods and briefly tightened her hold on his arm, to indicate that she understood, and giving him leave to continue.

'Ye'll be surprised, I don't doubt, Tabitha, at hearin' such words from yer friend's husband.'

She shook her head. 'No, not really, Conor. I'm not really surprised.' Because it now seemed to her as if she had already known it, and the only surprise was his decision to confide in her on such a matter. It was a measure of his own concern that he should do so.

'Ah, ye're a great girl, Tabitha, surely, and ye know her well. I heard her mother tellin' ye to look after her when we left Bloomsbury,' he went on. 'And I know that ye've seen more o' life than Mariette, born and brought up in a house o' brothers, and helpin' at the birthin' o' the last one. And I know how ye shouted at a fellow who was tryin' to kiss her, and gave him his marchin' orders. And Tabitha – I know ye've had an understandin' with a decent young fellow for some time – him who ye're goin' to marry when the time's right. You're a girl with greater knowledge than Mariette. She's always been sheltered from the world.'

Good heavens, does he think I'm not a virgin, just because I'm a tradesman's daughter and promised to one of my own kind? thought Tabitha. They stopped walking, and she stood with her head lowered.

He seemed to read her thoughts, for he continued anxiously, 'I haven't offended ye, have I, Tabitha? I'm only sayin' what Mariette has told me, and she thinks the world o' ye, as ye know. Tell me you're not angry, will ye?'

'No, Conor, not angry. Only – what do you want me to do?'

'Help me, Tabitha. Speak to her. Tell her that I love her desperately and wouldn't hurt her for the world, but she'll have to yield herself up to me to make our marriage real.'

'I can tell her, certainly,' answered Tabitha, still looking down at the path. 'But – haven't *you* tried to tell her that?'

'I've tried every night, but she won't have me near her.'

'Ah.' Tabitha cast her mind back to that night at Mrs Kelso's school when the girls had told her what she had not then wanted to know. Now she felt almost grateful to them, and out of the love she had for Mariette, she had to risk speaking very directly to him.

'It may be that Mariette has never been told by her mother exactly what a wife's duties are, Conor. Forgive me for speaking bluntly, but have you tried, very gently, and with words o' love, to tell her clearly what you must do to show your love for her?'

He turned to her with relief and thankfulness in his voice. 'Oh, Tabitha, dear girl, how well you understand! Didn't I know I was right to speak to ye, after all my doubts! The fact is, y'see, I have tried tellin' her, but I'm mortally afraid o' shockin' her – or hurtin' her – she says she only wants to lay in my arms and let me kiss her lovely body – as far as *here*, y'know –' he touched his chest – 'but no further.'

'And you want *me* to speak to her and tell her what you have to do?' Tabitha could hardly believe that she was uttering these words to a man. What her mother would say, she did not dare to think.

'Yes, Tabitha, if ye would – speak to her – seein' that ye've always been so close to each other – if it's not askin' too much – knowin' how well she trusts ye.' He hesitated for a moment, and then continued, 'Yes, that's what I'm askin', as her friend and mine.'

'Leave her to me,' she said quietly. 'I can't say when, I'll have to wait for the right moment.'

'Of course. Today's Thursday, and I could go into town tonight, to see Mr Shenstone—'

'No, not tonight,' she said quickly, feeling that she needed time. 'Maybe tomorrow, Friday – or possibly not until you're in your own home in Gerrard Street. I – I can't say exactly when.'

'Tomorrow my parents and brother are goin' home, along with Moira and Roisin. They'll be callin' here to say goodbye.'

'Then it'll be after they've called – and gone. We don't want to risk them seeing her upset in any way.'

'That's true. Ah, Tabitha, ye're a good woman. I'll be forever indebted to ye.'

'Let's go back to the house,' she said. She wanted to be alone: her head was spinning, her thoughts were in a whirl, for she had given Conor her word that she would speak to Mariette on his behalf.

Just as he had asked her in the dream – and she had told him she would.

'What do you think, Mother's taking us on a picnic party this afternoon, and she's told cook to boil a dozen eggs hard for us to put in a basket with a game pie. We're going down to the river at Strand-on-the-Green,' Hester gleefully informed them on their return.

'A dozen! But there are only five of us,' said Conor with a smile.

'And you are the only man among us, so you can carry the food!' laughed his new wife, but Tabitha's heart plummeted. She would have welcomed an afternoon alone, rather than having to exert herself to be agreeable, but she had already learned that a maidservant can have no preferences, not even a specially privileged lady's maid. Accordingly, she put on a pleasing expression, only to discover that Lady Farrinder had planned a big surprise for her guests, and the picnic party was to be much larger than Hester had thought. Conor's and Mariette's parents had been invited, together with Conor's brother and his wife Roisin and sister Moira, which made a party of twelve.

'It will be like the wedding all over again, but without the nerves!' exclaimed Mariette, and the guests were greeted on their arrival with much gaiety and good-will. The St Aubyns brought Sir Bernard and Lady Townclear in their carriage, and a light two-horse chaise had been hired for young Mr Bernard to drive his wife and Moira. The St Aubyns were overjoyed to see Mariette, and there was some rearranging when they set out to Strand-on-the-Green: the newlyweds travelled with the St Aubyns, the senior Townclears with Bernard and Roisin in the chaise, and Lady Farrinder took

Hester, Moira and Tabitha in her carriage. The three conveyances set out soon after two o'clock, followed by a wide-seated pony-trap driven by a manservant with a maidservant on either side of him; the well-packed food hamper was tied to the back of the Farrinder carriage.

'Lead on, O Master o' the Caravan!' quipped Conor as they filed past the gates of Heathfield House in stately procession, and the Comte told the Comtesse that he was King Louis XVI and she, his lovely wife Marie Antoinette, travelling from Paris to Versailles. Their journey took them past several great houses set in their extensive grounds and interspersed with farms and market gardens, all planted out for a new season of fruit, flowers and vegetables.

'That's what's so amazin' about London,' Conor remarked. 'So many things are goin' on there, but ye can so soon get out o' town and into the country.'

They reached their riverside destination, and climbed down on to a wide grassy area near to Grove House, known for its beautiful trees and park that ran down to the water's edge. The coachmen took charge of the horses, with young Bernard Townclear's willing help, and the party sorted themselves out into groups, sauntering by the river and exclaiming at the views it afforded. Tabitha chose to walk with Lady Farrinder's party with the young Townclears – Bernard and Roisin along with Moira and Hester – while the two older couples wanted to share the newlyweds, the Townclears' son and the St Aubyns' daughter, definitely the most handsome couple in the world, or so both sets of parents declared.

At one point Tabitha found herself listening with Moira to Conor's brother, Bernard, and his red-haired wife who was just beginning to show that she was carrying their first child. They had been introduced by their hosts to the social attractions of London, the shops and the pleasure gardens of Vauxhall and Ranelagh, and had been to see *The Relapse* by Mr Sheridan at the Theatre Royal in Drury Lane.

'It was the most terrible crush ye ever did see,' said Bernard. 'Talk about brazen women, all paint an' powder, holdin' up fans and lookin' over the tops of 'em – and the men struttin' around with eyeglasses to see who was there—'

'What, on the stage, Bernard?' asked his sister, smiling at Tabitha behind her hand.

'No, no, the ones in them boxes or stalls or whatever they're called, shoutin' out across the spaces to each other, not givin' a blind bit o' notice to what they were sayin' on the stage!' he said disgustedly. 'Such a chatterin' turn-out o' wigs an' hoops an' shoes they could hardly walk in – we were glad to get out o' the place, eh, Roisin?'

'Ah, sure, ye're right, Bernard, I was shamed to look at 'em,' replied the down-to-earth Kerry girl, a farmer's daughter who was clearly out of her depth with the fashionable *bon ton* of London. Observing the practical but drab colours of their homespun clothes and stout laced-up shoes, Tabitha concluded that the Townclears were country people at heart, and probably longing to get back to the rugged coast of the Iveragh Peninsula and their farm and tenants. She glanced at Moira who smiled back and whispered in her ear, 'All they think about is the price o' pigs and who's got a bigger bull! It's lucky for Mariette that Conor wants to stay in London, for she'd die o' boredom at Tahilla, surely.'

The two maidservants spread the picnic fare on a large white cloth, and the older one expertly cut the enormous game pie into wedges. Plates, knives, forks and glasses were produced, the hard-boiled eggs shelled, and the manservant opened two bottles of wine. The company sat themselves here and there on the grassy bank, and gave themselves up to enjoyment.

'This is capital, Lady Farrinder!' said Sir Bernard. 'We never thought to see such good fare on a ride into the country!'

Tabitha saw Madame la Comtesse nudge her husband and point to Mariette and Conor who were teasing each other and laughing; the parents exchanged approving nods and smiles. At a convenient distance the two coachmen and three servants sat eating their own share of the picnic, and Tabitha wondered what they thought of her, where exactly she fitted into this mix of family, in-laws, friends and those who waited upon them. She thought of Prudence and her place in the Prewett household – cheerful, hardworking Prudence who had no close relatives but who had become indispensable to the tailor's family, so that Tabitha was no longer needed at home; but Rob Drury was waiting to claim her as his wife, with her parents' approval . . .

91

'Tabitha! Tabitha! Come over here and settle an argument for us!' It was Mariette calling to her, and she got up and went over to where her friend was seated with Conor on a stone slab that formed a useful seat. Mariette patted the space beside her.

'Now then, *ma chérie*, Conor says that Shakespeare is a greater playwright than Molière, and I say he is mistaken. We appeal to you to tell us which is right – and remember I can read Molière in French, which is more than he can.'

Tabitha made a face, sensing national prejudice. 'How could I possibly dare to judge between two great geniuses?' she asked, sitting down beside Mariette who immediately whispered in her ear, 'Do not worry, *ma chérie*, I only want to have you here beside me, instead of wasting your words on those rustics! I've seen practically nothing of you today. Tell me, how does London life suit the Townclears? Did they like going to the play?'

Avoiding Conor's eye, Tabitha answered quietly, 'I think Bernard and Roisin found it rather – er – artificial, especially the audience in the boxes who talked all the way through it.'

Mariette giggled. 'Did you hear that, Conor? Your brother does not think as you do! It's as well they are returning to Ireland, and you are staying in London.' She lowered her voice to a whisper again in Tabitha's ear. '*Ils sont paysans*! Or as the girls at Mrs Kelso's would say, country bumpkins!'

Tabitha frowned and shook her head. It was indeed just as well that the Townclears were returning to Ireland; Conor's wife was not likely to endear herself to them.

The picnic was agreed by them all to be a great success, and Lady Farrinder was thanked for her generous hospitality – and for her essential part in making the match between the young man and woman. She graciously acknowledged their appreciation.

'And you can bid farewell to your parents now, Conor, for it won't be necessary for them to call at the beginning of their long journey tomorrow,' she added, smiling.

Conor agreed, but then he said he had an idea. He said he needed to see Mr Shenstone on a matter connected with that gentleman's library, and asked if he could travel back with the St Aubyns and beg a night's lodging with them.

'It would be doin' me a great favour if ye would,' he told

them, so of course they agreed, and if Sir Bernard Townclear wondered what could be important enough to take his son away from his lovely bride for a whole night of their wedding trip, he kept his own counsel.

The St Aubyn carriage left with Conor waving goodbye to his wife and hostess – and casting an imploring look in the direction of Mariette's dearest friend.

She could not fail to understand his meaning, and knew exactly why he had taken this sudden measure. She would have to speak to Mariette tonight. Yes, for both their sakes, she was bound to do what she could. She trembled at the prospect, fearful that she might do more harm than good, even though guided by love for the two people concerned.

When the moon rose high and all the house had settled into silence, Tabitha set about her duty. It was a truly beautiful night, and the scent of lilac drifted up to the window of the master bedroom. A nightingale burst into joyous song in a tree close to the house as Tabitha opened the connecting door.

'Are you awake, dearest?' she whispered, and Mariette stirred, sighed, sat up and held out her arms.

'Ah! I knew it was you, *ma chère*, Tabita,' she said, reverting to her earlier pronounciation of the name. 'Conor is not here, so come to me, my love. Let's sleep in each other's arms while we have the chance – like when we were at school.'

She pulled the bedcovers aside for Tabitha to get in beside her. She put her soft arms around Tabitha's neck. 'You smell so fragrant – is it lavender? Mm-mm! Delicious . . .'

'Mariette, my own dearest friend, I must speak to you very seriously. Oh, darling, I've promised Conor, and I must say it.'

'Say what, *chérie*? You can say anything. What does Conor want?'

'He only wants what is his by right, Mariette. Your obedience to him as his wife – to let him love you as you promised at your wedding.' Tabitha spoke very quietly, interspersing the words with gentle kisses, putting her left arm under the fair head, and holding the girl close. How I would weep for sheer joy, she thought, if he would take me in his arms! But it is for his sake that I must persuade my dearest friend to let him be her husband in very truth, to let him show his love for her as his wife.

'Listen, my Mariette, and let me tell you how to make him the happiest of men,' she whispered. 'You are so – so beautiful, and he adores you. It is your duty as a wife to lay in his arms and let your legs open – let them fall apart so that he can enter your woman's place when his – when that part of him is big and ready to do what all husbands must do. It is your duty, my Mariette,' she continued, as the girl lay in the crook of her enfolding arm. 'And 'twill give him great pleasure – and in time, as you get used to it happening, it will pleasure you, too. And if God wills it to be so, his seed will grow inside you, and you will bear him a child. Think of it, darling Mariette – a little son or daughter! What greater happiness could there be for you?'

'But Tabitha, such pain! Think of your poor mother on the kitchen floor!' cried Mariette, and looked up into her friend's face in such dismay that Tabitha was almost inclined to laugh. How different they were as women, she realized.

'That was unfortunate, but it won't ever be like that with you, dearest,' she said, kissing the cool cheek, imagining Conor's lips pressing softly on Mariette's neck and breasts. She was unable to stop herself wondering what a delicious sensation it would be if she herself could lie in his arms, as his wife now lay in hers. Perhaps an intimation of these forbidden thoughts passed to Mariette, for she gave a little smile.

'It is almost as if you wished you were in my place, *chère* Tabitha,' she murmured slyly.

Tabitha could hardly trust herself to speak. 'Oh, Mariette, Mariette, there are women who would give everything they possessed to be in your place! Take to heart what I've said, my own dear friend, and give yourself willingly to him. Oh, take him, love him, make him happy!'

She could speak no more as she lay back on Mariette's pillow, trembling and half afraid that she might weep, and choke aloud on her tears. Had she chosen the right words to awaken Mariette to her duty as a wife? Or had she made matters worse by her frankness? Would Mariette now submit herself to her rightful duty, and would Conor thank Tabitha for her counsel on such a matter? She waited almost in fear for Mariette's answer.

Mariette spoke at last, a little shakily. 'If that's what Conor wants, then that is what I have to do. For his sake and for your sake I will submit to his love. But oh, my Tabitha, God knows how much I wish it were otherwise.'

Tabitha did not ask her to say more, but looked at her as she lay with her eyes closed, her lovely mouth slightly open, her cheeks wet with tears that Tabitha had not realized she had shed. 'If that's what you tell me I must do for him, my Tabitha—'

'He's your lawful wedded husband, Mariette, and he loves you.'

'*Oui, ma chérie.* I will give myself. I will let him in. But for this night let us sleep with our arms around each other, as we did at school.'

It was enough. They kissed and nestled together, falling into sleep.

Tomorrow night, thought Tabitha, she will give herself to Conor. I've kept my word and eased the way for him. Ah, Conor, Conor Townclear. He had asked her to help him, and she had done her best. God grant that this husband and wife might have joy in each other.

Conor returned to Heathfield House later than expected, but full of hope and excitement over his plans for Mr Shenstone's library – and not only that. He had been unable to resist taking a look at No 21 Gerrard Street, now wonderfully refurbished and almost ready for occupation by its latest tenants. He was able to report to his wife that it was a perfect home with every comfort and convenience, and in a fashionable part of Soho, much patronized by artists and writers who were drawn to its superior taverns and coffee houses.

'That's where our married life will truly begin, my love, in our own home.'

And when he took his wife in his arms that night, he found her dutifully submissive.

Seven

At Number 21 Gerrard Street all was movement and bustle; when the new owners Mr and Mrs Townclear arrived with Miss Prewett at ten o'clock on Monday morning, Madame de St Aubyn was already there, giving orders to the four servants she had engaged for the young couple.

'Mrs Clark is your cook, Mariette, well recommended by my own, and Bartlett is a general manservant and handyman who may call himself a butler in a year or two if he works well. You have two housemaids, Deborah and Minnie. Deborah is a steady girl who may train to be your lady's maid in due time –' She glanced at Tabitha who would be leaving to get married – 'and Minnie, who is sixteen, will work under Mrs Clark in the kitchen and scullery. Now, *ma chérie*, your new furniture is all in place, and I've given you a few pieces from Bloomsbury Square. Your living rooms are on the ground floor at the front, with the kitchen at the back, next to the scullery and a little room for Bartlett, so that he may guard the house at night. There are four bedrooms on the first floor, the largest for you and Conor, and one for Tabitha. The female servants will sleep on the second floor, Mrs Clark in a room by herself, the maids together—'

'Are the two empty bedrooms for guests, Maman?'

Madame smiled knowingly. 'Ah, in a year or two you will need a nursery, and a room for a nursemaid. Do not blush, *ma petite châtelaine*! Perhaps by this time next year there will be a big difference in your life!'

She laughed softly, but Mariette bit her lip and seemed disinclined to share a sentimental exchange on this subject, for she immediately engaged Tabitha in a discussion about curtain material. Later that morning Madame took Tabitha aside to ask how Mariette had seemed during her wedding trip at Heathfield House.

'She was laughing and joking with Conor at the picnic, Tabitha,' she said, having told the servants to address Mrs Townclear's lady's maid in this way. 'The Comte and I thought them both very happy. Do you think that all is well? Please to tell me if you think she needs a quiet word from me – or perhaps Monseigneur should speak to Conor?'

Tabitha thought it would have been more sensible of the Comtesse to have had a quiet word with her daughter before the wedding, but she smiled and assured her that Mariette was indeed happy, though naturally married life had been a little strange at first.

'Mr Townclear seems very loving and patient with her, Madame. There is no need for any more to be said, I'm sure.'

And indeed, the less said the better, she thought to herself. Conor had found an opportunity to thank her briefly for her wise advice to Mariette, which had made his way easier, he said.

She had inclined her head and made no reply, sensing his embarrassment and not wanting to show her own. His new occupation at Mr Shenstone's house in Queen Anne Street took him away each day, and after Madame had returned to Bloomsbury Square, Tabitha found herself fully occupied with helping Mariette to settle into her new role as *châtelaine,* and in finding her own place in the hierarchy of a small establishment. Mrs Clark was a good plain cook with a few specialities that she could produce when the occasion demanded; she was happy to take both Deborah and Minnie under her wing, but looked askance at the lady's maid who had to be called Miss Prewett, and was clearly unwilling to take orders from her.

'I reckon she's got that delicate little Mrs Townclear under her thumb,' she muttered to the three other servants over their mid-morning cheese and beer. 'She'd better not start tellin' *me* how to do my work – not likely! When she asks for somethin' to be sent up, I say to her, "Is that what Mrs Townclear has asked for?" An' if she don't answer, I asks her again, pretty sharp!'

Tabitha was aware of the resentment against her, and always prefaced orders with 'Mrs Townclear would like—' or 'Mrs Townclear will be going out this morning, and asks for a late dinner', trying to sound suitably polite. She always spoke in a friendly way to the maids, putting herself on their level; Deborah was a butcher's daughter, one of a large family and used to hard work; Minnie was from an orphanage, like so many maidservants, chosen because they had no family ties, and Tabitha went out of her way to be kind to the girl who considered herself in luck to have found such a place.

'The grub – er, the food 'ere ain't 'alf good, Miss Prewett – cor! I wish I could take some back to them kids I lef' be'ind!' she confided, and Tabitha thought of poor Nan. Minnie was just the sort of girl to fall for a sweet-talking butcher's boy or milk roundsman, and Tabitha felt she should give her a friendly word of warning when the opportunity arose, though no doubt Mrs Clark would disapprove of her presumption.

'I hear that one's goin' to be married soon, thank the Lord, so we'll only have to put up with her till then,' said the cook, and was annoyed at getting no nods from Bartlett or the maids.

A spell of hot weather towards the end of May aggravated the tensions in the air, and Mrs Townclear was prostrated on her couch with headaches accompanying the usual discomforts of her monthly menses. Tabitha almost envied Mr Townclear his daily escape to work; he walked each morning to Queen Anne Street where he lost himself among the thousands of calf-bound volumes of essays, natural history, philosophy and theology. All the wisdom of the ages seemed to be contained within their covers, and in the course of classifying them, Conor admitted to his wife and her maid, he was often tempted to sit down and read some particularly interesting passage. Mr Shenstone was an amiable bachelor in his fifties whose scientific dabblings had gained him membership of the Royal Society and the possession of the library, willed to him by a friend he had made there.

'I sometimes wonder who'll inherit it after himself,' Conor told Tabitha over breakfast. 'I just hope it doesn't go to a pack o' relatives with no interest but to divide it up and sell it.'

Meanwhile it provided him with a pleasant daily occupation for which Mr Shenstone paid him well and bought him a midday dinner at the Rose of Normandy, a tavern on Marylebone High Street. Not only was the fare excellent, but the tavern was known as a meeting place for gentlemen's clubs and debating societies, and there was often good conversation to be had in its congenial atmosphere.

'What d'you make of all this anti-popery talk, Townclear?' asked Mr Shenstone. 'Seems to me that this Lord Gordon is something of a fanatic – and by the way, no offence intended, but I presume you're a Roman Catholic yourself, being an Irishman married to a Frenchwoman?'

'Ye presume rightly, Mr Shenstone, though I only want to live in peace and harmony with my fellow men. Anythin' else is against the teachin' o' Christ – who was a Jew, and none the more popular for that,' answered Conor in his direct way. 'I think it'll blow over all the sooner if people don't take too much notice of it.'

'I'd like to believe you, Townclear,' replied Shenstone in a lower tone. 'But I fear there could be trouble. There's a huddle of gentlemen over there who are brewing something up if I'm not mistaken. Let's pretend to be talking, don't look in their direction, but keep your ears cocked.'

Conor obediently put his head closer to Shenstone's, and they nodded and mouthed as if in deep conversation, but in fact they listened intently to the murmured sounds coming from a group of half a dozen men seated at a table in a corner of the room. Three of them were dressed like gentlemen, and one could have been a clergyman, but one was from a distinctly lower order of society, and it was his harsh voice that carried the words 'St George's' and 'up'ards o' twenty thousand stout men' to the listeners. He wore a bright blue scarf round his neck and tugged at it as he spoke. Suddenly one of the group caught Conor's eye, and made a warning movement to the others. He put his finger to his mouth, then pointed to the clock on the wall. It was clearly a signal for them to leave, and each one picked up his glass to finish his drink.

'Here's to our man, then, gentlemen—' And then followed a muttered name, which Conor suspected might have been Lord Gordon – and having drunk to their hero, they rose and disappeared in different directions. One minute they were seated at the table, the next they had completely vanished.

'What did you make of 'em, Townclear?'

'They got wind of us listenin', I think.'

'That's because you turned your head and caught that villainous one looking in our direction!'

Conor grinned. 'What d'ye think they meant by St George's – the church?'

'Could be, though there's several St George's. Did you pick up the name Pole?'

'Mm – don't think so – they mentioned a Gordon or Jordan.'

'It was Lord Gordon, and they drank to him. Well, if I were you, young Townclear, I'd keep guard over your home. If ever I saw a bunch of conspirators – we could be in for some kind of revolution, and they'd use the No Popery label to make a lot of trouble for people like yourself. Be careful, Townclear, and lay low. Keep away from crowds. Tell your wife to stay indoors.'

Conor thanked the well-intentioned bachelor, but did not intend to frighten Mariette with any words of warning – though there might be no harm in dropping a hint to Tabitha. Thank the Lord above and all the saints for that girl's good sense!

The girl of good sense was planning a visit to Orchard Court, having not seen her family since the wedding, and feeling a need for familiar surroundings where she was accepted by all.

'Go to see them whenever you like, *ma chérie*,' said Mariette. 'We could hire a phaeton for an afternoon, and go together, for I would like to see Maman and Papa.'

'To be truthful, my love, I'd rather go and spend a whole Sunday at home with them,' said Tabitha. 'My father and Jeremiah would be free from the shop, and Thomas home from school for the week's end. Andrew's nearly nine, and I'd love to talk to him – and dear Michael and Prudence – and my mother, of course.'

'Oh, if you want to go for a Sunday, I would have to stay here with Conor and go to Mass with him at that house in Westminster,' answered Mariette with no great enthusiasm.

'Which would give *him* great pleasure, I'm sure,' said Tabitha. 'So shall we say this Sunday, the first in June? And I can go to Morning Prayer at St George's Bloomsbury with – er – my family.' The slight hesitation was because she knew Rob Drury would also attend with them, and might reproach her for her long absence. Her mother certainly would, and perhaps with good reason. Tabitha sighed, pulling off the white cap she usually wore in the house, and shaking out her hair. The weather had become uncomfortably hot.

'Yer could fry an egg on the paving stones,' remarked Joe

Bartlett, sitting on the kitchen doorstep and peeling off his sweat-stained stockings, to the loud indignation of Mrs Clark and Deborah who wrinkled their noses, though the entry of Miss Prewett turned the cook's ill-will away from the man and redirected it to the lady's maid, who was carrying a glass.

'If ye're after fresh milk, there ain't any,' said Mrs Clark. 'It soon goes orf in this heat.'

'No, it's your excellent ginger cordial that Mrs Townclear needs,' said Tabitha, determined to be civil. Mariette was stretched out on a couch in the living room, holding a wet handkerchief to her forehead, and Tabitha had come for a glass of weak ginger beer from the covered jug on the stone floor of the pantry.

'I only set that lot up yesterday, so it ain't ready till tomorrer,' was the surly reply.

'Nevertheless, I'm sure it will be good for her headache,' said Tabitha, filling the glass from the jug as nobody offered to do it for her, though they would doubtless blame her for helping herself. Her own head ached, and she suddenly longed for the familiar kitchen at home, where Prudence would welcome her with a kiss. She always felt like a stranger in this kitchen, a servant yet not a servant, resented by all except poor little Minnie. And she even had to try not to show too much friendliness to *her*, because of the unkind comments that would be made.

The next day, Friday, was the second of June, and London shimmered in a heat-haze; even with all the windows open, rooms were like ovens. Women streetsellers hoisted up their petticoats and dispensed with scarves, leaving shoulders bare and bosoms more exposed, and Bartlett was chided by Mrs Clark for stripping to the waist. On the first floor of Mr Shenstone's house where two bedrooms had been converted into one large area for his library, Conor sat among the five thousand volumes, his shirt unbuttoned and his feet bared; he wiped his arm across his forehead, sticky with sweat, and tried to give his whole attention to what seemed a never-ending task, but his thoughts took another direction. He looked back to a carefree country boyhood at Townclear Hall, and now here he was, a married man in London, hired to organize the construction of a library: what was he doing with his life?

God knows I have a lot to be thankful for, he told himself,

considering his new circumstances as a husband and house-holder. A more beautiful wife he could not wish for, nor a more virtuous, though he sadly acknowledged to himself that virtuous women do not enjoy the grosser intimacies of matrimony. Thanks to Tabitha's timely intervention, Mariette now allowed him to claim his rights, but her silent acceptance of her duty and tightly closed eyes had the effect of cooling his own ardour, sometimes with a humiliating result – enough to get any man down, he thought gloomily. He could only hope that in time she would grow accustomed to his lovemaking, and imagined the joy they would share when it resulted in news of an expected happy event. He passed a hand through his damp hair, making it stand up on end.

'Conor Aquinas Townclear, ye're nothin' but a great booby,' he said aloud. If he was to be a father, he had to stop dreaming and idling the time away; he must rise above this melancholy mood, and apply himself seriously to the work he was fortunate to have.

Up until now he had made a great many lists, but these were getting him nowhere, and a better system was needed. He remembered reading about the method used by Dr Samuel Johnson when compiling his great Dictionary some thirty years before, using small cards of about the size of playing cards. In Johnson's case each card was numbered and represented a word; Conor's cards would each stand for a book, and would be placed in a box representing a category, indicated by a coloured ribbon. Where a book fell into more than one category, a second identical card – and maybe even a third, was made and labelled Card B – or even C, and put into the appropriate categories. Conor felt that he'd made a real discovery, and warmed to his theme: Dr Johnson had taken eight years to complete his Dictionary, and Conor reckoned that his five thousand books would be organized in well under a year, maybe six months if he got a move on. He visualized tall bookcases with shelves on both sides, and glass-fronted cupboards for the more valuable volumes, not to mention Shenstone's admiration as he showed visitors round this treasure-house.

Fired by new enthusiasm, Conor immersed himself in his mammoth task, and his mood lightened; he was deaf to the sounds that rose from the street below, where footsteps hurried past the windows and some sort of rallying cry was being repeated. A long way off there was a low rumble rather like distant thunder, but the sky was cloudless. The hours passed, and the solitary scribe wrote upon his cards and stacked them up. He did not hear the front door open.

'Townclear!' It was Mr Shenstone, back from his morning walk. Conor hastily began to adjust his clothes, tucking his shirt into his breeches and doing up the buttons.

'Townclear, are you there?'

'Coming, sir!' He pulled on his shoes and smoothed down his hair. Footsteps sounded swiftly on the stairs, and Shenstone burst into the room, his face flushed, his wig awry.

'By heaven, sir, what's happened?' Conor asked.

'Do you mean to say that you've heard nothing, seen nothing, Townclear? There are great crowds converging south of the river, in St George's Fields – thousands of 'em, all wearing blue cockades and scarves, and Gordon's there, spouting anti-Catholic speeches!'

'Ah, I thought I heard a lot o' footsteps goin' in one direction, and a fair bit o' shoutin', but ye get that most days, bringin' the traffic to a standstill. Now, Mr Shenstone, I've got this great new system for the library – ye'll be able to find any book ye want in a matter o' minutes—'

'Hang the library, Townclear, go home to your wife and see that you come to no harm. Gordon's got a great petition to take to the House of Commons to repeal the Catholic Relief Act, and there's half of London following him, waving blue flags and howling "No Popery!" like a pack of ravening wolves. Off you go, and keep your wife and servants indoors!'

Conor accordingly set off for Gerrard Street, missing his usual dinner, and cursing the show of bigotry that had taken him away from his new system.

Something was up, and Joe Bartlett was highly intrigued. Life at 21 Gerrard Street had not turned out to be as diverting as he'd hoped; the street's taverns, coffee-houses and superior lodgings should have yielded a rich variety of cronies – boot-blacks, pot boys and messengers to trade jokes and play tricks on. His last place had been with three young law students who drank, smoked, stayed up all night and brought in ladies from the town – until they'd been sent back to their families in disgrace, leaving Joe unpaid and out on the street. He'd then got work as a sedan chair-man and found it damnably hard on his arms and shoulders, carrying large ladies and gentlemen to and from social occasions, and his fellow chair-man was drunk more often then not. One day a charming French lady had hired him, and was much taken by his snub-nosed, honest face. She'd asked him a few questions, and finding him to be the son of a respectable widow, she engaged him as manservant for her newly married daughter and son-in-law. It had seemed like a stroke of luck, but he'd found himself at the beck and call of a sharp-tongued cook who was always finding fault with him. She said he had to wash himself every day, though there was only the stone sink in the kitchen, and he'd been discovered there by one of the maids who'd screamed her head off at seeing what she'd never seen before, or so she said, and earned him another rebuke from Mrs Clark. The mistress was seldom to be seen, but she had a nice, sensible lady's maid, and the master was an easy-going Irishman.

'You and me have to look after the women o' the house, Bartlett,' he'd said with a grin, whereas an Englishman would have said 'ladies', and in a much less familiar way.

The women were now all in a flutter because a great crowd had gathered in St George's Fields and some Lord High-and-Mighty was leading them across Westminster Bridge to Parliament Square with a petition to the House of Commons. It sounded as if it could be a bit of a lark, but Mrs Clark had said he was to stay away from it. Miss Prewett had come to the front door and looked at the scruffs who were going past with their blue cockades, scarves and flags. She seemed worried, and he asked her if he should go and try to find out more.

'No, Bartlett, we must all stay indoors in case there's trouble,' she said. 'Let's hope it will pass off peacefully, and not give rise to deeds of hate and wickedness.' She looked up and down the street again, and gave a cry of relief when she saw the master hurrying towards them, though he didn't usually come home at this hour.

'Conor! Oh, thank heaven! Bartlett here says he'd like to go and see what's happening at this meeting. Do you think we could let him go if he promises not to get drawn into the rabble?'

'Yeah, go on, Mr Townclear, let me find out summat for yer!' cried Joe eagerly.

'Not on his own, Tabitha, and I have to stay here to guard all o' ye,' answered Conor, who would dearly liked to have gone himself, but Mr Shenstone's warning restrained him. 'Have ye got a friend at all, Bartlett, some young fellow who could go along with ye?'

'Yeah! I'll find somebody, Mr Townclear, if I 'as to grab 'em by the scruff o' their neck!' And off ran Joe in search of any young lad from the servant fraternity who could get leave.

'We won't say too much to Mariette, Conor, there's no sense in worrying her, is there?' said Tabitha, and he agreed, while privately wanting to reassure her too.

'But it's one devil of a nuisance, just as I was gettin' into a good way o' sortin' out this library. Now I shall spend the rest o' the day twiddlin' me thumbs an' wastin' time for what will probably be no good reason at all.'

'Pardon me, but what time do Mrs Townclear want dinner sent up?' interrupted Mrs Clark, coming out into the front hall and looking pointedly from one to the other.

'I'll let you know, Mrs Clark, when I've talked with Mari— with Mrs Townclear,' replied Tabitha, cross with herself for blushing, as if she and the master were doing something improper.

Joe Bartlett returned jubilantly with a pot boy from the Turk's Head, and an ostler whose master had said he might go and see what was brewing, but not to join with any mob and to keep with the other two fellows. Conor emphasized this with strict instructions to the three.

'And mind ye come back by six o'clock and not a minute later – are ye hearin' me, now?'

'Oh, ah, we'll be back to tell yer all abaht it!' roared Ned the pot boy as they tore off leaving the household at No 21 to wait and watch and privately worry, especially when Mariette got up from her couch and demanded to know if her parents would be safe in Bloomsbury Square.

Conor heaved a huge sigh of relief when the three youths turned up just before seven in a dirty, dishevelled state, with cuts and bruises. Ned's forehead was bleeding, a tooth was

105

broken and his clothes torn. Joe Bartlett admitted that they'd been in a fight.

'But it wasn't our fault, Mister Townclear, honest it wasn't! We kept our distance from the big march, but when they got to Parli'ment Square this Lord Gordon stood up an' started spoutin', an' they all yelled like fury, and follered 'im into the 'Ouse just as some o' the big-wigs was comin' out. They knocked one ol' feller's wig off, an' started overturnin' carriages – yer never saw anyfin' like it, an' ev'rybody yellin' "No Popery!" Some great bully asked us why we wasn't wearin' somefin' blue, an' started goin' for us, so we 'ad to kick an' punch our way out of it – and then somebody said, "Look, they've called out the 'Orse Guards", an' everybody scarpered. The redcoats came an' took some prisoners, and we 'ad to leg it pretty sharpish, or we'd've got taken as well. Cor, what an 'ullaballoo!'

Tabitha and the two maids set about washing their cuts and bruises, and Conor went to apologize to the landlord of the Turk's Head and the ostler's master, admitting that he had sent Bartlett to find a couple of companions.

'An' it's a good thing yer did, sir – better three than one. Let's hope that'll be the end of it.'

But it wasn't. Later that same evening a division of the original gathering in St George's Fields crossed the river by Blackfriars Bridge and made for Lincoln's Inn Fields where the Roman Catholic chapel of the Sardinian Ambassador was attacked and looted. Terrified bystanders watched as the rioters – as they now began to be called – marched down Duke Street, brandishing statues, chalices, priests' vestments and the sacred treasures of the chapel where Conor and Mariette had been married less than a month before. The news travelled fast, and by midnight on that Friday all London trembled for what might happen on the morrow.

'But I *must* see Maman and Papa, and make sure they are safe,' wept Mariette who refused to go to bed.

'My dear Mariette, I'm just as worried about my parents, but we'll have to wait until morning for news,' said Tabitha sensibly. 'There's no sense in walking across London in the middle o' the night while these devils are prowling around. You can be sure our parents are just as worried about us.' She nodded at Conor as she spoke, inviting his confirmation.

'O' course Tabitha's right, darlin' Mariette – and I'll go over to Bloomsbury first thing tomorrow to see how they all are—'

'And I'll come with you, Conor! Let me come with you!'

'*No*, Mariette. You two must stay here within doors. Write a letter to your parents, and I'll take it with me – and you, too, Tabitha, I'll be your messenger, but I will *not* allow either o' ye to walk abroad, and that's final. Now, can any of us hope for a wink o' sleep?'

They retired at last to bed, but their sleep was fitful, troubled by anxious dreams. Mariette stayed in bed until late, and Mrs Clark sent her breakfast up on a tray. Tabitha sat at the table and watched Conor eat bread and cold bacon before he buttoned up his jacket, picked up a heavy club he had brought over from Tahilla, and set out on his errand soon after eight.

'Take care o' yourself, Conor – don't take any risks, for God's sake.'

'Don't worry, Tabitha. I'll give your parents your note and your love.'

'Hurry back,' she whispered, half under her breath. 'Keep out o' trouble.'

She went back upstairs to sit with Mariette, but soon afterwards there was a loud knock at the front door. Both girls stiffened, expecting they knew not what, and heard Minnie going to answer it. She came straight upstairs to tell Miss Prewett that a Mr Drury wanted to see her.

'O mon Dieu!' cried Mariette, and Tabitha muttered 'Oh, my God!' at the same time.

'He has come with news that my parents' home has been attacked!' said Mariette, bursting into tears, but Tabitha rose at once and told her friend quite sternly to be quiet.

'Let's wait to hear what he has to say before we think the worst. I'll go and see him, and bring you back word,' she said, glancing in Mariette's looking glass to check that her hair was neatly tucked into her cap. On her way downstairs she told Minnie to go and sit with her mistress.

Rob Drury had been left standing on the doorstep, and Tabitha beckoned to him to follow her into the drawing room. She drew a deep breath, and faced him. He was dressed as befitted a tailor, in a well-made light-brown jacket and waistcoat, with buckskin breeches. He was bareheaded, and the first thing that Tabitha noticed was the wide blue cravat around his neck, its ends hanging halfway down his chest. She stared at it.

'Good mornin', *Miss Prewett*,' he said with a hint of irony. 'Yer can guess why I'm here.'

'M-my father and mother—?' she faltered.

'Yer parents are very worried about yer, Tabitha, and I told them I'd come an' fetch yer home.' His unsmiling grey eyes met hers, and his manner was stern.

'Fetch me – home?' she echoed. 'Oh, Rob, I can't. I can't leave Mariette.'

'Why not? Is she yer father and mother, yer brothers and yer betrothed husband? D'yer care that *she* be worried, and take no notice o' yer own family?'

'You know that's not true, Rob. I – I do appreciate you coming over, and I'm relieved to know that they're safe – but Mariette's parents are – are—'

'Are French papists.' He finished her sentence with bitter emphasis. 'And I have no cause to be grateful to them. They took yer away from me.'

'Rob—' She wanted to protest, but the words would not come. What would be the use of arguing with him if she was not prepared to let him take her back to her parents' home? She pointed at the blue scarf. 'Does that mean that you've joined the Protestant Association?'

'Yes, though more for safety than on principle – my mother's safety, and your family's. I've advised Mr Prewett to hang a blue flag outside his shop, and yer could tell the St Aubyns to do the same – and the Townclears, too, if they don't want to be singled out for attack.'

She could not miss the contempt in his tone when he spoke of the two Catholic families who were her friends, though she could hardly accuse him of being unreasonable.

'Mr Townclear has gone to Bloomsbury to see Mariette's parents and mine,' she said. 'You may even have passed each other. Rob – dear Rob, I can't blame you for the way you feel, but it's just that – well, Mariette and I have been as close as sisters ever since we met, and I've looked after her, seeing that she's so delicate, and—'

'But Tabitha, she's *married* now, she's got a *husband* to take care o' her, for God's sake!' he burst out angrily, walking to the window, not looking at her. 'Oh, Tabitha, how can yer turn away from me – and yer own people – to go chasin' after foreigners an' Irish with nothin' but their titles to recommend 'em – yer mother's that grieved about it, and as for me – well, it's just about broken my heart. If yer knew how much I've loved yer – and for how long—' He swallowed, turned round and looked her straight in the eyes. 'But I'm not goin' to beg, Tabitha. Yer can come with me or stay here, but I'll tell you this: if yer stay here, there'll be no weddin', and ye'll end up a lonely spinster 'cause *they* won't want yer, 'specially when they've got their first child. So what's it to be, Tabitha?'

Her eyes flashed. 'I'm not going to bargain with you, Rob. I've told Mariette I'll stay here up to my birthday, that's only another two weeks – but if you expect me to obey you and come home *now* – well, then, we'd better tell the vicar at St George's that we've changed our minds. No, don't let me detain you, Mr Drury,' she said as he tried to take hold of her hand. 'Please give my parents my love, and tell them they've no need to worry about me. Good day to you.'

'*Listen* to me, Tabitha!' he shouted – but got no further, because there was a tap at the door, and Mariette entered with bare feet, wearing a shawl over her nightgown. She glanced from one to the other. 'I couldn't wait any longer,' she said. 'Are my parents all right?'

'Yes, yes, Mariette my love, they're all right, quite safe. When Conor gets back, he'll give us all the details.' In re-assuring her friend and encouraging her to hope that the rioters had given up and gone home, Tabitha almost managed to persuade herself as well. She held out her hand to Rob who shook it briefly, and strode away, as bewildered as he was hurt and outraged; for surely she couldn't possibly prefer to stay with a married couple and turn her back on love.

Conor returned at midday with first-hand news of the St Aubyns and the Prewetts, who were unharmed and relieved beyond measure to know that their daughters were also safe.

'Ye'd hardly expect Bloomsbury Square to be the scene of a riot, now would ye?' joked Conor, adding his assurances that although the St Aubyns had been horrified by the sacking of the chapel where they had worshipped for nine years, the uprising had now been put down, and English tolerance had triumphed over bigotry. And he told them something else: that John Prewett had promised the Comte and Comtesse de St Aubyn that in the event of any danger, they would be welcome to use his home as a hiding place. Although the necessity had passed, Mariette said that such a gesture of true friendship would never be forgotten.

That afternoon the three of them strolled out to take the air in Marylebone Park where five hundred acres of Crown land formed a green oasis, partly woodland and partly leased out as farms to supply London's hay and dairy produce. After the shocks of the past twenty-four hours, it was an idyllic place to restore calm, and they decided that on the morrow, Sunday, they would all go to Bloomsbury to visit their parents.

On their way back they met Mr Shenstone walking with Mr Burke, a fellow member of the Royal Society, and a neighbour of theirs in Gerrard Street. Conor greeted his employer warmly, and began to introduce his wife and Miss Prewett. To his surprise Mr Shenstone cut him short.

'After what happened yesterday, I think you'd be well advised to keep your ladies safe indoors, Townclear. Do you realize that there were fifty thousand marchers yesterday? That's a mob, Townclear, and don't tell me that they've all gone to ground. Good evening to you, Mrs Townclear – and Miss Prewett.' He smiled at the ladies and frowned at Conor before they proceeded on their way, and Tabitha felt a stab of anxiety, though she hid it from Mariette.

On Sunday morning the three of them set out on the walk to Bloomsbury, but did not get very far. As Shenstone had predicted, there was new trouble in the air. Few legitimate pedestrians were about, but there were groups of disorderly riff-raff, half of whom seemed to be drunk, and all were carrying implements of destruction: hammers, pokers, axes, saws and rakes that could be used on people as well as property. They growled at the man with two women, and somebody asked where Conor's blue cockade was.

''Ere! I know 'im, 'e's a bloody Irish papist!' shouted one of them, and Mariette shrieked in terror. In that moment Tabitha knew that it was up to her to talk them out of a dangerous situation, for the accents of her friends would betray them. She faced the small group of men, and shouted back.

110

'Don't be daft, 'e's me young fancy man from up norf, an' she's 'is sister – we're all good Protestants, only 'e ain't got 'is blue what'sit yet, 'cos 'e only got 'ere yes'day!' she said in the best cockney she could manage, and even gave the men a knowing smile and a wink.

'Cor, she's a proper little goer, she is! I'd up-end 'er any time!' one of them said with a grin as Tabitha steered her companions round to retrace their steps, and when Conor and Mariette tried to whisper their thanks, she muttered 'Be quiet' out of the corner of her mouth, adding aloud, 'I reckon ol' Lord Gordon's 'avin' anuvver go at the 'ouse o' Commons today!'

'Not on a Sunday, 'e won't, sweet'eart! 'E ain't no Sabbath-breaker!' somebody called out.

'Ooh, no, ye're right – then maybe 'e'll 'ave a go at anuvver papist chapel!' rejoined Tabitha, quickening her pace as she hung on Conor's left arm while Mariette clung to his right. They reached No 21 Gerrard Street without any further challenges, and the first thing that Conor did was put up a blue flag outside the house.

'Yer father gave me a length o' blue cloth yesterday, Tabitha, and I didn't think I'd use it at all, but I've changed my mind now.'

Tabitha nodded, remembering Rob Drury's advice and shuddering. She did not despise Conor for concealing his religion; he had his duty to protect his household, and for the rest of that Sunday it became increasingly clear that the danger was by no means over. Hoarse shouts filled the air, gangs of men and a few women of the lowest sort roamed the streets, going into alehouses and demanding free beer. Mariette was terrified, and again wanted reassurance about her parents in this new outbreak of violence. Tabitha could not console her, and Conor absolutely forbade Joe Bartlett to risk his life taking a message to Bloomsbury. The latest news was bad enough: Catholic chapels had been sacked and looted in Westminster and Moorfields, and the rioters had returned to the Sardinian embassy and finished their work of destruction there by burning the ruined chapel to the ground. The mob had become a mindless monster, no longer confined to harassing Catholics but focussed on doing as much damage as possible. From a religious rebellion it had become an army of the disadvantaged, turning in drink-fuelled vengeance upon property owners and politicians, especially those who'd supported the Catholic Relief Act, and magistrates who had sent law-breakers to prison. And it seemed that the constabulary were powerless to restrain the rioters, afraid of having their own homes ransacked in reprisals if they did. That night Conor slept downstairs in the kitchen with Joe Bartlett, and Tabitha took his place in the matrimonial bed, where Mariette clung to her and wept for the danger to her parents. Not much sleep was had by anybody, and on Monday the rioting continued unabated.

'Lord George Saville's 'ouse in Leicester Fields 'as been set on fire, and so 'as Sir John Fielding's,' reported Bartlett. Neither man was a Catholic, but they had acquired a reputation for leniency towards that religion.

'It's no good, I'll have to take ye all away to safety,' said Conor. 'I'll go out and see if I can hire a chaise or some sort o' conveyance from the coachin' inn up the Marylebone Road. Ye're to stay here in the house, all o' yer, till I return.' He added in a lower tone, 'Ye'll have to watch Mariette very closely, Tabitha, she's been threatenin' to run away to her parents.'

Hardly was he out of the house when Rob Drury returned, begging Tabitha to come with him to her parents' home or his mother's humble home in Spitalfields. She knew that a part of her longed to take heed and live an honest, easy life with such a husband as Drury, but she told him again that she could not leave Mariette, especially with rioters inflicting mayhem on the law-abiding population. He apologized for his behaviour on Saturday, and pleaded that it was only his love for her that had made him show such jealousy and anger. 'Think about it, dear Tabitha,' he said, putting his hand over hers as they sat in the drawing room. 'Yer have the rest o' yer life to consider, and if yer make a wrong decision now, yer may spend years regrettin' it.'

He looked into her face, demanding an answer – but he never received it, because the door burst open and little Minnie stood trembling on the threshold.

'She's gorn, Miss Prewett, she's runned away!'

'What? Do you mean Mari— Mrs Townclear?' cried Tabitha, starting up. 'Oh, my God, when did she go?'

'I don't know, Miss Prewett. Yer was sittin' 'ere wiv this

gen'lemun, I fought I'd better 'ave a look to see if she wanted anyfing – an' there she was – gorn!'

'God forgive me, I must go after her,' cried Tabitha. 'She'll be on her way to Bloomsbury.'

'I'll come with yer,' said Rob, equally promptly. Minnie was given instructions to tell the master where they had gone when he returned, and the pair set out, Tabitha reproaching herself bitterly for not guarding her dearest friend as Conor had emphatically ordered her to do, and praying with all her heart that Mariette might soon be found.

Mariette hurried along with Ned the pot boy from the Turk's Head. She had ventured out of the front door into the street, anxiously looking up and down for a sight of Conor returning; Tabitha was closeted *again* with Rob Drury, and Mariette both distrusted and resented him. She had half a mind to go in search of Conor without telling Tabitha – and then to her surprise poor Ned with his bandaged head and his face still swollen from his broken tooth had suddenly appeared in front of her and said she must come to her parents' home at once.

'No, don't stop to tell 'em nothin', you're to come wiv me right away, Missus, yer muvver sent me to fetch yer – 'ere, come on!' And he grabbed hold of her by the arm and led her swiftly out of the street and up towards Charing Cross and St Giles; she recognized the very poor area that she and Tabitha had visited many years before with little Thomas, when they'd seen the clock with seven dials and met that poor girl with the sick baby.

'Is this the right way to Bloomsbury Square?' she panted, longing to see her maman and papa, and wishing she had told Tabitha – but Tabitha might have prevented her from coming.

'There's a lady an' gen'lemun waitin' to take yer there, Missus,' Ned replied, and she was much relieved by the sight of a smiling couple standing outside St Giles's church. The young lady came towards her with open arms.

'Thank you, Ned – and *hallo*, dear Mariette! Don't you recognize your old school friend?'

She knew the voice – and yes, she saw the face of her one-time friend, Cynthia White. The well-dressed gentleman with her wore a high-crowned hat; he was putting some money into Ned's hand and some warning words into his ear.

'Don't worry, my dear, we're going to take you to your parents,' Cynthia reassured her. 'This is Mr Pole, a friend of mine and yours, too. This is the lady I told you about, Nathaniel.'

'Mademoiselle de St Aubyn, *je suis enchanté*,' he said with a respectful bow and there was surprised admiration in the look he gave her.

'Oh, Cynthia, how glad I am to see you!' And poor Mariette bestowed a kiss on her old school friend. 'Tabitha Prewett told me that she'd met you at a house her father visited last year, but she didn't say much about you. How well you look!'

'I'm very pleased to meet you again, Mariette, and you are as sweet and lovely as ever,' Cynthia said, smiling. 'But let's waste no more time. Take my arm, and Mr Pole will take the other – and we'll escort you to your home to meet your parents again!'

Mr Pole smiled and nodded, and Mariette was overwhelmed with gratitude.

'Oh, how *good* of you, Cynthia! I haven't seen them since this awful trouble began. My husband Conor has tried to keep me in our house at Gerrard Street, but he does not understand how much I need to see my darling Papa and Maman.' She wiped away a tear, and Miss White and Mr Pole looked at each other and nodded.

'We will walk with you all the way to your house, Mariette.'

Firmly supporting her on each side, the couple led her up towards Holborn and reached Bloomsbury Square. Cynthia carefully inquired about Tabitha, and noted that Miss Prewett had obviously not repeated what she, Cynthia, had said to her about keeping away from the St Aubyns, no doubt for fear of frightening this silly, spoilt French girl. Well, that was all to the good, for the girl would now lead them to that pair of Catholic parasites the St Aubyns, French immigrants living on the fat of England's land and plotting to put a Jacobite king on the throne.

They loosed their hold on her outside No 9, and Mariette happily ran up the stone steps leading to the front door. She rang the bell. She knocked on the door. She went to one side and tapped her fingers against a window. She called out, 'It's Mariette! Is anybody at home?'

There was no answer, and Mariette turned very pale. 'O, mon Dieu, they have been taken!' she cried, and tears began to flow again.

'Come on, Nathaniel, is this one you can unlock?' asked Cynthia, suddenly brisk. 'Looks as if the birds might have flown.'

Mr Pole produced a bunch of keys from an inner pocket, and tried them in turn. None of them opened the door, but Mariette then remembered a little key that she had always kept in an inside pocket. It opened the servants' door at the bottom of the basement steps.

'Well done, Mariette!' cried Miss White. 'I had no idea that you were so cunning! You go first, my dear, this is your home. We'll follow behind.'

Mariette ran straight in and up the stairs, crying out for her parents. 'Maman! Papa! It is I, Mariette! Where are you?' There was no answer. The house was silent. They were not there.

She turned to find Cynthia and Pole close behind her. 'Let Nathaniel have that little key, my dear – no, I insist you hand it over to him for safety's sake. We don't want anybody else coming in here, do we?' Mariette saw that her old school friend was no longer smiling.

'Right, Mademoiselle de St Aubyn, where are they? Where are your parents hiding?'

'You can see for yourself, Cynthia, they are not here,' answered Mariette, utterly bewildered. 'They – they have gone away, or – been taken away. Oh, please help me to find them!'

'You must have an idea where they are,' said Pole. 'Come on, speak up, where are they?'

'No, no, I do not know. I wish I did, I want so much to see them!' Mariette was chilled by the change in the atmosphere, and began to feel very frightened. Cynthia's eyes were as hard as glass.

'If you don't tell us where they are, it will be the worse for you, you spoiled, stupid, French papist, making yourself out to be such a fine lady at school! You'll stay here as our prisoner until your precious parents return, or until you tell us where they are – and then we'll burn this house to the ground – do you understand?' A stinging slap landed on Mariette's cheek, and she was about to receive another when Pole quickly laid a restraining hand on Cynthia's shoulder.

'Don't you dare hurt her,' he ordered. 'We've got time, we can wait. Don't lay a hand on her, she could be more valuable as a hostage.'

Mariette now saw that she had been led into a trap. She closed her eyes to blot out the sight of the couple, and two thoughts came to her mind: firstly, that John Prewett had offered her parents a hiding place in his own home, and she now desperately hoped that they were there. And secondly, that for their sake she must never tell these people what she knew. Mariette had always been protected, shielded from even the mention of evil, by her parents, by Tabitha, by her husband Conor. Now there was nobody to turn to – except for La Sainte Vierge. This was her testing time, and she would have to be brave and keep silent, no matter what this couple did to her. Instinctively she began to say inside her head, silently, *Je vous salue, Marie, pleine de grace, le Seigneur est avec vous, vous êtes bénie entre toutes les femmes . . .*

Aloud she said, 'I do not know the whereabouts of Monseigneur le Comte et Madame la Comtesse. You can keep me here and slap me for as long as you like, but I cannot tell you.'

'We'll get it out of you, you hoity-toity French heretic, I'll knock your teeth out!' Cynthia's face was contorted with hate, but Pole quickly interposed again.

'Shut up, you vindictive little bitch! This one's going to be harder to crack than we thought.'

For Pole realized that the beautiful French girl was turning out to be unexpectedly uncooperative. Her face was pale but composed as she finished her prayer silently, in her head.

Priez pour nous pauvres pécheurs, maintenant et à l'heure de notre morte. Amen.

Eight

Conor Townclear was not the only pedestrian desperately seeking transport out of the city, and he soon discovered that there were no conveyances for hire, nor were there places on stage or mail coaches for anybody suspected to be of the offensive religion. When he applied to hire a horse so that he might ride to Heathfield House and return with Lady Farrinder's carriage for his wife, her maid and such of their servants who had no other refuge, there was not a mount to be had, not so much as a wheezy, broken-down old nag for all the money he could offer.

Anxious and dispirited, he returned to Gerrard Street where Mrs Clark awaited him with yet worse news. Mrs Townclear had gone!

'That's right, sir, an' it pains me to tell yer,' she said with relish. 'No sooner 'ad yer left, when a gen'leman comes to see that Miss Prewett or whatever she calls herself, an they sat talkin' very close, heads together, an' she made tea for 'im. I saw 'em with me own eyes—'

'For God's sake, woman, come to the point! Where was Mrs Townclear while this visitor was here?'

'I can't really say, sir, 'cause after them two 'ad been 'ead to 'ead for 'alf an 'our, I went to see if poor Mrs Townclear needed anythin' – an' there she was, *gorn!*' Mrs Clark gave Minnie a quelling look when the maid seemed about to interrupt. 'Oh, the shock it gave me, sir, to see she'd run away, poor lady. I'd've gorn after 'er meself, only that Miss Prewett nearly 'ad a fit when I told 'er, and orf she went with 'er gen'leman friend, sayin' they was goin' after 'er.'

'Who was this man who visited Miss Prewett?' demanded Townclear, running his fingers through his hair till it stood up in black clumps.

''E tol' me 'is name was Mr Drury, sir,' ventured Minnie timidly, and Conor gave a nod.

'That'll be the man she's to marry, surely. Have ye any idea, Minnie – any idea at all o' where they went?'

'They just said they was goin' after Mrs Townclear, sir,' said Mrs Clark, adding importantly, 'An' *she* must've been goin' to Bloomsbury Square, seein' as 'er parents live there.'

Conor momentarily put his hand over his eyes, as if praying for guidance or to hide his face, and then addressed the servants. 'Ye must all stay here and don't draw attention to the house by looking out o' the windows. These rebels are out to sack and plunder like an invadin' army. Remain here and keep the blue flag up while I go after my wife, for I'll have no peace till I set eyes on her again.'

There was a length of blue cloth on the table, left from the roll that Prewett had given him. He tore about a yard from it, and wrapped the piece round his neck like a scarf, muttering, 'I'll be a Protestant for ye, Mariette, if it only gets me to yer side.'

'There's no need for you to come with me, Rob,' said Tabitha as they hurried across the city.

'I won't let yer walk alone at a time like this,' he said firmly. 'Too many scoundrels about. And we'd better avoid Oxford Street, where most o' the shops are boarded up against looters.'

He led her north of the main thoroughfare among back-streets where they walked between dilapidated sheds, barrows and casks; the air was thick with the stench of refuse from butchers' stalls and rotten fruit. A few drunken rioters were sleeping off their excesses of the night before, and practically everybody now wore a blue cockade or sash.

'This is where they retreated to plan the next stage o' their campaign,' observed Drury, drawing her arm through his as they picked their way through the territory. 'Thank goodness for the redcoats! The government'll have to call out the army in force if this goes on.'

When they reached Bloomsbury Square he stopped. 'Ye'll be all right now, Tabitha. Are yer goin' straight to your parents?'

'No, I'll go to Number 9 first, to see if she's there, with hers,' she replied. 'Oh, if I could but see her and know her to be safe!'

'I'll stay until I see yer go into their house,' he said, having nothing to say to the St Aubyns or their daughter, but wanting to see Tabitha received by them before he left her.

Standing a few yards away, he watched as she pulled the bell-rope twice, then knocked on the door. She tapped on the front window and peered through the letter box. She called out, 'Mariette! Mariette, are you there?' There was no response, and she turned back to Drury in dismay.

'She's not here, nor her parents,' she said. 'Not so much as a cast-off servant. Oh, Rob, wherever can she be?'

'Sssh!' he warned. 'Walls may have ears, they say, and so may windows. Ye'd better go to your parents, Tabitha, because –' He lowered his voice to a whisper – 'they may be hidin' there, the parents, daughter or both. I'm off to Spitalfields to see my mother, and see how things are at Davidman's workshop. All right, then, Tabitha – be careful – good-bye!' He briefly touched her hand, and then added, 'I'll maybe call on yer family tomorrow mornin'.'

She nodded her thanks, then went out of the square into the familiar mews and down the Frenchman's stairs to Orchard Court. A blue flag drooped over Prewett's shop front, and the door was open. With some trepidation she went in, causing an overhead bell to jangle. A young man appeared, and gave a whoop of delighted surprise.

'Tabitha! At last! We've been that worried – at our wit's end about you.'

'Jeremy! Are you all right? And mother and father – and all o' you?' she asked, embracing him.

'We've had our ups and downs, Tabitha, but – er – I'll call Pa.'

She was shocked at the sight of her father who looked care-worn and anxious – and more than anxious, for there was fear in his eyes. 'Tabitha, my girl, I didn't know whether yer were alive or dead. Praise be to God for the sight o' yer.'

'Yes, Papa, I'm very much alive, as you can see,' she said with a smile, kissing his pale cheek.' She lowered her voice. 'I'm looking for Mariette. She's run away from home, and I thought she'd be with her parents, but their house is empty.'

John Prewett's face closed up, as if afraid to speak, even to his daughter. 'She's not here, Tabitha. I can't tell you anything about her, nor her parents.'

'Oh, Papa, I'm so sorry to hear that. I shall have to go on searching for her.'

He was looking over her shoulder at the open door, and suddenly stiffened. 'There's a man coming here. Did he follow you, Tabitha? Oh, my God. God save us all. Have mercy on us.'

'Good day to you, Prewett,' said the newcomer in silkily polite tones, raising his high-crowned hat. 'We meet again, you and I and your charming daughter. D'you remember me?'

'I never forget a face,' replied the tailor, holding up his head and returning the man's stare. 'You're Mr Pole, and I met you at the house o' the Reverend Sands and his wife and daughter.'

'Correct. They were expecting you to call again with the

jackets you were making for them, but you sadly disappointed them. However, *Miss* Prewett was of use to us, and now I'm here to search your premises. I have good reason to believe that you are harbouring traitors.'

Tabitha gasped as she too recognized the man, and as they faced him, another man came into the shop; in contrast to Pole, he was uncouth both in appearance and manner.

'Mr Granby is an assistant of mine, and we shall go through this house together, Prewett. How many rooms are there? Is there an attic? A cellar?'

Tabitha's blood seemed to run cold, even on such a warm day. She was sure that the St Aubyns, with or without Mariette, were hiding in the house. Her father had promised them a refuge if things became dangerous, and where else could they be? Prewett's stricken face was proof enough: he was terrified. But he faced Pole with dignity.

'I can't stop yer,' he whispered.

'No, you most certainly cannot stop us, Prewett. And do you know what happens to householders who harbour traitors? They are guilty of high treason against the King's Protestant Majesty, and they are hanged – with all members of their family who have conspired against justice. Did you know that, you moth-eaten tailor?'

'You shut yer great mouth, yer bully, talkin' to my father!' roared a voice from the back of the cutting room, and Michael Prewett came crashing into the shop, a big, strong man with arms of iron. He struck out at Pole, and in a moment laid him on the floor: but the next sound was a tremendous crack as a short wooden club wielded by Granby crashed down on Michael's head. Prewett gave a loud groan as his firstborn fell to the floor where he gave a convulsive twitch and blood oozed from his head.

Pole heaved himself up from the floor and stood upright. He looked at Michael's inert body, and grimaced. He glared at Granby, who had put his weapon back into its bag on his belt.

'You were too hasty, Granby.'

'E'd've killed yer, Mr Pole. It was 'im or you.'

'Is he dead?'

'I reckon 'e is, or soon will be. Y'all right, Mr Pole?'

Tabitha and Jeremiah knelt beside their brother's body,

shedding tears as she tried to find his heartbeat. Prewett groaned again and muttered, 'How can I ever tell his mother?'

'Come on, then, Granby, let's get on with it,' said Pole. 'Let's find them!'

They went off to start their search, pulling at furniture, opening cupboards, emptying linen chests, knocking on walls, pulling bedclothes on to the floor; and while their pitiless footsteps clumped up and down the wooden stairs, Tabitha led her father into the kitchen where his wife sat at the table beside Prudence. The maid was white with shock, but Martha Prewett glared.

'Don't start on at me!' she told her husband. 'I'm not sorry I said I wouldn't give 'em house-room, not after the way they took my daughter away from me! I wasn't goin' to risk all our lives just for them French papists. And I don't regret it, neither, whatever yer say, John – even if yer blames me for the rest o' me life. I don't care what yer say!'

Martha's refusal to give refuge to the St Aubyns had turned out to their advantage, for no trace of the Comte or Comtesse was found, and with an oath Pole and his henchman departed, tipping over the work table in the cutting room as a parting shot. John Prewett stood with his clenched fists at his side, while a weeping Prudence helped Tabitha to straighten Michael's body and cover him with a blanket. Tabitha wiped the blood from his face and head, while her father told his wife that her beloved Michael was dead. She gave a long, low moan and laid her head on the table.

'Can yer stay with us for a bit, Tabitha?' her father begged. 'There's nothin' ye can do for Mariette, and it's up to her husband to find her now. It's too dangerous for you to be wanderin' the streets, and besides, I'll need help with yer mother. There'll have to be a funeral, and a lot to be done. Thank heaven Thomas is safe at school.'

Tabitha told him she would stay for a while, certainly until after the funeral, though she knew she should be out looking for Mariette who would be constantly on her mind.

'Whoever would've thought such things could happen, Papa?' she said, holding his hand. 'Our dear Michael killed before our eyes – and heaven only knows where Mariette is, or whether her parents are still alive.'

He whispered close to her ear. 'I can tell yer they're alive, my girl. They're next door, in Mrs Markham's coal cellar. Went there yesterday, when yer mother said she wouldn't have 'em.'

Mademoiselle Mariette de St Aubyn believed that her last day had come. She lay on a maidservant's bed in the attic of No 9 Bloomsbury Square, a prisoner in the charge of Miss White, her erstwhile friend; she was bound at the wrists and ankles with her own silk scarves, and gagged with a handkerchief in her mouth and another scarf tied over it, allowing her to breathe through her nose, but not to utter a word. Her gown had been stripped off her, and she lay in her white shift; she could heave herself off the bed when she needed to sit on the chamberpot beside it, but could not walk or wipe herself. At intervals her gaoler came up to check upon her, to see if she had worked the gag loose by facial contortions or attempted to release her hands, both of which had been bound with a piece of stout cloth before being tied together, so that she could not use her fingers or thumbs. She had not been given anything to eat or drink, and she was subjected to bitter humiliation when Cynthia came up to show herself off in Mariette's gowns, shoes and hats.

'I think this suits me far better than you, *Mademoiselle de St Aubyn*,' she mocked, parading up and down the small room, tossing back her head so that the ostrich feathers waved to and fro; she also decked herself in Madame's jewellery, and flashed it in front of her victim. Forbidden by Pole to hurt Mariette's body in any way, this was the only form of torture she could employ.

'We need her untouched for when we come to bargain with the family, and I know how spiteful you can be, White,' he had said bluntly. 'I'll be back before the day's out to see that she's unharmed.'

Cynthia therefore did all in her power to hurt her foe by jeering at her, pouring scorn on her religion and nationality and calling her family and friends by obscene names; but the result was disappointing, for the girl, who could not answer anyway because of the gag, seemed strangely impervious to her surroundings; she lay with her eyes closed, as if in a world of her own. Cynthia's fingers itched to slap her, pinch her, make her respond in some way, any way – but she feared

Nathaniel Pole, and suspected that he might have his own reasons for wanting Mariette's beauty preserved. In the end it was no longer sport to torment her, for she remained apparently unaffected: it was almost as if somebody was watching over her, and Cynthia found it unnerving, though there was one moment that gave her satisfaction: it was when the doorbell and the door-knocker sounded, followed by Tabitha calling through the letter box in the hall below. Mariette had then writhed upon the bed, and a silent tear trickled from the corner of each eye. Cynthia had stood beside her and put her hand over the gagged mouth to make doubly sure that Tabitha would get no answer. It pleased Miss White to see her prisoner suffer for a moment, but it was the only occasion when Mariette showed any reaction to her situation: nothing that Cynthia herself could say or do had any such effect.

The hours went by, and night fell over the city; Pole returned and untied the gag while he gave the prisoner a drink of water. She took a few sips, but refused to eat, and he reapplied the gag. Outside the city lay in the grip of terror, with houses burning and the shouts of drunken gangs roaming the streets and looting. Still Mariette lay helpless and inaccessible to whatever bitter words were said to her.

'It's as if she had the Devil and all his angels looking after her,' muttered White, thoroughly wearied by her unresponsive charge: she could not have explained to Pole or anybody else why Mariette made her feel so uneasy.

Conor Townclear's emotions churned within him as he set off in pursuit of his wife, and he bitterly reproached himself for not taking better care of her, for not listening to her repeated pleas to see her parents. He judged that she must have fled to Bloomsbury Square on the spur of the moment when Tabitha's back was turned. How could he blame her? He had said himself that the fashionable square was not likely to be a venue for rioters.

Unless . . . might it be possible that the St Aubyns were a special target, being both Catholics and foreigners? His fears became more sharply focussed, and he hurried on through streets that had been ravaged, past houses reduced to a smoking ruin, their contents spilled and charred, lying in the gutters. There were now mobs all over the city, and Townclear tugged at his blue scarf when a gang of men with sticks and clubs came bearing down upon him at Charing Cross. His efforts to avoid them by dodging down an alleyway brought him up against another band of rioters brandishing rusty implements and yelling, 'No Popery! No Popery in London! No Popery in England! Down with all poxy papists!'

He turned back to Charing Cross to find that the rioters were being set upon by a body of the militia, some armed with the dreaded muskets that it was said could kill a man from several feet by firing a miniature cannon ball called a bullet that entered the head or the heart. He heard several loud shots and smelt gunpowder as howls of pain were heard from men struck down by these firearms.

'Stop it!' he shouted. 'Stop killin' men in cold blood!' It was hardly an appropriate metaphor, as blood was running high and the sun still beat down on dusty paved streets that reflected the heat back on the scene of mayhem.

'And who d'you think *you* are?' Townclear spun round to face one of the soldiers, who pointed to the blue scarf round his neck. 'You and your kind've been doing enough killing!'

'No, I'm a loyal Protestant subject of His Majesty the King!' Townclear returned loudly, though his voice was lost in the pandemonium raging all around.

A redcoat mounted on a horse came forward and further accused him. 'Yes, you're one o' the ruffians who've been doing all the damage!' he shouted, waving an unsheathed sword with which he made menacing circles in the air. It was amazing how quickly this caused the rioters to disperse, leaving Townclear and a knot of men at the mercy of the military. He received a punch in the face from a foot soldier, just as he was about to repeat his denial of all connection with the anti-papist rioters. He staggered back, his hand over his right eye, only to receive a further blow on the back of his neck which sent him reeling literally into the arms of another peacekeeper.

'Right, that's enough from you, weasel – take him in, sergeant, along with the rest – march 'em up to Newgate!' ordered the cavalryman. 'Put 'em on special detention in time o' riot and civil commotion!'

And before he knew what was happening, Townclear's hands were manacled and he was chain-locked to another man and forced to march with other prisoners in twos along the Strand

and up to Fleet Street where the newly built Newgate Prison had been erected on the gutted foundations of the old. The great iron gate clanged open and in they went, down a dimly lit stone corridor and into the cells, two men to each one, still manacled together.

'Look, ye can't lock me up in here!' roared Townclear, having kept reasonably quiet until now for fear of making his situation worse. 'I'm not a rioter! I have not attacked anybody, not even when falsely accused! I—'

'Aw, shut yer potato trap,' muttered his unwilling partner. 'Give yer tongue an 'oliday. If it ain't bad enough to be 'oled up in Newgate, wi'out bein' chained up to a murphy!' And he spat.

So Conor Townclear was left to reflect on the irony of being thrown into prison for rioting against Roman Catholics. Within Newgate's thick stone walls that night he learned something about human degradation: the stink of the shared slop-pail, the dirt, the fleas, the lice, the oaths and obscenities; worst of all were the scornful eyes of his fellow inmate upon him, his sour breath and unwashed flesh, always uncomfortably close, being joined to Townclear at the hand. It was impossible to pray in such company: Conor had not even the privacy to bemoan his fate, and his right eye was swollen and painful from the punch he had received on arrest.

Night fell upon the city where fires blazed and buildings were laid waste, to the glee of the rioters who danced among the flames like limps from hell.

John Prewett and Jeremiah carried Michael's body into the cutting room and laid him on the longest table there. To carry him upstairs to his bed would be difficult, for he was heavy and the stairway narrow. The shop would be closed until after the funeral, which would need to be soon in the continued heat, and Prewett sent out young Andrew with a note to the coffin maker, naming Thursday as the likely date but subject to alteration in the present turmoil.

Martha Prewett went to sit and weep beside her son in the cutting room. Mrs Carter had been sent for to do the necessary offices for the dead, and while they awaited her arrival, Tabitha told her father that she had to visit the St Aubyns in their hiding place, much as she dreaded telling them of their daughter's disappearance, for which she blamed herself. Prewett told her to slip quietly out of the back door to the shared drying area, and under cover of the flapping sheets, to enter Mrs Markham's house by the door to her scullery.

Mrs Markham looked flushed and wore no cap in the heat. She led Tabitha into a small room off the kitchen in which she usually took breakfast, and there were the Comte and Comtesse de St Aubyn sitting dejectedly side by side on a wooden settle. They started up in fear when they heard the door open, but on seeing Tabitha they both rose to greet her eagerly.

'Monseigneur and Madame,' she whispered, as the lady embraced her and Monseigneur bowed and kissed her hand. Of course they were desperate for news of Mariette, and Madame burst into tears at hearing that she was missing since morning in the chaos of the rioting.

'They will ravish her, my poor, beautiful child!' sobbed the Comtesse in French. 'How terrified she will be – oh, what a barbarous country this is! Nothing like this would ever happen in my own fair country of France!'

Tabitha tried in vain to console her by saying that Mr Townclear was out searching for Mariette. The Comte caught her eye, and holding his afflicted wife against his chest, he addressed Tabitha in a low tone.

'Is it possible that she may be in our home? Has anybody searched there? Mariette has a key to the servants' entrance, and she may be in there and afraid to come out, especially if she has been – attacked by the rioters. Could you go in there, Tabitha, and look in every room? I have a spare key to the front door.'

Tabitha knew that her father would forbid such a dangerous venture without having at least one able-bodied man to protect her, but she told the Comte that when Mr Drury next came to see her at Orchard Court, probably tomorrow, she would ask him to accompany her to search No 9 Bloomsbury Square. She informed the couple of their lucky escape from Pole and his henchman, and with a break in her voice she described what had happened to Michael, at which they sympathized deeply. She pocketed the key and took her leave, saying that she might be needed to assist Mrs Carter in her duties to the dead.

With a heavy heart she returned to her father's house, where she was told wonderful, incredible news: Michael was not dead! Mrs Carter had arrived to do the last offices and, as she was taking off the victim's bloodstained shirt, he had moved his head!

'I stared at 'im, 'ardly able to believe I'd seen right, and then 'e fluttered 'is eyelids and gave a sort o' sigh,' she told the Prewetts breathlessly. 'Better send for Mr Appleyard, an' ask for some poultices for 'is 'ead an' medicine for 'im to take! Oh, my! I never saw this 'appen before!'

Mr Appleyard was the apothecary who attended the Prewetts, and once again young Andrew was despatched with a note, begging his immediate presence. He arrived within a quarter of an hour, and shook his head over Michael.

'He's in a very bad way, Prewett, and I think it hardly worth my while to intervene.' He looked at the tailor meaningfully. 'You know and I know, Prewett, that this lad will always be one of nature's simpletons. You have Jeremiah and Thomas – and thank heaven the boy's at school while this anti-popery uproar's going on – and Andrew, he's a bright lad. One or other of 'em will have the care o' this one when you've gone, but now might be the right time to let him pass quietly away.'

Prewett stared at the apothecary indignantly. 'Good God, Appleyard, ye're forgettin' that we all thought him a corpse up to half an hour ago, when Mrs Carter came to prepare him for his coffin!' he retorted. 'Simpleton or not, he's flesh of our flesh, as much as the others. Prescribe whatever'll do him good, an' I'll pay yer well, but no more o' that sort o' talk, if yer please!'

So Michael was helped to his own bed to rest and recover from a broken skull, and Appleyard went to fetch leeches. Mrs Prewett's tears were wiped away as she and Prudence nursed the son who had been brought back from the dead; but Tabitha was still fretting over the whereabouts of Mariette, especially since the Comte had suggested that his daughter might be in his house, unwilling or unable to leave it. How could Tabitha sleep in peace, knowing that she had failed to guard her dearest friend?

In Spitalfields the riots were taking their toll, and the house of a Catholic family near to Rob's mother had been plundered and torched. The Davidman workshop had closed and its staff

127

sent home in such a time of danger and uncertainty. Before returning to his worried mother, Rob went to look at the little house off the Whitechapel Road that Prewett had settled on as a first home for his daughter and Drury after their wedding. Rob knew in his heart that this was not likely to take place, now that she had become so involved with the St Aubyns; yet he could never banish her from his mind, and resolved that he would go to the Prewetts again on the following morning to hear what news there was, if any.

Tuesday morning dawned on more scenes of terror: the rioters seemed to have the upper hand and rampaged their way through the city without opposition; even the Lord Mayor was unwilling to issue orders to arrest them, for fear of reprisals. Doors and windows were barred as Londoners prepared themselves for further violence, dismayed by the failure of the authorities and dreading the next wave of fire and destruction.

Nathaniel Pole was getting worried about the French girl who lay a prisoner in her own home, in the dubious care of that unstable creature White. She seemed to be fading away before their gaze, lying on the bed with her eyes closed, her face chalk-white.

'Have you given her any medicine or such?' he demanded. 'Have you been dosing her with tincture of opium? If that girl dies in your custody, I shall hold you personally responsible.'

'I haven't enough interest in her to care whether she lives or dies,' Cynthia White retorted, for she had become disillusioned with the Protestant Association. At first it had been so exciting, a great cause for her to serve with pride, but all she wanted now was to get away from that girl on the bed, so helpless and yet so strangely unassailable. And frightening . . .

Pole's eyes flashed and his fist flew, landing Cynthia a sharp box of the ears that made her head spin. Any hopes she might once have entertained about a romantic attachment with this man were finally shattered, but she made no protest for fear of another blow.

In the foul atmosphere of the prison news filtered through from the outside world, mainly through new arrivals, that fires raged all over London. Conor Townclear, unwashed and unshaven, his right eye closed and throbbing, felt sick with despair, and could only guess at the whereabouts of his wife and Tabitha, though he presumed that the latter had young Drury to look after her. He cursed himself for a lazy, careless husband, and vowed that if he and Mariette were spared after this ordeal, he would devote his life to her, humbly grateful for such favours as she allowed him in the matrimonial bed. Yes! If he ever got out of this stinking cell and freed from the chain that shackled him to his fellow prisoner, he would show his repentance of past selfishness by striving to do good and living a better life than heretofore.

Tabitha had passed a restless night in the plain wooden bed she had slept in since childhood, with Andrew on a straw palliasse beside her; he had been moved out of the room he shared with Michael, now being tenderly nursed by their mother. In her dreams Tabitha saw Mariette, lying white and still in death, and woke with a cry on her lips; sleeping again she heard Mariette's screams of terror as her delicate body was ripped and desecrated – and again woke with a start, to find Andrew at her side, alarmed by her own nightmare cries.

'There's nobody here to hurt yer, Tabby,' he was saying. 'Ye're safe at home in bed now.'

The early summer dawn made further sleep impossible, so Tabitha wrapped her shawl around her, and went to see Michael, now asleep, slack-jawed and snoring. Martha Prewett sat on a chair with her head resting on her son's bed, worn out by watching for any sign of change for better or worse. Pity for them stirred in Tabitha's heart, but her fears for Mariette over-rode all other concerns. She was tempted to go over to the St Aubyns' house at this quiet early hour, use the key and creep in silently to see whether her friend lay there, and if so, in what state. Common sense warned her to wait until a man could accompany her: had Rob Drury said he would call on her again today? If he did, she would beg him to help her, but to enter the house alone would be foolhardy; she would just have to be patient and wait.

This decision was vindicated later, when at half past eight Mrs Prewett sent Jeremiah out to call at Mr Appleyard's for oil of rosemary to apply to Michael's head; when he returned he had news for his sister.

'I just saw a man coming out o' number nine,' he told her eagerly. 'He was slinking out o' the tradesmen's entrance with his head down, but I knew him – he was that villain Pole.'

'Jeremy! Are you *sure*?'

'As sure as I can be, Tabby. It was he, and he must've slept there.'

'Oh, my poor Mariette!' Tabitha wailed, wringing her hands, and her brother imagined how he would feel if it was his sweetheart Betty held captive by such a man as Pole.

'I'll come with you, Tabby, and we won't say anything to Pa. I'll take a knife with me, and we'll go across together.'

This threw Tabitha into a quandary, for not only was she reluctant to encourage her brother to disobey their father, but she was even more unwilling to put Jeremiah in danger; they already had one brother seriously injured as a result of their involvement with the St Aubyns. And yet she *had* to know if Mariette was there, and might have already delayed for too long. What on earth was she to do?

Relief came in the form of Rob Drury, who presented himself soon after nine. Tabitha threw herself into his arms, taking his breath away in joyful surprise: but he was quickly brought down to earth when she explained what she wanted him to do.

'Her parents are sure that she's in there, Rob, being kept a prisoner—'

'But who'd want to keep a young lady prisoner, Tabitha?' he asked doubtfully. 'The rioters are after Romish chapels and homes, lootin' and burnin' 'em to the ground. They're stealin' valuables and whatever they can lay their hands on. The St Aubyns' home hasn't been touched, has it?'

'Maybe not yet, but a couple of Lord Gordon's followers were here yesterday, and searched the whole of this house and shop, trying to find the Comte and Comtesse who are – who are in a secret hiding place,' Tabitha told him. 'There's no doubt that the ringleaders are after known Roman Catholics, maybe to capture them and hold them to ransom, or – or to kill them – oh, Rob, please, you must come with me, just to see if she's there! Her parents have given me a key.'

On learning about the ransacking of the Prewetts' home and the injury done to Michael, young Drury became sufficiently indignant to agree to a search of the St Aubyns' house, though he flatly refused to involve Jeremiah.

130

'I'll go and find a couple o' soldiers, Tabitha, armed with swords or muskets,' he said. 'Not much use tryin' to get hold o' constables – they're too scared to risk havin' their own homes torched. I know where some o' the military are stationed – wait for me, I won't be long. Get Jeremiah to keep yer father talkin'. We won't tell him till afterwards.'

It was nearly ten when Tabitha followed Drury to No 9 Bloomsbury Square, and watched as he quietly unlocked the front door and stepped inside, putting the key in his pocket. Two armed militiamen stood talking a few doors away, ready to pounce on anybody leaving the house, or to enter if nobody had left within five minutes. Wearing her housegown, apron and cap, and with Jeremiah's knife in her pocket, Tabitha followed him inside. The air smelled unpleasantly of stale food, with overtones of unemptied chamber pots, having had all the windows closed during the heatwave; there was no sign of recent occupation, though a famished black cat mewed pitifully at the foot of the stairs; Drury began to climb to the first floor, then the second, and seeing and hearing nothing suspicious, he continued up to the attic rooms where the female servants had slept. Here on the bare wooden landing he paused, and glanced back at Tabitha who had followed him. She pointed to a cup and a plate on a window ledge; her eyes were bright with expectancy, for now she sensed the nearness of her dearest friend. Three doors opened off the landing, all of them closed. Tabitha silently pointed to the middle one, knowing it to be the largest of the attic rooms. Drury drew a knife from his belt. Tabitha held her breath. He put his hand on the latch, and tried to lift it noiselessly, but it gave a loud click, and they heard somebody gasp, then a smothered cry. Rob Drury threw open the door and stood facing a strange girl who had leaped up and was gazing back at him, half-afraid, half-defiant. They stood staring at each other, and Drury was about to ask who she was, when Tabitha flew past him to the girl lying on the bed behind her: a slender young woman whose huge blue eyes stared out of a transparently white face above a gag, and whose hands and feet were bound.

'Mariette – Mariette, my own – what have they done to you? Let me get these accursed things off – oh, Mariette!' She tugged at the knots of the gag, and taking out Jeremiah's

131

knife, cut through the scarves that bound Mariette's wrists and ankles. Over her shoulder she shouted to Drury. 'Grab that witch, Rob, hold her till I can throttle her – I'll rip her tongue out – I'll break every bone – I'll – I – I—'

'H-hush, Tabita.' The hoarse sound from Mariette's throat was scarcely audible, but freed from her gag she could mouth the words at her friend. 'She – has – not –' The act of speaking was difficult after having her mouth filled with a handkerchief for nearly twenty-four hours, and her tongue was swollen. 'Not – touched – me.'

Tears sprung to Tabitha's eyes as she gently slid an arm under Mariette's shoulders and eased her up into a sitting position. Her whole body was stiff and her wrists and ankles chafed from being tied together. She leaned against Tabitha who sat down beside her.

'Do – not – hurt – her,' she said slowly and with difficulty. 'She – has – not – hurt – me. L-La Vierge – is – is—' Her head lolled against Tabitha's shoulder, and Rob Drury, holding the other girl and pinning her arms behind her back, saw the tenderness with which Tabitha supported her friend, the tears on her face as she embraced her. His captive saw, too, and began to tremble with fear. She made no attempt to struggle free.

'What d'yer want me to do with this one?' he asked. 'D'yer know her?'

'Yes, she was at school with us, but fell in with some o' Lord Gordon's fanatics – like that rat Pole,' replied Tabitha contemptuously. 'Tie her up as she tied Mariette, and leave her here for him to find when he returns.'

Drury hesitated. 'But she'll talk, won't she?' He had no stomach for tying up a shaking, whimpering girl, but by now the five minutes were up, and they heard the two militiamen come through the front door.

'Up here in the attic!' called Drury, and the men raced up the three flights of stairs to burst in on the extraordinary scene before them.

'One prisoner released, another taken,' Drury told them, and saw them grin at the sight of such an unlikely pair of prisoners: one pale young woman in a half-fainting condition, and another in a state of abject terror, her arms held behind her.

'She's dangerous, and mustn't be allowed to go free,' Tabitha told them emphatically. 'Can't you throw her into prison? Bridewell? Anyway, I need to get this lady to safety. Can one o' you assist me to carry her down the stairs?'

The rescue of Mademoiselle de St Aubyn, followed by her hungry black cat, had been noted by the amazed residents of Bloomsbury Square, and within half an hour she was joyfully received by her parents at Mrs Markham's, while Cynthia White had been led away in handcuffs by the peacekeepers. Drury was welcomed by John Prewett who gave him bread and beer in the kitchen, while Tabitha, having left her friend with the St Aubyns, experienced a sense of restlessness and anti-climax; she went up to Michael's room to give her mother a rest from nursing, and after checking that her son was sleeping peacefully, Martha Prewett accepted the offer and went to her bed.

Seated beside her brother, Tabitha wondered where Conor Townclear could be: surely he would not have stayed at Gerrard Street without his womenfolk? She could hardly ask Rob Drury to help her find Mariette's husband in a city racked by riots.

Her thoughts were interrupted by a visit from Mr Appleyard, calling to see the invalid. He peered into each of Michael's eyes, pulled down the lower lids, and examined the wound on the top of his head.

'The leeches have lowered the pressure on his brain, and he seems to be recovering quite well, Miss Prewett,' he said, wanting to dispel the impression he had given the previous day. 'I'm reasonably hopeful that he'll sleep off his head injury if he's kept still and quiet.'

In the kitchen, Drury was told by the man he had hoped one day to call father-in-law that the St Aubyns' hiding place was in fact next door, and therefore they were still a considerable danger to the Prewetts and Mrs Markham.

'Couldn't they go back to their home in Bloomsbury Square and have a soldier posted at the door?' he asked the tailor. 'It's not right that you should all be put in danger.'

'I don't know if that'd be possible,' Prewett said doubtfully. 'How would we go about it?'

'I'll speak to a sergeant I know,' said Drury, making up his mind to do whatever he could for Tabitha's family; God only knew he had done enough for Mariette's. 'By the way, Mr

Prewett, what do you know about this girl White, the one who was keeping the other one prisoner?'

The tailor proceeded to tell him how he and his daughter had met Cynthia White at the home of the Reverend Sands in Clerkenwell, and had recognized her as a former school friend.

'I can't fathom how an old school friend could turn so vicious,' marvelled Prewett. 'My girl was always so good to her.'

Drury shook his head. 'I don't know, Mr Prewett, but I'll tell yer one thing. Tabitha was like a wildcat over there. I've never seen her in such a fury. She'd've thrashed that girl to death if the French girl hadn't held her back – and yet it was *her* – Miss Aubyn, I mean, that the girl was most terrified of, not Tabitha. There's something about her that I can't make out, but Tabitha worships her.'

Rob Drury sighed deeply, and the tailor shook his head. Their conversation was ended by the entry of Appleyard who came to give his favourable report on Michael, and at the same time the coffin maker arrived to measure the body, apologizing for the delay due to the riots. He was sent on his way without business.

Late that afternoon, as Jeremiah was closing the shop, he quickly climbed the Frenchman's stairs to take a look at Bloomsbury Square and No 9 in particular. He came racing back, all excitement.

'Tabitha! He's come back, that fellow Pole!' he shouted. 'He's used his key to get in the basement door, and if we could board it up somehow, he'd be holed up in there! There's some planks o' wood by Holmes's bookshop, for more shelves – I'll go and grab one and some nails!'

'Oh, Jeremy, be careful!' cried Tabitha, but she eagerly accompanied him to the bookseller to explain their urgent errand. Silas Holmes willingly supplied half a dozen long nails and a hammer, and set off with them both to help place a thick plank crosswise across the wooden basement door at No 9, nailing it to the frame on each side. Within seconds they heard a furious hammering on the other side as Pole, finding both captive and gaoler gone, was trying to leave the house.

'Oh, but he'll do the most dreadful damage in there!' cried Tabitha.

'Not for long he won't, if we go out and find a redcoat to arrest him,' answered her brother.

'Yes, but we must be quick,' she answered. 'I saw some soldiers hurrying towards Holborn a little while ago – there's always some around there – but hurry!'

As soon as Jeremiah had rushed off, her conscience accused her of sending him into danger, and she followed after him, towards a roaring of voices and a tramping of feet pouring eastwards along High Holborn where she stopped and gasped with horror at the raging torrent of rioters armed with every kind of diabolical instrument and bunches of twigs ready to be lit and turn to flaming torches in the dry weather.

'To Newgate!' was the rallying cry. 'To Newgate! And the Borough Clink and the Fleet, we'll burn 'em all down! On, on, to Newgate!'

There was no sign of Jeremiah, and Tabitha was seized with fear. I must turn back and go home, she thought, but it was too late. At that moment she felt her skirt pulled towards the heaving crowd; there were other women, loud of voice and coarse of manner, being swept along on the edge of the surging body of men, and she was unable to turn back against the tide, but was caught up in a frenzied mob of hundreds of men, many of them drunk, some falling down where they stood and being trampled underfoot. She herself was carried along, the object of bawdy jests and laughter.

'Wot're yer doin' 'ere, my pretty maid?' asked an evil-smelling fellow close to her ear, and when she screamed he tried to put his bear-like paw over her mouth; somehow or other she managed to slip between the bodies pressing all around her, and thought she would die of suffocation, until all of a sudden she found herself pulled by the arm through the crowd and dragged through the door of what appeared to be a shop. In a dark and dingy corner she was pushed by her captor – or rescuer? – who was panting too rapidly to speak. Outside the mob was roaring past, and the noise made her think of a pack of wolves out for blood.

'Who are you? What is this place?' she whispered.

'They're goin' to – to set Newgate on fire, Miss,' he gasped. 'When they've all gorn past we might be able to give 'em the slip an' get away.'

She cried aloud in relief at hearing the voice of Joe Bartlett.

'Oh, thank God – thank God, an angel must've sent you, Joe! Oh, blessings on you! How did you get involved in all this?'

'I been lookin' for the master an' missus, an' I'm thankful to find yer, Miss, but d'yer know where they are?'

'Mrs Townclear's with her parents in hiding from the rioters, but I don't know about Mr Townclear. London's at the mercy o' wicked men, Joe. I've lost my brother in the mob – oh, shall we ever get out o' this alive?'

She became aware of other fugitives hiding in the darkness of the boarded-up shop, and could only pray that they would prove friendly and that all would eventually escape. Four or five terrible hours passed as night fell over the city again, during the whole of which time they heard shouts and shrieks and crashing stones. A flickering light was visible under the door, and the heat of a huge, blazing fire could be felt, though Joe said that Newgate Prison was at least half a mile away. Then a tremendous cheer went up, and they heard the clanking of chains.

'They've let the pris'ners out, Miss,' whispered Joe. 'It'll be like Bedlam out there.'

He spoke more truly than he knew, for the mob was threatening to burn down the notorious Bethlem lunatic asylum not far distant, and fill the city with madmen as well as criminals. After a further half hour or so the noise began to abate. Shuffling footsteps were heard, and the sound of axes severing chains as prisoners walked the streets.

'If they find us we're done for,' muttered Joe, but Tabitha put her hand to her ear.

'Ssh-ssh, I think I hear a voice I know, Joe – listen!'

The huddled group stood silently as shouts were heard outside in the street, but the voice she thought she'd heard had either stopped speaking or she'd imagined it.

And then the door burst open, and three redcoats rushed in on them.

'Found 'em! Here they are, skulkin' be'ind an empty shop! Quick, don't let 'em get away!'

'We're not rioters, we're honest citizens hiding from the mob!' pleaded Tabitha. 'We've been here for hours – oh, please let us go home!'

One of the redcoats stared hard at her, and gave a roar of triumph, hitting his right fist into his left palm.

'Well, Mistress Tabitha, we meet again! Don't worry, little dear, I'll take good care o' yer tonight!' He turned to his fellow peacekeepers. 'Take these others, and be off with yer. I'll stay here an' see justice done to this little maid. You can see to the others, fellers – take 'em away an' do what yer like with 'em – this one's for Corporal William Feather!'

She screamed and tried to cling to Bartlett, but he had no chance against an armed soldier, and received a bloody nose as Feather landed a punch in his face. Then the soldier turned to his erstwhile master's daughter and savoured the prospect of some unexpected good sport.

Nine

It was later said that the City appeared as a scene from hell that night, surrounded by a circle of flame that lit the sky with a lurid glow. Thirty-six major fires had been started, and timber dried by the heatwave blazed like matchwood, and reduced to ashes within minutes. Lead roofs melted and stone walls cracked: the very paving stones of the streets gleamed with an unearthly reflected light from the ring of fire: it was as if the whole world of law, order and justice had been overturned by a lawless mob; people cried out that it was a second Great Fire of London, and not a stick or a stone would be left standing by morning.

Conor Townclear, unwillingly chained to his fellow captive, began to be aware of something momentous happening outside the prison. Shouts and sounds of violent activity grew louder and seemed to be moving inside the building, while the degree of heat, already unbearably high, continued to rise steadily. Unable to see what was happening, the prisoners lay gasping in their cells listening to the sound of crashing masonry, and heard blood-curdling yells getting nearer; the air seemed to thicken, and a horrible smell of burning drifted through to the hapless inmates. Cries of fear rose from the cells as they thought the worst.

'Them devils're goin' to roast us alive,' gasped Conor's companion, trying to lick his parched lips, and when Conor contemplated the death that awaited them, he no longer cared what the other man thought, but fell to his knees and called upon the Holy Trinity to have mercy on his soul and the souls of all in this place who were soon to meet their Maker. Believing that his bodily discomforts, the dust-dry throat, the throbbing pain in his right eye and the chafing of his clamped wrist would soon be ended by a hideous death, he asked forgiveness for his sins and prayed that his wife would survive to find a worthier husband than he. While other prisoners bewailed and blasphemed against the fate soon to overtake them, Townclear stoically resigned himself to it, and prayed to die like a Christian.

And then within two or three minutes everything had changed. There was one more enormous crash, followed by the shouting of many voices as the prison was invaded by yelling mobsters running up and down the passages, armed with axes, clubs and hammers.

'Here we are, brothers, we've come to set yer free!' they roared, and the sound of hammering resounded all around. Conor saw the door of his own cell shake and rattle, and realized that it was being battered down from the outside.

'Stand back!' he cried out, jerking his partner away from it, and a few minutes later both lock and hinges gave way and the door fell inwards, leaving a gap through which they could walk free. They had a future again!

'Come on, we can *go*!' Conor urged, dragging his chained partner along the passage through clouds of billowing smoke, treading on red-hot embers of charred wood and molten metal – and out through the blackened gap where the great gate no longer stood. The prison keeper's house was blazing like an inferno, sending up more flames and smoke as every item of its contents was consumed.

All around them prisoners were shuffling out in their chains; Conor and his partner were among some three hundred men released that night, bewildered by the change in their fortunes. Not all went free: several of the badly injured, the drunk and the unconscious were suffocated in their cells; others whose doors had not been battered in were burned to death.

'This way, this way!' the rioters were shouting to the released men. 'Make a clear way – clear the way!' Conor found himself and his companion pushed into a line of other manacled pairs that moved forward towards the towering figure of a huge, sweating blacksmith standing behind an anvil and wielding a short-handled axe. On one pair after another, the axe descended on the linking chains, smashing through them, usually in one blow. When it came to the turn of Conor and his partner, other hands roughly grabbed hold of theirs and laid them on the anvil. Conor closed his eyes and held his breath while his partner swore and tried to remove his hand: then *whack*! Down came the axe, followed by a *crack*! Sparks and metal splinters flew up as the chain was severed, and Conor shouted in agony as his wrist was wrenched by the jolt – but he was freed from the other man who took to his heels without another word. Still wearing the heavy metal cuff round his aching right wrist, Conor truly realized that he was out of prison and no longer tied to another man. He turned to thank the blacksmith, but was quickly hustled out of the way to let the next couple be separated.

He leaned against a wall and closed his one sighted eye, marshalling his thoughts together, trying to assess his present situation, ascertaining where he was and what he should do now. He had just come out of Newgate in what seemed like the middle of the night, and Holborn lay ahead of him, illuminated in the eerie light cast by the conflagration. Beyond that was St Giles's, and continuing eastwards in the same direction was Bloomsbury. So – he could now put one foot in front of the other and continue along the way he had started to follow that morning, all those hours ago, from Gerrard Street to Bloomsbury Square. Oh, God, please let him find his wife there!

But somebody was shouting after him. 'Hey, Mister! Mr Townclear! Stop, *stop*!'

Conor turned his head to see who was calling out his name, and in the confusing half-darkness could only make out a wild-eyed youth who sounded vaguely familiar.

'Stop, Mr Townclear – thank Gawd I found yer – she's over there – they're over there, where we been hidin' – go on after 'em, sir!'

To his astonishment Townclear realized that it was Joe Bartlett who had grabbed hold of his arm and was babbling out his message.

'See that burnt-out shop wiv boarded-up winders? 'E's in there wiv 'er, sir – I couldn't stop 'im – go in after 'em!'

The young man's distress struck a chill into Townclear's heart and filled him with a new and terrible dread. Joe must be talking about his wife, Mrs Townclear – Mariette! Christ in heaven, what new horror was this? Without stopping to question Joe further he started to make his painful way towards the gutted frame of the shop on the other side of the street, the one Joe was frantically pointing at. What new disaster was this in a night of disasters? What was he about to witness? Stiff and weary as he was, he broke into a run.

Tabitha thought she was losing her mind. She could not understand what had happened to her world – or what was now happening to herself. Throughout the past five days her familiar city of London had been turned upside-down; the riots had separated friends, terrorized families and nearly killed her brother Michael, while her beloved Mariette had suffered untold humiliation at the hands of those two fiends, Pole and White. Throughout all this confusion Tabitha had associated the colour blue with the Protestant Association, the Gordonites, the No-Popery fanatics – whereas red stood for the redcoats, the army, the forces of law and order, the peacekeepers. Blue was bad, red was good, for it was soldiers who were out to quell the rioters.

Yet here she was, powerless in the hands of a peacekeeper: in his red coat and white breeches, his tricorn hat and with his sword at his side, he should have been a friend – but he was an enemy, a man she had never liked, a lecher and a seducer, and now fired by the excitement of the riots, his hot breath and bloodshot eyes showed how he lusted for mastery over her. He had been drinking, enough to make him bold, not enough to render him incapable. He threw her against the wall and pinned her to it with his left arm across her chest.

'Sweet little apple-dumpling,' he muttered, pressing his mouth over hers. 'You always were a devilish good piece, Tabitha—' And he kissed her again, pushing his tongue into her mouth and pressing her against the grimy brick. His right hand slithered down over her body, grabbing hold of her skirt and petticoat, shoving them up out of the way, brutally forcing her thighs apart, tearing at the light cotton material between

140

them. A huge erection bulged against his breeches, and he furiously tried to unfasten the buttons.

But he only had one pair of hands, and was unable to hold her in place and force his swollen member into her at the same time, especially as Tabitha was fighting, biting, punching with her hands and kicking out with her sturdy legs.

'Damn and rot you, bitch!' he growled as she spat in his face. It was not going to be possible to give her an 'upright' as he'd done with easy girls who'd charged him threepence for the favour. He'd have to throw her down and get on top of her. With an oath he heaved her up in his arms, still kicking and shrieking, and dropped her on the stone floor. When he threw himself down on top of her, she spat at him again, and he struck her across the mouth with the back of his hand.

'Take that, you spitting little cat, you – you—' He didn't want to knock her senseless, for that would spoil the sport, but he needed to get on with the job: Christ, he was so hard that it was painful, and if he didn't get in soon, he'd start spurting and wouldn't be able to stop. He'd miss the pleasure of laughing in her face as he thrust her up and down, hearing her squeal like a cat dipped in scalding hot water – oh, damn the woman to hell, he was spending: he groaned aloud as his pent-up stream shot forth, and almost immediately he went limp. At the same moment she opened her mouth and screamed at the top of her voice, a penetrating, despairing wail that unnerved Feather.

'Shut up, shut *up*, you screeching madwoman!' he shouted, slapping her face again.

Neither of them heeded the approaching footsteps, for there were still a great many people wandering about, released prisoners trying to get their bearings, others searching for relatives in the aftermath of the storming of the prison; but one pair of footsteps was coming in their direction, and a man stumbled into the gutted room, nearly falling over them in the dark.

'I'm here,' he announced. 'I'm here, Mariette – Mariette? Where are ye?'

'*Conor*!' was all she said, and heard him draw a breath and whisper, 'Oh, my God, 'tis Tabitha, my darlin' dear.'

He bent down and grabbed at Feather with both hands, using all the strength he still possessed, lifting the man up from the woman's body. Feather quickly wriggled from his grasp, and put his hand to his sword. Townclear was half-blind, weakened by the blows he had lately received, and stiffened by his hours of detention in the Newgate cell. He had no weapon to use against a soldier.

But he had, he *had*! – the heavy iron ring around his right wrist, and he blindly swung it against the man's head. A sharp, sickening thud was followed by a yelp which meant he had hit Feather somewhere on the head. He swung his arm again before his adversary had a chance to recover from the blow, and the sound of the crack was like the breaking of bone; Conor continued to swing his arm round and round for as long as he could, catching the man on his face, on the side of his head and on top of his skull. There were groans and choking noises as Feather put his hands up to protect his head, and in the half-dark Tabitha staggered to her feet. She felt in her pocket: Jeremiah's knife was still there. Her fingers closed around it, and as Feather lurched and howled under the blows raining down on his head from Conor's iron cuff, she lifted the knife and thrust the blade into the side of his neck.

This time there was no howl, no groan; the redcoat slid silently to his knees, then doubled forwards on the stone flags, pouring blood from a vein in his neck. Conor and Tabitha could not see him clearly, neither did they linger, for they wanted only to get out of the place. Townclear put his left arm around her and they helped each other out into the street, picking their way among ashes, charred pieces of wood, scorched rags and all the debris of the fire, including a couple of bodies that had either been trampled to death or died of injuries received. There was no sign of Joe Bartlett anywhere. A couple of redcoats approached them.

'Will you be able to get home, sir?'

'Sure, I'll look after the lady and get her home,' Townclear told them shortly, and they did in fact support each other all the way to Bloomsbury Square, though their progress was slow.

'Tell me, did he have his way with ye, Tabitha?' he asked in a low voice.

'No, you came just in time, Conor. I couldn't've gone on living if he had.'

'Don't ever say it, Tabitha, don't ever say it. We need ye. We both need ye.'

They stopped. He was in great pain from his injured eye and bleeding wrist. She was faint and nauseated. And yet he gently kissed her cheek, and repeated what he had said when he had come upon her and Feather in the burnt-out shop. 'My darlin' dear.'

After that nothing more was said, for there was no need. Their lives were inextricably entwined, the one with the other, and each with Mariette. There could be no separating of their three selves.

A guttering candle gave a last flicker and expired, sending up a thin wisp of smoke; no night light was now necessary, as the first rays of dawn were streaking the eastern sky. Michael Prewett lay sleeping peacefully, his skin cool; his mother lay exhausted in her chair, worn out with nursing and anxiety. Neither of them heard the quiet tapping at the back door, but the tailor dozing in his kitchen chair got up at once and opened to his daughter who was in a half-fainting state and Conor Townclear, also scarcely able to stand. Prewett wept aloud for joy at the sight of Tabitha, having dreamed that she was dead.

Up in her attic room Prudence had heard their arrival, and came downstairs with a shawl wrapped around her nightgown. The fire was coaxed into life with a couple of kindling sticks, and a saucepan of water heated. Prudence was alarmed at the swelling and discoloration of Mr Townclear's eye, and bathed it with a handkerchief soaked in vinegar.

'Oh, ye've got a handcuff on!' she exclaimed when she saw the iron ring around his wrist. Prewett came over to look, and said he would send for a locksmith to release it.

Tabitha was anxious for news of Jeremiah, and her father was able to reassure her about him, for he was now likely to become a local hero. He had quickly found an army officer to come and arrest Pole as the man was in the very act of climbing out of a window he had broken at No 9 Bloomsbury Square. Identified as a ringleader of the riots, he had been taken to the Tower of London to await trial, and Cynthia White was also there.

'That's enough o' talkin' – I'll take yer to yer bed, Miss Tabitha, soon as ye've drunk this,' said Prudence, pouring a cup of weak tea. 'Where shall we put the gentleman, Mr Prewett?'

Townclear was settled down on a straw mattress in a corner of the kitchen, and as soon as it was properly day, Andrew was sent out to fetch Mr Appleyard who gravely regarded the eye and feared that the sight might be affected by the inflammation that had set in. Compresses of witch-hazel bark were ordered, and the apothecary said he would come back to apply a few leeches to reduce the swelling.

Thus began the day which became remembered as Black Wednesday by Londoners. The stories of the mob's atrocities became more and more grotesque as the day progressed. The threat to storm more prisons was carried out, and the Fleet, the King's Bench and the Borough Clink were all burned and their inmates released, though Bedlam remained untouched. A distillery in Holborn, owned by a Roman Catholic, gave the mob a very good reason and excuse for breaking into it and broaching the wooden casks of strong spirit that lay in its vaults.

Nobody at Prewett's had time or attention to give to what was going on in the beleaguered city: there was too much to do in caring for the casualties of it. By midday Prudence took her master aside and told him that Mr Townclear had a high fever and should be properly nursed in a bed, not on the kitchen floor.

'Now that Master Michael's better, he could sleep with Master Andrew again, an' then Mr Townclear could—'

'No, Prudence, Mrs Prewett would never have that – an' Mrs Markham's already got those three hidin' in her home. No, what I'll have to do is ask Silas Holmes if his wife wouldn't mind givin' sleepin' space to young Andrew, and we'll put Townclear in Andrew's bed.'

'But that's in with Tabitha, Mr Prewett!'

'We'll have to move it out. Thomas is at school, so we can find room somehow. Thank heaven I've got yer to help me, my girl,' he added with a sigh, for he sadly missed Tabitha.

That afternoon young Mrs Townclear came quietly into Prewett's, using the back way, and asked to see her husband. Prudence led her to the room where he lay, and she was shocked by both his appearance and the state of his mind, which was delirious with fever.

'Conor, dear husband, don't you know your wife?' she asked tearfully, holding his burning hand in hers, and wiping his forehead with her lace handkerchief. There was no response; he muttered unintelligibly and stared into space.

'Oh, take me to Tabitha, please do!' Mariette begged, though Prudence was loth to disturb her young mistress from a much-needed rest. Nevertheless she led Mariette into the room where she lay, and Tabitha at once woke up and held out her arms. 'Mariette!'

'Oh, my Tabitha! How glad I am to see you again! Are you feeling better? Oh, Tabitha, Conor is so sick – his eye looks dreadful, and his mind wanders – he does not even know me. What is to be done?' cried the young wife, sitting on the bed and wiping her eyes.

'Come now, my Mariette, remember how brave you were when you were held by that wicked pair. Let me get out of bed – yes, Prudence, I must, I'm much better after a good sleep, and I must see him. Give me your arm, dearest.'

And in spite of Prudence's frowns, she let Mariette lead her to the room where Conor lay. She went straight to his side.

'Conor – Conor dear, don't you know me? And your Mariette? Does your eye hurt very much? How is your poor wrist?' She gently lifted the arm that Appleyard had bandaged after the locksmith had removed the iron cuff, and looked intently into his face.

'Yes . . . yes,' he muttered, his unfocussed eyes running to and fro between the three young women. 'Lord – Lord have mercy on all – on all souls under this roof tonight.'

'Ah, yes, Conor, that's good,' said his wife, nodding. 'That's what kept me safe while I was a captive. I'll say a decade of the Holy Rosary for you now – the Sorrowful Mysteries.'

So Mariette prayed and Tabitha gently bathed his eye in vinegar as his wife's voice rose and fell in soothing repetition. He closed his good eye and gave a half-smile. 'My darlin' dear.'

A shout from the courtyard below demanded their attention. 'They're comin'! The rioters are comin'! They're up there in Bloomsbury Square to burn the houses down!'

Within minutes a great crowd had surged into the Square, and the residents of Orchard Court held their breath, thinking of the St Aubyns and their son-in-law in hiding. They did not doubt that the mob had come to plunder and loot their home at No 9, and then set fire to it, as they had done to so many other homes of Catholics and Catholic sympathizers.

But they were wrong. It was not the St Aubyns' house but Lord Chief Justice Mansfield's which was due for destruction. To the horrified disbelief of the genteel neighbourhood, the porticoed front door was forced open with an improvised battering-ram, and in they poured, shouting for Lord Mansfield and his lady who escaped by the back way only just in time, and fled to their country seat at Hampstead.

The beautiful house that the judge had taken so many years to build up to its present state of excellence was now systematically demolished. The antique furniture, picture gallery, rare manuscripts and law library were summarily destroyed by fires lit in various parts of the house. A bizarre procession was formed, of rioters marching round the square waving priceless ornaments, books, pictures and pieces of furniture, shouting and exulting over the damage they had done. They were preceded by one of their number, a young man capering along like a marionette and banging Lord Mansfield's dinner-gong for all he was worth.

'But why Lord Mansfield's house and not the St Aubyns'?' everybody asked; it was only later that they learned that No 9 had recently acquired a reputation for being haunted, or as one rebel put it, the house was believed to be in the possession of a powerful Romish spirit who guarded its followers and brought bad luck to intruders.

A troop of soldiers arrived when most of the damage had been done, and a sergeant attempted to read the Riot Act to the mob. When this was disregarded, the soldiers levelled their firearms and shot into the crowd, killing or wounding six men and a woman. After this the remainder quickly melted away, leaving the dead and injured on the pavement of the square.

News arrived later of damage done to the Theatre Royal in Drury Lane because it was said that French, Italians and other papists had performed there, but the worst stories of all were about Langdale's distillery on Holborn Hill. Silas Holmes had gone to see the scene from a discreet distance with his brother-in-law, and returned white-faced.

'You never saw anything like it in your life, John,' he told the tailor in awed tones. 'Langdale's house was just one great blazing ball o' fire, but that wasn't the worst. The rabble had got into the vaults by the back way, and the gutters o' the street were running with gin, every crack and fissure of it – men were lying there on the ground, lapping it up, or singing and dancing until they dropped down dead-drunk – or actually dead. Women as well as men, I saw, drinking out o' hats, shoes, pails, anything, and there were poor little children wandering around, looking for their lost parents. And I even saw –' He lowered his voice so that none but Prewett would hear – 'I even saw some of 'em laying senseless, soaked in spirit – and then it *caught fire*, and they blazed like torches. Oh, it was the worst I ever saw o' my fellow men – something I'll never forget.' He shuddered, and then remembered something else. 'And d'you know, I heard too that an army officer, one o' those brave young peacemakers was killed in the line o' duty last night, quite close to Newgate. Stabbed in the neck he was, and his face beaten to a pulp, so's his own mother wouldn't have known him, they said.'

'Such savagery! What times we live in, Silas,' replied the tailor, shaking his head, and wishing his neighbour would stop. He had seen and heard enough of horror in the last few days.

Tabitha and Mariette knew nothing of this apart from the distant shouts as Lord Mansfield's house was sacked; every moment of their time was taken up with nursing Conor who continued to worsen, his one eye wild, his beard unshaven. Appleyard shook his head, and said they must prepare for the worst; meanwhile they sponged his body with wet towels, cooled his forehead with lavender water and gave him wine and water to drink. At night Mariette refused to return to her parents at Mrs Markham's, and she and Tabitha slept on a mattress on the floor of Conor's room, much to Prudence's disapproval.

'Please don't worry, Prudence dear, I'm quite recovered,' Tabitha insisted, and Michael was getting quite cross with his mother for keeping him in bed.

And there in a dream-world of his own, Conor Townclear lay on his bed of sickness, only dimly aware of his surroundings. Soft hands touched him, cooling his fevered body, holding a cup to his dry lips, gently removing his nightshirt and replacing it with another, clean and freshly laundered. A man came and sat beside him, speaking quietly, removing the bandage from his eye and bathing it with something astringent; a glass jar was opened, and a basin held to his face, and he felt three or four small pricks as something soft and wet was applied to the area around his eye. The man's voice murmured, the women's voices replied, the application was removed and the eye re-bandaged. The pain in his wrist was lessening, but he felt sick and light-headed as the soft hands smoothed his pillow, and a sweet voice intoned the Our Father and Ave Maria in Latin and French. He heard the consoling words of a psalm:

'I sought the Lord, and he heard me, and delivered me from all my fears . . . this poor man cried, and the Lord heard him, and saved him out of all his troubles. The angel of the Lord encampeth round about them that fear him, and delivereth them.'

Conor Townclear was waited upon by angels, and what man would not be content, even if death hovered near? He heard their heavenly voices murmuring as he drifted into sleep.

That night the fires burned themselves out. On Thursday the King took strong measures, and the army was called out in force, with extra regiments of cavalry and foot from the surrounding counties. An attack made upon the Bank of England was decisively repelled, and the militia were aided by bank clerks who made bullets, it was said, from melted-down inkpots. This overwhelming defeat marked the end of the reign of terror inspired by the Gordon Riots; it passed as quickly as it had arisen on the previous Friday, and the end came with the arrest of Lord George Gordon who was taken to the Tower, accused of high treason.

Suddenly it was over: suddenly London was safe again, and Catholics who had fled from their homes began to return. The Comte and Comtesse de St Aubyn, wearied by their close confinement in Mrs Markham's coal cellar and the little room on the ground floor, made their way back to their home, thankful to find it substantially undamaged, but appalled by the ruin of Lord Mansfield's, inflicted upon him simply because of his sympathy and tolerance towards them and other members of different religions.

Madame la Comtesse was never to feel secure again, but railed against the barbarism of the English as she saw it, and begged her husband to take her and their daughter and son-in-law to live in the pretty and peaceful countryside of Compiègne. The Comte urged that they should wait for a while to see how life settled after the rebellion. They had enjoyed nine profitable years in Bloomsbury, and he had good connections in London. Conor, if he survived, had a home and employment here, and might not want to live in France, in which case they would have to part with Mariette, an outcome none of them wished for, so for the time being, the Comtesse had to comply with her husband's opposition to an immediate departure to France.

Conor Townclear opened his one eye and demanded to know where in God's name he was, and what day it was. His two ministering angels had turned into his wife and the woman who was her friend and maid. Their smiles of joy were wonderful to see, greeting him back to the land of the living and his rightful mind again. The fever had left him, and it was Sunday, the eleventh day of June, and church bells were ringing. The swelling and inflammation around his right eye had healed, but he could only see a blur out of it, and Mr Appleyard recommended that an eye surgeon should be called to give an opinion on the likelihood of the restoration of sight.

The St Aubyns took him into their home with their daughter, and Tabitha stayed with her parents until the Townclears returned to their home in Gerrard Street, which took place a week later; on her nineteenth birthday she was to accompany them to take up her previous situation as Mrs Townclear's friend and personal maid.

But before she left she had to face Rob Drury.

On her birthday eve her father sent Andrew to ask her to come to the cutting room, and guessing that Rob Drury had arrived to ask for her hand in marriage one more time, she obeyed the summons at once. Wearing a plain grey housegown and a white linen cap that covered her hair, she entered the room. It was evening, and the shop was closed, but taking advantage of the midsummer daylight, John and Jeremiah Prewett had been doing some after-hours work on important orders.

Sure enough, Rob Drury was there, dressed in a light, sand-coloured jacket and buff breeches; his hat lay on a chair. His face was stern, and so, thought Tabitha, must hers be. She had always liked Robin since he first began to train as her father's apprentice at fourteen, when she had been ten. A lot had happened in her life since then: she had gone to boarding-school for four years, and lost the broad London accent of her parents: she had met the St Aubyns, aristocratic émigrés, and become an inseparable friend of their daughter, in fact her life had been changed on the day she met the French girl. Then when Conor Townclear had come courting Mariette, Tabitha had been their bridesmaid, and had so far shared their home as Mrs Townclear's maid.

'Here's Mr Drury to see yer, Tabitha,' said her father seriously. 'I'll leave yer both here in the cutting room, for 'tis as good a place as any to discuss such matters as he has to speak of.' He looked from one to the other, and added, 'Tabitha, I hope ye'll show some sense, and make a good man happy, for that's where yer best hope lies. Right, then I'll leave yer.'

He went out, closing the door behind him. The young man and the girl faced each other.

'I won't beat about the bush, Tabitha. This is my last word to yer, unless ye've had a change o' mind since I last spoke.'

Drury did not smile, though his clasped hands betrayed his nervousness. She inclined her head, inviting him to continue, though her heart sank at the thought of his disappointment.

'I want to hear it from yer own lips, Tabitha, the reason yer won't agree to accept my love and marry me. I'm a respectable tailor, skilled in the craft taught me by yer own father. That makes us equals, an' we follow the same faith we were taught by the Church of England. There's every reason to expect that we'd be happy, if yer could only love me –' He hesitated, and his voice shook for a moment, then he cleared his throat and continued – 'If yer could only love me half as much as I – as I've loved you for the past three years.'

'Oh, Rob,' she said, shaking her head. 'Oh, Robin, ye've been too good to me.'

'Maybe I have, maybe I've let yer step on me, to use me, to – but Tabitha, I'll forgive yer an' go on my knees to yer if ye'd only say yer love me.'

His words seemed to hang in the dusty air of the cutting room. There was not another sound to be heard.

'Rob, I'm so sorry, I can't marry you.'

He made an impatient sound, a sort of 'Pah!' and waved his hands in dismissal.

She said again, 'I can't marry you.'

'Then let me ask yer this, Tabitha. D'yer love that French girl more 'n a man who loves yer and wants to marry yer?'

150

'I – yes, I suppose I do. I've always been very close to – to Mrs Townclear, from the day we met.'

'And let me ask yer this. D'yer love her husband, the Irishman?'

'Yes, I'm close to him, too.'

'Yer love a married couple, then? An' what about them, do they say they love yer an' want yer to live with them as a sort o' second wife?'

'I don't know, Rob. They do need me, I'm sure o' that.'

'Then it's unnatural, it's not right,' he said emphatically. 'The Bible teaches that marriage is between one man and one woman – an' anythin' else is wrong.'

'The Old Testament of the Bible shows that men were allowed more than one wife,' she answered with a half-smile. 'King David, King Solomon, Samuel's parents – and Jacob had Leah and Rachel—'

'An' it caused 'em nothin' but trouble, as I remember – an' that was in the olden times, before our Lord's life on earth. It wasn't allowed after that,' he said impatiently. 'I wouldn't ever want anybody else but *you*, Tabitha, nor would I share yer with any other. That couple won't want yer when they start havin' children!'

'How can you be sure? They might want me even more, to look after the children. Mariette's delicate, and—'

'Oh, I've no time for this foolery!' he broke in, hitting the table with his fist. 'Ye're makin' a terrible mistake, Tabitha. That pair'll break yer heart between 'em, just wait an' see if they don't, just as ye've broken mine. Well, there's no point in stayin'. Tell yer father I did me best to try an' talk some sense into yer, but there's nothin' else to say now but goodbye.' He picked up his hat, and did not hold out his hand to her.

'Rob, I—'

'I don't want to hear any more. Goodbye, Tabitha.'

He was gone, and she was left standing alone in the cutting room. She would have to face her father's reproach and her mother's angry contempt – but by this time tomorrow she would be back at No 21 Gerrard Street with her dearest friends, and at that thought her heart lifted.

Tabitha stood at the window of her little room with its connecting door to the master bedroom, and breathed in the warm evening air with satisfaction. Soho was a much more interesting neighbourhood than Bloomsbury. Poets, artists and musicians found good company in its taverns and coffee houses, as did men of letters like old Dr Johnson and Mr Boswell, and forward looking philosopher-politicians like Mr Burke who was a neighbour at No 37, a friend of Mr Shenstone who had become a friend of Mr Townclear, and was much concerned about the loss of sight in his librarian's right eye. Tomorrow Tabitha would be helping Mariette to give a little dinner party to introduce Mr Shenstone to the Comte and Comtesse de St Aubyn – and she herself would sit down with them at the table for six, to be waited on by Joe Bartlett in a smart dove-grey livery, and Deborah in a simple gown with an apron and a ruched cap with an impressively high crown. Mrs Clark would labour in the kitchen, assisted by little Minnie, and they would all be paid an extra shilling for their services. Tabitha smiled to herself: the next dinner party would be for Mrs Markham, in recognition of her courage in providing the St Aubyns with a refuge. Townclear wanted to invite Mr and Mrs Prewett, but it was rather awkward, as Mrs Prewett had refused to shelter the St Aubyns, and they could hardly invite the husband without the wife. Tabitha knew that her mother would not accept, anyway. Conor was unconcerned, and said he had become friendly with two gentlemen who regularly took dinner at the Rose of Normandy, and they would be delighted to meet the beautiful Mrs Townclear and her friend. Dear Conor! Life was good . . .

Joe Bartlett's bravery on the night of the storming of Newgate, and his care for Miss Prewett had endeared him to the Townclears. He had managed to escape arrest by the redcoats, and made his way back to his mother's dwelling in a courtyard off the Strand, but finding her engaged with a gentleman client, he had returned to Gerrard Street and stayed there with the three female servants who had received a message from the St Aubyns to keep house until the return of Mr and Mrs Townclear.

Life was not quite the same as it had been before the riots. Miss Prewett now occupied a position as Mrs Townclear's companion, and had to be treated with the same deference as the mistress. Mrs Clark had to keep a civil tongue in her head when Miss Prewett gave her an order, though Tabitha some-times thought she saw an odd look in the cook's eye, and wondered if the woman suspected any kind of special under-standing with the master . . .

A month had elapsed since the end of the riots, but the after-math was still to come: at least two hundred were known to have lost their lives, but the real figure was believed by some to be nearer twice that number, taking into account the deaths by burning and suffocation, those who had been trapped in cellars or had leaped from roofs of burning houses, and those dead after the orgy at Langdale's distillery.

And now began a final reckoning: the punishments meted out to the ringleaders. Lord George Gordon was tried and found guilty of high treason by his peers, but was acquitted on grounds of insanity. Nathaniel Pole, the Reverend Sands and Cynthia White, along with some twenty-two others, were found guilty and hanged. Some of these executions were carried out on a platform erected outside the ruined Newgate prison, but a number were performed at the places where their crimes had been committed, and two young men were hanged on a gibbet set up in Bloomsbury Square in front of what remained of Lord Mansfield's house. John Prewett reported to his daughter that a huge number of sightseers had filled the square to watch the proceedings, and Tabitha was thankful not to be in the vicinity. However, she was in for a shock when a gibbet was erected at the end of Gerrard Street and crowds came to witness the hanging of the ostler, Ned, who was found guilty of betraying known Catholics for money. This was a great shock to Joe Bartlett who had looked on Ned as a friend, and he had no stomach for watching the young fellow's end. Tabitha sympathized with him, and when they talked about their experiences of the riots and he asked her outright if she had suffered harm at the hands of the redcoat on the night of Tuesday, the sixth of June, she told him she'd had a very narrow escape, rescued in the nick of time by Mr Townclear, just released from Newgate, who when warned by Joe that 'she' was in danger from a redcoat, had thought Joe meant his wife.

'Cor! That must've been a bad moment for yer, Miss, an' I'm sorry I wasn't able to 'elp yer, 'cause 'e was too big for me, an' 'ad a sword. What 'appened to 'im, d'yer know?'

Tabitha knew that she must never divulge the secret that

she and Conor shared, and replied that the redcoat had run off at the sight of Conor.

Joe did not mention the piercing screams he had heard coming from the burnt-out shop, for fear of embarrassing her, nor did he say anything about the report of a murdered redcoat's body discovered the following morning.

Tabitha never told anybody, and Conor told only his priest in the Confessional, and was given Absolution.

When Tabitha and her father were talking about the hangings, he told her gravely that his former apprentice Will Feather who had joined the army and was thought to be in America, had in fact been brutally done to death outside Newgate. She shivered and lowered her eyes.

'He wasn't a good lad, Tabitha, in fact he was a scoundrel, the way he treated that poor girl Nan – but he didn't deserve a death like that while he was defendin' law-abiding citizens against the rioters,' John Prewett said heavily. 'I wonder if his murderer – or murderers – have been brought to justice and hanged like so many o' the others.'

The words chilled Tabitha to the heart. It was something her good father would never know.

But now it was time to put the past behind, and look ahead to the bright future that stretched before her: years of happy daily contact with her two dearest friends.

Ten

1784

April had come again, bringing Mariette's twenty-third birthday and the fourth anniversary of her wedding to Conor Townclear. The little châtelaine, as Tabitha affectionately called her, sat at her dressing table with a pencil and paper, planning the guest list for the next lively dinner party at 21 Gerrard Street; invitations to dine with the Townclears were much sought after.

'Of course there will be my parents, and we must have somebody who will bring cheer to Maman,' she said as Tabitha combed out a strand of golden hair and pinned it in position at the back of her head. Minnie hovered near, being the personal lady's maid of both the mistresses, but Miss Prewett always dressed Mrs Townclear's hair.

'Well, there's always your devoted admirer,' said Tabitha, combing through another tress, and Mariette smiled, for dear Mr Shenstone openly enjoyed her company and pronounced her the most delightful hostess in London. 'He'll be happy to be a spare gentleman.'

'Oh, there's no lack of gentlemen at my table, with Conor's friends from Fleet Street and the debating society. And Mr Burke – in fact we'll need more ladies. Oh, Tabitha, do you think that Mrs Robinson might accept an invitation?'

'Hm. She's beautiful enough, I dare say, but she's got an actress's reputation, and might introduce a breath of scandal to your virtuous table,' teased Tabitha. 'Would the Prince of Wales have to be invited, too?' She exchanged a wink with Minnie, who smiled.

'Oh, don't be silly, his day was over years ago – well, two years, at least. Her name's now being linked with a Colonel Tarleton, he's a distinguished war hero, and very handsome.'

'Which war?'

'Why, the war against the American colonies, of course, the one we've just won.'

'How strange, Mrs Townclear, I thought the Americans won it. They've got their independence, haven't they?'

'How provoking you can be, Miss Prewett – and you're pulling my hair. Whatever you say, I shall send an invitation to Mrs Robinson and the Colonel – although now I come to think of it, there have been hints lately in the *Morning Post*, of – er – a friendship between her and Mr Charles James Fox, no less. You probably would not know of him, Miss Prewett, but he is a rising star, a young politician of the Whig persuasion, a brilliant talker and wit – ah, he would be an acquisition indeed!'

'He'd have to be extremely brilliant to outshine Mr Townclear for wit,' replied Tabitha drily. 'And by what I've heard about his big belly and black beard and double chin, Mr Townclear would win hands down on the point of looks, even with his eyepatch!'

This was too much for Minnie, who started to giggle, and all three young women collapsed in peals of good-natured laughter. Mariette's handsome, easy-going Irish husband had a charm that was all his own, and was universally liked, though men might envy his popularity and his beautiful wife, as renowned for her virtue as the lovely Mary Robinson was for her generosity with her favours.

'And we must have Lady Farrinder and Mr and Mrs – er – remind me of Hester's husband's name.'

'Mr Richard Leveret,' supplied Tabitha. 'D'you think she'll be all right to attend an evening dinner? She was such a size when we saw her last, poor girl, and looked so tired.'

Mariette shrugged and raised her eyebrows. 'It is for her to decide. Perhaps she will have the child by then, who can tell? The same applies to my good sister-in-law, Moira Seymour and that dull husband of hers – though she's not due to be confined until September, is she?'

Tabitha agreed. Moira Townclear's stated determination to find herself a husband in London had resulted in her catching the eye of a bank clerk at one of her brother and sister-in-law's social evenings, and within a year she and Mr George Seymour had married and were now expecting their first child. Her expectations of a busy social whirl of visits, theatre trips and shopping in fashionable Bond Street had been somewhat dashed by her stolid husband's lack of interest in the life of the *bon ton*, and finding herself expecting a child so soon, she had been thankful to have Conor and Mariette reasonably near to her home in Margaret Street.

'Poor Moira, she was perhaps a little too quick to take the first chance that came her way,' mused Mariette. 'I suppose she would have accepted anybody to get away from Tahilla and brother Bernard and that breeding mare that he has married. Is it number three or number four we are waiting to have news of? Townclear Hall must be like a farm indoors as well as out!'

She smiled at Tabitha's reflection in the looking glass, not appearing to notice the slight shadow that passed across her friend's face. 'Anyway, Tabitha my love, you will soon be able to indulge yourself in playing with two pretty little children, the Leveret and the Seymour!'

Tabitha returned her smile, for she knew better than to say

how much she longed to play with children of Conor's and Mariette's, her dearest friends. It was to her that Conor turned with his monthly disappointments, the news that Mariette had got her 'terms' again, and so his hopes of conception had once again been washed away in the menstrual flow. Mariette tended to be irregular in her painful menses, and on one occasion when thirty-five days had passed, Conor had been unable to eat or sleep for the suspense. And when the thirty-sixth day brought the hated flow of blood again, keeping Mariette in bed, he had secretly wept on Tabitha's shoulder as they sat together in the parlour downstairs. All around them couples seemed to be conceiving with ease, but there was never happy news for the Townclears in London to match the genial fecundity of the Tahilla branch.

'People must be wonderin' whether I can do it, Tabitha,' he confided wretchedly. 'It's a disgrace to a man if he can't give his wife a child.'

'I pray for you both every Sunday and oftener,' she told him. 'Madame la Comtesse has told her to eat apples every day, and instructed me to make an infusion of raspberry leaves for her to drink. Have you—?' She hesitated, but she and Conor were close friends and not unused to discussing intimate matters that concerned their beloved Mariette, so she continued, 'Have you spoken to Mr Davey at all?'

Mr Davey was the apothecary who lived in Gerrard Street and was consulted by the household at No 21, including the servants.

'Yes, and there's little he can suggest, seemin'ly,' Conor answered glumly. 'A steady way o' life, apples and other fresh fruit, though they're not in season now – and to take exercise every day, but not too much, and avoid gettin' tired. He mentioned that the leaves of the tansy can be eaten in a salad to encourage conception, and advised me to purchase some plants from a nursery garden.'

'The midwife who attends Mrs Leveret tells her to boil the roots of the motherwort, and said something else about the mandrake root,' said Tabitha doubtfully.

Conor gave a short, rueful laugh. 'Accordin' to Davey, and he doesn't believe it, the mandrake root encourages passion in men, and increases their – er – ability. That's not our problem, Tabitha, I can assure ye. I mean, not for me it isn't.'

Poor Conor did not say that his undoubted passion was sometimes chilled by the beautiful Mariette's lack of response to him, or that making love to her must be similar to doing it with a marble statue. Not even to Tabitha could he say such a thing. He sighed, for it had been four years since he'd last set eyes on Bernard, and he often thought of visiting his childhood home to meet his two little nieces, Siobhan and Sorcha: but Mariette showed no interest in going to Ireland, and he thought that perhaps the presence of the children would be distressing to her, and with another on the way . . . he guessed that the sisters-in-law would have little in common.

Apart from the one obvious lack, the household in Gerrard Street was a cheerful one, with an easy atmosphere and frequent laughter. Mrs Clark had mellowed over the four years, and Deborah had proved to be a reliable girl, though she was putting on rather a lot of weight. Minnie at twenty was a delight, and never tired of hearing her two ladies bantering with each other and commenting on local news. 'Dearest Mariette' and '*ma chère* Tabitha' became 'Mrs Townclear' and 'Miss Prewett' when they disagreed over something, but in fact they never once exchanged a truly cross word, nor did they with the master or he with them.

There had been additions to the staff. With Minnie promoted to lady's maid, another girl, Molly, had been taken on to help in the house, and Conor had bought a black boy aged about twelve or thirteen from a trader who had purchased half a dozen from a slave ship owner in Bristol, to meet a fashionable craze for owning black pages. The Townclears' boy had been called Cocoberry by his temporary owner, but the Townclears had shortened this to Berry, and the thin, bewildered boy discovered, as Minnie had on her arrival, that this was a good place to be. There was food, there was friendliness and a kindly interest that touched his sad heart – and after a while he found that he could laugh again, and even sing. Mrs Clark was heard to say that the boy was as spoiled as Mrs Townclear's cat that had come from Bloomsbury Square at the time of the riots, and was now a fat, contented creature who actually slept on the matrimonial four-poster bed. Berry had his own truckle-bed on wheels, stored under Mr Bartlett's bed in the little ground-floor room off the kitchen at the back, and the young butler taught him his duties, and showed him how to dress to the best advantage, in an English waistcoat, jacket and breeches with silver buckles on his shoes and a colourful turban on his head. Berry became a favourite with the many visitors to Gerrard Street, especially to Mr and Mrs Prewett who did not attend the dinner parties but came to take tea with Miss Prewett and the Townclears on Sunday afternoons. Mrs Prewett was especially kind to him, and brought little tit-bits, biscuits and honey cakes that she had baked for him. She was much younger than Mr Prewett, and always smiling and good-humoured. Miss Tabitha called her Prudence instead of Mother, but they were good friends.

Tabitha could not help noticing how much happier her father had become, though there had been some talk about how quickly he had re-married after Martha's miserable death from a growth of the breast that had spread and smelled dreadfully. Prudence had nursed her through the illness that Mr Appleyard said could only end in death, and this had come with merciful suddenness early in 1783, when Martha had fallen and broken both legs; Mr Appleyard had explained that the growth had probably spread to her bones, and hastened her death. Thomas had left the Reverend Wyatt's school that year, and was now assisting Silas Holmes in his bookshop. Andrew was still at school, and the big surprise had been Jeremiah's rather hasty wedding to Betty Topham, who had soon presented him with a little boy, John; a baby which poor Martha had not lived to see, but who was a joy to his grandfather. Prewett had set up his son and daughter-in-law in a small house off Southampton Row, and soon after had taken Prudence as his second wife.

'When Jeremiah left, there was talk that I was livin' with Prudence,' he told Tabitha. 'Then when I thought I'd put it right by marryin' her, there was more talk about bein' too quick after yer mother's funeral. All I can say, my girl, is that Prudence has made me a good wife, an' she's a good mother to Michael.' He sighed. 'She'll most likely have care o' him when I've gone.'

Michael was now in his mid twenties, a likeable fellow who not only swept his father's cutting room but regularly kept Orchard Court clean and free from dog's excrement. In autumn he swept up the leaves, and in winter he shovelled up the snow to make pathways to the various shops. He occasionally ran errands for the shopkeepers, and was called upon to help lift or carry heavy weights, but he seldom strayed further than the Court, for fear of being followed and teased by children of the lower sort, or tormented by loud-mouthed youths who thought it good sport to shout obscenities and make mock-accusations that he had tried to kiss their women. Prudence was kind and firm with him, insisting that he kept regular hours and got on with his tasks, for he was inclined to dawdle if not supervised.

'There were those who thought I'd've married Mrs Markham,' Prewett further confided to Tabitha. 'And to be sure, I could've done, an' I reckon she'd've had me, in fact I think she was a bit – yer know, surprised-like, when I took Prudence, 'specially after she'd took in the St Aubyns at the time o' the riots, when Martha wouldn't have 'em. But I reckoned Prudence'd be better with Michael. My poor son can't help bein' the way he is, and he might've been as clever as any o' the others, only Martha was a long time givin' birth, an' his bottom came out first. The midwife said he might be an idiot on account o' that, and in fact he could've been a lot worse than he is. It was nobody's fault, but it's hard on a family.'

Tabitha could only press her father's hand and say that she was entirely happy for him in his second marriage, and that Prudence was a gem. Nevertheless, she suffered a pang when on the Sunday afternoon following the birthday dinner party, the Prewetts came to tea as usual, and Prudence beckoned her aside.

'I got somethin' to tell yer, Tabitha, an' I hope ye'll be happy for me.' She blushed as she spoke, and Tabitha knew what she was going to say: she also blushed, and involuntarily put her hands to her face. Oh, not another . . .

'Yer don't mind, do yer, Tabitha? Yer father's happy about it, even though he says he's a bit old to be a father again, at fifty-five. I'm thirty now, an' I never did dream that it'd ever happen to me – a *mother* – oh, Tabitha, say ye're pleased for us!'

'O' course I am, dear Prudence, it's just that it's a bit of a – a shock, that's all—' Tabitha kissed her stepmother, and explained away her tears as being an overflow of emotion. But why should the news be a shock? A healthy, newly married woman of thirty was more likely than not to find herself expecting a child. But why, oh, *why* could not a married woman of twenty-three be equally blessed? As her father had said about Michael's damaged brain, it simply was not fair.

Was there anything more that could be done? Tabitha knew that women still consulted 'wise women' who were usually no more than gypsies and fortune tellers, and she had always looked upon such superstitious dabbling as foolish, and possibly even dangerous, being condemned by the Church and Bible. Nevertheless, when sufficiently desperate, the most outlandish remedies may be tried, and Tabitha had heard about just such an old wise-woman from a streetseller from whom she bought a brass ring. She was known as Mother Morrison, a former midwife who had also been known to help women to miscarry unwanted children; she lived in a cottage on a stretch of marshy land to the south of St George's Fields.

Tabitha made up her mind: it was worth a try. Without telling anyone where she was going, she put on her hooded cloak and set out to visit Mother Morrison.

She found her a formidable character indeed. If ever a woman qualified to be called a witch, it was she, and a hundred years before, or even less in some parts of the country, she would have stood a fair chance of being denounced and burned at the stake. As it was, she was still discreetly consulted about women's matters, and there were those who testified to her amazing powers. Tabitha introduced herself as Mrs Thomson, and wore the brass wedding ring.

The cottage was clean and comfortable, though there were some strange ornaments, like the child's skull on the mantelpiece, and a large map of the heavens, showing the twelve signs of the Zodiac. True to tradition, an amber-eyed black cat looked up at Tabitha in a way that made her nervous: unlike Mariette's sleek specimen of her race, this lean, agile creature seemed to be able to see into Tabitha's thoughts.

'Now, then, Mrs Thomson, let's sit down,' said Mother Morrison, putting away the sovereign that Tabitha had passed into her brown palm, and lighting a short clay pipe. 'Ah, yes, that's My Lady Moon lookin' at yer. She lets me know who's tellin' the truth an' who ain't. Ha!'

Tabitha realized that she meant the cat, and blushed scarlet. The old woman gave a deep chuckle. 'Ha! Most women who

161

comes to see me says they're doin' it for a friend, but *you* say it's yerself we're talkin' about. Right, then, to business. What d'yer want o' me, Mrs Thomson?'

'If – if My Lady Moon has told you that I'm really asking on behalf of a friend, I'd better admit it straight away,' Tabitha stammered. 'Only I can never, never tell the name o' my dearest friend, the lady I – I want to help.'

Mother Morrison inclined her head, her black mob-cap fastened by strings under her chin. 'Go on, then. Is she in trouble?'

'N-no, not that sort o' trouble, Mother. She's been married for four years, with as yet no sign of a child.'

'Ha! So that's the way of it.' The old woman then asked several questions about the friend's age and her husband's age. She inquired about the friend's menstrual cycle and her general health which Tabitha described as delicate. Was there any reason to believe that the man had ever got a child with another woman? When Tabitha replied that she was sure he had not, Mother Morrison pointed out that the barrenness might be on his side. Did the couple go to church and pray for a child? Tabitha replied that they most certainly did, and the husband had told her of their prayers offered up to St Catherine and St Brigit.

'Ha! So they're of the Romish faith?'

'Yes, Mother, they are. I am not, but I regularly pray to the Father, Son and Holy Ghost in my own church.'

The old woman was silent for a while, puffing on her pipe, and when at length she spoke, Tabitha felt that she was speaking nothing less than the truth.

'I could sell yer various cures and give yer a handful o' potions, Mrs Thomson, but the truth is that it's difficult, an' yer friend might get her wish in another year or two, maybe not. They could try lyin' naked under an oak tree an' doin' their business on the stroke o' midnight. With summer comin' in, it'll be easier than in the wind an' the rain, but yer might find it difficult to persuade her.'

'Oh, I'd put it to the husband, and let him explain it to her – and tell her where I got it from,' replied Tabitha, though her heart sank at such a drastic remedy. And it smacked of paganism.

'Ha! So ye're on good terms with the man, then?' Mother

Morrison raised her eyebrows. '*He* tells yer they pray to these women saints?'

'I'm on very good terms with them both, Mother – the best o' terms,' replied Tabitha simply.

'Ha! Well, now then – let him tell her about midnight under the oak, an' let 'em try it. May's a good month, an' they could try a couple o' times, between her menses. And then, Mrs Thomson – *then*, if no result's forthcomin', yer might have to think again.'

'But what then?' asked Tabitha in dismay. '*What* might I have to think again?'

The old woman stared long and intently into Tabitha's face. 'Think, think, Mrs Thomson. Yer answer might be for her to bear him a child in the house of a friend. That's all I can say now, I can see no further, and I'll bid yer good day.'

She rose from her chair and tapped out her pipe aganst the empty grate.

'But I don't understand you, Mother,' protested Tabitha, also standing up.

'Ha! I think yer will, Mrs Thomson. Good day to yer.'

'Ah, Tabitha, to think o' yer goin' to a witch for our sake.' Conor Townclear looked sad and grateful and wryly amused all at once, but shook his head. 'I couldn't ask it of her, not such a heathenish act. God knows the sacred duties o' the matrimonial bed are not always easy to carry out, but this would surely be impossible.'

Tabitha looked up at him pleadingly and took his arm in hers as they walked in Marylebone Park in the April sunshine.

'She said that May's a good time, Conor. Is it not worth trying? Shall I have a word with her?'

'Well, I'm certain *I* couldn't, for I'd only see shock an' unbelief on her face – an' disgust, which wouldn't make my work any easier. An' where in God's name can we find an oak tree in Soho?'

'We'd have to go to a quiet woodland place,' said Tabitha who had been giving the matter a great deal of thought. 'Lady Farrinder's estate at Heathfield House—'

'Good heavens, d'ye mean we should take that lady into our confidence and ask her to let us use her garden for such pagan goin's-on?'

163

'Remember that Lady Farrinder helped to bring about your marriage, and invited you to spend your wedding trip at that beautiful house,' Tabitha persisted. 'She must be wondering why there has been no – er – news since then.'

'Sure, an' the King an' Queen, the Prime Minister an' all the Whigs an' Tories must be wonderin' the same,' he answered, turning down the corners of his mouth in a grimace. 'But the good lady's waitin' daily, hourly, for news of her daughter's confinement, an' she surely wouldn't want us descendin' on her to play at bein' pagans in her woods!'

'But don't you see, Conor, that's even more of a reason for her to want to help – we'll wait until Mrs Leveret's safely delivered, and then you must write to tell Lady Farrinder of your joy at her becoming a grandmother. And in the same letter, tell her of your own lack, and ask her for the favour.'

'Ye'd have to help me write such a letter, Tabitha. But oh, I could never ask such a thing o' Mariette! I simply couldn't bring myself to form the words. If anybody can put it to her in such a way as to bring her round to it, 'tis likely to be yeself.'

'I'll speak to her, then, Conor. I'll do my best.'

'Oh, Tabitha, Tabitha, ye're a good friend an' more than a friend, nearer to us than a sister.'

He put his arm around her shoulders and drew her close to him. She trembled and closed her eyes as his lips touched her forehead. She could have wept for him.

When news arrived of Mrs Leveret's safe delivery of a fine baby boy, named Richard after his father, Mariette sent a carved wooden rattle for the child, and Conor sat down to compose a letter, aided by Tabitha. First came his felicitations on the happy event, and then he wrote of the disappointment he and Mariette had suffered by remaining childless.

'. . . And so I trust that I may count on Your Ladyship's sympathy towards us in a request. In order to carry out certain advice we have been given, we need the privacy of a woodland at midnight, and an oak tree. We would be accompanied by my wife's companion Miss Prewett whom you know, and we would cause you no inconvenience, but only beg your permission to use your private grounds for this purpose, and that the utmost secrecy be maintained.'

Conor shuddered at what Lady Farrinder might make of

this, but her prompt reply was favourable, for she had in fact felt very sorry for the Townclears in their unfruitful marriage. She cordially invited them to stay at Heathfield House for as long as they liked, and to bring 'dear Tabitha' with them; Mr and Mrs Leveret were at present also staying, so it would be a good opportunity for them to see little Richard.

'As to the other matter,' she wrote tactfully, 'you are perfectly free to use any part of the grounds at any time of day or night.'

'Oh, bless the dear woman!' cried Tabitha, kissing the letter. 'Now we have to put it to our darling Mariette.'

'*You* have to put it to her, Tabitha, not I.'

'It'd be best if you could take yourself away for a night, Conor, so that ye're not in the house when I speak to her.'

'Whatever ye say, Tabitha darlin'. Whatever's best for her.'

He accordingly found himself suddenly summoned to a book auction at Bromley in Kent, and left the next day.

Tabitha now had to inform Mariette of the extraordinary plan that had been made without her knowledge, and win her essential consent to it. It was the hardest part of the exercise, and Tabitha knew that she would have to use every means at her disposal for pleasing and persuading her friend.

On a warm, balmy spring evening Tabitha stood in her nightgown at the window of her room at 21 Gerrard Street: soon she must leave her room and go in to Mariette's. Her heart thudded and she took some deep breaths to calm herself. Suppose she failed? Suppose Mariette was so shocked and horrified by Mother Morrison's suggestion that she banished Conor from even the lawful bed, and ended her friendship with Tabitha? The thought of her reproaches made Tabitha tremble, and she shrank from opening the door into the corridor.

As she stood hesitating in her doubt and indecision, she heard a click and a slight creak as her door opened. She spun round to see her friend in all her pale beauty, smiling and beckoning to her.

'*Ma chère Tabita*, how long must I wait? Are we not sleeping in the same bed tonight?'

'O, Mariette dear, yes, we shall, only – I have something to say to you. Conor wants me to tell you of a plan we want to make, if you will but agree to take part.'

'Come to bed, then, and tell me of it. You know I would do anything for you.'

And when Tabitha hesitantly put the plan to her friend, the reaction was not what she had expected or dreaded. There were some tears, but these were for her childlessness; Tabitha could not bring herself to use the miserable word *barren* – and Mariette was more saddened than shocked by Mother Morrison's suggestion, and the length to which Tabitha had gone for the sake of Conor and herself.

'It is not that I want a child, dearest Tabita,' she said as she lay in her friend's arms. 'I have no wish to have a great belly and feel ill and look ugly, and I have heard – and seen – that the pains of childbirth are a taste of hell – but I know it is what marriage is ordained for, and Conor wants a son. I am a reproach to him, though he has never once reproached me for it.'

'Oh, you poor darling – poor, sweet Mariette,' whispered Tabitha, holding her close.

'To have you and Conor to love is all that I desire on this earth, and we are such a happy household,' Mariette continued. 'All the servants are content to be with us – our own little Minnie and Berry who smiles at me with his big eyes – oh, if only life could always go on as it is now!' She turned and looked up at her friend. 'But do not fret, *chère* Tabitha, I will do as Conor wishes, and accept Lady Farrinder's invitation to stay at Heathfield House. It will have to be at a time when I am without my terms, and I shall wear my silver crucifix to keep away the ancient spirits of the night.'

They were silent for a few minutes, and then Mariette gave a little chuckle. 'I wish I could have seen Conor's face when you told him about Mother Morrison! Only *you* could have talked him over!'

The weather was perfect. The woods were dark and magical, full of the rustlings of the spring night. The great oak, planted in the reign of Queen Elizabeth, stood in a small clearing, its thick roots spreading outwards in a circle above the ground, its new foliage whispering, a home to nesting birds. In the distance the clock on the tower of the old parish church struck the quarter hour before midnight.

The three of them arrived at the clearing, the man carrying

a rolled-up blanket which he put down on the grass. They spoke in low, hurried tones, and the man began to take off his clothes, while one woman helped the other to disrobe, until she was wearing nothing but the cross on a chain around her neck; then picking up the discarded garments, the other woman retreated to a clump of laurels, disappearing into their pitch-black outline.

The man picked up the blanket and led the unclothed woman towards the foot of the spreading oak, an innocent Adam and Eve, for there was no serpent in this English Eden.

She gave a little shiver as they lay down together on the blanket, and he gathered her into his arms, kissing her hair, her face, her lips.

'Are ye cold, my darlin'?' he whispered, running his warm hand down the side of her body as he drew her closer and felt the swelling of his own arousal.

'I am all right, Conor. Do what you have to do,' she answered quietly, closing her eyes. 'May we be blessed in what you wish for.'

'Oh, my darlin' – my precious, my beautiful wife . . .'

He gently shifted his body so that he was lying on top of her, and as the distant chimes of midnight echoed through the still air, he was at one with her. He shuddered, controlling himself, suppressing his own intensity of emotion into a few smothered gasps as he gripped her.

It was over. After a few minutes to regain his breath he rose and helped her to her feet. He picked up the blanket, and led her away from the tree; the other woman, the friend, emerged from the laurel bushes with their clothes. He dressed himself quickly, and the friend dressed the wife, quickly buttoning and hooking with nimble fingers. The man threw the blanket over his shoulder and put his arms around them both as they walked away from the clearing.

Mother Morrison's advice had been taken and acted upon. It was done.

Back at Heathfield House, Mariette went straight to her bed. Tabitha stood for a moment with Conor on the landing, and he saw her dark eyes shining in the glimmer of light from a window.

'Let us pray that this will bring you what you so much long for, Conor,' she whispered.

'May it be so, dearest Tabitha. She was prayin' herself while I loved her, the Ave Maria. She withdraws herself away, ye see, and speaks only to the Blessed Virgin at times like that.'

'Oh, don't say so!' Tabitha clasped her hands together in pity for the man. 'And yet, you see, that is her strength. That's how she protected herself when she was held prisoner by that evil pair. But *you*, Conor, God knows she needs no protecting from *you*!'

'It was ever thus, Tabitha. And who knows, I might still have got her with child. Good night, dear friend. I can never thank ye for all ye've done for us.' He kissed her cheek. 'Good night.'

'Good night, Conor.'

She was alone. Oh, Conor – Conor Townclear!

Whether it was the unusual circumstances, or whether Mariette had been chilled by the night air, the following morning brought her terms again, after only eighteen days.

Eleven

'I am so very sorry about poor Mariette,' Lady Farrinder said quietly to Tabitha. 'If ever she and Conor wish to try – er – to try the experiment again, please assure her that Heathfield House is always available to them.'

Tabitha thanked her, but thought it unlikely that the Townclears would wish to go through the strange ritual for a second time. Conor had returned to Gerrard Street the very next day, leaving Mariette and Tabitha to stay a further few days at Heathfield House, enjoying Lady Farrinder's hospitality and of course admiring the new baby. Hester as a young mother seemed completely different from the fifteen-year-old who had longed to go to school and meet other girls, and Mr Leveret was as proud and attentive as a young husband and father should be.

Mariette stayed in bed the day following the nocturnal ordeal, with the usual painful cramps and the nausea that invariably accompanied her terms.

'There, my love, take a glass of wine and water,' Tabitha said soothingly, having changed the cotton squares soiled with menstrual blood, and sprinkled the pillows with lavender water.

'I am so sorry, *chère* Tabitha,' moaned Mariette, and Tabitha was both touched and saddened that her poor friend felt the need to apologize for something entirely out of her control.

'I can hear the baby crying somewhere in the house,' Mariette went on. 'Wouldn't it be strange if he were *ours*, Tabitha, mine and Conor's! You would be attending to him a hundred times a day, talking to him and being just as proud as Lady Farrinder and Hester!'

'It must be as the Lord sends, dearest Mariette,' Tabitha replied, though in her imagination she could picture such a happy situation very much as her friend described it.

On their return to 21 Gerrard Street, Conor greeted Tabitha with a grimace and said that there had been 'ructions' in the kitchen, and that Mrs Clark had something very serious to say to Mrs Townclear.

'But I told her she wasn't to bother Mrs Townclear with this sort o' problem, Tabitha,' he said with a frown of irritation. 'I told her that Miss Prewett would deal with it and see that the right thing was done – so she'll be comin' to ye with a fine tale, I don't doubt.'

He said no more, but Tabitha did not have to wait long for the unwelcome surprise to be revealed. Joe Bartlett's sheepish looks and Deborah's red eyes and widening girth said it all.

'Speakin' for meself, *I* could see how it was at least a month ago,' said Mrs Clark, arms akimbo. 'There's them as can see what's in front o' their own eyes, and there's them as can't, or won't. Four months gorn already, and I must say I never thought it of *'er*, though I've given all three o' the girls enough warnin'. She'll 'ave to be sent back 'ome to let 'er mother deal with 'er, and as for *'im*, 'e ought to be sent back to *'is* ma an' all!'

Tabitha nodded and thanked her, privately pondering over the best way to deal with the dilemma. She decided to consult Conor about Joe Bartlett who had so much to recommend him as a willing worker and loyal servant who would be sadly missed if he was sent home.

Conor agreed. 'We're forever in his debt, Tabitha, for what he did the night Newgate was stormed. He's behaved badly

169

towards Deborah, though for sure it takes two, and I'll talk very
sternly to him – tell him he ought to be horsewhipped and such-
like, then give him a chance to make good by marryin' the girl,
and look forward to becomin' a father – the lucky young devil.'
He sighed heavily. 'And it'll be meself that pays for the weddin'
and settin' 'em up in a place o' their own, I dare say.'

'Oh, Conor, you're so good! Thank you! Give me leave to
tell Mrs Clark, and she'll have to pretend to be content, though
it will be a slap in the eye for her. And if you speak to Joe,
I'll speak to Deborah. When all is arranged and settled, that
will be the time to tell Mariette.'

But another baby! How could fate be so cruel?

If Joe Bartlett blushed for shame and embarrassment when he
was summoned to Mr Townclear's little study adjacent to the
living room, he blushed an even deeper crimson when he
heard the master's generous proposal: in fact tears came to
his eyes when he was ordered to marry Deborah within a
week at nearby St Anne's Church, and move with her into
modest lodgings in Gerrard Street, from where he could
continue to work for the Townclears by day, and Berry would
take over as house guard at night.

'Miss Prewett tells me that Deborah will be able to work
for another three months at least before she has to leave to
prepare for the birth o' the child,' Mr Townclear went on. 'I'll
let yer have the cost o' the weddin' as a weddin' present, and
start ye off in the lodgin's with a month's rent in advance.
After that ye'll have to take it out o' your wages.'

Conor paused for the manservant to make some kind of
response, but the young man hung his head as he stood like
a disgraced schoolboy on the headmaster's carpet.

'For ye must understand, Bartlett, that I'm not a rich man,
and I have a household to support,' Conor went on. 'Even so,
if ye do your duty towards the girl, I'll be happy to help ye,
and my wife and I want ye to stay.'

'Yes, sir, thank yer,' faltered Joe.

'But if ye were to fail in your duty to marry the girl, ye'd
be dismissed from my service forthwith. D'ye understand me,
Bartlett?'

'Yes, sir, I do, thank yer.'

'Good. Well, then, your next duty is to go to Deborah and ask

170

for her hand in marriage. She's of an age to give ye her answer, though 'twould be polite to visit her parents and ask them also. And – er – apologize to them for the haste while ye're there.'

'Thank yer, Mr Townclear. Very good o' yer, sir.'

'Twill be a quiet weddin', and Miss Prewett will see about arrangin' it with the rector o' St Anne's. Mrs Townclear and I will attend, and ye may invite your mother and Deborah's parents. All right, Joe, that'll be all. Go and find Deborah.'

Conor smiled and held out his hand, but was somewhat taken aback when the young man fell on his knees and kissed the outstretched hand, sobbing out his relief and gratitude after weeks of unrelieved fear and anxiety.

Miss Prewett had made up her mind to be stern with Deborah when she asked the girl to come up to her little sitting room, and to begin by giving her a severe scolding for the unmaidenly behaviour that had resulted in this inconvenience to the whole household; but the girl looked so wretched that all Tabitha's indignation evaporated; she told the girl to sit down beside her on the little sofa and they would have a serious talk. As soon as she was seated, Deborah burst into tears before a word was spoken.

''E said 'ow 'e couldn't afford to marry yet, Miss Prewett, an' said I ought to take castor oil an' clear it out,' she sobbed. ''E said 'ow I couldn't be sure, seein' as it'd only been the once – an' 'ow we'd bofe get into awful trouble wiv the master an' missus.'

'Oh, Deborah, don't cry – it isn't that bad, and I've got good news for you,' Tabitha said, putting an arm around the girl's heaving shoulders. 'Let me tell you what Mr Townclear has said to Joe Bartlett.'

And she proceeded to repeat the offers that had been made to Joe, and advised Deborah to go and wash her face, comb her hair and make herself presentable when Joe came to ask her for her hand. The quiet wedding at St Anne's was mentioned, and the invitations that would be sent to Joe's mother and Deborah's parents.

'Oh, Lord, me Ma'll half kill me when she knows!' wailed Deborah.

'No, she won't, not when she hears about Mr Townclear's kindness to you both,' replied Tabitha briskly, and as Deborah took in the significance of these words, she managed a wet-eyed smile.

'Just you mark my words, Deborah, a year from now you'll be a happy married woman with a little boy or girl to look after! And there'll be those who'll envy you your blessings!'

'Thank yer, Miss Prewett, but me Ma'll 'ave summat to say, just the same. Worse 'n Mrs Clark, she'll be.'

It was time to tell Mariette about the domestic upheaval, and how it was to be solved. Tabitha chose a moment while her friend was having breakfast in bed. As soon as Mariette understood that Deborah was with child by Joe Bartlett, she put down her spoon in the porridge bowl.

'She could stay here to have the baby if she likes, Tabitha. I'm sure Conor wouldn't mind.'

'But *I* most certainly would, Mariette. I won't have your sleep disturbed by a crying baby at all hours – and I'm sure Mrs Clark wouldn't approve!'

'As you wish, *ma chérie*, you always know best,' replied Mariette wearily, picking up her spoon. Tabitha saw how pale and tired she looked, and went over to enfold her in an embrace.

'Oh, Mariette, my poor love!' There seemed to be nothing else to say, but Mariette had a question to ask of her.

'Tabitha *ma chérie*, did that old wise-woman have anything else to say to you?'

'Er, no, not really.'

'Nothing else to suggest?'

'No, my darling, there was nothing else.'

'Well, I have been thinking that Conor could try again on Midsummer's Eve if Lady Farrinder doesn't mind. I shall be free of the menses by then, and – well, it is said that kind fairies are abroad that night, Queen Mab and her troupe. I don't really believe in it, but if Conor's willing, I'll give it one more try before—' Her voice trembled, and Tabitha gazed anxiously into her face.

'Before what, darling?'

'Nothing. I'll tell Conor that I'm willing to try again.'

The wedding was arranged for the seventh of June, a Monday. Thanks to Miss Prewett's good standing with the rector of St Anne's where she and the servants worshipped every Sunday, permission was given for a quiet early wedding at short notice, at which the curate would preside. They were to gather at ten o'clock that morning for the short ceremony.

Deborah's parents, a Mr and Mrs Pitcher, had been predictably shocked and angered by her news, but their hard feelings had quickly softened at hearing of the generosity of her master and mistress, Roman Catholics though they were. In fact the Pitchers were so gratified by this upturn in Deborah's fortunes, and her future husband's good prospects, that their initial shock turned to happy anticipation of a grandchild.

Joe Bartlett longed for the day to be over. He had suffered agonies of suspense and anxiety since that day in April when Deborah had muttered that she thought she might be carrying a child. At the beginning of May she said she was quite sure of it, and burst into tears because she felt sick and couldn't tell her mother. Too late Joe cursed what had happened one afternoon back in February when he had been left alone with Deborah in the kitchen. Berry had gone out on an errand for their master to Queen Anne Street, and Minnie and Molly were upstairs helping the ladies to make what they called an inventory of the household linen. They were opening chests of sheets, pillowcases and towels, patchwork quilts and such-like handmade treasures, taking them out, unfolding them and exclaiming over the embroidery and crocheted lace edgings, so were not likely to come down again for an hour or two. Joe took the liberty of giving Deborah a sly little kiss on her cheek, and instead of the rebuke he expected, she had put up only a token resistance. He'd kissed her again, this time on her full lips, and had felt them parting under his. He had pressed her up against the long cupboard where Mrs Clark kept her jars of flour, sugar, salt, tea, coffee and spices, and she had let his hands wander down over her ample hips. All sorts of forbidden pleasures now seemed to be possible, even obtainable, and it was only the work of a minute for him to lead her into the little room off the kitchen which he shared with Berry. There on his wooden bedstead with its straw-filled mattress she had let him help himself to her bounty, and it seemed as if he was drowning in her soft warm flesh: a moment of undreamed-of bliss that all too quickly came to an end.

173

'Cor, that was better 'n a slice o' steak pie an' a glass o' stout, Deb,' he'd whispered, kissing her again. 'But we'd better get up now, in case somebody comes down.'

The pair had been shy and awkward with each other for a few days afterwards, and then it seemed to recede into the past and be forgotten, like a dream.

Until that April day when she had murmured her suspicions in his ear, and he had actually knelt down in church the following Sunday to pray – to beg, to implore that she was mistaken. It never once occurred to simple, honest Joe Bartlett to accuse her of having other lovers, nor did he ever question his responsibility for her condition.

And now thanks to the beneficence of the Townclears and the good offices of Miss Prewett, he and Deborah were entering that same church to be made man and wife. He had met Mr and Mrs Pitcher, his future mother and father-in-law who had not had much to say, but told him that Deborah was a good worker, which was more important than looks.

'You must let your mother know, too, Joe,' Miss Prewett reminded him, for he had not mentioned taking Deborah to meet Mrs Bartlett. Instead he called briefly at her tiny dwelling in a court off the Strand, and told her of the forthcoming wedding, to which she was invited.

'The master an' missus 'ave been very good to us, Ma, even though they're Catholics – an' the weddin's on Monday at ten if yer want to come along.'

'Glad to 'ear yer done well for yerself, Joe,' she replied. 'An' I 'ope this girl's goin' to be a good wife. I dunno whevver I'll git to the church, but – er – I'll be thinkin' about yer, me boy.'

She kissed him and offered him a glass of gin and water. He longed to say something more, and awkwardly tried to tell her that he understood how hard her life had been bringing up a son on her own. He wanted to thank her for all she had done, but she had cut him short, saying that she'd only done what any mother would.

'I'm proud o' the way ye've turned out, Joe, an' now all I want is for yer to be 'appy wiv this girl. Tell 'er she's lucky to catch yer! Goodbye, son!'

And that had been that. He hadn't told her of the circumstances of the hasty wedding, because there did not seem to be any need, and she clearly did not intend to come to it.

And Joe was ashamed of himself for feeling relieved.

Mr and Mrs Townclear had invited the bride and groom and their guests to return to 21 Gerrard Street after the ceremony for a wedding breakfast, and Miss Prewett commended Mrs Clark on the excellent fare she had prepared before leaving for the church. Having understood that the errant couple were to be given sympathy rather than censure, the cook rose to the occasion, and the kitchen table fairly groaned under the mounds of home-baked bread, cold mutton and bacon, farmhouse cheeses and sweet pickles; there was also a splendid fruit cake decorated with almond paste and crystallized cherries.

'My word, Mrs Clark, there's enough to feed the five thousand here!' Miss Prewett exclaimed. 'Are you ready to leave now? Mr and Mrs Townclear have already gone with the maids and Berry, and the happy pair are waiting for their hackney cab. Come on!'

In the dim, cool interior of the church the small congregation waited for the arrival of the bridal pair. The Townclears and Miss Prewett sat in a front pew, with Mr and Mrs Pitcher behind them, looking rather self-conscious, while behind them sat Mrs Clark, Minnie, Molly and Berry, his eyes staring round at the memorial statues and intricately carved woodwork. The pews over on the bridegroom's side were empty, and Miss Prewett shook her head sadly to think that Joe's mother had not come to see him married; she wondered if he had any other relatives in the world.

There was no music, and the congregation were prompted by a sign from Miss Prewett to stand when the bride and groom entered through the west door, dressed in their Sunday best. When they began to walk forward, Mr Pitcher left his seat and went to his daughter's side, so the three of them walked up the aisle together, the bride's father in the middle, to stand before the curate who waited for them with his open prayer book.

'Dearly beloved brethren, we are gathered together here in

175

the sight of God—' he began, and at that moment there was a disturbance at the back of the church: heads turned to see two garishly dressed women, one with a large yellow bonnet and the other wearing a straw hat ornamented by three long and stringy feathers.

'Oh my Gawd, it's started, Sal – we'd better sit oursel's down quick – oops!' said she of the bonnet in a loud voice, pushing her companion unsteadily towards a pew.

'Can yer see the bride, Peg? Can't see nuffin' from 'ere,' answered Sal, and gave a hiccup.

'She ain't wearin' white, she's up there in front o' the parson – sssh, 'e's talkin' to 'em.'

For a minute or two there was silence, and the curate continued. When he reached the question, 'Who giveth this woman to be married to this man?' Mr Pitcher pushed his daughter forward, bowed and returned to his pew.

'Cor, looks as if 'e's changed 'is mind an' ain't goin' to marry 'er after all,' marvelled Peg, her bonnet shaking with her head movements.

'Oh, no, my Joe'd never change 'is mind, not when 'e's said 'e will,' answered the woman called Sal, and gave a groan. The congregation began to fidget, and the women received some very disapproving looks. The curate looked towards Mr Pitcher, raising his eyebrows in a mute appeal, whereupon that gentleman left his seat and strode towards the unwelcome visitors.

''Ere, you two – git out of it, git yer arses orf them pews an' out with yer,' he ordered, grabbing Peg's arm and hustling her towards the door. She turned round and hissed at him.

'Bloody shame on yer! Poor ol' Sal, she only wanted to come an' see 'er Joe git married! 'Er only son, 'im she brought up all on 'er own, an' yer won't even let 'er come to 'is—'

'Shut up, yer drunken whore, git out of it!' And out of the door hurtled Peg, her sunbonnet falling off her head as she landed on the grass of the churchyard.

Sal stood swaying beside the pew, and when she saw Mr Pitcher swiftly returning to give her the same treatment, she let out a shriek, but Mr Townclear reached her before the other man.

'Ye can go back, Pitcher, I'll deal with this one,' he said firmly, and led Sal by the arm to the west door, where he went outside with her. Peg had picked up her skirts and run away at the double, but Townclear sat Sal down on a gravestone and stood over her.

'Am I to understand that ye're Joe Bartlett's mother?' he asked her, not unkindly.

She groaned, gave another hiccup and whispered, 'Yes, sir. He's my boy, an' a good one.'

'I know, he's been in my service for the past four years, and he does ye credit, Mrs Bartlett. But the fact is, ye see, ye do him no honour by comin' here today in this state. Look, here's a guinea, take it and go back home. And keep away from the gin shop. Come on now, get ye goin', they'll be comin' out soon, and won't want to find ye here.'

She raised sodden, tear-drenched eyes to his face and seemed about to say something, but changed her mind and stumbled off across the churchyard to Wardour Street, leaving Conor Townclear, his eyes full of pity, watching her departing figure, the feathers streaming out behind her. 'God help her,' he muttered under his breath.

The new Mrs Bartlett had seen the horrified expression on her husband's face during the fracas in church, and not understanding the cause of it, had concluded that some difficult friend or relative had arrived in a state of intoxication to make trouble. Deborah was only too aware of her own good fortune that had saved her from disgrace, and she tightened her hold on her husband's arm as they walked down the aisle, ready to face life together, for better for worse, for richer for poorer, in sickness and in health. 'It's all right, Joe,' she whispered.

Joe certainly needed her love before the day was over, for when Conor Townclear quietly went out to see how Mrs Bartlett had fared after the scene at St Anne's church, he was met by sobbing friends who told him that she had drowned in the Thames at noon, after consuming half a bottle of gin.

'Died of a broken 'eart, she did – 'e was all she 'ad,' said a young prostitute, glaring at him. 'Brought 'im up to be respec'able, an' 'e never even arst 'er to 'is weddin'. 'Ardly ever come to see 'er these last four years or more, fought 'imself too grand. Bastard!'

Conor learned from them that Sarah Bartlett had never been married, and had worked as a prostitute to keep herself and her son; as with so many others of her sort, she had turned to gin to blot out the degradation of her existence, but after Joe had left to make a better life for himself, she had aged and coarsened. And then when he announced his marriage to a fellow-servant of the bountiful Townclears, Conor could understand her thinking that her son had cut himself off from a mother who shamed him – so what more had she to live for?

Mr Townclear sent for the anxious bridegroom on his return, and gently told him the news. He also remarked on how very well Mrs Bartlett had brought up her son, and that her last words were of her love for him.

'What else could I be sayin' to him, Tabitha?' he asked with a helpless gesture. 'The poor boy will forever be reminded of her death when his weddin' day comes round each year.'

'We must be thankful that she saw him respectably married, knowing that she'd brought him up to be a decent man, Conor,' Tabitha said earnestly. 'And aren't you glad that you gave him and Deborah a good wedding – and that you spoke kind words to that poor woman at the end? There are those who'd've thrown her out o' the church with curses, like Mr Pitcher, but you showed her pity. And d'you know, I think that Joe's probably made a good choice in Deborah, and that's where his future lies, not in the past.'

She spoke truth, for that night when Deborah lay in her husband's arms she comforted him, telling him to give thanks that his poor mother had finished with the troubles of this cruel world.

Mariette declared herself to be as shocked and as sorry as the rest of the household on hearing of the tragic death of Joe's mother, a woman whom none of them had met or even seen before the day of the wedding.

'I guessed there must be some reason why he so rarely spoke of her, but I did not imagine anything as bad as that,' she told Tabitha. 'My mother engaged him for me when I was married, after he had carried her in a sedan chair. He told her that he was the son of a widow, but Conor says she was never married. Poor woman!'

Tabitha could only sigh in agreement, but Mariette's next words made her look up in some surprise. 'When Conor spoke to her outside the church, he did not say a word about the baby. If you or I had been there, we would have told her she was to be a *grand-mère*, would we not, Tabitha? It might have given her a reason for living. Conor thought it would be indelicate for him to say it, but what happened was much worse.'

Tabitha was silent. She always tried to avoid mention of babies in Mariette's presence if possible. After a minute or two, Mariette went on speaking, calmly and deliberately.

'Tabitha dear, I have told Conor that we shall try again under the oak tree on Midsummer's Eve. He was not very eager, and said he did not believe in it, but I told him I wanted to try again. That night is on a Wednesday this year, and we shall go to stay with Lady Farrinder at Heathfield House on the Tuesday. I hope to be free of the menses then, and we have two weeks to pray and prepare for it.'

'Oh, Mariette my love, I'm sure Conor doesn't wish you to go through all that again! Let—'

'No, Tabitha. Conor will do as I say. You will pray and prepare, as I've told you.'

She spoke with a finality which silenced Tabitha, who for some reason felt an odd little shiver run down her spine. Her adored Mariette, so confiding, so lovingly childlike in many ways, could sometimes show an iron resolution that overrode all opposition.

The second time was very different from the first. It was Mariette who responded most cordially to Lady Farrinder's welcome, while Conor and Tabitha were somewhat subdued and not a little embarrassed. Their hostess had never been told exactly what was involved in the midnight ritual, only that it was an ancient fertility rite, and if she had any misgivings as a Catholic, she kept them to herself and tactfully assured them of her prayers. When she retired to bed on Midsummer's Eve, she left her three guests in the drawing room; Mariette rested on the sofa, and Tabitha got out Hester's old backgammon board and dice to play a game with Conor, rather than to sit in silence.

At twenty minutes to twelve they set out on their walk to the clearing where the oak tree stood. In contrast to the other warm, whispering night in May, this Midsummer's Eve was as disappointing as only a capricious English summer can be: chilly and showery, the moon and stars blotted out by banks of cloud.

Conor took the blanket over to the tree and laid it out on the ground. Turning his back on the two women, he quickly divested himself of his clothes and lay down on the blanket, waiting for Mariette to come to him, giving her every chance to change her mind; she had asked for this second attempt, he reasoned, and she could take the lead in carrying it out.

She stood as still as a statue while Tabitha undressed her, and when her friend had departed into the laurel bushes with her clothes, Mariette walked slowly but purposefully towards her husband, her white body gleaming pale in the dark of a moonless night. He sat up and held out his arms to her.

'Mariette!' was all he said as she lay down beside him, turning towards him so that they faced each other. An owl hooted above them, and was answered by another about half a mile off, and some nocturnal creature, a fox perhaps, chased a rabbit across the clearing. A breeze rustled the leaves, and there was a sudden downpour of rain, filling the air with its soft hiss; water dripped from leaves above to leaves below, and a few drops found their way down to the naked man and woman.

'You'll be cold, Mariette,' he said, and she put her arms around his neck, bringing her body closer: cold flesh met warm flesh, and with a sigh he rolled himself over on to her. She parted her thighs for him, and he gave a stifled gasp as he entered her, the familiar sensation of desire soon to be satisfied. He always tried to avoid thrusting, but pressed deep into her, suppressing the wordless sounds that rose in his throat; with her soft, damp arms around his neck and her knees raised up on each side of him like a gateway, it seemed that every nerve and sinew was rising to a peak of anticipation, a crescendo roaring in his ears, blotting out all else but his overwhelming need to become one flesh with this woman who was his wife, to enable her to conceive his child.

'Mariette, I'm comin' to ye!' His whole body shuddered as he reached his climax and the pent-up lifestream flowed, just as the midnight chimes echoed on the air and Midsummer's Eve passed into Midsummer Day.

Thus did Conor Townclear do his duty, unheeding of the rain falling all around them. His wife gave a smile of satisfaction, for her duty too had been done. They lay beneath the tree, Conor breathless and Mariette calm, each with their own thoughts, eyes closed, silent.

Tabitha emerged at last from the bushes with Mariette's clothes. She ran over to them.

'Come on, it's time to get dressed and get back indoors!' She adopted a scolding tone to cover the tremor in her voice and the tears she could have shed for them. 'You'll catch your death o' cold, the pair o' you!'

They obeyed her at once, and within half an hour were back at Heathfield House and in their beds, without another word being spoken; they had no need to be told of her love and pity, how completely she shared in their hopes and fears, for they knew only too well.

Conor returned to his home and his work the next day, while his wife and Tabitha spent the rest of the week with Lady Farrinder, admiring her needlework, playing backgammon, and taking gentle exercise, walking in the grounds when the weather permitted, though by tacit consent they avoided the clearing where the oak tree stood; they never referred to it in their conversations, though as the days passed and they returned to Gerrard Street, it was never far from their thoughts.

When June gave way to July and July to August, with no return of Mariette's terms, their hopes began to rise. Seven weeks went by from Midsummer Day, then eight weeks, then nine. Tabitha hardly dared to ask her friend how she felt each morning, and Conor's expectations rose: Mariette confided that she felt a sensation of nausea when she awoke, and could take only a little weak tea and a thin slice of dry bread for her breakfast, a known early sign that conception had taken place. She also told Tabitha that her small breasts tingled at times, and she was sure that they were increasing in size. Ten weeks: Conor could think of nothing else. It was the last week in August.

'D'ye think she can truly be with child, Tabitha? Has the midnight oak tree worked its magic – or has God above taken pity on her – on us? She has never gone this long before.'

Tabitha was very reluctant to raise his hopes, but he could read the joyful message in her eyes. She secretly studied the almanack, made calculations and looked ahead to a day in February of the following year, 1785. Monseigneur le Comte and Madame la Comtesse de St Aubyn heard their beloved daughter's whispered news with incredulity: could it be true, that at last they were to welcome a grandchild? Madame began to confide in her closest female acquaintances, and the news became official. They told Conor's sister Moira, now nearing her time, and the three women embraced with smiles and tears at this answer to so many fervent prayers. They began to talk of cradles and the merits of swaddling clothes for the newborn. Madame said that she knew of an excellent midwife, not the same one that Mrs Seymour had chosen, and Tabitha hoped this would not lead to a disagreement on the rival merits of each.

But then, on the last day of August, tragedy intervened. A messenger boy came running from Margaret Street with a note from Seymour, saying that Moira had been brought to bed suddenly after breakfast, and the midwife had arrived just in time to deliver a little girl; there had been trouble with the after-burden ('What in God's name is *that*, Tabitha?' asked Conor), and Moira had fainted and could not be roused. He begged that Mariette or Tabitha come at once.

'I'll go,' said Tabitha. 'You stay here with Mariette, and I'll see what's to be done.'

What she found was a scene to make the angels weep, as she said later. The red-faced, sweating midwife had tried everything she knew to stanch the haemorrhages that had borne Moira's life away, and she lay wax-pale, a still, silent figure in a pool of blood that dripped down right through the mattress. A tiny infant squirmed in a wooden cradle where it had been hastily laid, and downstairs George Seymour paced up and down like a caged lion, calling up the stairs at intervals to ask how his wife did.

'There's nothin' more to be done, Mrs – er –' muttered the midwife, shaking her head. 'It just poured out, there was no stoppin' it. God help the husband and the babe over there – if yer want to do an act o' charity, ye'd best take it away and care for it – find a wet-nurse.'

Tabitha stood for a moment, taking in the situation before her. She stifled her own feelings of pity and despair as she realized that the woman was right, she must first give care to the child. And there was something else she would have to do: tell George Seymour of his loss.

'I'll do what I can for the baby, nurse, and I'll tell the servants to come up and clear away this – this terrible flood.

The death will have to be registered in the parish, so the parson must be told – and the coffin maker – oh, my God.'

She picked up the little wriggling infant which seemed as light as a feather to her, and which she guessed weighed scarcely five pounds. The cord had been cut and knotted: it would need tying with string and then cut nearer to the belly. She wrapped it in the small flannel blanket on which it lay, and gathered it up in her arms. She carried it downstairs.

'Mr Seymour,' she said. 'George – this is your daughter. Have you got a name for her?'

He gave the baby no more than a quick glance. 'For God's sake, woman, tell me about Moira – my wife! Is she—?'

He looked into Tabitha's eyes, and turned away, putting an arm across his face. 'No! Oh, *no*, no, no – what shall I do? Oh, what shall I *do*,' he groaned out loud again and again, and Tabitha could hear the servants whispering and weeping.

'I'll take the baby to her uncle's house, George,' she said. 'I – I'll send Conor to you.'

After a quick word with the servants, she left the house carrying the newly born baby, and hailed a hackney cab. On arriving at 21 Gerrard Street she went straight to Conor and asked him to use the cab to go to his brother-in-law. There was no way to break the news gently.

'This is a very sad day for us all, Conor, for your sister lies dead. I'll have to find a nurse to suckle this child and take care o' her.'

'Oh, sweet Jesus, help us all! – but what about Mari—' he began, and she interrupted him.

'Your place is with your brother-in-law now, Conor. He's in no state to look after a helpless newborn babe. I'll let Mariette know.'

By the end of that day the baby had been installed at 21 Gerrard Street in the room that had first been set aside as a nursery, and a Mrs Wagstaff, recommended by Mrs Clark, was also accommodated in it with her ten-month-old son Jack. She was a wet-nurse who had successfully suckled several babies, and her own was being weaned on to semi-solid food: bread soaked in cow's milk sweetened with honey, and oat-flour porridge sieved into gruel. He was a fretful child, and his mother said that his first teeth were coming through: she asked for bread crusts for him to chew on. Molly the maid was told to wait on Mrs Wagstaff and see that she had everything she needed, which included two full jugs of porter brought up from the Turk's Head every day. This miraculously turned to milk inside Mrs Wagstaff, and ensured a constant, plentiful supply. The woman did little else but sleep, suckle and drink porter, and Tabitha and Molly between them looked after the babies until Tabitha sent for another maid from Margaret Street to come and assist them.

Madame la Comtesse was furious at this intrusion at such a crucial time in her daughter's life, but Conor asked her what else could he have done for his motherless niece and bereaved brother-in-law? Madame then demanded that Mariette come to stay at Bloomsbury Square, but Mariette said she would not come without Tabitha, and Tabitha could not leave the helpless baby, which Mariette herself had named Augusta Maria, because she had been born in August, and her life preserved by the Blessed Virgin.

'It can be changed if her father wishes,' she said, 'but we have to call her something. He has not yet been to see her, and I fear he may never forgive her.'

Two very busy weeks followed, and at last George Seymour put in an appearance, though he was not alone. He arrived with his parents, Mr and Mrs Seymour who had travelled down from the north to see their grandchild and claim her. It should have been a time of relief for the Townclear household, but it was to be forever recalled as the day when all their hopes and dreams departed. Mariette awoke with a cramp-like pain deep down in her belly, and when Conor turned back the sheet and saw the bright red blood, he leaped out of bed, shouting for Tabitha. Mr Davey the apothecary summoned a midwife to confirm that Mrs Townclear was miscarrying a child at three months, proved by the midwife's examination of the expelled contents of the womb.

The Seymours took their grandchild and departed with her, accompanied by Mrs Wagstaff and her son; Conor shed his tears in secret, and was unable to find any words of comfort for Mariette who lay dry-eyed, showing no emotion at this terrible disappointment. Tabitha ventured to cheer her by pointing out that she had proved herself able to conceive.

'Next time things may turn out better, my darling,' she said.

'Other women have miscarried and later borne a living, full-term child.'

'No, Tabitha, I cannot give Conor a child. That was my last hope, and now I know what must be done.'

'What do you mean, dearest? What is to be done?' asked Tabitha, afraid of the answer.

'I cannot bear my husband a child, *ma chérie*, so *you* must do so. You must conceive and bear a son for him – for us.'

Tabitha made no reply, but brought her a cup of hot milk into which she had added a few drops of valerian which Mr Davey had ordered.

'Drink this, it will help you to sleep, dearest,' she said, kissing Mariette's forehead and smoothing her pillow.

Would she remember what she had said in the morning? Yes, she would – for Tabitha now saw that Mariette had already planned this course of action if the magic of the oak tree failed.

And what had Mother Morrison said about conceiving a child in the house of a friend?

Twelve

It was as if a cloud had descended over 21 Gerrard Street, affecting every member of the household. In contrast to the scuttling activity of the past two weeks when the hours of each day and night had been measured by the cries of the two babies, Mrs Wagstaff's ringing of her bell for attention, the jokes about the brimming jugs of porter that Joe or Berry had to carry up from the Turk's Head, the extra washing, the constant footsteps up and down the stairs – all was now replaced by a mournful silence. Mrs Clark sighed deeply over her kneading and mixing, stopping to wipe her eyes on a corner of her apron, while Deborah, Minnie and Molly spoke in whispers. Joe Bartlett looked glum, and Berry's big eyes reflected the helplessness felt by all the servants. They longed to show their sympathy to the afflicted couple, but Mr Townclear could not bear to touch upon the subject, and Mrs Townclear was disconcertingly remote, lying on her couch and only receiving such visitors as her parents and poor George Seymour who came to be consoled rather than to give consolation. Miss Prewett's position as go-between for the domestics was now more essential than ever; she alone acknowledged their sympathy with gratitude, and assured them that Mr and Mrs Townclear were deeply touched by it.

'And yet she don't seem too happy herself, do she?' remarked Deborah to the others in the kitchen. 'She's restless, as if she was waitin' for somethin' worse. What's she like with Mrs Townclear, Minnie? Do they still pretend to fall out with each other, an' then burst out laughin'?'

'No, not like they used to,' answered Minnie who was lady's maid to both, and sensed a tension in the atmosphere which was more than just sorrow for the death of Mr Townclear's sister and the miscarrying of his child. Miss Prewett seemed agitated, and although she was as attentive as ever to Mrs Townclear, there was a certain constraint between them. Whereas before there had been a continuous flow of talk, teasing and laughter, there were now pools of silence – and Minnie noticed how abruptly they stopped talking when she entered the room. She suspected that if she'd been able to hear what passed in private between the mistress and her especial friend, she'd have had a good deal more to report.

Mr Townclear walked to his work each day, sometimes to Mr Shenstone's, sometimes to Fleet Street, but he lacked his former easy friendliness towards Bartlett, and had become quite careless over the way he looked; buttons were left undone, and there was a food stain on his shirt front. He only wore his wig on Sundays, and sometimes did not bother to put on the black eyepatch which had become part of his dashing appearance, and as the maids remarked, was much to be preferred to the pale, milky appearance of his blind right eye.

It wasn't exactly eavesdropping on Minnie's part: she had taken a tray with a jug of lemonade and two glasses to the ladies' parlour, and put down the tray before knocking on the door and entering at the usual 'Come in!' from one or other of them. She found that the door was not properly closed, and just as she was about to knock she heard their voices from within.

'But Conor would *never* agree to such a thing, Mariette! You're his wedded wife and he loves you!' cried Tabitha.

Mariette's voice was quiet but equally firm. 'He also loves *you*, Tabitha, we both do, and I would not dream of suggesting it with any other woman on earth. Surely you must see that.'

'Oh, say no more, Mariette!' Tabitha almost shouted. 'Conor would never agree to it!'

'Conor will do as he is told, *ma chérie*, whatever I ask him. And this is the only way.'

There was silence, and Minnie knocked on the door. 'If you please, Mrs Townclear – Miss Prewett – here's yer lemonade.'

'Thank you, Minnie,' answered Tabitha, giving her a quick, questioning look. There had been no sound of the door handle being turned, so it must have been already ajar; how much might the girl have heard? Yet even if she had overheard their exchange, the actual subject of it had not been mentioned; they might have been talking about persuading Conor to move back to Ireland, for all Minnie knew – and why should *that* unlikely idea cross my mind, thought Tabitha, trying to collect her confused thoughts together. Had Mariette spoken to Conor yet, or even dropped a hint? Poor Tabitha blushed for shame at the very idea of him taking her in his arms and making love to her as with a wife. No! She would not allow herself to think of it. I must not even dream of such a thing, she thought.

And yet . . . and yet . . . she had no such control over her dreams, the secret hopes and desires that they revealed, and the truth was that the image of him had come to her in sleep on many occasions over the past four years. He had taken her in his arms, but she had always woken up before the completion of the act of love, leaving her with an aching emptiness.

'Have you spoken to Conor?' she asked directly, as soon as Minnie had left them.

'Yes, on the same day that I first spoke to you.'

Tabitha gasped. 'And what did he—?'

'Nothing yet. He did not give me an answer, so I am giving him time to recover from his grief for our child and for his sister. When he is himself again he will acknowledge that I am right, and he will see where his duty lies.' Mariette suddenly snapped her fingers and spoke with a touch of impatience. 'Come, *ma chérie*, let us have more honesty and less of sentiment. *Mon*

Dieu, it will be no hardship to Conor! *Au contraire*, you are a friend equally dear to us both, and can only do him good. Don't you *want* to cheer him, to make him happy?'

To this Tabitha could give no answer, and she resolved to ask no more questions nor make any more protests unless – or until – Conor himself spoke to her.

Which he did that same day, on a mellow September evening that she would always remember. The servants were sitting out in the backyard, enjoying the last rays of sunshine, and Mariette's black cat basked on the window sill. Tabitha was watering and weeding the little herb garden that she had planted down one side of the fence that separated the back of No 21 from their neighbour, using water drawn from the street pump by Berry. The boy had just taken the watering can to fill again.

''Tis a lovely evenin',' said a voice close to her ear, and she drew in a quick, startled breath at finding him so near to her.

The only answer she could make was 'Yes, indeed.'

He leaned closer still, lowering his voice. 'I shall come to your room this night, Tabitha.'

On hearing this she did not turn round, but her heart hammered in her chest, and her breath deserted her completely for a moment. There was no question in his voice, no asking permission – and no mistaking his meaning. Her answer was a whispered, 'Very well.'

He put his hand briefly on her shoulder, and turned back into the house.

Berry returned carrying the watering can and smiling happily. 'You got enough, Miss Prewett? I fetch more?'

She shook her head and turned the rose of the can on to the flourishing clumps of parsley and borage, though the mint and the marjoram were not thriving in a London garden, and the thyme had grown woody. As with people, so with plants, she thought; they too had their successes and failures in keeping the species alive.

Tarts and pies made with seasonal fruit were served up daily by Mrs Clark, and enjoyed by the whole household, but Tabitha absented herself from the cold light supper she usually shared with Conor and Mariette. How could she face them or talk with anything like natural ease? Having finished her care of the herb garden she retired to her room next to the master bedroom. She tried to read, to pray, to concentrate her mind, but all efforts to calm herself were ineffectual. What would she say to him when he came to her? What would he say to her? Would he expect her to be in bed and waiting for him?

She stood at the window, looking out as the warm blanket of night fell over the roofs, the squares and fields of London, where lights twinkled in streets and windows. There lay reality, she thought, the comings and goings of everyday life, the people she knew: somewhere out there Robin Drury rested from his labours at Davidman's. What was now being proposed was *not* real, not possible, and she would have to refuse. Yes, she would stand before him and tell him it was not possible. Or if she locked her door, there would be no need for a confrontation, for that would be answer enough.

Oh, Conor! Conor Townclear, who had called her his darlin' dear.

She did not lock her door against him. She took off her clothes and put on her white nightgown. She stood waiting for him, trembling and fearful, her thoughts in confusion, her resolution wavering; her fingers shook as she lit a candle, for it was now quite dark.

Before the clock struck ten he opened the door, entered and closed it behind him. He was wearing his long nightshirt, and had put on his eyepatch. He came towards her on bare feet and held out his hand.

'Tabitha.' He clasped her right hand in his.

'Conor.' She lowered her head, but he put his left hand firmly under her chin and raised it until they faced each other. His eyes, dark like hers, gleamed in the candle light.

'Come, darlin',' he said, and led her to the narrow bed. She got into it and he got in beside her. 'Tabitha, my darlin' dear.' He put his arms around her, but she began to tremble violently from head to foot.

'Conor – oh, Conor, I love you, but I can't – not with Mariette under this roof, in the next room – my dearest friend, I can't betray her, Conor, I can't, I can't—'

'Hush, Tabitha.' He put his finger on her lips to stop her frantic whispering, the voice of her conscience. 'Hush, Tabitha. Mariette wishes it, and she's ordered me to come to ye.'

'*No*, Conor, I can't, please listen to me, I *can't*, I tell you!'

'Yes, my darlin' dear, ye can do it for her – and ye can do it for me. I love ye, Tabitha. I love ye above all women.'

The words fell from his lips like the most exquisite music in her ears. 'I love ye, Tabitha.' He kissed her forehead, her cheeks, her mouth, and buried his face in the warmth of her neck. He pushed aside her nightgown and cupped each of her milk-white breasts in his hands, first the one and then the other, licking each rosy tip as if they were already flowing with nourishment for the child she would bear him. And so her resistance melted, and she put her arms around his neck, sighing softly at the touch of his hand on her belly, her thighs; she willingly opened her legs and spread them apart for him. With his words resounding, echoing in her head, she would have done anything he desired of her, and when he guided his male member towards her secret place, now warm and moist, ready for him, aching for him, she heard herself say, 'Love me, Conor – love me now!'

He whispered her name as he entered her, and she arched her back, giving a little gasp as her virginity was yielded up to him, and then, instinctively, knowing how he had to suppress his emotion with Mariette, she whispered, 'Deeper, Conor – deeper!' and rejoiced as he thrust and thrust again, and again and yet again, until they both cried out in amazement at the mounting surge of pleasure, higher and higher until it almost seemed too much to bear, and then as he reached his climax she felt his life-stream flow, filling her and spilling over, a veritable river that sent waves all over her body. They gripped each other as if drowning in their passion, laughing and tearful as the tide slowly ebbed, leaving them in a glow of satisfied desire. It was her first experience of lovemaking, and for him it was better than any previous experience, a complete giving and receiving, without reservations or prohibitions. And he had made her happy beyond her dreams: cradled in his arms, bathed in his adoration, he was her whole world for this time-less moment. He stayed with her until morning.

As soon as she awoke, she knew that she had to go to Mariette, his lawful wife and her dearest friend.

'Ah, yes – come to me, *chère* Tabita. Is all well? Is it done?'

'Yes, dear Mariette, all is well. At first I couldn't do it, not in your – but I knew it was what you asked of me.' She took Mariette's outstretched hand and sat upon the matrimonial bed with her, trembling slightly. 'Oh, my love, how I hope there will be a child for you!'

'I have prayed to La Vierge all night, *ma chère* Tabitha, that his seed will grow in you.' She leaned towards Tabitha and softly kissed her cheek.

It was a strange yet sweet experience, this love between the three of them, the thanks and the gratefulness: there was no place for jealousy in it, no deception. Tabitha felt herself blessed by Conor's love and a deep certainty came to her mind that a child was already conceived from his seed within her womb – a child that would be theirs, belonging to the three of them.

In such overwhelming bliss, she gave no thought to the judgement of the rest of the world.

Thirteen

Overnight the atmosphere throughout the house in Gerrard Street had lightened, and it began to bustle again. Miss Prewett's agitation disappeared, and she was her usual quick, efficient self, talking over the daily requirements with Mrs Clark as one housekeeper to another. Mrs Townclear went through her wardrobe and discovered that with the approach of autumn she had no new clothes, so got her husband to accompany her on a few shopping expeditions; she also ordered a winter coat from Prewett's Quality Tailors, made up in the new style with a fur trim and matching muff. Ladies' fashions were changing, and becoming simpler and easier to wear, led by Queen Marie-Antoinette of France who had caused a sensation with the Empire style, high-waisted and flowing without the aid of stays, showing off the neck and shoulders, and revealing as much of the bosom as was decorous – a rule which varied from one lady to another. The lovely Mrs Mary Robinson had brought the traffic to a standstill when she rode out in her new carriage wearing the latest creation from Paris, said to be a gift from the Queen of France herself, for the two were known to be acquainted.

Halfway into October this pleasing state of affairs was suddenly interrupted. A messenger arrived from Bloomsbury while Miss Prewett was at breakfast with Mrs Townclear, with the news that Mrs Prewett had been in travail all night, and the midwife was at her side, though there was as yet no sign that the birth was imminent. Tabitha rose at once.

'My father needs me there, Mariette,' she said. 'I'll get Berry to call a hackney cab while I fetch my cloak. You don't mind, do you, dearest?'

'Of course not, *chérie*. Stay as long as you are needed. Send word to me if there is anything I can do to help.'

Within ten minutes Tabitha was on her way, feeling distinctly nervous, for inevitably the recent memory of Moira Seymour's death in childbirth came to her mind. She alighted at the corner of Bloomsbury Square, ran down the Frenchman's stairs to Orchard Court and into Prewett's Quality Tailors, conscious of the neighbours' observation of her. She found her father in the kitchen, anxiously awaiting news from the bedroom where Prudence lay.

'Mrs Carter's with her an' the midwife,' he told Tabitha. 'It's not Mrs Hitchcock now, it's a Mrs Newbold. They say she's skilled at her craft, but – oh, Tabitha my girl, I'm that glad ye're here! It's women's business, and I'm so helpless – there's nothin' I can do to ease the terrible pain she's in. Jerry's takin' care o' the shop, for I can't settle to anythin'.'

'Don't worry, Papa, she's a strong, healthy woman, and I'm sure she'll be all right,' said Tabitha, kissing him. 'I'll just go up and see how things are. Have you had any breakfast?' Her conscience smote her at the sight of his worried face, the lines around his eyes, the few remaining grey hairs on the top of his wigless head. She had not kept in very close touch with her family lately, and now reproached herself for her neglect. Resolved to give all the help needed and not to quit the house until the baby was safely born, she hung her cloak on the peg beside Prudence's, and went upstairs.

Her stepmother lay in her usual place on the right of the matrimonial bed that had seen most of Martha Prewett's children born; she was just recovering from a pain, and smiled gratefully when she saw Tabitha at the door.

'I told yer father ye'd come,' she said, but Mrs Carter signalled by a warning shake of her head that the midwife did not take kindly to visitors in the birth chamber. Mrs Newbold had learned her craft from her predecessor Mrs Hitchcock, who had approved the familiar presence of a neighbour like Mrs Carter as practical assistant at local birthings, but resisted relatives who came to peer over her shoulder and breathe down her neck, as she said. Mrs Newbold was clearly of the same mind, and did not even look at Tabitha, who offered to make tea for them all.

'I'll be in the kitchen, Prudence, keeping Papa company,' she said with a determined smile. 'Do you take milk, Mrs Newbold? I know you like two teaspoons of sugar, Mrs Carter!'

This proved to be a good move, and as the hours went by and Prudence's pains grew stronger without any apparent progress, the midwife became more forthcoming, though Tabitha suspected that she was also becoming worried. When the woman asked for hot water and soap to wash her hands, Tabitha quickly produced them and discreetly looked away as the midwife inserted two fingers into the birth canal. Prudence winced and groaned at this added discomfort, and Mrs Carter held her hand and whispered soothingly to her.

The midwife withdrew her exploring fingers. 'It's a big baby, and the head's high, so the womb's openin' but slowly,' she muttered. 'Twill be a long while yet, I don't doubt. Listen, Mrs Prewett, I'm goin' to get yer out o' that bed, an' standin' up.'

'Oh, but the pain – the pain,' gasped Prudence. 'I don't think I could bear it.'

'Yes, yer can. Up with yer, now, take hold o' my arm – and hers,' said the midwife, nodding to Tabitha. 'Feet on the floor, that's right, hold yer head up an' put one foot in front o' the other.'

'I *can't*! Oh, Mrs Newbold, help me, help me!' cried poor Prudence, slumped between the midwife and Tabitha as another strong contraction gripped her belly.

'Courage, Prudence, I'm here with you, and here I'll stay till you're delivered,' whispered Tabitha, though dismayed by the seeming endlessness of the pain Prudence was enduring.

'Let's sit her on the chamber pot,' ordered Mrs Newbold. 'An' give her more water to drink – ah, that's right,' she said when Prudence managed to pass a small amount of strong-smelling urine. 'Ye'll be better for that, Mrs Prewett.'

'Oh, it's coming again – coming again, let me lie down!' begged Prudence, collapsing on to the bed. As she did so, a trickle of cloudy liquid flowed from her.

'That's yer waters leakin' from behind the baby,' said Mrs Newbold. 'Pity yer couldn't've sat on the pot a bit longer, 'cause now we'll have to change the sheet.'

Morning crept on to afternoon, and Tabitha thought she had never known such a wearisome day. She contrasted Prudence's ordeal with what she remembered of her mother's delivery on the kitchen floor more than twelve years ago, and remembered in detail how she and Prudence had coped, and how Mariette had appeared and begun to pray to La Vierge: her prayer had been answered before she had even finished it, so quick and easy had the birth been. But then Tabitha recalled her father's memory of Michael's birth, a long, painful process that had ended with Michael being born bottom first, a fact that was said to be the reason for his slow wits. Might Prudence's travail end in the same way? Tabitha could understand her father's fears, and she did her best to comfort him, going downstairs to brew more tea, to simmer a hambone in a pot over the oven, to heat more water for Mrs Newbold to wash her hands again.

At about three o'clock she heard somebody come into the shop and speak to Jeremiah who then sent for his sister to come down. Mrs Townclear had called, and wanted to see her.

'How is she, Tabitha?' asked Mariette, looking from her friend to John Prewett who had joined them. Tabitha tried to sound hopeful, but could not hide her desperate anxiety.

'It's taking a very long time, and she's so tired,' she said helplessly.

'Can another midwife be sent for, to give an opinion?' asked Mariette, and Prewett eagerly took up this suggestion.

'Yes, er, ma'am, we could ask Mrs Hitchcock to come – she still goes out to a few women she knows,' he said, clutching at a hope. 'I'll go for her myself, straightaway—'

'I'd better tell Mrs Newbold, then,' Tabitha said quickly, and hurried up the stairs. At hearing what had been suggested, Mrs Newbold swallowed, then nodded glumly.

'Though I doubt she'll have any better success with this one,' she muttered. 'The child's head's jammed in the passage, an' she's lackin' the strength to push it forth.'

Mariette waited in the parlour while John Prewett went for Mrs Hitchcock, and Tabitha brewed yet more tea for everybody, privately confessing her worst fears to her friend.

'Poor Prudence keeps saying, "I'm not going to die, am I?" – and oh, Mariette, I fear that she may do so, and the child too – oh, my God, what a nightmare!'

'Hush, *ma chérie*, let us see what this older woman says, and meanwhile I shall pray to La Vierge to take care of the mother and child.'

Tabitha was afraid that this would prove too hard a case even for La Vierge, and when Mrs Hitchcock arrived, her hopes faded completely, for the older midwife frankly told the younger that their only hope was to send for a surgeon. She recommended a Mr Lyttleton who attended difficult births at the Lying-In Hospital in St George's Row, where, it was said, doctors practised on the poor, disgraced women who were confined there.

'Ye've no time to lose, and the best yer can hope for is that he'll save the mother,' she said grimly, having seen how a surgeon's destructive instruments were used to deliver a dead baby.

'Take my cab and go for this man, Mr Prewett,' ordered Mrs Townclear with commanding authority. 'I will pay for his services and – here, take this,' she added, lowering her voice. 'Offer him five sovereigns and say there will be five more if he can save your wife.'

Prewett hardly stopped to thank her as he rushed out of the house and up the Frenchman's stairs. Tabitha divided her time between Mariette who sat quietly praying in the parlour and her stepmother who lay exhausted on her bed of pain. The midwives applied cold compresses to Prudence's forehead, and gave her sips of wine and water to drink, though by the time Mr Lyttleton arrived with his bag, she was slipping into unconsciousness. Her husband, briefly allowed into the birthchamber, wept silently beside her until dismissed by the surgeon.

Assisted by the two midwives and with Mrs Carter and Tabitha to fetch and carry whatever he required, Mr Lyttleton set about his business. Experience had given him no belief in miracles, but having put his ear to the belly and ascertained that he could hear the child's heartbeat, he decided to take

195

this opportunity to attempt to deliver by means of the Chamberlen forceps he had brought with him. These were the invention of a French Huguenot, and Lyttleton had not used them before, but had seen a demonstration at the Lying-in Hospital. He ordered that the patient be turned to lie sideways across the bed, and her buttocks brought to the very edge. He asked the midwives to raise her legs high, and they each held one while they watched, holding their breath as first one blade was passed up around the child's head, and then the other. They clicked together, forming a protective cage around its head, and then the surgeon began to pull: a long, steady, sustained pull that slowly drew the head down and out of the mother's body. He dropped the forceps and gently rotated the shoulders, feeling for the umbilical cord. The rest of the body quickly followed, and Mr Lyttleton received a large, flaccid female infant into his hands. Bruised by the pressure of the metal, and her head elongated by the pressure in her mother's birth canal, the limp baby drew a convulsive breath, followed by a weak cry as if to announce her arrival, upon which she was handed to Mrs Hitchcock, who wiped her face and blew upon her nose, mouth and chest. The baby gave another, slightly louder cry, and the midwife nodded to the rest of them. It was just after six o'clock, and dusk was falling outside.

The mother lost a great deal of blood, and Mr Lyttleton had to stitch the torn outlet, but Tabitha Prewett was sent downstairs to tell the waiting husband and the lady visitor that a daughter had been delivered, and both mother and child were alive. Heartfelt exclamations of thankfulness greeted the news, which was soon spread to the whole of Orchard Court where neighbouring shopkeepers and their families breathed a collective sigh of relief, for Prudence was much loved.

Tabitha's self-control gave way at last, and she burst into tears. Her apron was stained, her cap askew, and strands of hair hung down untidily, sticking to her flushed face; but Mariette reached out to her and drew the dark head on to her shoulder.

'Praise God that it has ended this way, my love,' she whispered, 'and now you must stay with your family for as long as you are needed, to care for the new mother and baby. I will send Molly to help in the house. I shall miss you, *ma*

196

chère Tabitha, but – what is this? What in God's name are you doing? Get up, my love, stand up!'

For Tabitha had fallen on her knees before the beautiful French girl as at their first meeting, when Madame la Comtesse had called them two pretty little butterflies.

Tabitha remained at her old home for three weeks, devoting herself to Prudence and the new baby who was called Jane, or Jenny; the kitchen scales showed her to weigh over ten pounds, and her appearance greatly improved when her head regained its roundness, with a fuzz of dark hair; the bruises from the forceps blades also faded within days. Prudence had been weakened by loss of blood, but as Tabitha had pointed out, her basically strong constitution aided her recovery, and she waved away a suggestion that a wet-nurse should be engaged, and insisted on feeding the baby herself. It proved to be very difficult to get the child to suck at first; Mrs Newbold called daily and showed Tabitha how to give the baby feeds in the form of cow's milk diluted by half with boiled water, from a special spoon ending in a tiny spout that could be inserted into her mouth. A fair amount of the feed was dribbled away and lost, but enough was swallowed to tide her over until she was strong enough to fix on to the nipple.

Tabitha felt herself drawing close to her baby sister, and secretly imagined a time when she would hold her own baby on her lap: she had not had her monthly flow for October, and wondered if she had started on the nine-month journey to motherhood; though she knew it was too soon as yet to be sure.

Mr Lyttleton called back on two or three occasions, now regretting that he had not brought a couple of student surgeons to witness his success with the Chamberlen forceps. He had decided to write up an account of it as a case-history, hoping that it would gain him admittance to the Company of Surgeons, who were inclined to look down upon man-midwives.

John Prewett drew nearer to his grown-up daughter during this period, and told her how glad he was to have her at home. 'Ye've seemed so far away these days, girl, closer to them Townclears than to us. It seems a queer sort of arrangement, when yer could've been married to young Drury, and havin' a family o' yer own. He's doin' well, by the way, an' Davidman's is movin' to bigger premises next year.'

When she made no answer he reached out and touched her hand. 'I'm not complainin', girl, in fact I can't ever thank yer for the way ye've cared for Prudence an' the baby. We're both for ever in yer debt.'

She smiled back at him, but lowered her eyes and murmured that he had allowed Conor Townclear to be nursed here under his own roof at the time of the Gordon Riots, in spite of the danger of discovery. He gave a little shrug of his shoulders, and persisted with his question.

'D'yer think ye'll stay with 'em, Tabitha? Wouldn't yer be better off married to young Drury an' havin' yer own babies?'

Tabitha could not meet his eyes, but shook her head and held up a hand as if to fend off any more questions. Her father's words had a greater significance for her than he could have dreamed of, and for the first time in her life she was conscious of practising a deception on this good man who had loved her from the day she was born – for how could she ever tell him or Prudence or *anybody* the secret she shared with the Townclears? Gerrard Street had become home to her now, rather than her father's house.

October passed into November, bringing its chill fogs and early dark, and the day came for Tabitha's return, to be joyfully reunited with Mariette and Conor. Conor and Mariette. Molly was left behind at the Prewetts' as maid-of-all-work for as long as Prudence felt that she needed her; up until now, Prudence had not employed a domestic servant, but in her changed circumstances it was thought advisable that she should have regular help, and Molly was happy to reign over the Prewetts' kitchen, practising what Mrs Clark had taught her, but no longer subject to that lady's sharp eye and even sharper tongue. A new maid, Peggy, had been taken on in her place, and had settled in well, becoming firm friends with Minnie.

'Deborah – Mrs Bartlett, I should say – is nearing her time,' Mariette told Tabitha soon after her return. 'I have told Joe that she may come here when her pains start, so that we can be on hand for her. Their rooms are very small, and if she has a difficult time like poor Mrs Prewett—' She rolled up her blue eyes and left the rest unsaid. Tabitha could only agree that this was a kind gesture, and braced herself to witness another such ordeal, while as every day passed she was aware of changes taking place in her own body, six weeks after that shared night and eight weeks after her last menses, always so regular until now.

Deborah woke up with intermittent pains and continuous backache on a cold, raw morning, and Joe brought her to Gerrard Street at noon, accompanied by her mother Mrs Pitcher and a cheerfully talkative midwife. A bed had been prepared for her in the room originally set aside as a nursery, and Tabitha had made sure that everything they might require was at hand. While Mariette retired to the parlour, Tabitha took on the role of Mrs Carter, available to assist, fetch and carry and brew tea as the midwife deemed necessary. She began by removing Deborah's clothes and putting a clean white night-gown on her, rolling it up above the distended belly, and then helped the midwife to place a waxed, waterproof mat under her to protect the bed – and only just in time, because Deborah's waters gushed forth almost immediately, and her pains were hard upon her, causing her to gasp and grunt. Mrs Pitcher took hold of her hand and very soon the midwife announced that the top of the child's head was visible during a pain; on her orders Deborah began to strain down with all her might. Shortly before two o'clock a fine baby boy made his appearance, to the joy of his grandmother who cried out, 'It's a son! A little boy, thank Gawd!' The mother's flushed face lit up with a smile as she struggled to lift herself and view the squalling infant between her legs.

'Now for the after-burden, an' we'll have done,' said the midwife, highly gratified at such a short and easy labour. Looking over her shoulder, she added, 'Where's the handy lady who boils the water an' makes a good pot o' tea? We'll all be ready for one, I dare say!'

But the handy lady had fainted clean away and lay on the floor between the foot of the bed and the door, her face ashen.

'Quick, somebody, take her out,' ordered the midwife who was attending to the baby's umbilical cord, and Mrs Pitcher hurried off to fetch the mistress of the house.

When Tabitha opened her eyes she found herself lying on the floor in the corridor with a pillow under her head and Mariette looking down at her, trying to feel for her pulse.

'You are ill, *ma chérie* – you are so pale – I have never known

199

you to faint before. Have you got a pain anywhere?' she asked anxiously. Tabitha stared up into Mariette's face for a moment, and whispered, 'Go to Deborah, my love – she's had a son.'

Back in the birth-chamber, a jubilant Mrs Pitcher remarked that the young lady must have been overcome at the sight of seeing the baby born. The midwife did not reply, but gave a knowing look. She had her own ideas about Miss Prewett's indisposition.

When Conor received a note from his brother that had taken over a month to reach him, the news was that a third daughter had been born to him and Roisin in October. They had named her Grainne, and although the mother and child were said to be very well, there was clearly regret that they still lacked a son.

'Four babies born in the space of ten weeks, Tabitha, and none of them mine,' said Mariette flatly as they sat in the parlour with their sewing, while Conor sat a little apart from them, reading his newspaper. At first Tabitha made no reply, but on reflection this seemed as good a time as any to share her own news with her fellow conspirators.

'But there *will* be a child for you, my Mariette, at about the end o' next June,' she said very quietly, and heard Conor's newspaper rustle in his hands.

Mariette sat bolt upright, throwing her needlework aside. 'But can you be sure, *chère* Tabitha, as early as this?' she asked doubtfully.

'I am sure, dearest. This is the second time I haven't had my monthly flow, and I can feel my body getting ready to carry and bear your child,' Tabitha murmured, and for a moment her brown eyes rested on Conor's uncertain expression, as if he did not dare to hope. He now got up and moved his chair closer.

'I've been wonderin', but haven't said anythin', for fear o' losin' the luck,' he admitted to them. 'And it's my belief we should wait till Christmas before comin' to any decision. There's no sense in makin' plans before we need, only to have them all fall through.' His eyes regarded Tabitha with a look of tenderness. 'By the end o' the year when there's no doubt at all, an' no – er – disappointments – that'll be the time for us to decide what we must do – where we must go.'

Tabitha knew what he was going to say, but Mariette had not yet faced the inevitable.

'Of course we must leave London and hide ourselves away from my parents and all our friends until the child is born, Conor, but where do you propose we shall go?'

'To my family in Ireland,' he replied. 'I haven't set eyes on my parents or brother for over four years, and I've a mind to see them again. We shall journey to Tahilla, the three of us, and – and if indeed Tabitha is with child, it will be born there. Then we shall return, and your parents will accept the child as yours, Mariette. Nobody here will know any different – its birth will always remain a secret between us.'

'But not at Tahilla,' Mariette answered sharply. '*Your* family will know, and Tabitha will have to bear the disapproval of them all, especially from that sister-in-law of yours. Is there nowhere else that we can go?'

'No, it must be Townclear Hall, my home at Tahilla,' he answered gently. 'Roisin's just had another child, an' she'll be taken up with that and the other two little ones. My mother and father – and my brother – they will understand.' Conor spoke with conviction, because he knew of his parents' disappointment that he and Mariette had failed to give them a grandchild. He also knew how fervently Bernard and Roisin had prayed for a son, an heir to the baronetcy, without which Townclear Hall could be divided up on the death of Sir Bernard and possibly fall into the hands of Protestant landowners. A boy would be a safeguard, and a great comfort to them all, following the tragedy of Moira's death; and Conor hoped to supply that male Townclear heir.

'So when do you plan for us to go on this journey?' asked Mariette, thinking of her parents' shock at the very idea of her crossing a stormy sea in winter, to travel to a remote place inhabited by the kind of outlandish country people she had described as peasants.

Again he turned his eyes towards Tabitha who sat with her hands clasped in her lap, listening to these plans being made for her life.

'If Tabitha is still sure by the end o' the year, we'll travel to Tahilla at the end o' January.'

There was silence as the realization swept over both women of the upheaval they would have to undergo, the lies and deceptions they would have to take part in; how both the St Aubyns and John Prewett would worry about the dangers that might befall their daughters all those miles away. It now appeared as a wild scheme, full of pitfalls and hazards, and both women thought themselves mad to have embarked upon it without due consideration of what it would entail. Their doubt and apprehension showed all too clearly in their faces, and Conor saw it as his duty to try to raise their spirits.

'Ah, now, don't forget that we're each of us here to give comfort one to another, my darlin' dears,' he said with laughter in his dark eyes. 'Ye've got each other, and it's meself who's the luckiest o' men to have both o' ye. Let the rest o' the world envy me, an' when heaven allows me to hold our son in my arms, then won't we all rejoice together!'

It should have been enough, and when she was with either of them or both, Tabitha could forget her misgivings. She was even able to reassure Mariette about life at Townclear Hall and the response of Conor's mother when she understood the situation.

'Conor says that Sir Bernard and his brother will understand, so she will most likely feel the same way, Mariette, but in any case she'll have to get used to it for Conor's sake.'

'And the looks we'll get from that Roisin woman when *she* sees that you're carrying our child,' sighed Mariette. 'She probably won't speak to either of us.'

'Now, my love, remember what Conor said – Roisin's got three small children of her own to care for, and she'll be far more interested in them than in one of ours,' Tabitha reminded her.

'Unless ours is a boy,' Mariette pointed out. 'Conor has quite set his heart on having a son – though of course we must be thankful for whatever the good Lord sends,' she added without much enthusiasm.

'And we would love a girl just as much as a boy, wouldn't we, my Mariette?' Tabitha prompted, a little smile upon her lips as she remembered her new half-sister, Jenny, who was now doing well, the delight of her doting father.

'My dearest Tabitha, if it is a girl, you will have to try again,' replied Mariette unequivocally.

The winter days went by, and the season of Christmas festivities was soon upon them. The St Aubyns gave a dinner at 9 Bloomsbury Square a week before Christmas, and Tabitha was an invited guest as Mariette's friend and companion.

Although the table talk was convivial, Tabitha knew that Conor was still grieving over the loss of his sister Moira, whose baby daughter Augusta was with her paternal grandparents; George Seymour had not kept in touch lately with his brother-in-law, and Conor was sad for the little niece he feared he would not see very often, if at all. He spoke of his three nieces in Ireland, and Tabitha noticed that the Comte and Comtesse fell silent at hearing this, and made no reply. Conor then followed this up by dropping a hint that he was hoping to visit his family in County Kerry as soon as his work allowed him, adding that of course Mariette would accompany him and they would take Tabitha and one of their maidservants.

When the ladies withdrew after dinner, the Comtesse took Tabitha aside for a quiet word.

'How can Conor think of taking my daughter over there – to make her regard the difference between his brother's family and his own?' she demanded. 'Heaven knows that the Comte and I have suffered for our poor dear daughter's disappointment in having no children! And that unhappy *fausse-couche* – when she lost the child at three months – quite broke our hearts. Yet now he takes her away to a place in Ireland, and we do not know how long he will stay. The Comte is in his seventies now, and I am – er, a little younger, but when shall we see her again? What do you think of it, Tabitha? My only comfort is that you will be going with her.'

Tabitha smiled and replied that Conor had not seen *his* parents or brother for almost five years, and that since the death of Moira he had felt that he should go home for a while. There were matters concerning the Townclear estate that he needed to discuss with his father and brother, and perhaps it would be good for Mariette to get to know more about his family.

'Ah, if only she had a child of her own, it would be so much easier for her!' sighed Madame, and Tabitha felt that she should add a word – only a word – at this point.

'Forgive me, Madame, for saying this, but I think you should not give up hope. There have been cases where a change of air, of circumstances or – or even in the humours of the mind, has led to a woman conceiving after a long time of—' Tabitha was on the point of saying *being barren*, but changed it to, 'not being able to have a child.'

'Do you really believe that, Tabitha? It is what my husband says, but even he has given up hope now, and we are so sad for her.'

'Don't give up hope, Madame – that's all I have to say,' said Tabitha, and moved away as Lady Dersingham came over to speak to the Comtesse. If Lady Dersingham ever recognized the tailor's little daughter who had brought her father's swatches of material for inspection all those years ago, she gave no sign of it, and Tabitha took this opportunity to leave the company for half an hour to visit her father and Prudence. She found all her brothers at home, Jeremiah and Betty having brought little Johnny, and baby Jenny was now ten weeks old, charming them all with her dribbly smiles.

Following Conor's example, Tabitha decided to drop a hint to them that she would be accompanying the Townclears to Ireland in the New Year. Her father merely shook his head.

'Ye've thrown in yer lot with 'em now, my girl, so ye'll have to go where they take yer an' do as they tell yer,' he said with a resigned air, adding, 'Young Drury was in the other day, an' asked after yer. I said yer wasn't married, an' nor is he.'

Tabitha heard the reproach in his tone. 'How's his mother?' she enquired.

'All right as far as I know, but it was a disappointment to her, the same as for me. He's talkin' o' goin' up north to take a look at this new machinery that can spin an' weave at a great rate, faster than ever hands can do it. He reckons they'll be buildin' great mills that'll give work to all the people. Yer never know, he might find a nice Lancashire girl an' settle down with a second choice. I hope he does, anyway – he's a good man, is young Drury.'

There seemed to be no reply to this, except to say that she hoped Robin would be happy, after which she took her leave and went back to the St Aubyns. The Prewetts were a complete household who no longer needed her, though they would always hold a place in her heart, and she was glad to have had this opportunity to call on them at Christmas time.

Mariette herself gave a party at Gerrard Street on December 22nd, a Thursday, a lively affair with guests including the St Aubyns, Mr Shenstone and many younger friends that Conor and Mariette had made, happily crushed against each other in rooms and on the staircases. Wine flowed freely, and there was much laughter at Conor's witticisms and admiration of the ladies' low-necked gowns and feathered turbans, the latest evening wear. Everybody complimented their hostess who had never appeared more beautiful, and Mr Shenstone made up his mind then and there to give a New Year concert at his home where there would be music both for listening and for dancing.

'And you won't mind, Townclear, if I engage your wife to be my hostess, seeing that I'm only a poor old bachelor?' he asked amidst laughter, and Conor made no objection.

If the Townclears' party had been lively, Mr Shenstone's was a truly glittering affair, with one room set aside for a chamber ensemble who played works by Italian composers and the concertos of Mr Handel, still very popular more than twenty years after his death, and a separate room for dancing to a pianoforte and violin. A splendid supper table was set between the two, and ladies and gentlemen could cross from one to the other, picking up a glass of wine or sitting down to roast pheasant and game pie. The lovely Mrs Townclear set the tone, spending time listening to and applauding the musicians, then making her way across to the floor for dancing, where she was besieged by partners.

Tabitha did her share of smiling and curtseying, and then finding herself unoccupied, sat down to listen to the musicians for a while. To her annoyance there was a great deal of banter going on among a group of gentlemen and three ladies, punctuated by shrieks of laughter which prevented her from enjoying the music. Thoroughly irritated, and feeling oppressed by the warm atmosphere, she quietly got up and took refuge in the library. Here it was cool and relatively quiet, and she leaned against the wall, shielded by one of the double-sided bookcases that Mr Shenstone had installed to show off part of his collection, the books that Conor had so laboriously catalogued. The sound of the music drifted through, but not the trivial talk, and as she stood there alone, Tabitha experienced a sudden chilling sense of alienation. She thought of how her father and her late mother would regard her present situation: an unrelated one-time servant of the Townclears, unmarried and yet carrying a child. She was soon to face danger on sea and land, a long journey and a sojourn in a strange place among unknown people. What was she doing? Panic rose up in her throat, and she turned to face the wall, resting her head against the panelling, trying to calm herself, yet at the same time longing for the release of tears. She put her hands up to her burning cheeks, and tried to say a prayer, but no words would come.

And then – what was this? Oh, praise be to the heavens above, she was not alone! Conor had silently followed her into the library, and now stood directly behind her. Two strong arms encircled her, two hands met and clasped beneath her breasts. He leaned his head forward to put his cheek against her flushed face, and instinctively she covered his hands with her own.

'Heart o' my heart,' he whispered, and she felt her whole body soften as the tension drained from every nerve and muscle. Unclasping his hands, he pulled away the gauze scarf that covered her neck and shoulders, and put his lips to the bare flesh.

'Tabitha.' His hands roved over her breasts, cupping and caressing them in turn. She leaned back against him, and his hands reached down to her belly, softly stroking it. 'Our child, darlin' Tabitha. Our son if God pleases.'

'Conor – oh, Conor.' She was breathless, and her legs had turned to jelly. His hands on her belly was an incredible sensation, and she knew that he desired her at this moment, and she returning his need, could not hide it, nor did she wish to pretend. Turning round to face him, she put her arms up around his neck and they kissed long and deeply, his hands roving in her skirts, urgently pushing them up so that she could feel his hard male member thrusting against the softness of her woman's parts, and realized that he had already unbuttoned when he came to her. Pressing her hard against the wall, he raised her left leg to give himself entrance, and almost before she was aware of it, he was within.

'I'm comin' to ye, darlin'.' She hardly heard his urgent whisper, for she only longed for a return of the pleasure she had known at their child's conception. The time, the place, the incongruity, even the discomfort of their position, went unheeded. Conor was again inside her, bringing her up to a climax of satisfaction. She gripped him tightly as his stream flowed, filling her, spilling between her thighs, warmly trickling down her right leg, her left leg hooked behind him. She could have laughed and wept, but he stopped her mouth with his kisses. Conor! Conor Townclear, her lover, the father of her child, husband of her dearest friend, here he was, totally at one with her, and so suddenly, so unexpectedly, with no time to agree or refuse, while the sound of music and gaiety continued under Mr Shenstone's roof.

It had to subside. He had to withdraw and release her without another word. She straightened her skirts, he buttoned with shaking fingers and gave her one last, lingering kiss before he left the library.

Alone again, she smiled to herself. Why should she be afraid, why dismayed, now that she was to bear Conor's child, the most precious gift in the world for her two dearest friends? The future no longer troubled her. She would go to Tahilla or anywhere else on earth for his sake and Mariette's – and for the sake of their son, their Townclear heir.

But suppose it was a girl?

Fourteen

1785

'I shall die, Tabitha, I'm dying without a priest to absolve me from my sins – *O, mon Dieu*! Ugh! Quickly, give me the basin again – *O Sainte Vierge*, have mercy – help me – ugh!' Mariette moaned in garbled French and English.

'Ssh, my love, you're not dying, you're just very seasick,' said Tabitha, holding Mariette's head while she vomited into the basin, then hastily grabbed the basin as another roll of the ship sent them sprawling to the back of the bunk bed they shared in a small, airless cabin. 'Steady, dearest, I'm here with you and Minnie. Courage, Mariette! Remember how our blessed Lord stilled the storm, and He'll guide us to – to—' Another roll sent them towards the edge of the bunk, and they would have fallen out of it if Tabitha had not clung on to the post that connected the upper and lower bunks; poor Minnie groaned below them, terrified that they were about to capsize and be thrown into the raging waters where St George's Channel meets the Atlantic Ocean. Tabitha knew that both women looked to her for aid, and hid her own dread of imminent shipwreck. She longed to see Conor, who was somewhere else in the hold of the *Ocean Star*, tending poor Berry who, like Mariette, lay prostrated by sickness, while their crates and boxes were stored in some other inaccesible place, and Tabitha could not get a fresh towel or even a handkerchief to wipe Mariette's mouth of the vomit that filled the cabin with its sour smell. A pail had to serve as a privy, and was emptied overboard by Conor or one of the sailors at intervals.

How long was it now since the five of them had set out by post-chaise from London on a raw February morning? They had stayed overnight at Reading and reached Bristol the following day. Berry had wept and trembled at the sight of the tall ships by the quayside, remembering his own terrible journey from his native African shore to this place, and Conor had difficulty in assuring him that they were not sending him away, but were taking him to Conor's own home in Ireland where he would continue to serve the master and mistress and Miss Tabitha as before. The boy brightened a little at the sight of the comparatively small sailing ship on which they were to continue their journey; the owner, a Mr Smithson, was a trader in general cargo, happy to take a few paying passengers on board, and the *Ocean Star* was ready to set sail for Cork harbour. She was a vessel of twelve tons, thirty-five feet long, and the little group boarded her hopefully, in company with Mr Smithson himself, a skipper and two swarthy sailors. At first they had danced along across the waves, but Mariette had quickly become seasick and took to the cabin down in the fo'c's'le, as it was called, where she lay wretchedly heaving, tended by Tabitha who was thankful not to suffer any worse discomfort than the slight nausea of a pregnant woman. She was now into her fifth month, and her body was thickening, but thanks to the high-waisted fashions and the need for warm winter clothes, her condition had so far been concealed from all but the two for whom she was bearing the child.

They had boarded the vessel yesterday at some time around noon, in winter sunshine. During the night a storm had got

208

up, and the ship rolled violently; Tabitha had no idea what the time was, only that it was endlessly dark, and they could hear the voices of the men up on the deck, shouting to each other. She longed to see Conor and ask him where they were.

Conor had in fact gone up on the deck where a ship's lantern swung from side to side, rain and sea-water lashed down on the ship, and the sailors were up in the rigging, trying to shorten sail. It was so impenetrably dark all around them that Conor felt a qualm of fear in his stomach: he learned that the ship had blown a long way off course southwards, and Mr Smithson was having some sort of argument with his skipper.

'We'll have to goose-wing our way before the wind!' roared the skipper.

'Them sails'll be torn to ribbons!' Conor heard one of the sailors say with an oath.

Oh my God, have I brought my nearest and dearest to perish at sea? thought Conor, and returned to his tiny cabin to pray, though his time was taken up with attending to Berry who was in a pathetic state, having vomited over himself and the bunk he was to share with the master.

Even the longest night ends in morning, and by daybreak the storm had abated, leaving the sea relatively calm. Mr Smithson told Conor that they would have to sail back north-east to bring them to Cork harbour, and hoped to make landfall by noon. At hearing the cry of 'Land ahoy!' Conor uttered a heartfelt prayer of thanks, and he went to tell the women. Once anchored in the harbour, in sight of firm ground, they took new heart. Conor helped his wife to stumble ashore, more dead than alive, she said later, and Tabitha assisted Minnie and Berry to disembark.

'Before God, I'm sorry for all I've put ye through, and I beg yer to forgive me,' Conor said to them all. 'Praise God that we're all safe on land!'

'Amen,' replied Tabitha on behalf of herself and the others. 'You can't be blamed for bad weather, Conor, but where do we go now?'

'There's an inn, The Prospect o' Cobh, ye can see it from here,' he answered, pointing to a white-painted stone building near to the quay, and pronouncing the Irish word as *cove*. 'Ye can all rest there on beds that won't roll from side to side.'

And to The Prospect of Cobh they went, to be shown rooms

with low wooden box-beds and straw mattresses. Mariette sank down fully clothed, saying that she could sleep on a bed of nails, and pale-faced Minnie curled up on the floor beside her. A stout woman in a woollen gown with a large apron tied round her middle offered them tea but recommended a little brandy and water to settle their stomachs; Tabitha accepted the latter for the other two women, and having drunk her tea, laid down on a narrow truckle-bed that she pulled out from under Mariette's.

Having similarly settled Berry, Conor asked the landlady for whatever victuals she could produce and tucked in heartily if somewhat guiltily to fried bacon and potato cakes, washed down with a pint of porter, giving thanks both for the food and his healthy appetite.

While he ate he was approached by a cheerful, broad-faced man wearing a coachman's hat.

'So ye got here at last, then, Master Conor.'

Conor turned round quickly. 'Seamus! Where in God's name have ye come from?'

'Where d'ye think? From home, o' course – Sir Bernard sent me to meet ye, and here have I been hangin' around since the day before yesterday,' the man replied with a grin. 'I was gettin' ready to give ye up for lost, surely, in that merciless storm. Where's yer lady wife, Master Conor? And the three servants ye was bringin' with ye?'

'God love 'em, they've gone to rest for a few hours, and don't ask me to wake 'em, Seamus, not after all they've been through. We'll spend a night here in the Cobh before we set forth again. What have ye brought with ye? A carriage or a farm-cart?'

Sir Bernard had thought it practical to send a covered wagon and three horses, one for Conor to ride while Seamus drove the ladies and their boxes of belongings along the Killarney Road as far as Poulgorm Bridge, where they would turn off on to a rough track that led down to Kenmare and so on to Tahilla and Townclear Hall – some seventy miles in all; but Conor insisted that they all had a good night's sleep first, for the sake of the ladies and Berry.

'Berry, Master Conor? And who might he be?'

'One o' the three servants ye're expectin' – ye'll find out when ye see him. Come on, Seamus, we'll go and get a sight o' Cork – sure 'tis good to be back in the old country!'

Early next morning they set off, a journey that started before daylight and ended after dark. The wagon wheels jolted on the stony track, in places very narrow, and every part of Tabitha's body ached when at last they drew up before the entrance to Townclear Hall. She dimly saw the outline of a roof with many gables and chimney pots, and a lighted hall behind the huge stone porch: the massive front door stood open, framing Sir Bernard and Lady Townclear with their eldest son, Bernard, waiting to welcome them.

Conor helped Mariette down from the wagon, then herself and Minnie. Berry stood back a few paces, his big eyes taking in the scene.

Tired and travel-sore as she was, Tabitha curtseyed and prepared herself to meet Conor's family again; he embraced his mother, father and brother in turn, then held out his hand to Mariette who stepped forward without curtseying or smiling.

'If ye'll forgive my wife, Mother – she's been very ill on a long journey, so would ye mind—'

'Of course, my dear Mariette, you must come straight up to bed,' said Lady Townclear at once, gesturing to a dark-browed maidservant to bring hot water up to Mariette's room. 'We both said that it was not a good time to make such a journey, much as we longed to see you after poor Moira—' She broke off, and her eyes were sad. 'Roisin is attending to the little ones, and will see you in the morning.' She turned to Tabitha. 'We're so pleased to have you here, Miss Prewett. I've put Conor and Mariette in a room on the second floor with views across the harbour, and you and the maidservant are in an adjoining room, so as to be on hand. Oh, my goodness, who is the boy?' she asked, staring at Berry who stared back at her, fearful of so many new sights and surroundings. He soon found himself accommodated in a room with the stable boys who slept above their charges in the stables, with Seamus in charge. It was warm and dry, and like the rest of the party from London, the African boy soon fell fast asleep.

The young women woke to a new day, and as they soon realized, a completely different way of life. Conor rose early and went out riding with his brother, impatient to be in the saddle again, while his wife and Tabitha dressed at their leisure, sharing with Minnie their first impressions of the Townclears' home and its surroundings, now seen in the light of day. Built from local stone on the lines of an English manor house, it was more rugged than gracious, though it had some fine points like the curving main staircase and splendid fireplace that took up almost the whole of one wall in the central living room, or hall, as the family called it, where daily life was lived, and to which the visitors descended for a good breakfast of soda bread and milk, with cold bacon and mutton on a huge sideboard. Lady Townclear joined them, and at once called Seamus to remove two of three enormous dogs who were loudly gnawing at bones beside the fire. Mariette breathed a sigh of relief.

'They are just like wolves!' she said with a shudder. 'And why does the other one stay?'

'Oh, Belle is nursing her puppies, so she stays in,' explained Lady Townclear. 'Look at them, they're only two weeks old. The children love them, needless to say!'

Siobhan and Sorcha, now aged four and three, came running into the room with their mother who was carrying the baby in her arms. The little girls stopped in their tracks and stared when they saw the visitors, and Roisin reassured them that this was Aunt Mariette from London and her friend Miss Prewett. They all sat down to breakfast with a woman called Mrs Shea who had been nurse to Bernard, Conor and Moira, and now helped with Roisin's little ones. Minnie was given a place at the same table, next to Tabitha.

Lady Townclear asked how they were now feeling, whether they had slept well; she was particularly anxious about Mariette, who had little to say. Tabitha found herself speaking for them both, and was determined to make a good impression: it was so important that Conor's wife, the beautiful daughter of a French aristocrat should be accepted by her husband's family. She therefore set out to be a useful go-between, and to get to know the children. Baby Grainne was now five months old, and being breast-fed – Mariette's eyebrows rose when Roisin opened her bodice at the table – so Tabitha had an opportunity to play with Siobhan and Sorcha during the morning, while Lady Townclear tried to talk with her daughter-in-law. There were a great many impressions to take in, and ways to be learned; it felt very strange.

When Mariette took herself off upstairs, Lady Townclear asked Tabitha to sit down and have a talk.

'Sir Bernard and I saw only a little of you, Miss Prewett, when we came to Conor's wedding, but we know that you're a great friend to both of them. Conor told me how good you were when our dear daughter Moira – I'm sorry, I still can't bear to think about that tragedy.' Her eyes filled with tears, and Tabitha took hold of her hand. 'We lost a daughter *and* a granddaughter, for it doesn't seem likely that we shall ever see poor little Augusta.'

Tabitha pitied the woman from her heart, but gently pointed out that she had three little granddaughters living under the same roof.

'Yes, Miss Prewett, but it was a great disappointment to have another girl. Without a male heir this family home could fall into the hands of a Protestant landlord, and be lost to our family for ever. It has happened to other Catholic houses, and our numbers are falling all the time – my husband says we're only about ten per cent of landowners, half of whom are absent for much of the time, and treat their tenants disgracefully. We are such a happy family, we take care of all our people, and they attend Mass in our own chapel. It would be a terrible shame if – but oh, Miss Prewett, I wonder if you will let me ask a question? Poor dear Mariette is still feeling ill after that dreadful journey, and I wonder – oh, Miss Prewett, I just wonder if—'

Tabitha closed her eyes and braced herself for the question she knew was coming.

'Could it be possible, Miss Prewett, that Mariette is again expecting a child? It was another bitter blow when she miscarried last September, but do you think that—?'

Distressed by the awful irony of the situation, Tabitha's hasty reply was misunderstood.

'I'm not in a position to say anything, ma'am. It's not for me to say.'

'Of course not, my dear, I quite understand, and of course I shouldn't have asked you,' said poor Lady Townclear, obviously taking this as an encouragement to believe that Conor and his wife would break the news at a suitable time. 'But thank you, Miss Prewett – thank you!'

Tabitha could not bear to hear the hope in the woman's voice, or look at the new light in her eyes. Her one idea was to get hold of Conor and demand that he inform his parents and brother of the true situation – the sooner, the better, and before the day was out, she decided.

The brothers spent the whole day riding over the estate and beyond, and she did not see Conor again until they dined with the family at five o'clock. Immediately after the meal she drew him aside into a small room full of boots, hunting coats and hats on pegs, walking-sticks and all the paraphernalia of a country house.

'Tabitha, darlin',' he protested. 'My father's asked Bernard and myself to take a glass o'—'

'I can't help that, Conor, you have more important business with Sir Bernard than taking a glass of anything.' Her dark eyes were serious and unsmiling. 'Your mother's a good woman, and she's suffered a lot o' trouble lately, a lot o' sorrow. I've had to fend off her questions, in fact I've practically lied to her. You must tell your father today – *now* – that she *is* going to have a grandchild from you, but not by Mariette.'

'Oh, forgive me, Tabitha, I've been waitin' for the moment, y'see, and I—'

'The moment's *now*, Conor – you must tell your father, and he must then tell her. It will be a shock, and I don't know how she'll take it, but I refuse to be a party to this deception any longer. *Tell him.*'

'I will, I will, Tabitha, and I'm sorry. Of course it's not fair on my mother – or on Mariette or yeself. I'll speak to Father this evenin', and Bernard. When I see ye again, darlin', it'll be done.'

And it was. He was true to his word, and over a bottle of port wine, he told his father and brother together, and that night, in bed, Sir Bernard told his wife, and young Bernard told Roisin.

On their second day at Townclear Hall, the atmosphere had changed. Conor's mother looked bewildered, and had little to say to either of her daughters-in-law or Miss Prewett – or rather Tabitha, because she said that the girl's Christian name was more suitable, thus relegating Tabitha to the status of maidservant rather than an equal. But when Roisin asked that Tabitha and Minnie be moved out of their bedroom to sleep in the servants' quarters, Mariette simply stood up and forbade it.

'Tabitha is my friend, and Minnie is my personal maid, so they will sleep next to my room,' she declared, and when her husband nodded his approval, nothing more was said.

The little girls were disappointed that they were not encouraged to speak to Tabitha, let alone play with her, and as Mariette had predicted, their real opponent was Mrs Roisin Townclear. She scarcely spoke to either of them, and they met her silence with silence, which sometimes made for a strained atmosphere, especially as the wintry weather kept them all indoors for much of the time. Tabitha persuaded Mariette to go for walks when they could, accompanied by Minnie, and this way they got to know something of the life of Tahilla; behind Townclear Hall a mountain range rose up, and in front the land swept down to a small harbour with fishing boats. The estate was also an extensive farm, with sheep, cows and the much-admired horses. They saw Berry going about his duties as a stable lad, learning how to ride, then taking the reins of a farm-cart. His colour made him something of a curiosity among the cottagers, but his smiling good humour won him acceptance, and as the days grew longer and signs of spring began to appear, he became a familiar figure among the indoor and outdoor servants.

The same could be said for young Mrs Mariette and her friend Tabitha, now obviously carrying a child and looking very well. The friends drew even closer together, if that were possible, and became known to the cottagers' wives and their large families who lived in crowded thatched cabins, shared, to Mariette's horror, with their pigs and chickens. They discovered that these people spoke a strange foreign tongue, the Gaelic Irish language that had been spoken for centuries, and Tabitha tried to learn a few words of it, so as to be able to give a simple greeting, a remark about the weather or a new baby; but it was a barrier to real conversation, and Roisin used it to exclude her sister-in-law and companion when she spoke to Mrs Shea or other servants. Conor's mother was English, a woman of good Catholic family background, chosen by her husband in much the same way that Mariette had been chosen by Conor, but Roisin was a local farmer's daughter, and Tabitha suspected that she was jealous of Mariette, and considered her as bad as an adulteress for allowing her husband to father a child on a mere maidservant, a nobody and a

215

Protestant into the bargain. Even so, she could not fail to notice that Mariette's beauty won admiring glances from everybody they met.

One of these was the travelling priest, Father Aengus, who took Mass in the little chapel within Townclear Hall, and in other small places of worship around the county, sometimes in barns made into temporary chapels, sometimes in the open air. He was a cheerful, sport-loving man who rode to hounds and liked a whiskey with the menfolk after Mass, was always happy to talk about the price of livestock and attended county fairs where farmers bought and sold animals and produce. He was a natural speaker of the Gaelic, had little English and knew only the Latin of the Mass. This lack could be used to advantage when hearing confessions, and though he could not understand much of Mrs Mariette Townclear's words of penitence, he absolved her without hesitation. What Conor told him was between themselves, but Father Aengus sympathized with the need for a male heir; Tabitha of course was not under the priest's spiritual direction, though he noticed her and thought her a fine, healthy-looking woman, likely to bear a strong child for the younger Townclear son. He told Conor that they would have to wait and see if it was a boy: a daughter was not likely to cause any family complications. In fact the menfolk adjusted to Conor's situation with less difficulty than did the women; Sir Bernard himself was as polite and friendly towards Tabitha as before, possibly explained by a piece of family history that Conor told her.

'My father went to find a wife in England, ye see, and when he found my mother, her parents thought her too young to marry and leave home, and said they must wait a year. Well, that was agreed upon, and Father came home again, and – er – there was a little bit o' bother with the innkeeper's daughter over at Sneem, that's a little village a few miles up the Kenmare river – and this girl had a daughter, and everybody in the village and for miles around knew whose daughter she was. Anyway, the girl went off to Cork an' made a good life for herself, and ye can see the daughter any time ye like, for she's married to a sailmaker here in Tahilla, and a fine, handsome woman she is, too.'

Like father, like son, then? No, Tabitha decided, because whereas Sir Bernard's bastard daughter had been an accident, so to speak, Conor's child was the result of a serious decision, for which he took full responsibility. The thought occurred to her that if the innkeeper's daughter had had a boy, he would have had no claim on the estate over the two legitimate sons, even though he was the eldest; but if *her* child was a boy, there were no legitimate sons to stand in his way. Not yet.

February gave way to March, and March to April. Life at Tahilla was busy indoors and out, and the coming of spring to County Kerry was a transformation. The Cala mountains rose up blue against the clear sky, and Tabitha had never imagined grass so green, pastures so lush or air so clear; she smiled to herself when she saw Mariette striding out across the fields or down to Coongar harbour with the great Irish wolfhounds bounding along beside her, guards against danger from ruffians who might rob her or be tempted by her beauty. She had quite got over her fear of them, and Conor was teaching her to ride. Tabitha felt no envy, for she thought herself the most blessed of the three, and rejoiced as she felt the child moving within her. She had mixed feelings about the birth, now drawing nearer; while she carried the child in her womb, it was undeniably hers, but once it was born it would be *theirs*, Conor's and Mariette's, and only partly hers. Remembering the births that she had recently witnessed or heard about, she knew that the event would be an encounter with great pain, possibly even death, as had happened to Conor's sister, and so nearly to Prudence and her daughter. The midwife, she knew, was to be Mrs Shea who had delivered Lady Townclear's babies and Roisin's, and also many children born to cottagers' wives. She had never lost a mother yet, she boasted, but Tabitha had no illusions, and prayed that she would face the ordeal with courage and commonsense.

'And if one of us has to die, Lord, then let it be me and not the child.'

'At last, Tabitha, a letter from Maman and Papa! Oh, I am half afraid to see what they say about the baby – will you read it for me, please, Tabitha? No – I must read it for myself. Stay with me while I do!'

Her eyes quickly scanned the page covered with her mother's close, sloping handwriting.

'Oh, it is just as I thought! They are so much worried about me – Maman says I must have known there was a baby coming when I left London. Oh, *mon Dieu*, she says she wants to travel to Ireland to see me! – ah, but thank heaven, my father is not willing – says that Conor will see that I have good care – they send their compliments to Lady Townclear – and she has enclosed a letter for *you*, Tabitha – yes, look, here it is, folded up inside the envelope – she will pray every morning, noon and evening—'

While Mariette chattered on, Tabitha unfolded the small square of paper on which her name was written:

> Dear friend Tabitha,
> I rely on you more than ever to take care of our beloved daughter. Do not let her tire herself, ensure she avoids too much exercise, let her rest often and eat only what is wholesome. Make sure that Lady Townclear finds her a good midwife . . .

It went on for a whole page in the same vein, and far from being amused by the welter of misdirected advice, Tabitha felt a sense of unease, much as she had when Lady Townclear had been similarly deceived. Whichever way she viewed the situation, Tabitha knew that it could not be right to lie.

'Can't you write and tell her the truth, dearest Mariette?' she asked. 'It would be better for our consciences if we explained, as we've done to Sir Bernard and Lady Townclear.'

'What? Have I endured all this upheaval, banished to the back of beyond and nearly dead on that terrible voyage, only to tell everything to my parents? Good heavens above, Tabitha, can't you see how shocked they would be, how they'd turn against Conor? It would do nothing but harm in every way! – but as long as they believe that the infant is mine, they will rest content.'

'But Mariette, my own dear love, Sir Bernard and Lady Townclear have accepted the truth, and so would your—'

'Once and for all, my Tabitha, let me tell you that I don't care a fig for what Conor's parents think, nor that low-born peasant, Roisin. *My* parents must believe that the child is mine, and so will all our neighbours in London. It will be *ours*, Tabitha – yours and mine and Conor's, and if God answers all our prayers, it will be a son. Oh, look here at the bottom of Maman's letter, she says, "If the baby is a boy, we suppose he will be called Conor, for his father – but if we get a little girl, I would like her called Marie-Therese after my sainted mother." Well, Maman, let it be so – but we shall be far happier with a Conor!'

Mariette spoke gaily, and Tabitha smiled. It sounded as if Conor was going to have little choice in the matter of a name, and she herself even less. Marie-Therese was a pretty name, though very papist, but there seemed no point in arguing over names at this stage. As Father Aengus had said, they would have to wait and see.

By the end of June, Tabitha was feeling very tired. Her belly seemed enormous, and her back ached as the weight of the child dragged on the rest of her body. Mrs Shea waylaid her in the house a couple of times, and asked her about the due date for delivery, which Tabitha reckoned to be about now, the end of June. The woman enquired about her bowels and how often she needed to get up in the night to pass water. One matter that Mrs Shea did *not* mention was Tabitha's unmarried state, nor did she ask questions about the father of the baby, or any personal details. Tabitha concluded that Lady Townclear must have confided in her and mentioned what attitude she should take.

It was in the early morning of the second day of July, a Saturday, that Tabitha awoke just as the first light of dawn was breaking in the east, and knew that her ordeal had begun. Minnie was sleeping soundly beside her, and Tabitha lay listening to the silence of the household in which every member, including the dogs, was wrapped in slumber; she was the only one awake.

There it was again, a tightening of her belly which rose in board-like hardness, accompanied by a bearable degree of pain. It subsided after about a minute, and recommenced after about ten minutes. There was no need to call Mrs Shea and wake the whole house just yet; she would lie beside Minnie in the growing daylight, and think of Mariette and Conor. Conor and Mariette. This was the gift she was giving them: perhaps by the day's end they would hold their treasure in their arms . . . She closed her eyes, dozing between these early pains. She was a traveller at the start of a hazardous journey. An hour passed, and the pains got stronger: she realized that she was moaning as each one reached its peak. Minnie was awake and sitting up.

'Are y'all right, Miss Tabitha?' The girl had never learned to drop the Miss. 'Shall I get Mrs Townclear to come to yer?'

Mr and Mrs Townclear were only in the next room, and Minnie's knock roused them. Mariette wrapped a shawl over her nightdress, and came at once to the bedside of her friend. She scarcely moved from her post throughout the day, but sent Conor out to do his duties on the estate – 'and don't come back till afternoon, this is women's business!'

'I shall remain with her and see the birth of the child,' she informed Mrs Shea. 'I want to share every moment, just as if I were there in her place.'

This was not good news for the old midwife, used to reigning supreme in the birth-chamber, but Mariette turned out to be a more useful assistant than expected. She spent the hours wiping Tabitha's face and hands, offering her sips of water, holding her hand during the strong, painful contractions of the womb, and supplying Mrs Shea with hot water, towels and cups of tea. And she did not disdain clearing away soiled linen, the discharges from the bowel and gushes of fluid from the womb.

'I was mistaken in Mrs Townclear,' the midwife admitted to the serving maids of Townclear Hall. 'She's a tidy little body, careful as a hen hatchin' chicks, an' doesn't mind what she has to do. Ye'd think it was her own child she's havin'.'

Lady Townclear overheard these words as she walked to and fro, anxiously awaiting the outcome, but Roisin's mouth was set in a stern, straight line. If a son was to be born to this nobody, then God grant that she too would give birth to a boy in the fulness of time, an heir to Townclear house and the baronetcy!

The hours went by, and the sun was well past the meridian when Mrs Shea noted that Tabitha's cries of pain had deepened to a straining, almost grunting sound. Mariette's lips moved in silent prayer, listening to the new, encouraging tone in the midwife's voice.

'Come on, now, Mrs Tabitha, it's time to be pushin' down! Will ye be takin' a big breath in an' holdin' it while ye push – push – push down as hard as ye can. An' again – an' another – all right, have a rest before the next one.' Turning to Mariette, she said, 'Ye can help her when she pushes, Mrs Townclear, by holdin' on to her knees. Ah, now, here comes another pain – do as before, that's right, that's good, that's the way, keep goin' – well done, both o' ye!'

And so Mariette Townclear, who would not have gone near any other birth-chamber, now saw and heard and understood every moment of her friend's birthing.

'Another push – and another – you're nearly there, my Tabitha!' she breathed as the midwife nodded and placed her hands on the emerging crown. 'It's coming, it's coming!'

A little face appeared as the midwife extended the head with her practised hands.

'The head's born, Tabitha – oh, my darling, it's nearly over – oh, let it be a boy!'

The shoulders rotated and the left shoulder appeared; Mrs Shea gently pulled down the left arm, and then the right arm was freed. Immediately the rest of the body was born, and Mrs Shea received into her hands a fine, healthy, crying baby.

'*O, merci, Sainte Vierge*! It is a boy – our own little Conor! Dear, dearest Tabitha, you have given us a son!'

The two women embraced with tears and smiles while Mrs Shea attended to the baby's umbilical cord. The fleshy afterbirth was speedily expelled into a basin, and the midwife called out for Minnie to go and tell the news to the waiting relatives and to ask that Conor be sent for.

Lady Townclear covered her face with her hands when she heard that she had a grandson, but Roisin's tense features hardened. A son to Conor posed a threat to her own brood, even though there was plenty of time yet for her to produce a boy. She did not follow Lady Townclear into the birth-chamber, where the new baby was being admired and exclaimed over.

'Here he is, yer Ladyship, as fine a boy as ever was, an' heir to Townclear Hall!' cried Mrs Shea triumphantly, and Conor's mother gave a sob.

'Let me call you daughter now, Mariette, for giving my son this blessing—'

The two women embraced, the mother and daughter-in-law, and Mrs Shea gently placed the baby in his grandmother's arms. 'He's got his father's eyes, God love him, a true Townclear!'

'Has anybody sent for Conor?' asked Lady Townclear.

'Sure, the maid Minnie's taken a message to tell Berry to fetch Conor home straightaway!'

Laughter, tears, exclamations of joy – the happy sounds wove in and out of Tabitha's conscious mind as she lay exhausted after her ordeal. It seemed that a chorus of voices was rejoicing over the son she had borne in pain to Conor Townclear. Suppose the child had been a daughter, Marie-Therese – she knew there would not have been the same elation, and in due course she would have had to conceive and bear another child, and perhaps yet another, in order to give Conor a son. A girl would have been more truly hers, more equally shared between herself and Mariette; but now there was no further need for Conor to use her body in this way; her duty was done.

Tabitha closed her eyes as the excited talk went on over her head, until another sound reached her ears: the hammering of a horse's hooves getting louder: they all heard it approaching the house, and there was a shout as a man dismounted in the yard below. Conor's rapid footsteps were heard on the stairs, and as he burst into the room, Mariette took the newly-born baby from Lady Townclear and held him out for her husband to see.

'Here he is, Conor! Our own little son, another Conor! Isn't he beautiful?'

He hardly seemed to notice her, or the baby who was crying lustily. His single eye saw only the woman on the bed.

'What? How is she?' he demanded. 'Tabitha – oh, Tabitha, my darlin' dear – my own darlin' dear.' Blinded by tears, he knelt down by the side of the bed and took her hand.

Mrs Shea silently but firmly took the baby from Mariette's arms and placed him in his father's. 'There now, Conor, 'tis a fine, healthy boy,' she said, 'and he's yours, so ye'd better be raisin' yer head an' lookin' at him.'

Fifteen

And so began those blessed months that Tabitha was to remember as the Tahilla summer, when skies were cloudless above the Cala mountains and fresh breezes blew in from Coongar harbour. Up in the room she shared with Minnie and her precious baby, Tabitha looked out on an emerald-green countryside where sheep wandered over open common land and cottagers' children played barefoot in the sunshine, their shouts echoing through the long July afternoons. Sunny days and warm, velvet-dark nights passed in worshipping the child she had borne and now nourished with a plentiful supply of rich, sweet milk; as his eager lips sucked from one breast, the other dripped with overflowing bounty. Tabitha knew that she had never been so contented, so deeply at peace with herself.

Mariette watched in fascination. 'Mrs Shea says there's a cottager's wife with childbed fever who can't feed her baby, so it is having cow's milk, poor little thing,' she said, whereupon Tabitha at once called for a clean basin to collect her own surplus milk.

'Send it to them, and let Mrs Shea give it to the baby with a teaspoon,' she said. 'She can show some responsible woman how to do it, as I did for my little half-sister.'

Mrs Shea was delighted by the success of her stratagem; knowing that Mrs Tabitha, as she was now titled, could never deny Mrs Townclear anything, the midwife was now able to collect and supply good fresh breast-milk to more than one unsatisfied child on the Townclear estate.

'Call me the milch-cow of Tahilla!' laughed Tabitha, cuddling her baby and kissing the top of his downy head before offering him the breast yet again.

'*Mon Dieu*, I've never seen you looking better, my Tabitha!' exclaimed Mariette.

'Truly, I've never known such happiness as this,' replied her friend, smiling down at the baby and reflecting to herself that she had chosen right, even though her father had thought her a fool. I was right to choose Mariette and Conor, she thought, and now I have my reward – oh, such a reward, far beyond anything I could have imagined possible!

When the baby had finished sucking, and lay drowsily content in her arms, she gazed on his sleeping face with wondering love. Some of this love communicated itself to Mariette.

'He is adorable – my little Conor – *oui, mon petit*,' she whispered, leaning over to kiss the son given to her by her dearest friend. All the obstacles, all the difficulties and deceptions that had dogged them over the past year now seemed of no importance, for the baby made up for everything they had endured. Lady Townclear was never tired of looking at her grandson, while his grandfather and Uncle Bernard agreed that he was a fine little fellow, a regular Townclear who might one day protect the family estate and save it from falling into other hands.

But Conor could never see enough of his son, and whenever he was able he made his way to Tabitha's room, simply to watch her feeding his little namesake. One afternoon when Mariette was out with the dogs he came and knelt down between Tabitha's knees while the baby sucked vigorously at her right breast. Minnie had just brought her another glass of water, and discreetly withdrew when the master entered.

'Tabitha, my darlin'—' he murmured, kissing her mouth; she smiled and offered him her left breast to fondle. He licked the drops of milk that trickled from it, and put his arms right around the two of them.

'I'd make love to ye if ye weren't so busy with my son,' he whispered, and she laughed softly, for there would be opportunity enough when the satisfied baby was laid down in his crib.

'Thanks be to ye, darlin' Tabitha, for givin' me a son – our son, our little Conor.'

'And thank you for giving him to *me*, Conor. I've never known happiness like this,' she answered simply, for it seemed as if the very angels in heaven must look down and envy her.

July gave way to a warm and mellow August, and Tabitha wrapped her baby in a shawl to take out and show to the tenants and their families. Mariette always accompanied her on these visits, and they took turns at carrying the child. They invited Roisin to come with them and bring baby Grainne, but she could not overcome her bitterness at the way she had been supplanted.

'Ah, now, Roisin, ye can't hold out against a little baby who's never yet done anythin' wrong,' her husband remonstrated. 'It's not his fault, is it?'

But poor Roisin, a farmer's daughter who felt her humiliation keenly, would only sulk in aggrieved silence, unable to express how she felt towards these two shameless women who shared her brother-in-law and proudly showed off the bastard son as if he belonged to both of them. It galled her when Sorcha and Siobhan pursued their aunt Mariette who showed them how to make daisy-chains, but she could hardly prevent them, and knew that her resentment would gain her no sympathy. She could only pray for the day when Conor would return to England and take his two wives with him. And if her prayers were answered, she herself would produce a son – a legitimate heir – before they showed their faces at Tahilla again.

And when September came, bringing misty mornings and burgeoning fruit, Conor had to face the fact that their summer idyll was coming to an end; he needed to take his family back to London before the winter storms set in over the Irish Sea.

'Yer parents'll be wantin' ye home, Mariette, an' they'll be dyin' to see the child,' he told his wife, now tanned brown by summer suns and ready to return to their London life of dinner parties, theatre outings and studying the latest fashions.

By contrast, Tabitha shrank from the artificiality of that life, and the deceptions they would have to practise on their relatives and friends, especially the St Aubyns who must never suspect that baby Conor was not the natural born son of Mrs Townclear. Minnie was the only servant who knew the truth about the child's parentage, and she was fiercely loyal to her master and the two mistresses. Berry, who had been too busy to notice otherwise, was simply told that the baby belonged to Mr and Mrs Townclear, and that Miss Tabitha was his nurse.

When the time came for leave-taking at the end of September, Tabitha experienced the first real sinking of the heart since the birth of her baby. She was reluctant to leave Tahilla, where the most important event of her life had taken place. She told Conor's parents that she would always regard Townclear Hall as home in the truest sense of the word, but even as she spoke she felt a chill foreboding that she might never see them or their home again.

All too soon the morning came when the five of them, plus the baby, climbed on to the farm wagon that was to take them the seventy miles to Cork. Everybody except Roisin was sorry to see them go, and Lady Townclear wept at parting from her beloved little grandson. She stood watching and waving as the wagon, driven by Seamus, jolted away into the mist and out of her sight.

On arriving at Cork there were no small sailing boats available to take passengers to England, and they spent a night at the Prospect of Cobh, thankful for tolerable lodgings. The next day Conor spent much of his time looking out to sea and scanning the horizon with a borrowed eyeglass. When eventually a large ocean-going vessel weighed anchor to drop a couple of passengers, Conor eagerly applied to the captain for a passage to the port of Bristol. He learned that the ship carried a cargo of raw cotton and sugar, and would be continuing from Bristol to the west coast of Africa. It seemed like a godsend – until the servant boy Berry saw it.

Tabitha had never seen such cowering terror as on the boy's face. He fell on his knees and begged Conor not to make him board that dreadful slave-ship, he wept and held his hands up as if to ward off blows, he trembled like a leaf as he spoke of the human cargo that had lain chained in its hold on its former journey from West Africa to America. Nothing that Conor could say would persuade him to embark on it, for he vowed he would rather die.

'This is ridiculous, we cannot miss a passage to England just because of a servant-boy's fear,' complained Mariette, but Tabitha for once disagreed with her. She had caught something of the boy's horror, and there was something about the captain – a slave trader – which repulsed her. Conor admitted that he could not step on board with a good conscience, and so the ship sailed off without them, and they spent a second night at the Prospect of Cobh. The next day they boarded a small schooner which carried them across the Irish Sea within hours, though Mariette and Berry were again struck down by seasickness, and Mariette declared that she would never go to sea again. After a night at a Bristol inn, they travelled by stagecoach to London, arriving tired and travel-stained at Hyde Park Corner, and from there by hackney cab to 21 Gerrard Street. Mrs Clark and Peggy were there to welcome them home and exclaim over the baby; a message had been left by the Comte and Comtesse de St Aubyn, to be informed at once of their arrival, but to Tabitha's relief Mariette said they all needed a day to rest and recover before meeting anybody, even her parents.

In any case, there was a very important matter to be discussed before word was sent to Bloomsbury Square. The St Aubyns had been told of the baby's birth on the second of July: but what should they be told about his feeding routine?

How could they be prevented from knowing that it was Tabitha and not Mariette who was nourishing him?

'We shall have to say that I insist on strict privacy when he is fed,' said Mariette, 'or rather, that I only allow Tabitha in the room with me, to help me with him. After all, we were always alone at Townclear Hall, not like that Roisin who uncovered her breasts at the dining table!'

'But your own mother will surely want to see you feeding him, it's only natural!' Tabitha pointed out.

'Do not make objections, Tabitha! It is your duty to help me in this matter. I shall tell Maman that I cannot feed him if I am watched – and *you* must make sure that *mon petit* is always full of milk when we have visitors, so that he will not cry.'

'Can't we say he has a wet-nurse to feed him?' begged Tabitha.

'Of course not, Maman would wish to see the woman and approve of her. No, Tabitha, we must make sure that she never suspects that you are his nurse. I will put pads over my breasts – under my gown, so – and you must flatten yours as much as you can. Come, my Tabitha, we must make a promise to each other over this, for our little son's sake. My parents must believe that he is mine – as indeed he *is*, in every other way, both mine and Conor's!'

And somehow or other the deception was maintained, though the constant anxiety of it affected Tabitha's milk supply and little Conor became fretful. Whenever he cried in his grandparents' presence, she would pick him up and whisk him away to her room where she would feed him behind a curtain in the window alcove, and only Minnie knew of it. Fortunately he was on the whole a contented baby, and the Comte and Comtesse were so delighted with him, the Comtesse in particular smothering him with kisses and pretty French endearments, so that Mariette's sensitivity over breastfeeding was not much remarked on, and Tabitha was praised for taking good care of the young mother at the time of the birth and during these early months of motherhood.

Nevertheless Tabitha looked back with longing to those carefree summer days at Tahilla, where there had been no need for deception. These days her conscience troubled her from time to time, even as she fed her little son and revelled in his early smiles and attempts to hold up his head on its flower-stalk neck. His eyes were dark like her own and Conor's, and his hair a light brown with a little curl on the top: he was in every way a darling, but life was not the same as at Tahilla. Conor had to resume his work for Mr Shenstone and in Fleet Street, where he was embarking on a history of the Gordon riots, and the popular Townclears had many engagements to attend. With a houseful of servants it was not often convenient for Conor to visit her in her room, and in any case Tabitha felt that having borne him the longed-for son, it was no longer right for her to continue their relationship. What had seemed to be so natural was no longer the same: and the word adultery came to her mind with all its implications of sinfulness, of breaking one of the Lord's explicit commandments.

It was perhaps for this reason that she was reluctant to go and visit her own family in Orchard Court, and indeed she could hardly do so while the baby needed her for regular nourishment. She had sent word to her father and Prudence that she was back in London with the Townclears, but added that she was very busy helping Mrs Townclear with the new baby; Prudence had replied briefly but kindly to say that they would be glad to see her if she could manage a free afternoon to take tea with them, adding that their daughter Jenny was toddling around happily, and that Jeremiah and Betty had another baby, a little girl called Amy.

I really must go and see them for a couple of hours, thought Tabitha, but no sooner had she made up her mind than she was suddenly confronted by her father: he had called at 21 Gerrard Street in response to a request from the Townclears for new winter clothes. He had come with a basket of swatches and a measuring tape, and Peggy had shown him into the parlour, telling him that Mr and Mrs Townclear were out, but expected home shortly. Meanwhile she called to Miss Prewett, and Tabitha put baby Conor into his crib and went downstairs to face her father.

'Hallo, Papa—' she began, and he held out his arms to her. 'Oh, Papa, I'm sorry it's been so long – I'm sorry,' she said confusedly as they embraced, and she was conscious of the soft fulness of her breasts against his jacket. He smiled and held her at arm's length.

'Hm! I'll have to take yer measurements again before I make anythin' new for yer, girl. Ye've put on a bit o' weight.'

'Er – yes, I have, a little. How are you, Papa? And Prudence and all the boys?'

'Growin' up fast enough. Did yer know I've got another grandchild?'

'Yes, Prudence told me. I – I really want to come over and see you all, only—'

They were interrupted by the arrival of Conor and Mariette, who greeted John Prewett very cordially, and Mariette at once asked if he had seen the baby.

'You mean Tabitha has not shown him to you? Oh, let him be brought down at once!' cried Mariette, though Conor hesitated and glanced at Tabitha. She had mixed feelings about her father seeing her baby son, but there was no real reason why he should not, and she left the room to go upstairs and fetch him from his crib.

'There now, Mr Prewett, isn't he a lovely little boy?' said Mariette proudly as the tailor looked at the child in Tabitha's arms, and nodded.

'Yes, Mrs Townclear, he does you credit. I'm happy for you,' he said pleasantly, glancing towards Conor who stood back and watched in silence.

'Mr – er – Prewett has come to take your measurements, so I'd better put him back to sleep, Mrs Townclear,' said Tabitha, her embarrassment making her sound fussy. 'You must excuse me, please.'

She left the parlour and took the baby back to his crib in her room; half an hour passed while John Prewett discussed the coats he was to make for the Townclears. Then Mariette called up to ask Tabitha to come and assist with the measuring, and also to be measured herself.

'It's only right that you too should have a new coat for the winter, Tabitha! Come on, while your father's here!'

Tabitha stood still and raised her arms while the tape measure was passed around her chest, waist and hips, and the figures put down in the tailor's book.

'Thank ye very much, Mr Prewett, we're obliged to ye. My wife and I'll be lookin' forward to the fittin',' said Conor, steering Mariette out of the parlour. 'Let her have a moment with her father,' he whispered, and then raising his voice again, 'Ye can see Mr Prewett out when ye're ready, Miss Tabitha.'

He had deliberately left them alone. She looked into her father's face, and knew his thoughts.

'He's the image o' Jeremiah when he was born,' he said bluntly, and she lowered her eyes, having seen a passing resemblance to both Thomas and Andrew in baby Conor's features.

'But he takes after his father most closely, Papa.'

'Oh, ah, he's a Townclear right enough, a handsome little fellow. Is his mother still feedin' him?' Prewett asked suddenly.

'Yes, o' course she is.' Tabitha could not meet her father's penetrating look. 'But I'm his – his nurse, Papa, I do everything else for him.'

'He won't always need a nurse, my girl, not when he starts walkin' an' talkin'. But there it is, it's the life yer chose, and yer can't go back an' undo it.'

She understood that he was not to be deceived, and therefore she too could no longer pretend. She raised her head and looked directly at him. 'Yes, Papa, he's mine, but he's also theirs,' she said very quietly.

He nodded, unsurprised. 'Ye've done them a service, my girl. I hope they won't forget it.'

'You won't tell Prudence or – anybody, Papa?'

'I won't tell anythin', my dear, but if Prudence sees him, she won't need tellin', I reckon.'

'Thank you, Papa.'

'Goodbye, Tabitha. I hope ye'll be happy with the boy.'

'Oh, I am, Papa, very happy!' But her eyes filled with tears when he kissed her and said goodbye. There was a certain relief in knowing that he knew, and did not condemn her, but he had also made it clear that he thought her future uncertain.

As the year declined towards Christmas, Conor Townclear came to a decision about the practice of his Roman Catholic faith. He no longer wanted to be dependent upon embassy chapels or friends who, like Lady Farrinder, had set aside rooms for worship in their homes; he said they would have a small chapel at 21 Gerrard Street, and provide hospitality for any priest who would come and administer the sacrament to the family and a few Catholic relatives like the St Aubyns or any of their friends. Lady Farrinder put him in touch with an itinerant priest, Father Braine, a Jesuit, and this man became a regular visitor to celebrate Mass and hear confessions. Among the servants Peggy and Berry, neither of whom had an attachment to a church, were now received into the Roman Catholic church as baptized members. Mrs Clark and Minnie attended the Anglican church of St Anne's, and Tabitha had not attended any church for many weeks. Her round-the-clock care of little Conor, now approaching six months, allowed her little time to leave the house: on Christmas Day she stayed up in her room within her baby's call while the Townclears received the sacrament from the hands of Father Braine.

Even though she was not under the priest's authority, she was somewhat in awe of him, a thin, angular man with piercing blue eyes that rarely smiled. It was said that he had once been tortured for his faith, and had refused to yield the names of other persons supposedly involved in a popish plot. He seemed to glare at Tabitha if she crossed his path in the house, whether in the entrance hall or on the stairs leading to the little room set aside as a chapel, and she wondered what Conor might have said to him at confession. Conor and Mariette seemed to have been absorbed back into London life with all its commitments and engagements, whereas her own life revolved around baby Conor. She took care of him day and night, and he had become her whole world; he was her passion, her chief delight, the apple of her eye – and he clearly looked upon her as his mother, smiling and following her with his eyes, holding out his arms to her.

There was no joy equal to feeding him at her breasts, and she did not look forward, as Mariette did, to his weaning in another two or three months' time, when he would be started on barley bread soaked in broth or milk, and a little mashed potato with gravy.

'I shall be able to feed him with a spoon, and you will be much more free, my Tabitha!' Mariette predicted happily. 'I shall become as necessary to him as you are!'

Tabitha said nothing, for she dreaded losing the very special intimacy of feeding her son from her own body; more freedom would be no compensation for such a loss. However, for the present time he was still entirely hers.

On Christmas Day they invited the St Aubyns to dinner after attending morning Mass, and on New Year's Day the

231

Townclears went to dinner at Mr Shenstone's while Tabitha stayed at home with the baby, which she greatly preferred. She gazed in doting admiration as he crawled across the hearthrug of the nursery, which was also the bedroom she shared with Minnie, his bright eyes following each object he saw, his chubby hands reaching out to explore every inch of his surroundings. Tabitha knew that there was nowhere else in the world where she would prefer to spend the New Year than here with her precious darling.

And yet suddenly her thoughts turned to Tahilla, and she pictured the family there – Conor's parents and his brother Bernard, his sister-in-law Roisin and the three little girls. Would Roisin ever manage to produce a son? And if not, would this child of hers inherit the title and the estate in due course? Conor had talked of growing unrest among tenants who were rebelling against tyrannical Protestant landlords who charged extortionate rents although they were often absent from the land. At Tahilla there were no such grievances, for the cottagers were treated as an extension of the family; but if there were no male heir to carry on the estate, this could all change, the estate could be carved up and taken over by neighbouring Protestant landowners, as had happened in many other cases. For some reason Tabitha gave a shiver, although the room was warm. A blazing log fell in the grate, sending up a shower of sparks, and she tried to picture a different life, the great hearth at Townclear Hall, where they would all be seated after dinner, the dogs gnawing the leftover mutton bones, and Father Aengus sitting in his corner with his glass of whisky, talking over the times in the Gaelic Irish that they all understood.

Ugh, there was that shiver again, like a messenger of ill tidings at the door. Tabitha rose and picked up the baby, hugging him to her heart. The house seemed very silent.

'Is somebody there?' she called out. 'Is that you, Minnie?' But Minnie had gone out to tea at the home of the young man who delivered the milk, and the other servants were no doubt seated around the kitchen fire, talking, dozing or playing at cards, perhaps. The long-case clock on the landing struck six: it was time to put the kettle on to make tea and eat a slice of Mrs Clark's plum cake.

Little Conor put his arms around her neck, and she kissed him, shrugging off her superstitious fears.

'Darling Conor, your Tabitha's afraid of shadows tonight – aren't I silly? *Silly* Tabitha!'

It took a month – almost to the end of January before the letter arrived from Lady Townclear, telling of the fatal accident on New Year's Day. There had been a storm at sea, and a ship had foundered on the rocks south of Coongar harbour. Sir Bernard and his elder son had gone out in a fishing boat with Seamus and a couple of men from the village. Whether a sudden strong current had drawn them out to sea to capsize under towering waves, or whether the wrecked vessel had sucked them down with her as she sank, the widow could not tell. All she knew was that neither her husband nor son had returned.

'Come home, Conor,' she wrote in anguish. 'For God's sake, Conor, come home again, my only son, as soon as you can.'

Sixteen

1786

No 21 Gerrard Street was thrown into turmoil. Conor broke down and wept aloud when he read his mother's letter and understood the extent of the loss he had sustained: his father and only brother gone, together with their faithful retainer Seamus who had been born on the estate and served the family for so long.

There was never any question as to where Conor's duties lay. His mother had already lived through a month of mourning, uncomforted by the presence of any relative other than a distraught daughter-in-law and three fatherless children. As soon as he had reasonably recovered from the first shock, he announced that he must go to his mother at once, and neither Mariette nor Tabitha could deny that this was his first duty. They could only heap their love and sympathy upon him and send their condolences to the dowager Lady Townclear, Roisin and all the bereaved household.

'I'll take Berry with me,' he told them. 'He's a good lad an' we'll be needin' extra outside help. An' besides, we don't want him fallin' into the wrong hands here.'

Taking Berry with him seemed to underline the permanence of his move to Ireland, and the women had to hide their own feelings, their reluctance to part with Conor at a time of year when the crossing might be dangerous; it was certainly not practical for him to take two women and a sucking child, placing an extra burden on the stricken household at Tahilla. He needed to be unencumbered when he arrived at his family home, and later they would make arrangements for them all to join him. Later, when the immediate needs of the estate had been settled. Later, when the spring brought sunshine and longer days. Later.

When he and Berry had set off by stagecoach for Bristol, the two women had time to reflect on what had happened, and what was likely to happen in the future. Without Conor, they still had each other to ease their loneliness, and of course there was his baby, their little darling who would soon have to be weaned. Yet in their sadness and bewilderment, each waited for the other to speak about what the new situation would mean. It was Madame la Comtesse who expressed their thoughts with tearful misgiving.

'If he is now Sir Conor Townclear and has to live far away in an Irish farmhouse with peasants, what will happen to my lovely Mariette?' she cried. 'It is impossible that she should live in such a way!'

Monseigneur le Comte gently pointed out to her that their daughter would be Lady Townclear, the mistress of a Catholic household and mother of the future Sir Conor. Even if she had no more children, her position was assured. The St Aubyns would be able to visit her when things were more settled, he said, and no doubt she would make visits to them.

And not only to London. After fifteen years of exile the Comte was now seventy and had for some time felt a longing for his native soil. This seemed as good a time as any to speak of returning to Compiègne, his place of birth, his homeland where he had family and grandchildren from his first marriage. If his youngest daughter was to settle permanently in Ireland, it seemed like the right time to move back to France, and his argument carried considerable force with his wife. Her thoughts turned to Paris and life at the court of King Louis and Queen Marie Antoinette, the elegance and luxury; she thought of their estate at Compiègne, currently held by a son of the Comte, a place where society was much more defined, and the lower orders knew their proper place. Outbreaks such as those dreadful Gordon riots would never occur there. The Comtesse smiled at her husband.

'Yes, *mon cheri*, in our own beautiful country we shall worship in a Catholic church, without any of the fear and secrecy we have here. I have been missing it more and more.'

Mariette was cheered by the prospect of travelling to France on visits to her parents, and taking her son with her. And she would be châtelaine of Townclear Hall!

And Tabitha? As soon as the terrible news reached Gerrard Street, she had immediately understood the long-term implications, though delicacy and her deep pity for Conor restrained her from speaking, and even after Conor's departure she stayed silent. Only when the Comtesse had expressed her own feelings and expectations did Tabitha openly talk about the facts as she saw them.

'It seems likely that you will live in Ireland, dearest Mariette, with Conor and his – and our baby son,' she said as they sat together on the chaise longue in the parlour. 'And it is such a beautiful place! Think of last summer, wasn't it heaven? You got on so well with the tenants, they will look to you as their Lady – and you'll ride a fine horse and go hunting with the dogs! It will be a wonderful life for us, and our little Conor – I know we shall be happy.'

Thus encouraged, Mariette began to imagine herself as the Lady of Townclear whose beauty would be a legend: men would admire her, women would try to imitate her, and she would have no rivals. She would miss London, of course, but life would have its compensations like those visits to France and appearing at court . . .

As for Tabitha, her heart swelled in anticipation of a healthy country life, the joy of seeing little Conor grow up to be the handsome heir of Townclear. Away from London and its many distractions, she would grow ever closer to the two people – no, there were three of them now – Conor and Mariette, and baby Conor who loved her with a generosity untarnished by jealousy. Their dear little son cemented their love. Tabitha closed her eyes and let herself dream that she might yet bear more children to Conor: she pictured a dark-eyed little Marie-Therese. Then she reproached herself for indulging in such sweet images when the Townclears were mourning the double loss of Sir Bernard and his elder son. She would have to hide her own thoughts, dress plainly and keep her eyes downcast when she eventually saw Tahilla and Townclear Hall again, out of respect for the tragically bereaved family. But oh, how her heart glowed within her!

Mrs Shea had done her best to keep the sorrowing household together, to maintain discipline among servants and also the tenants, for the reliable Seamus was no longer with them. In this she was aided by Father Aengus who visited every day to give spiritual consolation to the widows, talking to Lady Townclear of her younger son, now Sir Conor Townclear, who would surely lose no time in coming home to take over the running of a large and hitherto prosperous estate.

'The house will not fall into ruin, Mary,' said the priest in his limited English, and with the familiarity of one who had seen Bernard, Conor and Moira grow up. And now Conor, his own personal favourite, was the only survivor. 'Courage, Mary! Conor will come when he gets the letter, dutiful son that he is, and will see all to rights.'

And of course they both knew that Conor had a son. That fact was now of much greater significance, and Father Aengus looked ahead to a time when he would have to turn a blind eye to the circumstances of that son's birth. The whole future of the Townclear land could be at stake, for it seemed that the young Mrs Townclear – as beautiful a woman as Aengus had ever set eyes on – was unable to bear children and looked upon Conor's bastard son as her own, and his father's heir. The child was undoubtedly a Townclear, baptized into the faith of his fathers, and the priest was willing to accept him as such – but there must be no more bastards, and Conor as master of Townclear Hall must have only one wife, his lawfully wedded lady, the beautiful Mariette. The other woman had done her duty, and must be sent away now.

Father Aengus sighed, for he was not an unkind man. From what he had seen of Conor's attitude towards his wife, and to the woman who was – well, *not* his wife, he foresaw heartbreak ahead; nevertheless, he had to speak his mind as a priest of the church which decreed that marriage was between one man and one woman, a husband and wife. It could not be otherwise.

By the time Conor and Berry stumbled wearily over the threshold of his family home after a journey lasting four days over land and sea, his mother was full of reproaches, saying that she had looked out for him day after day, and concluded that he had either given her up or had drowned in the Irish sea. He tried to explain that her letter had been delayed.

'Yes, mother, yes, yes, o' *course* I'm stayin' – I've come home to look after ye an' see to everythin',' he told her as she clasped him in her arms. 'No, I *won't* be goin' away again, mother, this is my home now, an' twill be my wife's an' my son's. Don't cry, dearest mother.'

She seemed to need endless reassurance, and clung to him as if afraid he would vanish from her sight. She had grown thin, and the place had a cheerless aspect, though he learned that Mrs Shea had kept the fires burning and made sure that the maidservants were busy with their brooms and mops. There had been trouble when Roisin had made some half-hearted efforts to bake bread, but had let the dough spoil while she left it to attend to the demands of her three children. When her mother came over to the hall to help out, the maidservants had resented her scolding them, and Mrs Shea had angrily told her not to interfere. Conor longed for the kindness and commonsense of his own womenfolk, left behind in London.

It was with a certain relief that he turned to Father Aengus, and realized how much the old priest had done to keep the estate on an even keel, for he could speak the Gaelic to the tenants. He advised Conor to become more fluent in his native language.

'I'm glad to see young Berry again, we've room for a good stable hand,' he told Conor. 'I've put Dermot Flynn in charge o' the horses, he's a cunning little fellow – and his big soft brother Mick's as strong as a horse and works well enough as long as Dermot watches him. There's not much doin' in the fields at this time, an' yer father made sure there was enough winter feed to see 'em through, but now ye're here—'

As Conor began to understand the enormity of the burden

he had now taken upon his shoulders, and the degree of commitment he would need, he saw that it was no use harking back to his London life, his dreams of becoming a writer and chronicler. His place now was here, and so was Mariette's, and he feared that she would not take kindly to it. He would have to rely on Tabitha – oh, Tabitha, his darling dear! – to help his wife to settle into her new position as Lady Townclear. In these dark February days he felt desperately lonely for them and his son; but he resolved to give his best efforts and take on his father's mantle with honour.

At Gerrard Street too there was much to be done. As soon as Mr Shenstone learned that No 21 was to be sold, he applied to the Comte de St Aubyn on behalf of a business associate who was interested in the property and willing to pay the full market price for it, plus extra for such fixtures and furnishings as were to be left in it. The St Aubyns marked some pieces of furniture and gifts they had made to the Townclears at the start of their married life there, and which they would now retrieve. Mr Shenstone was then invited to choose anything he liked, to be saved for him at the time of the sale, to take place at the end of April.

As the days sped by and their departure approached, Tabitha made an effort to visit Orchard Court, to see her father and his wife and child, and all her brothers before leaving. She thought she might not see them again for a very long time, possibly never, and wanted to embed them all in her memory.

She arrived at her old home to be given an unexpectedly warm welcome. Mrs Markham was very interested in hearing about the Townclear estate in Ireland, and asked a great many questions about County Kerry and the kind of people who would be Tabitha's countrymen. Silas Holmes and his family were also intrigued, and asked what Tabitha's position would be at Tahilla, to which she replied that she would continue to be Mrs Townclear's companion and friend, as well as nurse to the child.

'Yer won't see young Drury, he's left London,' remarked her father. 'He's settled up in Manchester, an' likely to stay there, I reckon.'

Tabitha nodded, thankful not to have to see Drury's reproachful eyes again. 'And his mother, how is she?'

'He didn't like leavin' her, but she's got good neighbours, an' told him to go an' make a new start for himself,' replied Prewett. 'An' I told him I'd keep an eye open for her.'

'That's good, Papa – and I'm so glad that you've got Prudence and Jenny and your grandchildren. It makes me feel better about going so far away.'

'All I want is for yer to be happy, my girl, an' if that means settlin' in Ireland – well, ye'll still be my daughter, wherever ye go.'

Mariette became increasingly enthusiastic as she felt the approach of spring, bringing a new start in her life. Tabitha wished the move could be all over, but there were a great many things to attend to before they could set out on their journey. Little Conor was being offered soft, solid food in addition to Tabitha's breast feeds, but progress was slow, and he always needed a night feed.

The maidservant Peggy happily agreed to accompany her mistress to Tahilla and settle at Townclear Hall as lady's maid and nurse. Mrs Clark was to stay on as cook to the new owners of 21 Gerrard Street, and Minnie hoped that she might also remain, as she planned to be married within a year to her sweetheart. Joe Bartlett had found work with a wine merchant, as he said he had no wish to serve a new master at No 21 after serving the Townclears.

At Tahilla the lengthening days were welcomed with all the other signs of spring: the winter barley was already sown, and they would soon be planting the potatoes.

'We can see our way ahead now, Father Aengus,' Conor said with satisfaction. 'And in another four weeks or so I shall see my wife and son – and our friend Tabitha, too, God be praised! I've a mind to go over an' fetch them myself.'

As soon as the words were out of his mouth, Conor saw the old priest's face harden. 'No, Conor my son, that won't do. Not any longer, not now ye're master o' Townclear Hall.'

They were walking towards the house, and Conor felt a stab of alarm at his air of solemnity.

'What exactly d'ye mean, Father Aengus?'

'I think ye know my meaning, Conor, but we'll go indoors an' speak with yer mother. Come on, she's waitin' for us.'

And indeed Lady Townclear was standing in the hall, her face pale and anxious as the two men entered.

'It's time to speak to yer son, Mary,' said the priest, and Conor felt a tremor run right through his frame: he began to see where this was heading.

'*No*, Father!' he exclaimed. 'Ye're not goin' to tell me to – to—'

The priest nodded to Lady Townclear, who began to speak, her eyes full of sympathy.

'It's Tabitha Prewett, Conor, she can't come here again, you must see that. No, listen to me, please. Whatever irregularities there may be in the household of a younger son three hundred miles away may be overlooked, though that still doesn't make it right – but the present master of the house and estate must set an example of godly living.'

'Mother, I can't part with her, it would break her heart and mine – don't ask me!' Conor was running his hands through his hair, making it stand on end.

'For God's sake be a man, Conor! And don't insult yer mother,' Father Aengus said angrily. 'What she says is true, an' ye know it. Ye must get rid o' this woman an' send her away. She can't come back here an' show herself off as a—'

'What's that ye're sayin'?' demanded Conor, his one eye blazing. 'If ye weren't an old man, I'd make yer swallow them words, surely to God!'

It might have been one of the stable boys or farm hands speaking, as Conor spat out the words, his fists clenched. Father Aengus took a couple of steps back, and looked towards Lady Townclear. She was not afraid of her son, being full of compassion for him, but she was a woman of unbending principle.

'You have a choice to make, my son. Either you break with Miss Prewett and take over this family estate and the baronetcy, or you desert your inheritance and shame your father's memory. We are prepared to accept your son Conor as your heir, there being no other, nor can there be now, it seems. We welcome your lawful wife under this roof as Lady Townclear – but Tabitha Prewett must go. She has served her purpose, and no longer has a place here.'

'But can't you see that Mariette loves her?' groaned Conor.

'We both need her – our lives would be wretched without her – empty and miserable!'

'The more shame on ye both, then, to rely so much on a fellow creature instead o' puttin' yer trust in the Holy Trinity!' cried the priest.

'Don't say any more to him now, Father,' pleaded Lady Townclear, moved to greater pity by her son's unhappiness. 'Let him sleep on it, give him time to see the truth of what we're saying. Let's stop now. I'll pour whiskey for you both, and say no more.'

She proved to be right. On the following morning when the priest called soon after seven, Conor was already out in the barley field, and Lady Townclear sat at the breakfast table, her shoulders drooping.

'He scarcely slept last night, Father, and he got up before dawn. But I'm to tell you that he has made a decision.' She hesitated, and Father Aengus prompted her.

'And what has he decided, Mary? Please God let him be guided to do his duty.'

'He has, Father. After a night spent in prayer and – and agony, my son told me in his own words that he must sacrifice his child's mother's happiness and his own. Oh, my poor boy!'

'Praise be to God, then, that he's stayed faithful to his church,' said Father Aengus, greatly relieved. 'He may be unhappy now, Mary, but in time he'll have the greater peace o' mind.'

Conor had gone out to the barley field, and watched Dermot Flynn hitch up a pair of horses to a two-wheeled single-seater, at the back of which he fastened the Townclear harrow, invented by Sir Bernard's father and fashioned by the blacksmith of his day, a contraption of criss-crossing bars that carried sharp iron teeth at their intersections. On an impulse Conor leapt up to the narrow seat, grabbing the reins from Dermot and urging the horses forward and up the side of the field of young barley, dragging the harrow behind. The teeth dug into the earth between the rows of young shoots, so that by the time they reached the other end of the field several of the plants were adhering to them, having been wrenched out of the ground, while many of the others had been covered in earth. But harrowing had to be done, to ensure that the earth

241

was broken up around the young barley, and Conor steered the obedient horses round to drag the harrow back down the field; up and down, up and down he went all that morning, to the open-mouthed astonishment of the farm hands and Father Aengus who came looking for him.

'Save your breath, Father,' he retorted when the priest called to him. 'I've got work to do.'

He spared neither himself nor the plodding horses until the whole field had been harrowed.

And thought the iron teeth less cruel than the harrowing of his heart.

There were no loiterers in Bloomsbury Square to observe the Jesuit priest's visit to No 9 on a wet, blustery evening, and the maidservant who answered his knock saw nothing remarkable in his request to be shown at once into the presence of the Comte and Comtesse. As soon as they saw him they rose and stood for his customary blessing, after which the Comte begged him to be seated and Madame la Comtesse poured him a glass of red wine.

They were taken aback, however, when he began to explain his business with typical directness, coming straight to the point of his visit and the need to engage their cooperation.

'But Father, it will break her heart!' protested the Comtesse in dismay. 'She has always been so close to Miss Prewett, they have shared everything, ever since they first met in this very house, at barely ten years old!'

The priest was entirely unmoved, and told the Comtesse that the closeness between the two young women was the cause of much of the trouble; it was not healthy, and Mariette had been too much influenced by the low-born Protestant girl. Now that she was a titled married woman with a child to care for and bring up in the faith of his fathers, the friendship must end, as it should have done on her marriage. Father Braine went on to say that Conor's mother had agreed on this with their priest Father Aengus, and Conor himself had been brought to see the necessity for dismissing the woman who had made herself useful to his wife.

'But Mariette will never agree to it – she'll refuse to go to Tahilla without Tab – Miss Prewett!' cried the Comtesse, but the priest sternly told her to be firm. The Prewett woman was *not* to go to Ireland with Lady Townclear, as Mariette was now titled, and there was now the baby. He instructed them to say nothing, but that he would tell Mariette himself at the proper time. He then advised them not to go to 21 Gerrard Street on the day of their departure, but to meet with their daughter and grandson – and himself, for he was to escort them – at Hyde Park Corner where they would be able to make their farewells to their daughter when she boarded the stagecoach on the first leg of their journey. He bid them be strong and resolute, for her sake, and left them to ponder over what he had said and to acknowledge the wisdom of it.

When he had left, the Comtesse was far from convinced. 'But our darling daughter will be so lonely in such a place without her dearest friend!' she wailed in dismay.

Monseigneur le Comte sighed deeply, and shook his head. He was less surprised than his wife, for he had always had his doubts about the friendship, and wished that he had been firmer with his daughter in the past. He decided to lose no time in taking his wife to Compiègne, to spend their remaining years in their native land.

Father Braine surprised Mariette by saying that the child Conor would have to be completely weaned before being 'taken home' as he expressed it, by about the middle of April. Madame la Comtesse stepped in and said that they must be firm; her daughter was to give the solid feeds, she said, so Mariette sat daily with the baby on her lap, offering him teaspoons of soaked bread or mashed potato and carrot while Tabitha watched anxiously.

One afternoon when little Conor struggled and let out a roar of protest, Tabitha could not help herself, but took him from Mariette and opened her bodice, throwing aside the scarf that covered her shoulders. His eager lips fastened on to the nipple, and she smiled at Mariette who gave a mock grimace as she put aside the dish and spoon.

Suddenly there was a sharp knock at the door, and without waiting for permission to enter, Father Braine stood before them. Tabitha hurriedly pulled the scarf around her and the baby. The priest looked from one to the other, then spoke to Mariette.

'It is essential that Conor's child be weaned, and it is your duty, Lady Townclear, to see that it is done,' he told her, and before either of them could make an answer, he came forward and took the baby from Tabitha's arms. Looking down at the boy he allowed his features to soften into what was almost but not quite a smile; then he made the sign of the cross over the baby and handed him to Mariette. In that moment both women realized that he knew the situation, and Tabitha felt resentment rising up within her at such cavalier treatment on the part of a man, priest or not. He had totally ignored her, and she could not protest. Mariette glanced up at him, and obediently offered the spoon to her baby.

'Your mother will be visiting you later today, Lady Townclear,' he went on. 'I have impressed upon her the need for this child to be weaned.' He made the sign of the cross over her and Conor again, and added, '*Dominus vobiscum.*'

Mariette bowed her head and replied at once, '*Et cum spirito tuo.*' He turned and left them.

While Mariette talked to her baby, softly murmuring endearments in English and French, Tabitha felt dismissed by this Jesuit priest, and his hostility chilled her to the bone. Never mind! Her consolation would come when little Conor awoke in the night, and she would take him and hold him to her soft, warm breasts and feel the indescribable sensation of his hungry little mouth taking nourishment from her, and her alone.

When Conor's letter at last arrived at Gerrard Street, it was addressed to Mariette only, and told her briefly what she already knew: that Father Braine would act as escort when the time came to sail. By now it was well into April, and baby Conor was almost weaned – he still had that precious night feed so dear to Tabitha – and there was no further reason for delay.

Events moved quickly: Father Braine told Mariette that the stagecoach would leave Hyde Park Corner for Bristol in two days' time, on April 21st, a Friday. On that last night at 21 Gerrard Street the friends shared Mariette's bed, with little Conor sleeping beside them. They clung together, repeating the assurances of love and lifelong friendship that had bound them since their very first meeting.

In the morning they rose at six, and breakfasted in the kitchen with Mrs Clark, Minnie and Peggy who was coming with them. Mariette gave Conor bread and milk, with a hard crust to chew on, as his first teeth were coming through. At eight o'clock they were ready, their boxes packed as they waited, dressed in their travelling clothes.

When she looked back upon that fatal morning, Tabitha always remembered the terrible sense of inevitability which seized her from the moment the hackney cab drew up outside, and Father Braine got out of it, wearing his familiar black soutane, a dark shadow cast over the April morning.

'Good morning, Lady Townclear,' he said to Mariette, ignoring Tabitha and the servants. 'This will take us to Hyde Park Corner where I have arranged to meet with your parents to say their farewells. But first there is business to settle, and the sooner it's done, the better it will be.'

Mariette looked surprised. 'What is it, Father? Are not all the arrangements made?'

'Yes, and I am to travel with you and the maidservant with the baby for the whole length of the journey. But the other woman is not to travel with us. Where is she? I've got a letter for her.'

'What other woman?' asked Mariette, completely bewildered, glancing at Peggy.

'The Prewett woman, of course. There is no place for her at Tahilla.'

'But I don't understand, Father – she's always been with me, wherever I go. She—'

'Not any longer, Lady Townclear. Your husband has dismissed her. Now, let us get you and the maidservant into the cab with the baby. The driver's putting your boxes on at the back, and I want to get away on time.'

'I won't go without Tabitha!' cried Mariette. 'I'll *never* leave her! I'll stay here in London with her and my baby. Tabitha, where are you?'

She looked wildly round for a sight of her friend, and saw her leaning against the wall in the entrance, deathly pale, unable to move hand or foot in the glare of Father Braine's piercing blue eyes. Mrs Clark and Minnie rushed to her side.

'She's faintin' – help her!' cried Minnie.

As Tabitha sank to the floor she heard Mariette's voice as from a long way off, then Father Braine's stern tones telling her to be quiet, and then something else she did not catch.

245

When she recovered her senses, she was lying on the floor with a cushion under her head, and Mrs Clark was bending over her, holding a glass of water to her lips.

'Are yer feelin' better now, Miss Tabitha?' The cook actually had tears in her eyes, and Minnie was somewhere near, sniffing and wiping her nose.

'Where is she? Where is M-Mariette? And my baby?' asked Tabitha, her voice scarcely above a whisper.

'They've gone, Miss Tabitha, with that old sourface of a priest. He threatened her with – with somethin', an' then she didn't argue any more – she just went with him an' Peggy an' the baby, bless his little heart. There's a letter for yer, when yer feel up to readin' it.'

Mariette had gone, and little Conor. They were on their way to Tahilla, where Tabitha would never join them, though it took her some time to understand what had happened. She was to understand many other things that day as she sat in the parlour, looking out of the window. Minnie stayed close by her side, and when Tabitha asked her what Father Braine had said to make Mariette obey him, Minnie was at first reluctant to tell her.

'Oh, it was too cruel, Miss Tabitha.'

'Please tell me, Minnie, I want to know what persuaded her.'

'Well, she was cryin' an' sayin' she'd never go without yer, Miss Tabitha, an' then he said she was goin' to see her parents to say goodbye to 'em, an' – an' wouldn't it be a pity if they was to find out – oh, Miss Tabitha, yer should've seen her face, poor lady – she said, "No, no! They must never find out, it'd break their hearts for the shame of it!" – an' then that horrid man said, "Behave like a lady, then, an' they won't find out". An' the poor little baby was yellin' his head orf – oh, Miss Tabitha, it was the worst leave-takin' I ever did see!' And poor Minnie sobbed at the recollection of it until Mrs Clark told her to hush her noise because she was upsetting Miss Tabitha, though in fact Minnie's tears were comfort of a kind.

Yes indeed, it would have been disastrous if the St Aubyns had discovered the deception that had been played upon them, and to know that the heir to Townclear Hall and the baronetcy was not their grandson, especially after all the precautions that had been taken to ensure secrecy. And yet the irony of it for Tabitha was that just about everybody else knew – all the family at Tahilla, her own father – and as she now realized, Mrs Clark and Peggy, who like John Prewett had simply put two and two together and guessed the truth.

With trembling fingers she broke the wax seal on Conor's letter, delivered to her from the hand of Father Braine. There was one page of blotted and almost illegible writing:

My dearest Tabitha, Heart of my own Heart,
It is possible that this letter will not reach you, and if it is intercepted and read by other eyes, shame be upon them. It is to pass through the hands of priests, and I have no great love for them in my present state, but I have to trust Aengus and Braine to be honest couriers.

I have loved you above all women, Tabitha, and you gave me the Son who will be my only child – but we were not married, and there have been lies and deceptions. I was once the happiest of men, but now comes the Reckoning, and we are all three to be punished. I must lose you if I'm to carry out my Duty here, and so will live out my life with half a heart, though no doubt men will envy me my beautiful, virtuous Wife who will lose the wise help and advice you have always given her, and your Son must now be hers. Without your Friendship I fear that she will become restless and bored with country Life, but she must endure it, and that will be her punishment. It is when I consider your punishment, my darling Dear, losing the Child that you bore me in pain, that is when I weep in secret and try to find consolation in Duty. Townclear Hall is empty without my Father and Bernard, and Roisin has gone back to her father's farm with the three children. I cannot write more, Love of my Life, and if there are priest's eyes reading this, let them be satisfied that the three of us are duly suffering for the wrong I have led you both into.

Pray for me, dearest Tabitha, as I shall pray for you down the long days and weeks and years. May God comfort you. I have no more words. Goodbye.
Conor Townclear

It was to Father Braine's credit that the seal had not been broken. Only Tabitha's eyes saw Conor's last despairing farewell.

Seventeen

It took Tabitha some time to realize how completely her life had been changed in one brief moment. From being safe within a web of love, she was suddenly alone and adrift, the third point of a now broken triangle. Her beloved son, born to the man she loved, had been taken from her, as was her dearest friend for more than half her life. They had gone to Tahilla, but there were to be no more Tahilla summers for Tabitha. To whom could she turn now? She tried to pray, but could not truly repent of her sin, and she knew that repentance is essential for salvation, the forgiveness that her Saviour had earned for her by His death on the cross. Her words therefore sounded hollow and empty, like her heart.

The faithful Minnie hovered near at hand, bringing her drinks of tea and chocolate, and she drank a little but could not eat. She saw again her baby son rejecting the solid food he was offered, preferring to curl up snugly to her warm, flowing breasts, now aching and uselessly leaking milk. She could not concentrate on a book or her crocheting, which dropped from her hands as she relived the moment of separation and saw Father Braine's fierce blue eyes piercing through her like a sword, paralysing both body and mind. When she dozed, she dreamed of her baby being taken from her, and the misery of it woke her to consciousness again.

Mrs Clark and Minnie whispered in her presence as if she were an invalid, though at one point, Minnie asked gently if she wanted to go home to her father. She shook her head. She had no claim on her father, though she knew that he and Prudence would open their door to her. She had said her good-byes at Orchard Court, both to her family and the neighbours;

248

they thought she was now on her way to Ireland, and she could not bear for them to know that she was still in London, suddenly cast off, dismissed. She could not face the humiliation of going back and saying she was no longer needed by the Townclears: that she was *disgraced*. And she had been so much a part of Conor and Mariette that she had not made other friends; certainly nobody else was half as close to her. Her world had become a desert, and London a city of strangers.

That day passed, and the night, and on the Saturday another thought came to her. 21 Gerrard Street was sold, and the new owners would be arriving within a week. Mrs Clark and Minnie were staying to serve them, but she would have to move out, having no longer a place in the house. Her life with the Townclears had been comfortable and secure, with no lack of the necessities she had taken for granted, her food and clothing, a bed to sleep in, a roof over her head. Now that it had all come to an end, she needed somewhere to stay and employment to earn for herself those basic needs of life – otherwise she would be *homeless*. She remembered poor Nan who had been turned out by her own mother and by the Prewetts, to fall into bad company and suffer an early death. Where would she go? Who, apart from her father, would take her in? For a moment, only just one fleeting moment, Tabitha saw in her mind the cold waters of the Thames, the last desperate refuge for many a lost soul: she thought of the black, swirling descent into oblivion and shuddered. When the moment passed, it left behind a certain resolution: some reserves of courage, of pride perhaps, rose to the surface and she sat up straight. There must be work to be found for an able-bodied woman with some domestic skills – such as in the houses of the more fortunate, where maidservants mopped, dusted, scrubbed and polished from morning till night; and in the new clothing manufactories such as Davidman's where women were employed to strain their eyes sewing for long hours and low pay. She had to go out to seek for employment. But where to start? She had neither the energy nor inclination: sorrow had wearied her as much as any bodily labour. She gave way to tears, and Minnie gently hushed her, persuading her to take a little soup and bread and cheese; this time she forced herself to eat, and was grateful.

At about four o'clock that afternoon, Minnie told her that

she had a visitor. Who on earth could it be? She was at once aware of her crumpled gown and tear-stained face, and wished that she had time to prepare herself; however, she rose from her chair and Minnie showed in Mrs Deborah Bartlett, smiling shyly and looking well at about five months into carrying another child.

'Deborah! W-what's brought you here?' asked Tabitha, then instinctively remembered her manners. 'How are you? And how's Joe? And the little boy?'

'Little Joey's doin' well, Miss Tab— er, Miss Prewett,' replied Deborah, clearly shocked at Tabitha's woebegone appearance. 'A year an' a half 'e is now. Er – I heard that ye'd – er – not gone to Ireland, and – er – Joe an' me thought ye might want somewhere to stay for a bit – just till yer get yerself on yer feet, like. I hope yer don't mind me askin', Miss Prewett, our place is only small, it's just the ground floor, but ye'd be welcome to come an' stay – an' yer wouldn't 'ave to pay nothin', I mean.' Deborah paused in her gabbling and blushed, as if she were asking a favour rather than offering one.

Tabitha stared at this girl who had been a maidservant taking orders from her when she and the Townclears had first moved into 21 Gerrard Street, and who was now offering her a free lodging. She realized that the Bartletts could only have known from Minnie or Mrs Clark of her present predicament, and it seemed like a gift from above, at least for the time being. Her eyes filled with tears as she nodded and whispered her thanks, and then she felt Deborah's plump arms around her.

'Yer was a friend to me an' Joe when we was in trouble, an' so was Mr Townclear – an' we won't never forget it,' the young wife mumbled against Tabitha's shoulder. 'Come whenever yer want, Miss Prewett – today if yer like.'

And indeed there seemed to be no time like the present. Her box being already packed with clothes and a few books, and Joe ready and waiting to collect it for her, the move was made that same evening, after a tearful, grateful farewell to Minnie and Mrs Clark. Tabitha slept that night on a truckle-bed with a straw mattress, in the tiny room usually occupied by young Joey, now bedded down with his parents. Deborah's kindness and hospitality more than made up for the incon-venience of her domestic arrangements, and her cooking was wholesome. Tabitha stirred herself to offer help and show some interest in Joey, a bright little fair-haired fellow with his father's saucy grin.

On Sunday morning, the Bartletts asked if Tabitha wanted to accompany them to St Anne's, the church where they had been married, and together they set out with young Joey. Tabitha tried to listen to the words of the service, and when Psalm 147 was sung, she tried to take some comfort from the verse that said, *He healeth the broken in heart, and bindeth up their wounds*, but there seemed to be no healing for her own heart.

After a midday dinner the Bartletts had their usual Sunday visitors, Deborah's parents, Mr and Mrs Pitcher. They greeted Tabitha with great warmth, and Mrs Pitcher declared herself to be forever obliged to her.

'My Deborah could've 'ad a very different endin' to her story,' she said with embarrassing candour. 'I was very disappointed in 'er when she told us she was in trouble, an' I thought she'd be chucked out on the street when Mr and Mrs Townclear got to 'ear of it. But they was good to her, even though they was papists, an' I'll never forget all *you* did for her, Miss Prewett. Nobody could've done more, yer was kindness itself.'

Deborah now steered the conversation round to Miss Prewett's need to find suitable work, at which Mrs Pitcher beamed and said she was sure she could find something.

'As it 'appens, I got a sister, Mrs Goldie, she lives down south o' the river in the Borough. She runs a little workshop between the 'Igh Street an' Long Lane, makin' ladies' gowns and men's shirts an' such. It ain't a bad place, an' she's always tryin' to find the right sort o' girl. Are yer any good with a needle, Miss Prewett?'

When Tabitha revealed that she was a tailor's daughter, Mrs Pitcher was delighted.

'Oooh, she'll be glad to meet yer, Miss Prewett! Ye're just the sort she likes to 'ave, tidy an' quiet, a little bit older than most o' the girls – some of 'em are giddy little 'ussies, I can tell yer, an' they calls 'emselves sempstresses when what they really are is somethin' else altogether, which I won't repeat. What d'yer think? Would yer like me to take yer to see Mrs Goldie?'

Tabitha knew little about London south of the river, but agreed to go with Mrs Pitcher on the Monday morning. For all her sorrow and weariness, she had a sensation of life going on, and felt that she must accept any reasonable offer to earn a living, and not impose on the Bartletts any longer than was necessary.

She set out with the talkative Mrs Pitcher on Monday morning with Deborah's good wishes, and Joe paid for a hackney cab for them. It was a fair distance, but once they had crossed London Bridge, they were soon into the Borough High Street, the main road to the south, and it seemed a different London from the one that Tabitha knew. She noticed a great many inns on each side of the street, and roads going off into a maze of yards and courts; the cab turned left into Long Lane, narrow and crowded, with shops selling caged birds, second-hand clothing and cheap leatherware. The cab driver put them down beside a turning that was little more than an alleyway, and Mrs Pitcher led Tabitha to a tall building hemmed in by more recently built tenements, which seemed to be a hive of industry. They climbed up stone steps to the second floor, and Mrs Pitcher raised the brass knocker on a double wooden door, to make their presence known. A stout, rather formidable woman wearing a high mob cap opened to them, and at once her face broke into a broad smile.

'Sister Polly Pitcher!' she exclaimed. 'Come in, come in!' She showed them into a little office where a kettle simmered on an iron hob over a small fire, and on hearing Mrs Pitcher's business, she eyed Tabitha narrowly.

'I don't know whether this'd be what ye're lookin' for, Miss – er—' she began.

'I'm used to needlework and ladies' and gentlemen's outfitting,' Tabitha ventured, and Mrs Goldie put her head on one side and pursed her lips.

'Well, that sounds all right,' she said doubtfully, glancing at Mrs Pitcher, and Tabitha suspected that she would very much like to know the reason why this apparently respectable, plainly dressed woman was looking for work.

'The family she was with 'ave sold up their 'ome an' gorn abroad,' said Mrs Pitcher bluntly. 'An' she was very good to Deborah a couple o' years back, an' we're obliged to her.'

This was Tabitha's recommendation from a reliable source,

and Mrs Goldie nodded. 'Better come an' see the workroom,' she said, beckoning them to follow her through another door and into a wide room that had been enlarged by pulling down a wall. Windows at each end faced north and south respectively. A series of wooden benches filled the room, with forms on either side, where rows of women, mainly young, sat at sewing. Parts of garments lay on the benches: collars, sleeves, backs and fronts, all in the process of being stitched together.

The twittering of female chatter quickly faded to silence when Mrs Goldie appeared with her visitors. She exchanged a couple of remarks with a woman who sat at the top of a row and was in some way overseeing the rest, then she nodded and led her sister and Tabitha back to the cosy little office.

'Well, what d'yer think, Miss Prewett?' she asked, her tall mob cap wobbling slightly on her head, though she had already guessed that it was not really a question of whether the work would suit the young woman, but when she would be able to begin. Tabitha hesitated.

'I shall have to find lodgings,' she said, and Mrs Goldie waved her hand.

'I can recommend rooms in Tabard Street, where a couple o' the girls are stayin'. You could take 'er there now, Polly, and get her settled with Mrs Dove. Right, Miss Prewett, I look forward to seein' you again – when shall we say – tomorrow? Wednesday?'

Tabitha agreed to start on the following day, and after the sisters had parted with a kiss and messages to the Bartletts, she obediently walked with Mrs Pitcher to see the lodgings and meet Mrs Dove who seemed obliging enough.

'I got a little room up the top, as'll suit yer nicely, dear,' she said. 'If yer don't mind climbin' the stairs, ye'll be nice an' private up there.'

They followed her up two flights of stairs to a very small attic room with a sloping ceiling. It had a narrow bed, a hard-backed chair and a wash-stand with a bowl not much bigger than the chamber pot that could be glimpsed under the bed. Tabitha wondered if she would have to carry a pitcher of water up every day, and likewise bring the chamber pot down, duly slopped out with the water she had washed in, but she had no objection to the room, which was clean and would be pleasantly private.

'I only take ladies, dear, an' don't have any followers,' said Mrs Dove. 'I've got two other ladies from Mrs Goldie's establishment, so ye'll 'ave friends, and that'll be nice.'

Tabitha nodded, and said she would take the room; she had enough spare cash in her bag to pay a week's rent in advance, although Mrs Dove said it was not really necessary, she could see that Miss Prewett was the right kind of young lady; even so, she accepted the money.

Mrs Pitcher expressed her satisfaction at the way the morning had gone.

'I said to my Deb, Miss Prewett, mark my words, Deb, I said, that poor girl don't want to be mopin' around all day, thinkin' about 'er troubles. What she wants is to be *doin'* somethin', an' not 'avin' to rely on other people, no matter 'ow willin' they are.'

Tabitha managed a smile and thanked her sincerely; garrulous she might be, but her sentiments were correct: Tabitha needed to be independent. What had Conor said in his letter about trying to find consolation in duty? If duty meant hard work, she understood, and hoped that the prospect of having to work to earn her bread might ease the misery that enclosed her like a grey fog.

Spring passed into summer, and Tabitha's life took on a routine in which one day followed another, with little to distinguish each one from its predecessor. As she sat for long hours stitching shirts for gentlemen and putting endless tucks into the backs of ladies' summer gowns, she began to find out about the lives of her fellow sempstresses, as Mrs Goldie called her workers. At first she had tried to keep herself to herself, but her very silence made her an object of curiosity, and she had to fend off pert questions about her age, place of birth and family; they wanted to know if she had a sweetheart, and why she had come to the Borough and Old Mother Goldie's workshop. She told them her name and that she was a tailor's daughter, but said the rest of her history was her own business. This was met with giggles and grimaces, and she was called Madam Prewett by two or three bold-faced girls who exchanged whispers, some of them audible, about which one of them had been bedded and then deserted, the one whose father was in prison, and the one who had been caught stealing from a bakery.

'But with the mis'rable wages she doles out to us, yer can't blame 'er, can yer?' was the general attitude towards the petty thief, and there were whispers about handfuls of silver to be made from – the voices sank to a whisper, but Tabitha realized that they were speaking of streetwalking, and remembered what Mrs Pitcher had said about sempstresses.

'Ssh, yer don't know 'oo's list'nin',' hissed one of them, glancing in Tabitha's direction. 'Ol' Mother Goldie'd chuck 'er out if she 'eard about it.'

Not all of them were so defiant; one sad-faced girl bent short-sightedly over her work and had little to say. The others tended to leave her alone, and one of them whispered to Tabitha that poor Nell had had a baby and had taken it to the Foundling Hospital.

'It was a little girl, only Nell'd got nowhere to go, an' they'd've both starved else,' Tabitha was told by a chatty girl called Meg who also lodged at Mrs Dove's. Tabitha's pity was stirred, and when an opportunity arose she exchanged a few words with Nell, confiding that she too had had the experience of losing a baby, though in different circumstances. In no time at all this became common knowledge among the sempstresses, and though Tabitha was sure that Nell would not have deliberately repeated what she'd said, it could have been overheard or guessed at. Inevitably in their long hours of working at close quarters the girls came to know everything about each other, and the often tragic circumstances of their lives. Few of them had come from happy homes, and one, aged only fourteen, had to leave a crippled mother alone all day while she worked at Mrs Goldie's to keep a roof over their heads.

On Sundays they rested from their labours, and Mrs Dove provided a Sunday dinner at midday for her lady lodgers; there was Tabitha, Meg and Ida from the workshop and Miss Pepper who gave lessons on the pianoforte in her pupils' homes. She and Tabitha struck up a friendship of sorts when Tabitha asked about churches in the neighbourhood; Miss Pepper went to Morning Prayer at St George the Martyr in the Borough High Street, and said she would be pleased to have a companion, while Tabitha gladly resumed her habit of regular church attendance, taking comfort from the Book of Common Prayer and singing the hymns and psalms. After dinner she liked to walk out with Meg and Ida, and they found their way to St George's Fields, a large green expanse where couples courted and families enjoyed the fresh air and sunshine. It brought back memories of the Gordon Riots – oh, so long ago as it now seemed, and how Conor had rescued her from Will Feather after his escape from Newgate Prison . . . it was still too painful to dwell on.

One Sunday afternoon Meg wanted to cross London Bridge and join the crowds that always gathered around the base of the Monument, Sir Christopher Wren's memorial to the Great Fire in the last century, and famed as the tallest single stone column in the world. So the three of them crossed the bridge, lingering to gaze down on the broad river below them, crowded with boats and barges. Around the monument were booths selling trinkets and various kinds of refreshment, and the girls were counting their coins when Tabitha heard a familiar voice.

'It can't be – but it *is*! *Tabitha*, by my Bible oath! Oh, my sister Tabitha!'

Her heart gave an enormous leap. She turned – and there was her brother Jeremiah with his wife and children! Leaving Betty to take care of Johnny and Amy, he flew to her side, and the next thing she knew was his arms around her and his voice brokenly repeating her name.

'Tabitha, where in God's name have yer been? We thought yer were in Ireland, an' Father's been hopin' for a letter, but yer haven't sent a word. Oh, Tabitha!'

Tears filled her eyes as she hugged her brother while Meg and Ida stared. It was several minutes before she could say anything coherent, and when Betty joined them with the little ones, there were more kisses and tears. 'Why haven't yer been to see us, Tabitha?'

She explained as well as she could that there had been a change of plan at the last minute, and she had not gone to Ireland after all – and she had not liked to come home and admit as much. She assumed that her brothers had not been told about the baby she had borne, and Jeremiah was indignant that the Townclears had not taken her with them.

'The ingratitude of 'em, Tabitha, after all ye'd done for Mariette – an' for that Townclear, too, nursin' him in our own home – and then for them to chuck you out like that! But

256

Father'll be that pleased to know that ye're still here – where're yer livin'?'

There were a lot of questions to be answered, and Tabitha realized how much she had missed her family, but she still hesitated to show her face at Orchard Court.

'Oh, Jeremy, you mustn't tell Papa—'

'Yer don't expect me to keep it from him, do yer? Oh, Tabitha, *why* didn't yer come home?'

It was a perfectly reasonable question, and Tabitha knew that the time had come to see her family again. 'Tell Papa and Prudence that I'll write to them, and try to explain – and say I'm sorry for staying away!' The last words were accompanied by a gush of tears, and she clung to her brother again, while Meg and Ida looked on open-mouthed with astonishment. This was a fine discovery! Miss Prewett had been keeping away from her father and family! Why should she do that? Could it be something to do with the baby she had mentioned to poor Nell? Explanations would be needed!

In spite of her brother and sister-in-law's pleading to come home with them, she refused, saying that she would write to her father first. She told them that she was employed at a garment workshop in the Borough – and at this point she introduced Meg and Ida as workmates and friends, and they mentioned Mrs Goldie, of which Jeremiah took note.

When she parted from her brother, she knew in her heart that she was glad to have met him, and promised again that she would write to her father and Prudence.

But of course the letter never got sent. Jeremiah went straight to John Prewett as soon as he got home, and told him about the meeting, whereupon the tailor took hasty leave of his wife and hurried up the Frenchman's stairs to Bloomsbury Square, pausing to get his breath before walking down to Hart Street where he hailed a hackney cab to take him to the Borough High Street. Once there he enquired of the Sunday strollers still around where there was a garment workshop run by a woman called Goldie, and was advised to try Long Lane. Here he gave a penny to a beggar who pointed him to the alley where stood the building which had Mrs Goldie's workshop on the second floor, and after puffing his way up the stairs, he knocked at that lady's door. When she answered, he asked

257

if she knew of a Tabitha Prewett, and she was at first reluctant to tell him anything.

'Why d'yer want to know? I can't go givin' my sempstresses' names to every Tom, Dick an' 'Arry!' she told him haughtily.

'I'm no Tom, Dick or Harry, woman, I'm her *father*, John Prewett! Where is she?'

Ah, now this was interesting! Mrs Goldie remembered that Tabitha had said her father was a tailor, and it was from him that she had learned her skills.

'I hope there's no trouble in the family,' she hedged. 'It's not bad news, is it?'

'Look here, will you tell me where I can find my daughter? I just want to see her face again!'

Ah, this was worth leaving her supper for. Mrs Goldie took down her cloak from its peg, and pulled it around her shoulders.

'I'll take yer to her lodgin's, Mr Prewett.'

Mrs Goldie hoped to witness Tabitha's surprise – and perhaps consternation – when faced with the father she had obviously run away from; but when Mrs Dove brought her downstairs and her father cried out, 'Tabitha, my girl – my girl!' and clasped her in his arms while they both wept for joy, both ladies had the discretion to withdraw and leave the reunited father and daughter alone. The whole story was told, and Prewett found it hard to excuse the man who had used his daughter and then taken her child and discarded her, even though Tabitha herself said that she was just as much in need of forgiveness.

'Come home with me, my girl.'

She shook her head. 'I have to work tomorrow, Papa, and I can't just leave my workmates and walk out. I've supported myself for three months, and I'll go on doing so. You must understand, dear Papa, I need to work and make a life for myself – I can't just depend on you for my living, or anybody else. Let me come and visit you next Sunday.'

He saw that her newly acquired independence was essential to her, and it was agreed that she would go over to Orchard Court on the following Sunday, her one free day.

And so there was a happy family reunion, and Tabitha was welcomed at Orchard Court by relations and friends alike. Prudence and little Jenny, Michael, Thomas and Andrew,

Jeremiah and Betty with their children were all there to partake of Prudence's boiled bacon and mutton pies, her pickles, cheese and home-baked bread. Neighbours were told that owing to special circumstances, Tabitha had not gone to Ireland after all, and was working south of the river. She caught up with local news, including the departure of the Comte and Comtesse de St Aubyn to France. Their house had been let for a year, her father said, and nobody knew when, if ever, they would return; he spoke as if he did not much care, and turned his attention back to Tabitha.

'Ye've no need to go on sweatin' at that place for all the hours God made!' he declared. 'Mrs Markham says she'd like yer to assist her now that she's gettin' older, an' ye'd only be next door, so yer could have yer old room here. What d'yer think about it, girl?'

Tabitha said it was very kind of Mrs Markham, but she had an obligation to Mrs Goldie who had given her work; it was difficult to explain that she had become involved with the lives of the girls who worked alongside her as they stitched and hemmed, day after day. Mrs Goldie had lately put her in charge as supervisor for an extra shilling a week, and the added responsibility was giving her back a sense of self-worth. Happiness might have fled, but honest work and care for others brought its own reward, and Tabitha felt that at twenty-five she needed to live a separate life from her father and stepmother, much as she loved and valued them.

Back at the work bench the following week, Tabitha was amazed – and more than a little amused – to receive a letter from Lady Dersingham at No 14 Bloomsbury Square.

I have heard from your father that you have had an unfortunate disappointment in your plans to work abroad. You will therefore be pleased to know that I can offer you a very rewarding position as lady's maid and companion to my mother who is sadly becoming rather forgetful. She has a beautiful house in Belgravia, and other servants are kept. Your duties would simply consist of staying near at hand, reading to her, helping her with essential necessities, and generally making yourself agreeable. She does get a little impatient at times, but knowing you and your family background, I feel that you would probably be suitable.

Tabitha remembered the afternoon when she had called on Lady Dersingham on her father's behalf, on the day that the first Andrew Prewett had been buried. The lady's mother had been visiting at the time, and had questioned ten-year-old Tabitha closely about her family, showing surprise that the Prewetts employed a maid. Tabitha had thought her ill-mannered then, and could imagine what she must be like now, some fifteen years later, losing her wits and probably just as inquisitive. She sat down and wrote a polite note to Lady Dersingham, thanking her for her offer, but saying that she was happily engaged in useful occupation, with opportunities to befriend less fortunate workmates. There was nothing in the note that was objectionable – she had to remember that Lady Dersingham was a regular client of her father, so must not be insulted – but it might make her ladyship feel suitably rebuffed.

August sunshine poured in at the windows of the workroom which was inclined to be hot and stuffy for the inmates who sat there hour after hour at their benches, and Tabitha asked for a large jug of clean water to be supplied for them, not only for drinking but for wetting handkerchiefs to apply to flushed faces and aching heads.

Just as Meg was complaining that life was dull and nothing interesting ever happened, there was a diversion one Thursday morning, when Mrs Goldie entered the workshop and beckoned to Miss Prewett.

'There's a gentleman to see yer, an' he seems very insistent on speakin',' she said, with barely disguised curiosity, and of course all the girls looked up and exchanged glances while Tabitha rose and followed Mrs Goldie, wondering who on earth this could be. Was it one of her brothers with news from home? She felt a sudden qualm of alarm.

She stared at the man standing before her. He looked about thirty years old, and was well dressed without being dandified; his jacket was bronze in colour, his breeches a lighter brown, and a snowy-white shirt showed at his neck and wrists. His well-shaped calves were encased in dark-brown hose, and he wore brass buckles on his shoes. He had removed his hat to reveal a neat white wig such as gentlemen wore, and the overall impression he gave was of a well-to-do young man of business. And yet he seemed nervous, even agitated.

'Miss Prewett,' he said, and at once she knew him. She gave a quick gasp, and put out a hand to steady herself against the wall; he took hold of it, while Mrs Goldie watched them with interest. Tabitha was unable to believe her eyes.

'I – I never thought to see you again, Rob – Mr Drury,' she managed to say, and his eyes lit up at hearing her speak his name.

'Call me Rob, Miss Prewett – Miss Tabitha – and may I say what happiness it gives me to look upon you again.' She noticed that although his accent bore traces of the London dialect they both knew, his speech was more correct than in the days of his apprenticeship, his diction clear and pleasing. Mrs Goldie was obviously very impressed.

'Forgive me, sir,' she said with studied politeness, 'but would yer like to see Miss Prewett alone? Let me show yer into a nice little room.' She knew that if they were in her small office, even with the door shut, she would be able to hear every word through a discreetly placed panel with a hole in it.

'That would be very kind o' you, madam,' he said. 'I hope not to detain Miss Prewett for long, but yes, I would prefer to speak with her alone.'

She led them into the office, delighted at being called madam, and noted that Miss Prewett was trembling. Once they were alone together, he took her hand again, and bending over it, pressed it to his lips.

'Tabitha, forgive me, I can't pretend. As soon as your father told me you were still in England, I had to see you, and I've come down from Manchester, a journey of two days. I stayed last night with my mother. When may I speak with you at more leisure? Are you free for a day or a half-day?'

Tabitha's heart was thumping, and she hardly knew what to say. 'How is your mother?' she ventured.

'She keeps very well, I thank you, and I have hopes of her moving nearer to me,' he replied with a half-smile. 'But tell me, when may I walk and talk with you, Tabitha?'

She knew that she should answer that it was not possible, but the words came out quite differently. 'I only have Sundays,' she told him. Why had she said that? So much had happened to separate them for ever.

'Then dear Tabitha, let me see you on this coming Sunday, and give me an early hour!'

She must not make such an arrangement. She must tell him that it would be a mistake.

'I go to Morning Prayer at St George the Martyr in the Borough High Street at ten,' she said.

'Then let me meet you there at nine, and we can talk before the service begins.'

'All right, very well, but—' She hesitated, unable to finish the sentence, and lowered her eyes. This could not be happening – it must be a dream. But here he was, holding her hand and making her promise that she would keep their appointment on Sunday. And she knew that if she failed to keep it he would seek her out again: sooner or later he would have to be told the truth about her life and what had happened to her during those intervening years.

With every courtesy he took his leave of her, and thanked Mrs Goldie for her kindness. She returned to her work bench, and when questioned eagerly by the other girls, her self-control gave way and she burst into tears, begging them not to ask her; and because she had proved herself to be a good friend to them, they left her alone.

On Sunday Tabitha set out alone for church an hour earlier than usual, explaining to Miss Pepper that she had a friend to meet first. It was a beautiful August morning, but she approached the church of St George the Martyr in fear and trembling, certain that Robin Drury was going to renew his offer of marriage to her, and that meant she would have to tell him the whole truth about her life with the Townclears; she dreaded the shock and disappointment it would cause to him – the look of incredulity he would turn upon her.

He was already there and waiting by the west door.

'Tabitha – I feared you might not come, or that you would send a messenger – oh, I am so thankful to see you!' They shook hands and he linked his left arm in her right. 'Shall we walk in the churchyard a little way? There's a bench over there in the sun if you'd like to sit down.'

He was all kindness, all care and attention to her comfort.

They sat down on on the weathered wooden bench, and he took her hand in his.

'You must know what has brought me here, Tabitha. It was always my wish, and your father's, too, and your late mother's, that you and I would find happiness in sharing our lives—'

This was it, the moment she had dreaded. She drew herself away from him.

'No, Rob, no! My father had no right to tell you where I'm living. He of all people knows why I – I can't accept you or – or any man. I'm not what you think I am. Oh, Rob, if only you knew the kind of woman you are talking to, you'd see that marriage is quite out of the question.'

She rose from the seat, and he rose too. 'Hush, my Tabitha, I have no wish to cause you distress. Here—' He handed her a large white handkerchief. 'My own Tabitha, I can't bear to see you crying. Pray compose yourself, for I know—'

'I can *never* be your Tabitha!' she cried, wrenching herself free from his restraining hand and starting to run from the churchyard. She did not get very far, for he caught and stopped her.

'I will *not* let you go, Tabitha. Your father had every right to send me to you. Can you suppose that he, good man that he is, would leave me uninformed? I know about those people, the Townclears, and how they misused you, the more shame to them!'

'Don't blame others for my wrong-doing, Rob!' she cried, still trying to free herself from his determined grip. 'I have just as much need for mercy and forgiveness – you can't possibly know how much!'

'Hush, Tabitha, hush,' he said quite sternly, and putting both arms right round her, he drew her close to him and lowered his voice as he spoke in her ear.

'If you mean the child you bore to Townclear, the son you nourished and cared for, just so that his wife could call him hers – yes, I know of it, Tabitha. I know.'

'Oh, my God,' she whispered. 'Oh, my God.'

He put a finger under her chin and firmly raised her head until she had to look into his eyes. He saw the disbelief on her face, and confirmed his words with a nod and a loving smile. Then he softly kissed her cheek.

'Yes, I know, my Tabitha, your father told me. And I can

scarcely imagine the pain you must have suffered when the boy was taken away from you, and you were left alone.'

She leaned against him, speechless and still trying to believe the evidence of her own ears.

'Come, my Tabitha, let's say no more now, but go into the church to wait for the service to begin.' He put his arm around her and led her towards the door where early worshippers were beginning to arrive; and once inside its ancient walls, they knelt down together.

'Let us ask for God's blessing upon us, Tabitha. My heart is overflowing with thankfulness.'

And Tabitha found that she could pray again, from a truly contrite and grateful heart, asking forgiveness for herself – and for Mariette and Conor, that they might find happiness in each other, and in their son. From now on she knew herself to be freed from the bondage of the past, and able to look ahead with hope to a future with this man who had never ceased to love her.

Epilogue

The driver of the trim, two-wheeled open carriage drawn by two lively horses had to manoeuvre his way carefully between the trundling waggons and loaded pack-horses leaving Manchester by Deansgate and heading south-west towards Chester. Once out on the open road he soon left them behind, and smiled to himself: he was on his way home. About three miles out of the city he turned right into Stretford Lane, and was soon passing through farmland; over in the distance the river Mersey meandered through low-lying meadows. He passed one or two weavers' cottages, but did not stop to deliver spindles of yarn to be woven into cotton cloth, for he knew they were not yet ready for more. The spinning had leapt far ahead of the weaving trade, and in Drury's own small factory in Miller Street the spinning jenny could do in hours what had previously taken a woman days on a spinning-wheel at home. And now that the so-called spinning mule, powered by water, had increased the number of spindles per machine, Drury could foresee an accelerating growth of much larger factories all over the region. The working of coal-fields, building of canals and the harnessing of steam power was making an enormous difference to the cotton trade, and already there were protesting voices against the new machinery that would dispense with the need for labour.

He reached Orchard Villa, a pleasant free-standing house grouped with half a dozen other dwellings on the edge of a sprawling village. And there was his little Martha running to greet him as he got down, followed by Robbie aged three, toddling on his fat legs. Now nearly six, Martha was a pretty, confident child who chatted happily with her father, mother and Grannie who lived with them and looked after the chickens.

While Martha was telling him how well she could read her

story book, he saw his wife appear, her body burgeoning with another child; but instead of her usual welcoming smile, she looked solemn and anxious.

'The news from France seems to get worse every week, Robin – look here at what it says in the *Manchester Herald* – they're calling it a reign of terror over there, and some people are saying that the same thing could happen over here.'

Drury frowned. 'Nonsense, my love. The English nature is completely different from the French. We're not revolutionaries, we can keep our heads and wait for times to change. Besides, our workers aren't badly treated like the French peasantry, though I grant you conditions can vary a lot from place to place.'

'You haven't forgotten those riots in London, when was it, twelve years ago?' she asked.

'That was entirely different, a matter of religion, and half of them had no idea what it was about, they were just out to drink themselves into committing all kinds of wicked behaviour.'

Drury knew only too well what was going through his Tabitha's mind. That so-called Count and Countess had returned to live in France after their daughter and her one-eyed husband had gone off to some Irish backwoods, and there had been no word from them, not as far as the Drurys knew. If Mrs Drury's father had heard anything in Bloomsbury Square, he had not told them, for it was a forbidden subject in Orchard Villa, never to be mentioned, just as Mr Drury would never do business with Roman Catholics, of which Lancashire had quite a large number. But even Drury had to agree that what was going on in France sounded frightening; he said it was enough to make anybody thankful to be in England and at war with the damned French.

When the ragged, starving townspeople of Paris had risen up against a thoroughly corrupt system of government and stormed the Bastille prison four years ago, it had aroused the whole of Europe, and the rebels had been hailed as heralds of a new dawn of liberty and equality.

But it had not stopped there. Risings took place all over France as the oppressed turned upon their oppressors with terrible ferocity, and extremists seized power: the populace had tasted blood, and having no proper leaders, they followed opportunists like Robespierre and Marat who seemed to be intent on slaughtering all the former nobility and anybody remotely associated with them. King Louis XVI had gone to the guillotine earlier in the year, and his Queen, Marie Antoinette, was under arrest and likely to go the same way before the year was out. It was a Reign of Terror indeed, and Tabitha acknowledged to herself that she would never know if the Comte and Comtesse had shared the same fate as thousands of others, or whether they had escaped back to England in time.

Drury enjoyed living in Manchester, a thriving city with rolling moors and green countryside within easy reach. It had been a good move to bring his mother to share their home, much as she had objected at first to being pulled up from her London roots. Now that she was in her sixties, he felt the need to be near at hand for her instead of a two or three days' journey away, and if he'd had any doubts about how she and Tabitha would settle down together, he need not have worried. The old lady kept her own counsel about Tabitha's earlier refusal of her son, and Tabitha did not know how much she knew or might have guessed about the circumstances. They were polite but wary with each other until after the birth of Martha, named after both her grandmothers, for Mrs Drury, like the first Mrs Prewett, was a Martha. When little Robbie was born, he became the apple of his Grannie's eye, and Tabitha drew closer to her mother-in-law. It helped to ease her longing to be nearer to her father, but she knew him to be happy with Prudence, and more grandchildren, as Thomas and Andrew were both husbands and fathers. Prudence had not had any more children after her difficult childbirth with Jenny, and Tabitha thought her father was probably relieved.

Tabitha considered herself very fortunate, with a good, hard-working husband, a daughter and a son and another little one coming. She had a spacious house with all the latest comforts and conveniences, for Robin was an astute businessman and a generous provider: he sometimes used to say impatiently that the policy makers in London ought to come up to the rapidly expanding towns of the north, and see that England's true wealth lay in 'factories and finance'.

And did Tabitha ever look back on those six years of her life when she had shared her love with Mariette and Conor –

Conor and Mariette? Did she think of the precious gift she had given them – and given up? Their son would be eight years old now, and she pictured a handsome, dark-eyed boy going out into the fields with his father, and being a comfort to his widowed grandmother. There were rumours of unrest in Ireland, kindled by the French Revolution, of Catholic peasantry rebelling against Protestant landowners – but that would not happen on the Townclear estate, though they could become caught up in a general uprising. There were times when Tabitha wondered how they were, and she had even considered writing to Mr Shenstone who might still be in touch with Conor and have some information.

But she had never done so. She knew that it would be disloyal to her husband, and she owed Robin Drury everything; he had forgiven her for what had happened in the past, and had said he would never refer to it, which meant that she must not refer to it either. Only in her head did she sometimes hear a distant voice whispering, 'My darlin' dear . . .'

Such forbidden memories were quickly banished by little Robbie who climbed up on to her lap, and although there was not much room for him on her knee, she put her arms around him and held him close to his future brother or sister. The world was a dangerous and uncertain place, there were changes everywhere, and nobody knew what sort of a future awaited these dear children given to her and Rob. She could only do her duty in loving and caring for them, giving thanks for present blessings and leaving the past behind, where it belonged. She would not wish for anything more.